# God's Paradox

**Boniface Ossai**

**God's Paradox**

Boniface Ossai

Paperback Edition First Published in the United Kingdom in 2023 by aSys Publishing



Illustrations: One Pixel (www.onepixel.com) and Unsplash (https://unsplash.com)

**Disclaimer**

This is a work of fiction. Names, characters, businesses, places, events and incidents are either the products of the author's imagination or used in a fictitious manner. Any resemblance to actual persons, living or dead, or actual events is purely coincidental.

ISBN: 978-1-913438-75-3

*This book is dedicated in loving memory of my brothers, Emmanuel Ossai and Felix Ossai. You are deeply missed by the whole family. This book wouldn't have been a success without the effort of my wife, Nkem, who worked tirelessly to ensure the success of this book. Not to forget my children, Ikechukwu and Ifeanyichukwu.*

# CHAPTER

## ONE

### *The missionary Assignment*

It was a sunny Saturday afternoon, Reverend Fitzgerald was relaxing in his reclining cushion chair, after spending his Saturday morning tending to his garden. A hobby he takes on as a way of getting his hands dirty whenever he has some time to spare.

After gardening and a refreshing lunch, the reverend relaxed on a recliner chair in his conservatory as he enjoyed the sight of children playing by the water fountain in the church premises.

He had a glass of a mixture of strawberry and orange juice on a metal-glass side table by his side. Not long after the reverend made himself comfortable, his phone rang, and he reached for his phone. He took the call, and it was his beloved Evangelist, who is also a member of his congregation that was calling. It didn't take long before Evangelist Fredrick and the priest began laughing after they'd exchanged pleasantries. Their conversation borders on nothing but their Christian work, and after spending some time on general conversation, Reverend Fitzgerald had to inquire about Winnie, Evangelist Fredrick's wife, and then his boys, to know how they were doing even though he saw them in church just days back.

After some time into their conversation, Evangelist Fredrick then reminded the priest that he's calling to acquaint the priest that his annual leave is just two months away.

"Yeah, I understand, and I know it's that time of the year when you spend time doing missionary work for the Lord," replied Rev. Fitzgerald.

Evangelist Fredrick proceeded to inform the reverend he'll be going with Winnie, and they intend to revisit the Solomon Islands this year. The reverend on the other hand thinks a visit to the Solomon Islands this year will be one too many, not because such visit is unnecessary, rather he felt the Evangelist should spread the gospel to other part of the world where the word of God hasn't been preached. He then voiced his thoughts as he suggested to the Evangelist to go somewhere different this time so the word of God will spread across the face of the earth.

After realising the priest hesitated to give his blessing to his earlier intention for a missionary trip to the Solomon Islands before voicing an alternative, he kept an open mind and ready for any suggestion the priest has. However, aside visiting parts of the world where the gospel is scarcely heard, the priest has a fresh assignment for this missionary couple. The Evangelist then interjected and asked the priest if he has something else in mind, it's the work of God, after all, and wherever God sends a person is where they go.

"Yes, maybe, our sister church in Ukraine will be holding their annual conference and they have sent us an invite," said Rev. Fitzgerald. Obviously, Ukraine isn't one of those places where the word of God is scarcely preached, the priest wants them to visit Ukraine this time and visit other parts of the world on their subsequent missionary assignments in the future.

As an Evangelist not keen for the spotlight but the work of God, Evangelist Fredrick pointed out that the invite should be for the priest, yet proceeded to ask if the priest thinks otherwise.

"You're an Evangelist, a missionary who has given so much to advance the work of God, and I suppose you're the best person to represent the church," said Rev. Fitzgerald.

This isn't something the priest just pulled out of his hat, it seems the programme in Ukraine is something the priest had marked in his diary, but particularly as an assignment he hoped Evangelist Fredrick will be attending on behalf of the church.

"What are the programmes and activities outlined during the conference?" asked Evangelist Fredrick.

Revered Fitzgerald took his time to brief the Evangelist that there will be a workshop for couples, for singles, and also a workshop on church planting and evangelism. Evangelism, and the workshop on church planting is something the Evangelist holds close to heart, an area which attracted his interest.

"Hmm, this conference is packed with lovely activities," said Evangelist Fredrick.

Reverend Fitzgerald laughed and said he knew for sure this are activities that the Evangelist will be quite interested in, and then said the Evangelist will really be a blessing to all attendees.

This whole Ukraine mission is news to the Evangelist who has planned a visit to the Solomon Islands with his wife, Winnie. He then told the priest he'll discuss this with Winnie, to keep her abreast of the change in plan. Reverend Fitzgerald has no qualms about the need to discuss the change with Winnie, his worry is whether Winnie will be happy with the switch, and not find the priest to be too pushy.

Evangelist Fredrick on the other hand knows too well that there's not a cat in hell's chance that this switch in missionary assignment will send his wife carping at the priest. The Evangelist had to dissuade the priest of his worries, as he reminded the reverend that they're missionaries. Reverend Fitzgerald paused and listened to the Evangelist's assurances for a while, and appreciated his willingness. He then described the Evangelist as a man whose red mist never comes down and said considering the peaks and valleys of an average Christian's productivity, the Evangelists seems to have had everything but valleys. The Evangelist smiled and said the wind in their sails is supplied by God, and they've no choice in the matter when it comes to deciding when and where God sends them on an errand.

"Ok, we'll continue to look forward to the trip," said Rev. Fitzgerald.

Moments after they ended their conversation and said goodbye, the Evangelist turned on the ignition of his car, and went to pick his wife up from work, and funnily, he didn't bring up the subject of his conversation with the priest after picking Winnie up from work until they got home. Later that evening Winnie walked out of the bathroom and heaved a sigh of relief as she reminisces on her experience earlier in the day after having a long day at work. "Ooh thank God, there's nothing as refreshing as a warm bubble bath after a hard day's work," she said. Evangelist Fredrick was sat on the bed, with his back slightly slanted, he'd a pillow as a back rest and using the lighting from a bed side lamp to enhance his vision as he perused a new Christian literature he just bought, he then stopped momentarily. "Honey, I tried calling you earlier today even before I had a conversation with Reverend Fitzgerald," he said.

Winnie had to apologise for her inability to pick her husband's phone call because there was a road traffic accident with so many casualties rushed to the hospital, and as a nurse, it was quite a busy day for her. "We encountered some difficulties, but God intervened," she said.

He then proceeded to inquire of the nature of difficulties his wife was talking about, to at least have a better grasp of what his wife's day was like.

She then stopped walking as she narrated to her husband that the paramedics brought in an accident victim who was bleeding uncontrollably. The nurses tried all they could, but the blood was just gushing out and refused to clot, they got the doctor's attention, and he tried as well, yet the bleeding still didn't abate. "Really! What a bleed from hell, and how deep was the cut?" he asked.

Winnie confessed to her husband that the whole episode was quite a mystery, and then said the patient suffered a punctured artery, and even at that her husband was keen to know how the whole drama unravelled and how it was resolved. Winnie acknowledged she was confused at a point, and hurtled into the ladies to put herself together because her nerves were a shudder. At some point, she went back to the patient and laid her hand on the cut and prayed, and mysteriously the bleeding stopped. Her husband then jocularly asked why she used the word mysterious to describe the outcome, rather than miraculous, because it was a miracle. They laughed, as he urged his wife to focus on the miracle that saved the day rather than the bizarre mysterious bleed that threw everyone into utter confusion.

"Ok, it's a miracle, as you said," replied Winnie.

Evangelist Fredrick concluded by saying that his wife had one hell of a day, before Winnie interjected and requested, he tell her about his conversation with the reverend.

"It went well, but there's a change in plan," said Evangelist Fredrick.

She immediately asked him to elaborate further on the change he's talking about and said she doesn't seem to be following. Evangelist Fredrick told his wife that they aren't going to the Solomon Islands this time as planned, rather, they're going to Ukraine.

This sudden change piqued Winnie's curiosity and she's keen to know if there's anything particular about Ukraine that made it take precedence over the Solomon Islands.

Evangelist Fredrick understands too well that his wife criticalness has no undertone, but just the need for answers. He then intimated to her that their sister church in Ukraine invited the church to their annual conference and the reverend felt they should be the ones representing the church.

"What programmes and activities are we taking part in?" she asked further.

"We will be ministering at the couples' workshop, singles workshop and also teach on church planting," he replied.

"Not bad, it's all about God's work and we're up for it," said Winnie.

Two months later, it was Sunday morning and Evangelist Fredrick Douglas, and his family were preparing for church. While the Evangelist was knotting his tie, he walked into his eldest son's room, and asked Peter, his eldest son, if his car is ready but Peter seemed busy attending to other matters of concern. He replied to his dad, he's yet to get the car ready, but his dad who seems to have so much lined up for the day doesn't want any further dawdling as he asked his son to take the car out of the garage, warm it and get it ready to go.

"Ok dad, I'll do that right away before getting dressed," replied Peter. The Evangelist turned around as he attempts to leave, then stopped and asked Peter if he's joining him or perhaps driving his own car to church.

"I'm coming with mine, and Jordan is coming with me," replied Peter.

"Ok, suit yourself," his dad replied.

Unbeknown to Winnie that Peter has already told his dad that Jordan is coming with him, Winnie walked into Jordan's bedroom and asked if he's ready.

"Your dad and I won't be waiting for you," said Winnie.

"No worries, mum, I'm going with Peter," said Jordan.

"Ok, suit yourself," she replied.

Moments later, Winnie walked into the living room as she prepares to leave the house, Jordan looked at his mum and said he knows the shirt his mum was wearing. She interjected and asked Jordan what it was about the shirt, and said his dad bought this shirt for her two years ago as a Mother's Day gift but she only wore it once.

"It's nice, I like it, but why today?" he asked.

"I don't get you, why the why?" she retorted.

Jordan felt his mum was over dressed for the Sunday service, and this piqued his curiosity. He then asked his mum, if she consider this dress special, then why wear it today, before asking if there's anything special about today. Winnie wasn't captious, and neither did she make a fuss about her son's curiosity and said every day is special, they're in summer and the weather is wonderful, so she feels like wearing it.

"Though it's nice, and I like it," said Jordan.

"Thanks to your dad, he has eyes for good things," said Winnie.

Jordan became jocular as he reminded his mum that his dad takes care of her just as she does for the Evangelist. "He buys for you, and you buy for him," said Jordan.

His dad walks into the conversation and asks Jordan to go and get dressed and let his mum be because they're almost running late for church. Winnie on the other hand seem to be holding onto Jordan, as she said Jordan is helping her out, and perhaps if she had a female child, this is what she would've been doing for her. The Evangelist became jocular as he reminded his wife that Jordan can't fit perfectly into that role.

Moments later, Peter walked in and informed his dad that his car is ready, and ready to go.

"Ok, thank you," he then turned to his wife, "honey, let's get going," he said.

"Honey, I'm almost done, and I'll join you in a minute," replied Winnie.

The Evangelist then retorted and asked his wife to meet him in the car, saying he'll be waiting. It didn't take long before Winnie joined her husband and they drove off to church. As Evangelist Fredrick arrived the church premises and drove into the car park, Paul Luca, or Bro Paul as he's popularly referred to, walked up to Evangelist Fredrick to say hello immediately the Evangelist pulled into the car park, and not long after the Evangelist and his wife took their seatbelts off.

"Good morning, Fredrick," said Bro. Paul.

They exchanged pleasantries, and he then turned to Winnie as she smiled and said hello. "Hello Winnie, you look great in that dress," said Bro. Paul.

"Oh, thanks to him, that's his doing," as she pointed to her husband in appreciation, "and how are you anyway?" asked Winnie. After exchanging pleasantries, Bro Paul then informed the Evangelist that Reverend Fitzgerald wants to see him.

"You mean I should see him right away?" asked Evang. Fredrick.

"Yes, of course, he's waiting for you in the office," replied Bro Paul.

Evangelist Fredrick then said he'll be with the priest in a minute, and instead of alighting from his car and then walking in locked step with his wife into the church auditorium, the Evangelist turned to Winnie and handed his bible to her and then said he will be back.

"Ok, sure," she replied. Minutes later, Evangelist Fredrick walked into the Priest's office as he prepares for the Sunday morning Service. "Good morning, Reverend," said Evangelist Fredrick.

"Good morning, Evangelist, how are you doing?" asked Rev. Fitzgerald.

Evangelist Fredrick replied to the priest saying his morning is great and he just met Bro Paul who said he wants to see him.

"Yes, I want to see you, your trip is just two Thursdays away, I suppose?" asked Rev. Fitzgerald.

Evangelist Fredrick gave a nod in affirmation and said he and Winnie have concluded arrangements for the trip. The reverend then said he will put a phone call across to their sister church in Ukraine to inform them of Evangelist Fredrick and Winnie's itinerary, so they can prepare a good accommodation awaiting their arrival.

The Evangelist thanked the priest for the kind gesture, but the priest then proceeded to inform the Evangelist of the reason he sent for him, as he intimated to him that he'll be making an announcement concerning their mission to Ukraine during the church service to enable those who want to support the mission to do so.

Evangelist Fredrick seems not to think too much of this mission, as he interjected and asked the priest if such support will be necessary. He suggested that since he isn't going to the Solomon Islands or ends of the earth, he doesn't think there will be a lot of people in Ukraine in need of help.

The priest smiled as he stopped what he's doing then fixed his gaze on the Evangelist before saying there are always poor people everywhere, and they'll always be in need of help. He stressed further, saying even the richest of nations has a lot of people in abject poverty. He wasn't in anyway flummoxed about their differences in opinion even though this trip hasn't presented as a make or break. Evangelist Fredrick then changed his position on the matter and said donations are welcomed.

During the service, Reverend Fitzgerald called Evangelist Fredrick Douglas and his wife, Winnie, out to the front of the church and as this couple stood in front of the congregation.

**Rev. Fitzgerald:** Brethren, I've called Evangelist Fredrick Douglas and his wife out to inform you that they will be going on a missionary assignment in Ukraine in two weeks' time.

In the previous years, they've been to the Solomon Islands, Christmas Island, and other remote parts of the world advancing the work of God but this time, they'll be going to Ukraine to also advance the work of God. Brethren, I want you to pray for this couple as they embark on this missionary assignment, and I will as well solicit your assistance to donate towards this cause because we must continue to assist the poor and the needy in all our missionary assignments.

# CHAPTER
## TWO

*Thomas, the Spanner*

It was Wednesday, two weeks later, at the Hail Maria Hospital, just a day before the Evangelist and Winnie set off to Ukraine. Alisabel rushed as the paramedics brought in a patient to the accident and emergency unit. She asked the paramedics for update on the patient just as the paramedics wheeled the patient into the ward. The Paramedic was equally in haste as he replied saying the patient was burning with fever and at the same time, she's amnesic, but Alisabel was keen about the fever, as she then asked how long the fever has been for.

"That'll be three days ago, according to her," said the paramedic.

"Any other symptoms?" asked Alisabel.

The paramedic then said no other symptoms that he knew of but insisted that he know for sure the patient is very sick and a test will resolve the cause. Alisabel thanked the paramedic whom she has taken a liking to lately, and the paramedic then handed over the documentation on the patient's vitals before leaving. Alisabel then called out to Winnie, requesting she give her a hand with this patient while she attends to another patient. Winnie replied and said she'll be with her in a moment but she needs a minute to speak to Doctor Saul. "Ok, please be fast about it," replied Alisabel.

Just as Winnie walks into Doctor Saul's office, the doctor stopped what he was doing.

"Yes Winnie, what can I do for you?" he asked. Doctor Saul is the Medical Director of the Acute Assessment Unit and he's the go-to-person as far as this unit is concerned. Winnie then asked if she could have a moment with the doctor, but Doctor Saul was quite up for it, and said yes of course, Winnie should go ahead.

Winnie proceeded to say she has come to remind the doctor that she won't be here by tomorrow, and supposed he has the shifts covered.

Doctor Saul burst into laughter because this reminder doesn't need a glossy presentation. "Everyone knows you won't be here, and we all know you're going on a missionary assignment," said Doc. Saul. She smiled in return saying she'd just come to remind him about the fact that this is her last shift, and her handover note is already on his table.

"But you aren't closing now, the handover note seems early," replied Doc. Saul. Winnie became jocular and said she's aware that there isn't any need being censorious because she knows the day is still quite young, but she just wants to keep her boss in the know.

"I'm in the know, Winnie, let's wait, and when Rita comes in later today, you will hand over to her," said Doc. Saul. After their conversation Winnie then excused herself and returned to the ward because Alisabel needed her to help out in the ward.

Rita was meant to resume work that afternoon but hours before starting her shift for the day, she and her four-year-old son, Thomas, drove to Bright Mart Supermarket for shopping. Funnily, Thomas was quite elated as they alighted from the car, his excitement is likened to a child on a sugar rush. He couldn't wait to remind his mum, at least to be sure he's going home with the computer game his mum promised buying him if he remains a good boy. Rita smiled at her son who seemed to be looking at her for affirmation that he's leaving the store with his favourite computer game in his hand.

"I know you won't give me peace until I buy you your computer game," said Rita. Thomas seemed to have his ducks in a row, as he reminded his mum that his dad sure gave her money for the computer game and proceeded to ask his mum why she's still complaining.

"I know your dad gave me money, and I'm not complaining, you'll certainly get your video game today. Thomas's love for a new video game is everything but a healthy enthusiasm, and keeping him in a tight leash might be a tall order particularly when he's sure that his much-anticipated video game is within touching distance.

Thomas was taken by excitement, and as they stepped into the store, he ran to get the trolley for their shopping, funnily, he didn't take his mum's instructions seriously as his mum beckoned on him to stop running so he doesn't slip. "Don't worry, mum, I won't slip," he replied.

"Just be careful," Rita cautioned again.

Funnily, Thomas's excitement meant he didn't take due care and paid less attention to the floor as he ran to get his mum a shopping trolley. Sadly, he suddenly slipped into the trolleys with a bang and there was a sudden loud cracking noise from a pile of trolleys that got the attention of everyone in the store, as the trolleys moved all at once on top of Thomas. Rita screamed Thomas's name out loud as she rushed to pull her son who seemed trapped by the pile of trolleys. Sadly, Rita seemed unable to rescue her son, she then called out for help.

"Somebody, help me, help me," screamed Rita. A Bright Mart Security Person in the supermarket who was already rushing to help out, got to the scene to help, and as he approached, he asked Rita if the boy is ok. Rita wasn't quite pleased with the question of the approaching security person, she immediately turned and retorted. "Does he look ok? help me pull him out." replied Rita. The store Security staff immediately joined Rita in moving the trolleys apart and then pulled Thomas out. "Are you ok, boy?" he asked.

Thomas has a bleed from a deep cut, and while the security staff and Rita observed Thomas to assess his injury, Thomas muttered, telling his mum his hand hurts badly. Rita calmly assured her son, Thomas, that mummy is here, and assured Thomas he'll be fine as she attended to the cut to stop the bleed.

The security staff sensed Thomas was hurt, and decided to call the ambulance, he then informed Rita the ambulance is on the way, and urged her to just hold on. Rita replied saying she's holding on, but her son needs help right now because he's bleeding all over.

The security staff replied saying the bleeding is as a result of the bruises, "wait a minute, let me get first aid, while we wait for the ambulance," said the security staff.

Rita is a nurse, and not taken in by panic. She immediately advised the security staff not to bother getting a first aid if the ambulance is on its way and urged him to just stay with them while she had her hand on the cut to reduce the bleeding. The store security staff stayed with Rita and Thomas, and minutes later, the ambulance arrived, even as the security personnel continue to assure Rita her son will be fine.

"Ok, thank you," said Rita. The paramedics immediately began attending to the cut to stop the bleeding, and it didn't take long the ambulance left the scene and moments later the ambulance arrived at Genesis Medical Centre, where Doctor Kirsty was on hand to attend to Rita. "I'm Doctor Kirsty, and I guess Thomas is your son?" she asked. "I'm Rita Laats, I am a senior nurse and I'm his mum," replied Rita. Immediately after exchanging pleasantries, Doctor Kirsty proceeded to check Thomas out, and then a scan, was recommended.

An hour later, the doctor returned, but this time, she began by asking Rita which hospital it is that she works as a senior nurse.

"Hail Maria Specialist Hospital," replied Rita.

"Oh good, that makes my work easier," said Doc. Kirsty.

Rita seems not to be following, she immediately asked the doctor what she meant by "that makes her work easier." Doctor Kirsty has to put things back to perspective by explaining herself in a much clearer terms, she then said she meant to say she wouldn't have to do much of convincing since Rita can interpret X-ray results as well, because Thomas fractured his left hand.

Rita exclaimed, and said Thomas complained about his hand earlier, but she never knew it will be this serious. Doctor Kirsty continued and said apart from this and other minor bruises, she doesn't think there's any other serious cause for concern. Catching her usual forty winks before heading off to work is now the least of Rita's worries.

Rita was quite riled by how soon her day was ruined by this visit to the supermarket, she then muttered and said she's meant to resume work within the hour, but that wouldn't be possible anymore. Doctor Kirsty had to calm Rita down, assuring her that this accident shouldn't be interpreted as things falling off the boil, she then said the orthopaedic consultant will be around to attend to Thomas in thirty minutes time.

"He's in pain, and you just can't leave him like this until the Orthopaedic consultant comes around," said Rita.

Doctor Kirsty stopped and then turned around, as she assured Rita that she intends to give Thomas something to ease his pain. She also suggested to Rita to put a call to inform her workplace that she won't be coming to work today, except she has someone else to stay with Thomas.

"No, no, this isn't good, my colleague will start her leave tomorrow and she's meant to travel with her husband tomorrow as well," said Rita.

"What an ugly coincidence!" the doctor exclaimed.

Rita's heart sank at the thought of calling out of work, she went on to narrate to Doctor Kirsty, that her colleague and her husband have already booked for their travel and now she will look like a spoiler before her. Doctor Kirsty had to assuage Rita of her worries, assuring her this is no fault of hers, and urged her to put a call across to let them know and possibly delay their trip a little, even if it's just for a few days.

Rita's focus momentarily shifted away from her son's wellbeing as she attempts to reason out how this accident will impact on Winnie. Finding the best way of dealing with this situation that's fast turning into a carbuncle is her primary concern. She then braved it and put a call across to her boss because she doesn't know how to tell Winnie about this. Rita stopped and paused for a while, with her phone still in her hand. Her silence is undoubtedly the result of the possible quizziness among her colleagues who might consider her a spoiler that has done nothing but dampened Winnie's excitement.

After spending some time in mute silence and considering her options, Rita sulked for a while but then decided to put the call across to Doctor Saul to intimate him of the unfortunate circumstance. Immediately Doctor Saul picked the call, he didn't hesitate to ask Rita if she's already at work, but then asked if she's calling to inform him, she's running late.

Rita chuckled and said she wouldn't be calling if she's already at work, that she will rather be standing before him. She then muttered saying the reason behind this phone call could blow her boss out of the water. Doctor Saul proceeded to ask if anything is the matter.

Rita subtly informed her boss of her quagmire as she told him that Thomas had an accident at the Bright Mart Supermarket, and they're presently admitted at Genesis Medical Center.

"You mean my friend, Thomas, how did it happen?" asked Doc Saul.

"He ran into a set of trolleys, and they all closed in on him," replied Rita.

"You said he's admitted in the hospital, and how bad is it, is he hurt?" Doc. Saul queried further.

Rita replied saying her son's condition is bad enough to prevent her from reporting for duty, which makes her feel bad about herself. Doctor Saul became quite apprehensive, as he asked to know how bad Thomas's condition is. Rita became quite sober as she informed her boss that her son fractured his left hand and sustained some bruises, which could keep him in the hospital in the next four days.

Doctor Saul knows too well that Rita could be a lot of things but not a spoiler. He then interjected and reminded Rita that her son is hurt, and she has to be with him in the hospital because that's what any sensible parent would do, before asking why she should feel bad about herself.

Rita then reminded Doctor Saul that Winnie is going on holiday tomorrow, and this incident might likely throw a spanner into Winnie's plans, and her son Thomas is now that spanner. Doctor Saul who seemed to have forgotten about Winnie's planned holiday, suddenly came to his senses.

"Oh, yes, you're right! Winnie should be off tomorrow, isn't there anybody to stay with Thomas in the hospital? Because communicating this to Winnie will be quite difficult," asked Doc. Saul.

Rita replied saying there isn't, because Thomas's dad is out of town on official assignment, and she doesn't know how to start this conversation with Winnie. Doctor Saul isn't a man without a soul, he then returned his attention to Thomas as he asked to know if Thomas is responding to treatment. Rita quickly replied saying Thomas is stable at the moment, and there isn't much cause for concern.

"Don't worry, I'll speak to Winnie about this, and let's see how it goes," said Doc. Saul.

"Ok, thank you," said Rita.

Immediately after their phone conversation, the doctor immediately decided to call in a favour from agencies that supply nurses but couldn't get any because his request came at very short notice. After looking around and realising there's no replacement for Rita, Doctor Saul is now in a bind.

Moments later, Doctor Saul stopped what he was doing and walks out of his office through the hospital reception area. He stood with his hands on his hips, which signifies he's in trouble. He understands too well that this news will obviously take the wind out of Winnie's sails, yet he needed to find a way around this.

"Alisabel, where is Winnie?" asked Doc. Saul.

Alisabel replied to Doctor Saul saying Winnie is in the acute admissions area, and attending to a patient. Understanding that this is a difficult conversation, he asked further to know if Winnie is busy. Alisabel then informed Doctor Saul that she doesn't think Winnie is handling a serious case, but then said the look on Doctor Saul's face was quite unsettling before asking if anything is the matter.

Doctor Saul muttered as he said there's a little issue, and he has to discuss with her. He then proceeded to ask Alisabel to inform Winnie that he needed to see her right away. Alisabel couldn't let her boss who seemed reticent at the moment out of her sight without expressing concern. She quickly reminded her boss that Rita should be in by now because her shift starts in five minutes time, so she can take over from Winnie.

"Yes, you're right, and that's why I want to see Winnie," he replied.

"Is she running late or what?" asked Alisabel.

Doctor Saul couldn't remain inhibited any longer, he then told Alisabel that Rita's son, Thomas, was involved in an accident. Alisabel exclaimed and immediately asked to know how and when this happened. Doctor Saul proceeded to give a little flesh to the information, as he explained further that the accident happened about two hours ago, and the boy fractured his left hand and suffered some minor bruises.

"How is he, and is he admitted here in our hospital?" asked Alisabel.

"No, he was admitted in Genesis Medical Centre and Rita will be off duty for some days to care for her son," said Doc. Saul.

Alisabel exclaimed again and reminded her boss that Winnie is travelling tomorrow, her bags are already packed, and cruise ship booked. Doctor Saul smiled at Alisabel's comments and said he's well aware of Winnie's planned travel but Alisabel's description of Winnie's preparation makes it sound as if Winnie is going on a cruise party.

Alisabel smiled in return, yet urged her boss not to misquote her, and said everyone in the ward is aware that Winnie is going on a missionary assignment.

"Yes, I know, this is a difficult one," said Doc. Saul.

Alisabel seemed to be speaking up for her friend, as she insists, she doesn't think Winnie will be happy with this news, she then exhaled before muttering on the complexity of the situation.

Doctor Saul on the other hand needed an easy way out of this, as he urged Alisabel not to tell Winnie anything, and said he prefers to do the talking, he then urged her to go and drop off the items in her hand before passing his message across.

"Ok, I suggest you lighten up a little, and you know for sure, that look will put Winnie off," said Alisabel.

Doctor Saul then decided to put on a little smile, to at least lighten up a bit. He then asked Alisabel if this smile will do,

Alisabel then replied saying not bad, at least for a start and then walks away. Minutes later, the moment Alisabel walked past Winnie, she was quick to express her concern to Alisabel that Rita isn't in yet.

Alisabel had no choice but to come up with a plausible excuse, as she suggested to Winnie that maybe Rita is running late, though it's unlike Rita who loves coming in ten minutes early. Winnie on her part still thinks Rita might be nearby, as she informed Alisabel she's doing her last round of the ward, before signing off for the day.

Instead of informing Winnie Doctor Saul wants to have a word with her, Alisabel excused herself, so she could drop the stuff she's carrying, and said she'll be back. Winnie then proceeded to Alice's bedside, and said hello to Alice, before asking how Alice is feeling.

"I'm feeling a bit better, gosh, it was like, I was dying," said Alice.

"Yes, you were, but that's why the hospital is here, to do the magic," replied Winnie.

Alice exhaled, and thanked Winnie saying she's now feeling much better and more alive. Winnie reciprocated with a smile and said Alice is welcomed, but Winnie's benignity meant she can't proceed without asking Alice if she should ask the kitchen to get her something to eat, sensing she might be famished.

Alice on her part wasn't quite keen to eat anything as she insisted, she doesn't think food is necessary because she doesn't have an appetite yet.

"It's necessary, because you need to take your medication," said Winnie.

"Ok then, but where is my mum?" asked Alice.

Winnie had to spend some time with Alice who hasn't been much aware of her environment, as Winnie told Alice that her mum just stepped out, and that she went home to freshen up and change her clothes.

Alice interjected and exclaimed her pity for her mum, as she said her mum must have been terrified. Winnie concurred following the disposition of Alice's mum the moment they stepped into the hospital, she then replied "yes, of course, she was," before saying it's good she knows that parents feel the pain of their sick kids much more than the sick kids themselves.

"You're right," said Alice.

Alisabel walked into the conversation, and informed Winnie that Doctor Saul wants her.

"When, now?" asked Winnie.

"Yes, of course, now," replied Alisabel.

Winnie interjected and said she'll do that right away, but then urged Alisabel to please inform the kitchen to get something for Alice, so she can eat before taking her medication.

"Oh, ok, I'll do that," she promised.

Winnie thanked Alisabel and then turned to Alice to excuse herself, before informing her Alisabel will attend to her needs.

"Ok, thank you, Winnie," replied Alice.

Minutes Later, Winnie walked into Doctor Saul's office, and said she had it in mind to come and see him before signing out for the day, then got a message from Alisabel that he wants to see her. Doctor Saul seemed to misunderstand Winnie's comment about coming to see him, but then interjected and said he's glad to know that Winnie is already aware of the situation.

Winnie toed the line, thinking she's on the same page with her boss, as she said she's of course aware she's expected to leave her handover note because today is her last and she's travelling tomorrow. Doctor Saul suddenly realised he and Winnie aren't singing from the same song sheet.

"Oh no, no, no Winnie, that isn't what I meant," he replied.

Winnie then asked Doctor Saul what then it is, but then pressed on to ask if there's anything she should know of, and if there is, he should please tell her.

"It's about your holiday," said Doc Saul.

Winnie seemed lost as to the direction of travel of this conversation, yet stayed calm as she asked what it is about her holiday, saying her bags are already packed and her travel bookings concluded. This is one of those conversation that leaves people cringing and feeling like jumping out of their skin.

He subtly spoke on the subject saying he's aware Winnie had plans, but effort to get a handle on things can sometimes be overwhelming, because no matter how hard we work towards achieving our plans, they sometimes spin out of control.

Winnie interjected immediately, and urged her boss to stop speaking in riddles, saying he's quite aware she will be signing out in the next few minutes because Fredrick will be here to pick her, and then proceeded to ask why Rita isn't here yet.

"That's why I sent for you, Thomas was involved in an accident," said Doc. Saul.

"What, Thomas, when did this happen, I was on phone with Rita during my break, and why didn't she tell me?" asked Winnie. Doctor Saul replied saying it happened just a couple of hours ago, and he's presently admitted at the Genesis Medical Centre. Winnie exclaimed for a second time as she asked how bad the situation with Thomas is.

Her boss had to hit the nail on the head as he replied saying the situation is bad enough to stop Rita from work for some days.

"I mean, Thomas, how is he?" asked Winnie.

Doctor Saul then offered more details about the situation, as he informed her that Thomas fractured his left hand and suffered some bruises.

Winnie grappled with the news and she couldn't process the news immediately. It was as if she was hit by a ton of bricks, and all she could do was exclaim saying what's going on and why is all this drama happening now. She came to work with spring on her steps, but the day seem to be ending in such a bizarrely awkward note.

Doctor Saul on his part, continued to look for the right choice of words in his conversation with Winnie. The doctor knows her to be unassuming and hardly unnerved when confronted with surprises, but this could rattle her cage, and yet, he asked

Winnie if she knows the implication of this situation, even as he acknowledged that he knows that this is hard on her.

He then begged her to please make some adjustments. Winnie thinks this shouldn't be much of a problem because there are agency nurses who could take up the cover until Rita is back to work. Her boss informs her that this is far from it because he has already reached out to them and unfortunately, they're unable to help out in this circumstance.

Winnie struggled with the news, as she insisted that this is emotionally shattering for her, even when the humane thing to do is to show sympathy for the little boy, Thomas. Considering the delicate nature of this conversation, Doctor Saul then said he just felt that he needed to tread on egg shells because this isn't an easy decision as it relates to her.

Winnie took the whole thing on the chin, and reminded Doctor Saul that he has made his point, and masking or painting the situation to assuage her worries wouldn't have been fine by her.

"I know how much you desire this holiday," he said.

Winnie continued as she insists that this is cagey for her, because her desire to go for a planned holiday and her emotion for an injured Thomas ran into each other.

Doctor Saul, who's left with running an AAU that's already short staffed looked on, and asked Winnie what she intends to do about this. It's obvious that the promise of reimbursing her of all she has spent towards this planned holiday doesn't make it any easier.

"Give me some minutes to process this news, and I need to give Rita a call, I will get back you," she retorted.

"Ok, I'm sincerely sorry about this," said Doc. Saul.

Winnie left the office as she attempts to deal with the news, and funnily, she isn't known to be someone who's taken in by rage, yet her boss expected that this time, he might see Winnie kicking off, and displaying an incandescent rage. Despite being caught off guard by this news, Winnie is still trying to make good of her good intentions towards the injured little boy, but the news did actually rattle her cage. This news was more than a punch in the face, it was more like a punch in the gut.

Immediately Winnie stepped out of Doctor Saul's office, she reached for the phone and dialled Rita's phone. Rita reached for the phone, and realised it was Winnie on the other side of the phone, she cringed inside her and immediately developed cold feet, then muttered under her breath. "Oh my God, it's Winnie."

"Hello Rita," said Winnie.

"Hello Winnie, I don't know how to call and inform you about this, I'm really so sorry and I am quite ashamed for working against your holiday," said Rita.

Winnie sensed Rita's apprehension in her voice, she then toned the temperature down and subtly told Rita she doesn't have to be ashamed, Winnie then proceeded to ask how Thomas is doing. Rita became more forthcoming, as she informed Winnie that Thomas fractured his left hand, yet told Winnie on how laborious she tried to tell her son to stop running to avoid slipping but he didn't listen, and now see the troubles he has caused her.

Winnie smiled and asked Rita what else she expects from kids, saying all they do is throw the unexpected at their parents. Rita then returned to her earlier line as she reminded Winnie, she has just messed things up for her, and asked her about her planned holiday. She then muttered and said she's certain Winnie is meant to leave tomorrow.

Winnie affirmed she was meant to travel, yet asked what option is there now that this accident has presented a problem, and funnily, the agency has been unable to send them nurses for cover. Winnie is a devout Christian and attaches the will of God to every unravelling circumstance around her, she then said, man proposes and God disposes.

"Can you move your holiday forward, maybe for three or four days, till I resume, because there isn't anybody to stay with Thomas?" asked Rita.

Unbeknown to Rita, Winnie and her husband don't have the luxury of choosing what date suits them. She had to inform

Rita that if they push their holiday forward then they'll miss the programme they're going for, but then urged Rita not to worry, saying she will find a way around it because Thomas's health matters most.

Rita insists she can't stop worrying knowing full well she's standing in the way of her plans, and the sound of this makes her look like a spanner, and that's awkward. Rita loved the fact that Winnie wasn't presumptuous and wasn't making a fuss about Thomas's drama throwing a spanner in her planned holiday either. Yet, her apology to Winnie was accepted but it didn't bring Rita solace either, Rita just felt she couldn't take the edge off Winnie's disappointment even when that isn't the case. Winnie on her part, continued to play the adult in the room, as she pressed on Rita to take care of her boy, and leave her to find a way around it.

"Thank you, Winnie," said Rita. They ended their conversation and Winnie walked away to a quiet place to allow herself process this news.

Minutes later, Fredrick was at the car park to pick his wife as usual, Winnie then rushed to Doctor Saul's office, and said Fredrick is already at the car park, and she has to go. Doctor Saul, didn't even ask to know what Winnie's position is on the matter at hand before saying he'll be expecting her tomorrow. Winnie looked at Doctor Saul and said it's plausible, but she needed to discuss the matter with her husband, yet insisted that this news will shatter him.

Doctor Saul needed an assurance that the shift is covered as he told Winnie that he knows for sure that she needed to discuss the situation with her husband, yet he wouldn't want to be left holding the bag.

He then pressed on her, insisting he need to be sure she'll be here tomorrow. Winnie couldn't keep her husband waiting at the car park for too long. She then turned to leave, yet said it's already a yes in advance, but she'll affirm her position on the matter in a couple of hours' time after she'd discussed the matter with her husband. She didn't feel shafted in all of this, and there is no need attempting to avoid being perceived as a polarising character.

Doctor Saul voiced out as Winnie walks away, saying she shouldn't sleep on it, because he doesn't have all day. Winnie replied him saying that's why she said a couple of hours, and moments later she walked to the car park where her husband was already waiting.

"Hey honey, how was your day?" asked Fredrick.

"Work is good actually, but I know you won't like this," Winnie chuckled.

Her husband then asked if anything is the matter, she looked sober as she subtly informed her husband her holiday has been cancelled. The Evangelist exclaimed and said his wife must be joking, before asking if she's just having a laugh. Winnie's facial disposition speaks differently to prove she's serious, as she insists this is no joke, and the whole thing equally left her perplexed and heartbroken.

"You mean you cancelled your trip after all travel arrangements were made and bookings concluded?" he asked.

Winnie understands the gravity of the situation and the disappointment that will follow, she subtly told her husband it isn't her, it's Rita. Her husband turned his focus on her and asked. "What has Rita got to do with this?"

Winnie had to inform her husband that Thomas was involved in an accident a couple of hours ago, and he's admitted at the Genesis Medical Centre. Evangelist Fredrick exclaimed, before asking about the nature of the accident.

Winnie decided to give flesh to the information as she said Thomas had fractured his left hand and also sustained some bruises. Her husband felt pity for Thomas as he muttered, that's a shame, yet insisted that this shouldn't stop his wife's planned holiday because it's easy get agency nurses to cover until Rita resumes.

"There isn't anyone to stay with the boy in the hospital, and you understand what that implies," said Winnie.

"Yes, of course, it means Rita will be off work and does it mean, it must be you who should cover for her?" asked Evang. Fredrick. She then narrated her boss's effort to get someone come over from the agency, but the very short notice made that quite impossible. Winnie gestured with her shoulder saying that's it, their unit is short staffed and strained.

Evangelist Fredrick looked on for a while and began analysing the complexity of the situation at hand, he then said Thomas needs his mum, Rita needs to be there for her son, their unit needs somebody to cover for Rita and he needs his wife to go on holiday with him.

Winnie's response was everything except flattery and platitudes as she said the situation at hand leaves them at a crossroads. "Does your crossroads imply I should make the trip alone?" asked Evang. Fredrick.

Winnie then suggested to her husband that since they're attending a conference, and this isn't a trip to be moved forward, he should go alone. Her husband felt lost with this new twist in the mix, and the only solution to the problem at hand is one that pulls no punches. He then muttered saying he didn't see this coming and asked his wife how she'd expect him to make this trip alone.

Winnie encouraged her husband as she insists, they don't have a choice, and throwing the unexpected at them, is one of life surprises. With words of encouragement from his wife, the Evangelist now seem ready to get on with the planned trip after his wife persuaded him to go it alone. He then said he'll speak with Reverend Fitzgerald, and let him know of the change in plans. Winnie then picked one from the box of strawberries in the car, and said these strawberries are unusually big. She then asked her husband where he bought them.

"Oh" he laughed, "I just picked them from the fruit market," he replied.

She takes a bite, "hmm, it's juicy, and tastes very nice as well, I've always looked out for this species, but they are hard to come by," she said.

Her husband then urged her not to worry as he hinted, he knows how to get exactly what his wife likes, she nudged him with her elbow and they both laughed. He then turned on the ignition of his car and then drove off.

Later that evening, Evangelist Fredrick puts a call across to Reverend Fitzgerald, and after a brief exchange of pleasantries, the Evangelist then informed the priest that they have a little hitch. The priest listened carefully but asked Evangelist Fredrick what sort of hitch he's talking about, yet said he supposed they're leaving for Ukraine the next day. The Evangelist paused but then said of course the trip will go ahead, but Winnie won't make it because something came up in her workplace. No matter how nicely the Evangelist break this news to the priest, the news will still leave the priest with a feeling that things aren't going according to plan.

The priest didn't hesitate to ask why the sudden change occurred and asked if Winnie didn't inform her workplace in advance. The priest's concern was that travelling without his wife by his side, will make this trip a lonely one for the Evangelist.

"She did inform the hospital, but just at the point of hand over, something came up," said Evang. Fredrick.

"Ok, but how did she take it?" asked Rev. Fitzgerald.

Evangelist Fredrick confirmed his wife was broken, but she took it in good stride.

"What about you, how are you dealing with it?" asked the Reverend.

Evangelist Fredrick said there's nothing he can do about the situation because a missionary assignment without his wife by his side is odd to him, but he has decided to put God first.

Reverend Fitzgerald accepted the situation and was happy the Evangelist and his wife came to an agreement on how to deal with the situation without much fuss. He then blessed the Evangelist and said God will provide the company he needed and fill every void.

"Amen, and thank you, Reverend. I've to get ready for tomorrow," said Evangelist Fredrick.

"Ok, have a safe trip," said Rev. Fitzgerald.

The next morning, Winnie and Jordan accompanied the Evangelist to the cruise ship boarding point. Immediately they arrived in the car park, Evangelist Fredrick turned to his wife while still in the car, and said this trip will be dry without her but he's essentially faced with no choice but to work with the Ukrainian church's schedule.

They booked the cruise ship because they also considered this a holiday, which allows the couple some time together and to as well enjoy the cruise experience as a couple, but the Evangelist now prefers going by flight since he's going alone, and without the company of his lovely wife.

Winnie on her part, replied saying this whole trip has encountered too many twists and turns. "Yes, you're right, first was the redirection of the trip from the Solomon Islands to Ukraine, and now this issue with cancelling your holiday," said Evangelist Fredrick.

Winnie then shifted the focus away from the fact that her husband is going it alone and said participants in this conference will be blessed by her husbands' presence, and that's what matters most. They then prayed for a while as they commit the trip to God, and then Jordan alighted from the car, but Evangelist Fredrick dawdled for a while. He just didn't feel like stepping out of the car, as he tells his wife about this odd feeling inside of him. He continued, saying he just can't explain it, but his hunch tells him something isn't right.

Winnie remained speechless as her husband poured out his heart, she told him she feels the same, but she just can't place the feeling, and it's like a deep feeling of emptiness. After a while, they held hands again and prayed one last time. The Evangelist then alighted from the car, and said he thinks he should get going, so this feeling won't get into his mind.

Winnie also alighted from the car after her husband got out of the car, she then asked Jordan to take his dad's luggage to the boarding point. Jordan then moved his dad's luggage, but reminded his dad, saying he supposed his dad's cabin is number twenty-four.

Evangelist Fredrick affirmed, and urged Jordan to stop at the check-in, and he'll take it from there. After few minutes of going through the check-in, it's now time for the Evangelist to board his cruise ship, Winnie then hugged and wished her husband a safe trip and they said their goodbyes. He then muttered one final time and said it would've been much fun having his wife by his side, then told her he loves her.

Jordan stepped in and hugged his dad in his bid to say goodbye and wished him a safe trip.

"Thank you, Jordan, goodbye," said Evang. Fredrick.

He then left his wife and son and lugged his luggage into the cruise ship, but then stopped one last time to wave Winnie and Jordan one final goodbye before he was out of their sight, as he went in search of his cabin. It didn't take long after the Evangelist was out of their sight that Winnie and Jordan returned to their car and drove off.

Not long after sorting his luggage out and spending some time praying inside his cabin, he then made himself comfortable in his cabin. By evening of same day, Evangelist Fredrick Douglas left his cabin and came down to the deck of the ship. Chad Jackson the

Captain of the Octal Flamingo Cruise Ship was standing on the deck of the ship with his hands on the rail, as he gazed at the sea.

The Evangelist walked up to the captain who's dressed in his full uniform, adorned with gold epaulettes, his belt and buttons. He then said hello to the captain and asked if he's the captain of Octal Flamingo. Chad Jackson turned around with a smile and extended his hand for a handshake, and affirmed with a nod, then said the Evangelist guessed right, because he's the captain of the ship. The Evangelist began a conversation with Chad who seemed consumed with his observation of the state of the sea.

"You're observing the storm, I suppose?" asked Evang. Fredrick.

"Yeah, the storm is a bit boisterous, though I expect it will be calm shortly," replied Chad.

"This is bad for business, isn't it? I mean the storm," asked Evang. Fredrick.

Chad replied saying of course it is, and said he likes it when the sea is glassy calm, but it isn't within his gift to decide for the sea on how to behave. The Evangelist paused in a suggestive manner, then smiled and said he guessed the captain's desire for a calm sea is right, but also reminded the captain that he needs to speak to the sea and tell the sea what he desires of the sea.

"I'm Evangelist Fredrick Douglas, pleased to meet you," said Evangelist. Fredrick.

"Chad Jackson, it's a pleasure, are you travelling with us for the first time?" asked Chad.

The Evangelist replied and said this isn't his first trip in this cruise ship, rather his second. He went on to say he was with Winnie the last time.

"Sorry, who is Winnie and when was that?" asked Chad.

The Evangelist smiled and said Winnie is his wife, and that was the second week of June, two years ago, though he went on to say they didn't see much of the captain then.

"Hmm, oh, oh, I remember, I was down with a severe migraine. Though, I don't remember meeting you. I spent most of my time indoors, I mean, in my cabin," said Chad.

The Evangelist then asked why the cruise company is this cruel, and said he expected that they should've allowed him time away from work to take care of his health.

Chad had to absolve his company of any blame, as he intimated to the Evangelist that the decision to travel while sick was his and smiled, saying he's obsessed with his baby and he just can't do without her. Evangelist Fredrick smiled, without the knowledge that the captain was speaking metaphorically and asked Chad if his baby is here with him, he then asked where she is now.

"She?" asked Chad.

"Yes, you just mentioned your baby, where's she?" asked Evang. Fredrick.

"I meant my ship, I'm not referring to a person," Chad replied.

"Oh, now I get you," said Evang. Fredrick.

Chad became jocular and said he named her. Evangelist Fredrick then became quite interested in the conversation, as he asked Chad Jackson, if really it was him that named this ship. Chad Jackson was glad to tell this stranger who cares to know a little about the history of the ship he's travelling in, as he said of course he named the ship, and he's the first to travel with her.

Evangelist Fredrick exclaimed saying this is wonderful, affirming this captain does have a cherished history with this cruise ship.

Chad Jackson then shifted the conversation away from the ship and asked the Evangelist what part of Romania he came from. Chad suddenly realised himself and retorted, saying, no, no, and said he's sure the Evangelist isn't from Romania. Evangelist Fredrick smiled and asked Chad how he knew, and what made him say he isn't from Romania.

Their conversation was quite a friendly one as Chad Jackson burst into laughter, and pointed out to the Evangelist that his accent is what outed him, and proceeded to say the Evangelist is most definitely an American. Evangelist Fredrick affirmed that Chad is right, that he's from Mississippi and he's a missionary.

"Your wife, Winnie, what about her, is she an American?" asked Chad.

Evangelist Fredrick smiled and said of course Winnie is an American, and they got married twenty-six years ago in the United States, and came to Romania for their honeymoon.

Chad Jackson then laughed and joked with the Evangelist saying they seemed to like what they saw when they visited Romania during their honeymoon and decided to return to Romania for good.

"I was staying with my parents who are devout Christians at the time of our marriage, but during our honeymoon, Winnie and I felt as if the whole world was placed on our palm for us to explore," said Evang. Fredrick.

"Hmm, you felt the same? I had that feeling as well and I guess every new couple do have that feeling," replied Chad.

Evangelist Fredrick laughed and said as newly married couple he and Winnie considered the options before them and what to do with the world, then decided to throw all in for God. He went on to say, working for God became their life style and they haven't looked back since they made that decision.

Chad Jackson went to say his dad is an American, while his mum is from Romania.

Evangelist Fredrick's suspicion was confirmed as he told Chad that he now understands where Chad got his name from, and said Chad's accent is Romanian but his name is American.

Chad Jackson interjected and said his accent is because he was born in Romania, and he grew up in Romania. Evangelist Fredrick then asked Chad if he does make out time to visit America, at least to spend some time with his dad's siblings. Chad Jackson confirmed he does visit, saying his dad made sure he's acquainted with his relatives in America, and he enjoyed their company.

"My next holiday will be in the United States," said Evangelist Fredrick.

Chad Jackson smiled and said that will be nice, but suddenly realised his attention is needed in the office, he then turned to the Evangelist, and said he'll have to go. Evangelist Fredrick replied to Chad and said it's a pleasure spending some time with him.

Chad Jackson then said maybe later tonight, he will send for the Evangelist, so they can spend some time together.

"Ok captain, that will be great, and let me retire to my cabin," said Evangelist Fredrick.

Chad Jackson rushed back to attend to his ship, and the Evangelist retired to his cabin.

An hour later, as the Evangelist leafed through the pages of some Christian literature, Winnie called her husband's phone. She went on to say she hoped he's enjoying his cruise ship experience. The Evangelist became somewhat jocular even as he confirmed it's all fun, but then reminded her the fun would've been complete with her by his side.

Winnie laughed and said the fun would've been more if she's by her husband's side yet went on to say her ears are itching to hear about the fun he'd enjoyed thus far. Funnily, instead of sharing his cruise ship experience with his wife, the Evangelist went on to say that each time he tries expressing his satisfaction over the cruise experience, he gets this needling feeling of emptiness, meaning something is amiss.

Winnie interjected and said it's already glaring that he's on this trip alone and urged him to feel free with himself for once.

"Oh, alone? I think this feeling goes beyond mere loneliness," said Evang. Fredrick.

"Yes, of course, I suppose this is just a feeling of loneliness, though I'm with you in the spirit," said Winnie.

Evangelist Fredrick then joked and said the fact that she's with him in the spirit, gives him the comfort he seeks. "What do you think, aren't I always with you in spirit, this can't be any different?" said Winnie. The Evangelist then decided it's time to satisfy Winnie's itching ears as he now said the atmosphere in the cruise ship is wonderful and their service has greatly improved compared to their last trip.

Winnie laughed and joked with her husband, saying she's beginning to feel jealous, but the Evangelist decided to return the joke as he urged his wife not to be jealous and that since she's with him in the spirit, part of the fun will trickle down to her.

"Yeah, you're right," said Winnie.

The Evangelist then told his wife that it was a bit stormy earlier, and the wind has suddenly become boisterous, thick and fast, though the ship captain expects things to return to normal. Winnie then suggested the ship should've stayed behind about an hour or two, till the wind settles down.

The Evangelist played the situation down to stop his wife worrying, and said he doesn't think that was necessary, and if it was, they would have stayed back for things to calm.

"Have you eaten?" asked Winnie.

The Evangelist confirmed he has eaten, and said he ate lunch at the cruise restaurant and the meal was lovely. Winnie replied saying that's nice but asked about her husband's pack lunch.

"I decided to leave that for dinner, later today," he replied.

"Ok, not bad," said Winnie. After spending some time catching up, they ended the conversation, with Winnie promising to call back before going to bed.

# CHAPTER

## THREE

*The Kaija incident*

Later that night, Simon who's one of the sailors in the cruise ship walked into the captain's office and asked the captain if he sent for him. Chad Jackson nodded in affirmation, as he asked Simon if he's busy at the moment, Simon replied him saying he's documenting travel information.

Chad has always considered himself a pragmatist as opposed to a moralist. His brief meeting with the Evangelist was quite unravelling and left him wanting more of the Evangelist, and decided to invite him to the bridge of his ship.

Chad Jackson seemed keen to have the Evangelist by his side that evening, as he insisted that whatever task Simon has at hand can wait for now. He then asked him to go to cabin 24, and said the occupant is Evangelist Fredrick Douglas, and requested he ask the Evangelist to come with him.

"Ok Captain," said Simon.

Minutes later Simon knocked the door to the Evangelists' cabin and asked if there's anyone in. Evangelist Fredrick stopped and asked who it was by the door. Simon replied and said who it was, before proceeding to inform him the captain has a message for him. Evangelist Fredrick then asked Simon if he meant Chad Jackson.

"Yes, of course," replied Simon.

The Evangelist then asked Simon to give him a minute so he could make himself decent, he then puts on his pyjamas and opened the door. Simon quickly informed the Evangelist that the captain said he should come with him.

The Evangelist who really didn't think the captain will follow through with the promise of spending some more time with him, then asked if anything is the matter. Simon said he doesn't think anything is the matter because the captain's countenance doesn't suggest there is any. After their brief conversation, the Evangelist then requested a few minutes to get dressed, and said he will join Simon in a minute.

"Ok, I'll be waiting," said Simon.

Minutes later, Simon and the Evangelist got to where the captain was seated, and he turned to the captain and joked. "You sent for me?" The Evangelist isn't oblivious that there's nothing untoward about this call, but an opportunity for the two to catch up further.

"Are you surprised, I told you I will send for you and that's what I just did, or have you retired for the day?" asked Chad. The Evangelist smiled and said he hasn't retired for the day, and that he's just leafing through his favourite Christian literature.

Chad Jackson laughed and said the Evangelist answered to his call with a bible in his hand.

"I thought you wanted me to share the word of God with you, because that's what I do best," said Evang. Fredrick.

Chad Jackson replied saying it's their first day in the cruise ship, and he looks forward to hearing God's word from the Evangelist but that will be tomorrow. The Evangelist pressed and said since God has laid it in his heart to come with a bible, now is the best time share the word of God, because procrastination is a thief. Yet, after the back and forth, they decided that they will share the word of God the next day, the Evangelist then said he'll be grateful for the opportunity to share God's word with the captain.

Chad Jackson wasn't playing down the opportunity either, as he said the privilege of having missionaries around him is something he holds close to his heart and cherishes. Chad was a bit jocular with Evangelist Fredrick and said he wants to know more about the Evangelist because he thinks he's an unassuming character, and man with a dazzling personality. He then proceeded to ask the Evangelist what drink he should offer him.

The Evangelist laughed and thanked the captain for the kind gesture and said aside from the health implication, he doesn't drink alcohol because he's a Christian. The Evangelist's view on God doesn't necessarily make him some sort of recluse who is miles away from modernity. He's a man basking in the glory of God and believes that only those divinely positioned to understand this will know it.

Chad Jackson laughed and said he knows the Evangelist will say that and said he didn't invite the Evangelist unprepared. "Prepared, how do you mean?" asked Evang. Fredrick.

Chad Jackson then hinted his guest that he has some non-alcoholic drinks, good ones, and the Evangelist will like them. Evangelist Fredrick then laughed, saying the captain seem quite prepared before inviting him over.

Chad Jackson then turned to Simon who's still by the corner and asked him get the non- alcoholic drinks from the refrigerator. Moments later, Simon returned and handed the captain a bottle of wine, and two wine glasses. Chad Jackson then asked Simon to open the bottle of wine and serve them, after serving the captain and his guest, the Evangelist collected the glass of wine from Simon and took a sip, then muttered.

"This wine is lovely."

Chad Jackson laughed and said that's him, keeping his word about the quality of the wine.

Evangelist Fredrick then thanked the captain and told the captain he's beginning to make this cruise trip very interesting.

Chad Jackson interjected and reminded the Evangelist that he said he was with Winnie on his previous trip, and then asked why he didn't bring Winnie along this time.

Evangelist Fredrick didn't hold back as he said they planned to make the trip together but something came up in Winnie's place of work. "Do you work?" asked Chad.

"Of course, I'm an architect while Winnie is a nurse," said Evangelist. Fredrick.

Chad Jackson smiled again as he interjected and said, as for him, this ship signifies his retirement.

The Evangelist seemed not to understand what Chad meant, he then reminded Chad he's still strong and asked why the talk about retirement should come up in his conversation. Chad Jackson had to make himself clearer by throwing more light in his comment concerning his retirement, as he said he doesn't intend retiring now but intends to carry on with this ship until he's due for retirement.

"Ok, that's not a bad idea," said Evang. Fredrick.

Chad Jackson went on to suggest that if this cruise ship should break down before his intended retirement time, then that will mean early retirement for him. The Evangelist wasn't impressed with Chad, considering his view as morbid, because the idea of an early retirement is nothing but a tin pot, he then urged the captain to take a more positive approach to life. He reminded Chad that since he intends to travel with this ship for years to come, then he might as well better be positive, so this ship won't break down.

"Evangelist, I know, but I'm only being pragmatic, and I don't mind dying with this ship, if the need be, because she's my baby," replied Chad. He assured the Evangelist that his comments about his ship isn't some kind of egocentric trip, and if a man lives long enough, he definitely will have regrets, but the buck stops with this ship.

"Every decent captain of which I am one, should go down with their ship," he reiterated.

The Evangelist interjected and quickly admonished Chad Jackson and said he has just moved from being pragmatic to cynicism. Chad Jackson laughed after being rebuked by the Evangelist, he then said he understands that a step away from pragmatism is cynicism and there's a thin line between the two. Chad sensed that the Evangelist's claim of God having the moral high ground seems not to have diminished, and even at that, no love was lost between them because their disagreements wasn't physical, and neither was it bare chested.

Evangelist Fredrick felt the need to admonish this cruise ship captain further over his negative utterances, he then turned on his positivity and said, "I won't die today or any other day in an accident, and that's my resolve".

"I like your faith, and spirit of positivity," replied Chad.

While the conversation was going on, the ship was being tossed up and down by the mighty storm that suddenly gained momentum, the captain sensed the ship is losing its ability to stay steady in its course he then excused himself and said he will be back.

The captain immediately stood up and rushed to see how his crew was dealing with the boisterous sea weather. After a moment with his crew, he realised he will be needed by his crew to steady this ship and help it stay its course, he then turned around and quickly rushed to inform the Evangelist that their little get-together is over, because he now has quite a pressing issue to attend to.

Unfortunately, while he was passing the message to the Evangelist, the ship slammed into a rock causing a big shaking. Sadly, both the Evangelist and Chad Jackson, found themselves on the floor. Chad Jackson got up from the floor of the ship where he fell and realised his guest, Evangelist Fredrick, was still on the floor, the captain rushed to his side. "Evangelist, Evangelist, wake up," Chad screamed.

Simon rushed into the captain's office to inform him they have a problem outside. Chad is now torn between focusing his attention on reviving his guest, and going to attend to a ship that has just slammed into a rock. He got up quickly and he inquired from Simon about how bad the situation is. Simon's hand was quite a shudder, and the fear in his face was palpable, as he replied his boss saying the situation is very bad, Simon then proceeded to ask if the Evangelist is ok.

Chad Jackson interjected and said the Evangelist is unconscious, and that he seems to have hit his head on the metal edge of the table in the captain's office. He then pleaded with Simon to please attend to the Evangelist, so he could attend to the situation outside. Simon took over from the captain, trying to revive the unconscious Evangelist, he kept calling the Evangelist and asking if he could hear him.

Raphael who's the assistant captain of the Cruise ship immediately went on radio to call for help. "Mayday, Mayday, Mayday," he yells continually through the radio.

Chad Jackson rushed to his number two man in the cockpit, he then asked Raphael what the problem was, and what they have done. Raphael was now trembling, as he confirmed to the captain that they slammed into a rock and the ship is going down.

"Oh Raphael, no, no, what have you done, Raphael, and why did you do this to me?" Chad cried. "I'm sorry, Captain, the storm is just too powerful to keep the ship on course, and I just can't explain how this happened," replied Raphael.

"How can anything ever be simple, and have you sent SOS message?" asked Chad.

"Yes, captain," replied Raphael.

Chad Jackson was quite exasperated, even as he held his nerve while asking Raphael how much time at their disposal to evacuate the passengers to safety, despite his being worried sick that most of the passengers are already hurt by the accident.

Raphael muttered in response, saying they don't have time and the ship will possibly go down in the next two hours. "Oh, that's bad," said Chad, who didn't hesitate to order Raphael to begin evacuation immediately, and just as Raphael turned to leave, Chad beckoned on him again and ordered the crew to locate those who were hurt by this accident and let them get medical attention even as they evacuate.

"Ok, Captain," said Raphael.

Chad Jackson then ordered Raphael to start evacuation immediately, while he continues with his effort of trying to save the ship. Unfortunately, Chad's effort seemed impossible.

Raphael left in a hurry to begin the evacuation process, and even as he struggles to keep this ship afloat, Chad remained worried sick about his new friend, the Evangelist. He then rushed back to his office to see the state of his friend who was unconscious, and by the time he got there he met a medical team attending to the Evangelist and asked Simon how the Evangelist is doing.

Simon replied his boss saying the Evangelist is breathing but still unconscious, a member of the medical team then turned to the captain and said the Evangelist may have fractured his skull. The captain has to inform them that he has ordered immediate evacuation of the ship. He then asked Simon to evacuate the Evangelist from the ship immediately.

It didn't take long before the situation inside the ship became quite tense, thick and fast, with crew members running helter-skelter to save what's left of their ship. The passengers were suddenly overwhelmed, as they scampered for safety at the sight of rushing torrential sea water inundating their cabins.

While the ship crew were attempting to begin evacuation using the lifeboats, things took a sudden and dramatic twist as the cruise ship that was struggling to stay afloat and steady, sank within few minutes, and ten minutes later rescue teams began arriving.

**Rescue Crew**

The first respondent arrived the scene moments later from when the SOS message went out, which is about few minutes from when the ship went down to the bottom of the sea. Not long from when the ship went down, a ship on sea arrived the scene on a rescue mission and gave a landing platform to the helicopter with which the first respondents arrived. Jerome Baptist who led the rescue mission let down some boats for the survivors around the scene of the incident, he then sends divers immediately into the ship to find survivors.

After rescuing the survivors around the scene of the incident, particularly those on lifeboats and survival craft, there's now a need to expand the perimeter of the search while the rest of his crew search for both the living and the dead trapped in the cruise ship. Jerome Baptist who's the head of the rescue operation returned to the helicopter and urged his crew to embark on a further search.

Ned kristoff, who is a member of the crew in the helicopter turned to Jerome and said it's dark and there seem to be no more survivors.

"Don't tell me they're all dead!" exclaimed Jerome, he then instructed the helicopter pilot to just flash the light of his helicopter on the water. Ned flashed his head light on the water and the crew began to scream. "Is anybody out there, anybody alive, please answer me?" search crew screamed. The sea that suddenly turned glassy calm is now inundated with lights from the ship, as the rescue ship provided more visibility in support of the rescue operation.

Jerome Baptist urged his team members to keep screaming, and louder. Sadly, the troubled sea has dispersed some of the survivors far away from the scene of the accident. This implies that the search crew will have to do more than limit their search around the sunken ship to find survivors. Simon is still adrift at sea trying to keep afloat in water.

"Help, help me, I'm alive and I'm here," Simon yelled. Jose turned to Jerome Baptist, and pointed saying there's somebody out there, and he can hear him call out for help.

Jerome Baptist urged his team to move quickly. "Move, move, go for him, go for them, anybody out there, do that now," said Jerome.

He then turned to his crew and urged them to keep screaming and scream louder.

Minutes after his rescue, Simon wasn't self-indulgent and didn't sulk about his time in the water either, he immediately walked up to Jerome Baptist and introduced himself and said he's a crew member of this ill-fated ship, and then thanked them for coming.

"Ok, good you're safe, what really happened, and why isn't there any rescue attempt by the captain and the crew?" asked Jerome.

Simon was still shaken, yet informed Jerome, it all happened so fast, the ship went down as they're about releasing lifeboats into the water in an evacuation attempt.

"Oh shame, let's hope we will get everybody out in one piece," said Jerome. He then turned to the paramedics, and urged them to check Simon out to be sure he's ok.

# CHAPTER

## FOUR

### *The Breaking News*

*Breaking News*

Jordan was watching the television in his dad's living room when the breaking news of the accident came up on screen, and he immediately rushed to his big brother's room. "Peter, Peter, wake up," said Jordan.

Peter woke up, but still sleepy, he then asked Jordan what it was, and said Jordan scared him in the manner he woke him up. Jordan interjected and said there's a problem, something has just happened.

Peter was oblivious of the happenings out there, he focused on Jordan and asked if anything is the matter and if he's ok.

"It's dad, Octal Flamingo has gone down," said Jordan.

The sleep in Peter's eyes disappeared immediately as he asked his brother to explain what he meant by the ship going down, and what the problem with Octal Flamingo could be.

Jordan was still apprehensive as he informed Peter that Octal Flamingo has sunk, that they just aired the news on the television. Peter exclaimed and jumped up from bed immediately, and then rushed for the remote and switched on the television in his room. "Oh my God, my dad," he muttered, with his hands on his head and then fell back on the bed.

Jordan looked on, as tears rolled down his cheek, he then asked Peter what he suggests they do next. Peter was quite distraught yet constrained himself from crying, and all he could say to his brother was that he doesn't know how to break this news to their mum, because this is a hard pill to swallow.

"But we still need to tell her, so we can start contacting the authorities," said Jordan.

Peter nodded in affirmation and said it's obvious they'll have to tell their mum about it, he got up from his bed again and left his room.

"Lord, please strengthen us," Peter prayed.

A moment later Peter knocked the door to his mum's room, "mum, mum wake up," said Peter.

"Peter, is that you?" asked Winnie.

"Yes mum, wake up," said Peter.

"Come in, Peter, is anything the matter, and are you ok?" asked Winnie. This mum isn't such inept not to sense that something is off, considering the manner her sons came knocking at her door. Peter and Jordan walked into the bedroom, and in a quite subtle tone, Peter told his mum there's a problem and he doesn't know how to say this.

It was quite an eerie feeling for Winnie, as she muttered and said seeing the two of her sons walk into her room at this time of the night sent jitters down her spine. She then asked Peter what it was because she's scared already.

"Mum, Octal Flamingo has sunk," said Peter.

"What, Jesus! she exclaimed. She then asked when and how this happened.

Peter then informed his mum that the news of the accident is being aired on the television as they speak. Winnie rushed to the front of the television in the living room and finds the news and even the rescue operation being aired live.

"No, no this is a joke," Winnie cried. Sadly, it isn't a joke, and she knows that. Her heart sank as she watched the news with her heart in her hands, wishing the television reporting isn't true. Unfortunately, this isn't the case, and even the mighty Oak tree understands when the forest is troubled. The news was so shattering to Winnie that she turned to Peter, and crying, begging him to please tell her this news isn't true.

Peter had no choice but to insist the news is true, and then suggested to his mum that they pray that his dad is ok. He then said the rescue team is already at the scene, and there's a contact number displayed on the screen for concerned families to reach out.

Winnie decided that they call that number immediately and said she and her sons needed to be at the scene of the accident for their dad, and to make sure he's ok. Peter quickly typed in the emergency phone number displayed on the screen, he then dialled the number.

"Hello" said Peter.

The customer care person on the other side of the phone, said hello, and asked who's on the line. Peter introduced himself as Peter Douglas, and then said his dad is on board that ship, I mean the Octal Flamingo. "Ok Peter, this line will be open all through this period, to give family members all the support they need," said the customer care person.

Peter quickly interjected and said the support they need right now, is to be at the scene of the accident to give whatever support they could to their dad.

The customer care person replied Peter saying that would be fine but it's already late and the rescue team are still searching for survivors. Peter proceeded to ask to know how many survivors have been rescued so far. The customer care person who was quite courteous in her choice of words replied Peter saying only thirty passengers have been rescued, and the search for survivors is still on. "Oh my God, thirty out of two hundred and seventy-nine, that's quite poor and that's the more reason why I should be there for my dad.

"It's late already, Peter, and how do you intend to do that?" asked the customer care person.

"I need to be there for my dad, please help me," replied Peter.

"Ok, hold on," said the customer care person.

Peter held the phone to his ear and hoping for an opportunity to visit the scene of the accident immediately. A moment later the customer care person returned to the phone and informed Peter that a rescue team will be leaving for Kaija in the next hour, and they are headed to the scene of the incident.

"Oh good, can I join them?" asked Peter.

The customer care person then said the resource team will be ready to make space for him since he's determined to be there. Peter quickly interjected and pleaded with the lady on the phone to please make space for three, to accommodate his mum, his brother and himself.

The lady smiled empathetically for the grieving family, but considered Peter's request to be a tall order, and said all that's available is just a space, and suggested that his brother and mum can join him at the scene tomorrow. Peter thanked her for the available opportunity and promised he will be there in thirty minutes from the time of their conversation, and he then ended the phone conversation.

Immediately Peter dropped the phone, Winnie asked to know what he concluded with the lady. "I'm going to the scene of the incident with the emergency services," replied Peter.

Winnie was oblivious of the agreement reached between her son and customer care person on phone, but then suggested she and Jordan will quickly get dressed, so the three of them will leave immediately.

Peter had no choice but to inform his mum that the space is just for him alone, he then urged them to stay back, and that he'll feed them on the happenings.

Winnie is already quite exasperated, and she isn't going to take a no for an answer in this circumstance, and insisted she has to go with Peter because she must be by her husband's side right now.

"Mum, they have just one space, and it's only one of us that will make it to the scene tonight," Peter said.

Winnie finds it bizarrely awkward and couldn't imagine staying back while her husband's fate remains unknown, she insisted that staying behind leaves her disturbed and traumatised. Peter himself is worried sick as the fate of their dad remains unknown, yet he had to comfort his mum, urging her not to worry that he'll keep her abreast of the happenings.

He immediately turned to Jordan, then suggested he stay with their mum, and keep an eye on her. This family held their breath, as they are now faced with the difficulty of reconciling the uncertainty of the grim news concerning the fate of survivors with the possibility of finding the Evangelist safe and well.

They now have to deal with the peril of the ill-fated Octal Flamingo. It didn't take long before Peter arrived at the take off point, and the resource team set off almost immediately, and thirty minutes later, they arrived at Kaija the scene of the accident.

Immediately Peter alighted from the helicopter, he walked up to Oscar a member of the rescue team and said hello to him before introducing himself as Peter Douglas. Oscar replied and introduced himself as Oscar, and a member of the rescue team.

Peter quickly dispensed of all the pleasantries, and said his dad is in this ship, he then asked Oscar if his dad is among the survivors rescued so far.

"What's his name?" asked Oscar.

"He's Fredrick Douglas," replied Peter.

Oscar looked through the list in his hand, and then said he doesn't know the names of all those rescued so far, yet urged him to go over there and meet Jerome Baptist.

Peter interjected and asked Oscar who Jerome Baptist was, and how he could find him. Oscar told Peter that Jerome Baptist is the head of rescue team and urged him to ask of the rescue head. Peter hurriedly walked to the pack and asked for whom the supervisor was, and with a little help, he was able to locate Jerome Baptist. "You're Jerome Baptist, I guess?" asked Peter.

"Yes, of course, what can I do for you?" replied Jerome.

Peter quickly informed Jerome that his dad is in this ship, and he needed to know if he has been found. Jerome Baptist understands the apprehension inside Peter, he then toned his voice down, and said they've rescued thirty-five passengers and all those rescued so far are all being attended to by the paramedics.

Peter rushed and looked at those rescued, and quickly returned to Jerome and said his dad isn't here, and that means he's still beneath the sea. Jerome Baptist could see through the disappointment in Peter's eyes to the disappointment in his heart, he then asked Peter to be hopeful, and they'll find his dad.

Peter hesitated for a while, but then reminded Jerome that the rescue of just thirty-five out of two hundred and seventy-nine passengers was quite an appalling record and isn't good enough. Peter urged them to up their game because time is now of the essence. Jerome Baptist took Peter's outburst on the chin, after all anyone in Peter's shoe will possibly do same, the guy wants his dad, that's all. He then subtly informed Peter he understands how he feels, and they're doing all they could to reach out to survivors, if there are any.

Peter took exception to Jerome's choice of words, and asked what he meant by if there are any, he then stressed that his dad is in there, and he believes he's still alive. While the conversation persists, Winnie called Peter and asked if he has reached the scene of the accident. Peter affirmed, and said they arrived the scene about fifteen minutes ago.

Winnie then interjected and said she hopes Peter has seen his dad and inquired to know how he's doing. "They haven't rescued dad yet, he isn't among the survivors so far," said Peter.

"What! Do you mean your dad is still beneath the sea, and what have they been doing?" asked Winnie. Peter had to calm his mum down saying the rescue team is doing all they could and urged her to be calm, even as he assured her that their dad will be safe. Winnie expected more from Peter who took the only space available in the helicopter, she stayed back to allow Peter go to Kaija with the rescue team. She seems troubled by the needling feeling that Peter has been dawdling around with the rescue team while his dad is trapped somewhere in the ship underneath the water, and expecting his family to facilitate his rescue.

Winnie quickly urged her son to get involved and give the rescue team all the support, to make sure his dad is safe. Peter concurred and said he's doing that already, but then asked his mum to pass the phone to Jordan so he could have a word with him. Winnie passed the phone to Jordan, and immediately he received the phone, he quickly asked to know what's happening, and asked if there's any news about their dad. Peter was left bereft by the situation on the ground and finding the right words to communicate the situation he's faced with without the obvious and uncomfortable squawky reaction that would follow meant he still had to be economical with the truth.

Peter subtly relayed to Jordan that their dad hasn't been found, and he's afraid time is running out. Jordan urged Peter to make himself much clearer, as he asked what he meant by time running out, and what about their dad.

"Jordan, you have to be strong for mum, make sure you comport yourself and comfort her."

"This makes the situation much scarier, but mum and I will join you by morning," Jordan insists.

"I'll be expecting you, just try to be calm," said Peter.

This accident has just by one stroke cut off the thousands of threads that holds together everything this family holds dear. The cannonade of images spouting out from the crash site shown on the television increased Winnie's desperation. While on the phone, Peter realised his mum was sobbing louder, Jordan paused for a while but then told Peter he needed to be with their mum. She's inadvertently looking like a cry-monger, and no one will wish to be in her shoes at such a grime moment.

By morning, just as many family members of victims of this ill-fated ship began trooping to the scene of the accident in droves, Winnie and Jordan also arrived the scene of the accident. Peter rushed to welcome his mum, but she didn't hesitate to ask Peter of his dad's whereabouts and said he should be out by now. Peter sadly informed his mum they haven't found him yet, and they're still hoping they'll find him alive. Winnie understands full well that the situation gets grimmer with every passing minute and took exception to Peter's comment of saying they're still hoping, asking "what have they been doing?"

"Mum, they've been working, and I felt the same way when I arrived last night," said Peter. Winnie had to remind her son that as at last night he informed her that only thirty-five people have been pulled out from the wreckage alive, and then asked how many more survivors have been rescued since them.

"They pulled out fifty more, all dead, no survivors," said Peter.

"Jesus! No Peter, don't tell me all they recovered were corpses," she cried, and then accused her son of virtue signalling, for excusing the laziness of the rescue team. Peter on the other hand pleaded with his mum, urging her to please be patient, saying they should hope his dad is somewhere in the ship and will get back to them alive.

Winnie isn't satisfied with this new revelation, she quickly asked Peter to know who the head of this rescue operation is, so she can have a word with him. Peter then replied to his mum that she will have to speak to Jerome Baptist right there.

"Jerome Baptist, who is he?" asked Winnie.

"He's the head of this rescue operation and that's him," Peter said and points to Jerome Baptist.

As Winnie approached, she met Jerome Baptist speaking to the father of a victim, "sir, please be patient, we are doing everything to get your daughter back to you safely," said Jerome.

Winnie walked into the conversation. "Excuse me, Mr. Baptist, my name is Winnie and my husband is in there," she said.

Jerome Baptist protested against Winnie's premature interference, telling her off that she should have allowed him to finish with this man, before cutting in. Winnie's knee jerk reflex implies that she was all ears and keen for news concerning her husband, but wasn't willing to accept fibs as news. She immediately reminded Jerome that her and her son can't twist in the wind any longer, and so would like to know the true situation of things.

Jerome's reply to Winnie was sort of riveting, as he insisted, they're trying to be as expeditious as possible, to make sure they find survivors. She isn't anything like her son at this point, she's like an open wound, a live wire sort of, and highly irritable with the possibility of exploding at the slightest suspicion of dawdling.

There's no cat in hells chance that Winnie would want her anxiety to be contained, courtesy at this point is overkill, and a smokescreen that could prevent victims' families from demanding haste, now that time is of the essence. Winnie stood speechless for a while, trying to process the reality before her, but wasn't too keen to be presented with damage control codes, she then opened her mouth and asked Jerome if he's repeating the exact words of her son, and insists she wants to hear something different.

"Your son, who's your son?" he asked.

Winnie quickly pointed to Peter, and said "that's him over there."

"Hmm, Peter?" asked Jerome.

"Oh, you know him already," said Winnie.

"Yes, of course, he has been pacing up and down," replied Jerome.

Winnie wasn't smiling, and she isn't about theatrics either as she asked Jerome why Peter shouldn't be pacing up and down, knowing that time is of the essence, in a rescue operation of this nature.

"Winnie, I know this is a difficult moment for you and for your boys, but I promise you, we'll do everything within our power to get Fredrick back to you," said Jerome.

Winnie quickly asked if any member among the crew of the ill-fated ship was assisting with the architecture of the ship. Jerome Baptist points to Simon who's a crew member of the Octal Flamingo, and said they're working with Simon, and that's him over there.

Jerome then hinted her that Simon is among the three surviving crew members of the Octal Flamingo. It didn't take long before the scene of the accident dawned on Winnie who was basking in the euphoria of going on a holiday, unbeknownst to her, a tragedy was lurking around. Jerome Baptist tried his best to keep Winnie calm, using known clichés and said sometimes life throws the unexpected at people.

Winnie began to sob, and began speaking metaphorically, saying the euphoria of going on a holiday with her husband has turned into a surreal drama. Jerome did his best to encouraged Winnie to be positive, urging her not to resign her husband's fate to death with negative thoughts.

Winnie replied and said that's good, let's hope on hope, because that's the only thing they have got left. Jerome Baptist thanked Winnie, and said he has to go now, because there are lots of things needing his attention.

"Thank you, my sons and I will be hanging around for my husband," Winnie said as she walks away.

Just as Winnie walks away from Jerome, Peter suggested to his mum, they should have a word with Simon, maybe he might know something about their dad. Winnie wasn't keen to hear siren voices repeating what she had been told already, as she insisted that asking Simon about her husband would do nothing but relying on mere serendipity. This is a cruise ship with over two hundred passengers, and the possibility of Simon having met their dad is quite slim. She then reminded Peter that there are two hundred and seventy-nine passengers in that ship, and asked him how he expects Simon to know his dad.

Jordan was more upfront with Peter's suggestion than his mum, as he suggested to his mum that him and his brother would like to speak with Simon if she doesn't mind, maybe he knows something about their dad.

### The grim reality

Peter and his brother then walked up to Simon, and he immediately called out Simon's name just as he said hello to Simon.

"Hello, do I know you?" asked Simon.

"Oh, I get it; we called your name just as your acquaintances do," replied Peter.

Simon nodded in affirmation, and said of course, Peter's tone sounds as if they knew him long before now. Peter wasn't apologetic about being upfront with Simon, he went on to say, he learnt that their interest seems aligned.

Simon then focused his attention on Peter and asked what interest it is that he's talking about. "Just as you wished all the passengers and crew members are safe, all we want is for our dad and other passengers to come out of this," said Peter.

Simon isn't too keen to attend to words laced in riddles, he went on to ask Peter what's it he want to know about his dad. Peter dipped his hand into his pocket and brought out his dad's photograph and asked Simon if he saw his dad, Fredrick Douglas, the Evangelist.

Simon then asked them if their dad is the Evangelist, about 6ft tall, ginger hair and blue eyes. He then looked at the photograph and said, yes, the man in the photograph is the Evangelist he's referring to.

"Are you sure about this, and do you know him?" asked Jordan.

Simon affirmed he knew the Evangelist and said the Evangelist was with the captain all through, until the accident. Peter interjected and said it mean Simon saw his dad before the accident.

"Yes, of course, he was having a drink with the captain just before the accident," said Simon.

Jordan quickly pointed out to Simon that his dad doesn't drink alcohol, and suggested Simon might be talking about the wrong man. Simon then went into specifics to prove to this pair he isn't telling them fibs, and that he really knew their dad, he then reminded them their dad was lodged in cabin 24.

"You're right, you know him, what happened before the accident?" asked Peter.

"The captain served him a non-alcoholic drink, and when the accident happened, your dad hit his head and lost consciousness at the impact of the accident," said Simon.

This new twist left Peter speechless, now that providence has brought them face to face with someone who had a direct encounter with their dad. He then asked Simon if he's implying that his dad was already unconscious even before the ship sank.

Simon opened up to these siblings that the ship captain did ask him to resuscitate the Evangelist while he steers the ship to safety, but the sea water inundated the ship thick and fast and suddenly the ship sank.

Peter became critical and even accused the ship's crew of negligence, as he reminded Simon, he isn't a medical person, how come the captain would ask him to resuscitate an unconscious man. Simon quickly rephrased his earlier comment by saying he meant the captain asked him to get paramedics to do the resuscitation.

"And my dad didn't return to consciousness before the ship sank?" asked Peter.

"Yes, he didn't, I'm sorry," replied Simon.

Jordan rushed to his mum who has been on her knees praying, to inform her Simon knew their dad, saying Simon said their dad was already unconscious even before the ship sank.

This new revelation left Winnie reeling from within, it did leave a bad taste in her mouth, as she quickly asked Jordan what it was that Simon had told them about their dad. Jordan replied to his mum and said Simon hinted them he was with their dad before the ship sank.

Winnie is inclined to hear directly from Simon whom she earlier dismissed, she then said she needed to see Simon because she needs to know everything he knows about her husband. Jordan supported the move and urged his mum to have a word with Simon.

Winnie immediately hurtled over to where Simon was and speaking with Peter. She quickly said hello to Simon and said her son said he met with their dad. Peter paused as his mum approached and joined the conversation. Simon replied and said of course, he was with the Evangelist before the ship sank.

Winnie is a nurse, and her first question to Simon was to clarify what he meant about her husband being unconscious because she doesn't seem to follow. Simon had to relay the chronology of events leading to the accident again, but this time to Winnie, as he said the Evangelist was having a drink with the captain when the accident occurred.

Winnie pleaded with Simon not to get them confused saying her husband doesn't drink alcohol. Simon then explained further saying he meant her husband was having a non-alcoholic drink, he then fell and hit his head on the side of a metal table, at the impact of the accident.

"And that made him unconscious, why wasn't he revived before the accident?" asked Winnie.

Simon understands the crew of this ill-fated ship is now being perceived by this grieving family as a heartless bunch, who cared less for their passenger. He'd to clear any misconception, as he informed Winnie that he was doing that with the paramedics when the ship suddenly sank.

Winnie then muttered and said this seems to be a lot harder than expected, because if her husband is unconscious as at the time the ship sank, then his chances of fighting to stay afloat and alive will be limited.

Winnie then reached for her phone, Peter looked at her with keen interest but wasn't sure what his mum was up to, he then asked her who it is she's itching to call with her phone. "I need to talk to Reverend Fitzgerald," said Winnie.

"Mum, does it matter, what can he do for us at this point?" asked Peter.

Winnie insisted that calling to inform the Priest is the right thing to do, he's part of this from the beginning, and he should know. Winnie puts a call across to Reverend Fitzgerald who serendipitously, hasn't seen the news headlines until a few minutes ago. He was standing in front of the television, faced with the surprise of the shocking news when Winnie's phone call came in, and she immediately said hello reverend, immediately he picked up.

He exclaimed and said he was just about to call Winnie, before her call came in. Winnie interjected and asked the Priest if he heard the news. Reverend Fitzgerald replied and said he just saw the news and was about to rush into his bedroom to get his phone but Winnie's phone call came in first.

Winnie began to sob saying they haven't found Fredrick, and that he's still beneath the water.

"Calm down, Winnie, please be strong, my hunch tells me Fredrick is alive," said Reverend Fitzgerald. Winnie continued sobbing saying she doesn't think she can handle this, and there's no way she can be calm, when her husband's whereabouts' is still unknown. Reverend Fitzgerald then asked to know where Winnie is right now.

"I'm in the coast of Kaija, the scene of the accident," said Winnie.

Reverend Fitzgerald then proceeded to ask about Peter and Jordan.

"Peter and Jordan are here with me, though Peter actually got here last night," said Winnie.

Reverend Fitzgerald then interjected and said he will join them shortly, he then said he need to find a way to navigate to Kaija. Winnie doesn't seem to like the idea of the priest coming to Kaija, she then reminded the Priest of his frail health, and urged him to just stay behind and continue to pray along with them, but promised to feed him with the happenings. The reverend insisted it's necessary, as he reminded Winnie that it was him who advised Fredrick to make this trip, and as such he can't stay behind in times like this.

It's common knowledge that Reverend Fitzgerald is a notorious enabler of Fredrick Douglas Evangelistic missionary assignments, and now that things have suddenly gone south, sitting on the fence isn't the most idyllic thing to do. Winnie pleaded with the Priest not to feel guilty over this and urged the Priest to just continue praying and look forward to receiving Fredrick alive.

Reverend Fitzgerald then decided to stay behind and promised to be calling Winnie for regular updates. Peter took some steps away and stood by the seaside imagining his dad beneath the sea, but shortly after, he had this brief moment when he forgot about his dad and was admiring the sea. The sea looked glassy-calm, harmless, and patronising, but he immediately reminded himself that this is a shipwreck site, and nothing but a relic of bad memory.

Three days after the accident, Winnie and her boys have hoped against hope, but the Evangelist wasn't recovered whether dead or alive. This time Peter and his mum walked up to Jerome Baptist who was busy addressing families of victims, and asked what's going on, saying his dad is still in there.

Even the nuance of the gesticulation when he addresses the crowd is something many find fascinating, but this nuance meant nothing to Winnie and her sons because Jerome have been unable recover their loved one. Jerome Baptist muttered, and said he knows the Evangelist is still in there and he understands their frustrations. Winnie interjected and urged Jerome to please stop telling them about knowing how they feel.

"I have told you earlier he's in cabin 24 or the captain's office, send your team to get him," said Winnie.

Jerome Baptist became more cautious with his choice of words and asked what else he could say if not to encourage Winnie and her boys to be strong, while they continue with their search and rescue effort.

"Look Jerome, I'm tired of these platitudes, cliché, or whatever you call it, just search the captain's office thoroughly and you will find him," insists Winnie.

Jerome Baptist emphasised and said they've searched the captain's cabin, time after time, and didn't find her husband. Peter then urged them to keep searching, stressing that his dad is in there, and they want him alive.

Jerome then specifically assigned Petru to go into cabin 24 in search of the Evangelist, if per chance the Evangelist serendipitously find himself in his cabin. Petru went into cabin 24 in search of the Evangelist but was faced with an empty cabin. He looked around and saw a Christian literature among other things, the Evangelist was reading this literature before his invitation by the ship captain.

Interestingly, Petru needed evidence to show to Winnie that he did visit her husband's cabin, and among other items in that cabin, this literature seems to be one thing that captured this diver's attention. He immediately reached for the book and opened it. He couldn't believe what he saw next. He practically saw the letters in the book leaving, in what looked as if the inked letters in the books were being lifted out.

As an experienced diver who is used to the mystery beneath the sea, he knew immediately that this counts as one of those unexplained mysteries, as he could suddenly feel goose bumps all over his body. He then hurried out of the cabin as he reports back to Jerome who seem keen for answers.

Yet, he held onto this literature, as he needed something to prove to Winnie and even Jerome that he was actually in the Evangelist's cabin.

Things suddenly got weirder when Petru came out of the water and reached for the literature, only find the book dry and not looking like something that has had contact with water. More confusing for this diver is that all the letter in the book left, except the word "God", and "Jesus."

These two words remain where they originally appeared in the book, while the rest part of the book is blank. No one at this point is able to corroborate Petru's story and no one could disprove it either.

One thing everyone present agreed on was the mystery of how this Christian literature came out of the water dry, and how this literature is suddenly wiped blank leaving only the word "God" and "Jesus" in their original locations in the book.

"It's like I am going crazy, Jerome, and is my mind playing tricks on me or what?" Asked Petru.

"Petru, please sit down, the dry book in your hand explained your encounter with something divine," replied Jerome, who seemed confused with the mystery surrounding this literature.

"Do we have a priest here? get me a priest, Jerome, I need a priest," said Petru.

Jerome has worked with Petru for years, and he knows for sure that he did have an encounter with something, but that something is what Jerome himself couldn't explain.

"Are you suggesting that some spirit entered inside you, that you need a priest to exorcise?" Jerome curiously asked.

"I came in contact with something, Jerome, " replied Petru.

There wasn't any priest around to help calm Petru. Peter was at the scene and watched as this drama unfolds, he realised the guy that was meant to get his dad may have experienced the finger of God at work the moment he entered his dad's cabin. He immediately reached out to Petru, they then stepped aside from the crowd, and minutes later Winnie joined her son as they prayed and counselled Petru, then led him to Christ.

"Please repeat after me," said Peter.

"Lord Jesus, I come to you a sinner, and from today onward, I accept you as my Lord and Saviour. Please forgive me of my sins and write my name in the book of life in Jesus Name," Petru professed. Winnie then reached into her handbag and handed Petru a spare bible she carries with her for an occasion such as this.

This family had to step aside to carry out the command of Jesus Christ by leading Petru to Christ, and later returned to the drama of searching for their loved one. Petru had to go somewhere quiet where he stayed for a while, reminiscing his experience in the missing Evangelist's cabin.

Hours later, divers returned and painstakingly searched inside the wreckage of the ship as it lays on the sea bed, beneath the water, in search of this Evangelist that has suddenly become a sensation following Petru's experience in the missing Evangelist's cabin, but couldn't find him.

Now that divers specifically went into cabin 24 in search of the Evangelist following Winnies' insistence, that her husband may have rushed to his cabin while the ship was being inundated with water, and didn't find the Evangelist but returned with the Christian literature he was reading before the invitation by the Ship Captain. Jerome has proved he has a listening ear, by acceding to Winnie's suggestion.

Winnie's dogged determination to recover her husband wasn't misconstrued by Jerome as offensive, moreover she apologised for her earlier outburst and reminded Jerome she doesn't in anyway intend to spit in his face, rather she's doing what any sensible wife will do in the current circumstance.

Jerome Baptist wouldn't want to give this family a false hope, he quickly corrected Peter's request to have his dad back and alive, by saying the operation is now a recovery operation and no more a rescue operation. It's now undeniably obvious that Peter must be illusory to expect the rescue team to recover his dad alive except there's a divine hand at work in this rescue operation. Winnie however quipped at Jerome's assertion that this is now a recovery operation.

"What! That's a harsh thing to say, that comment makes me feel a sharp pain tearing through my heart," Winnie cried. She knows not what fate has befallen her husband, yet she is determined to continue the search for her lovely husband whom she is overly fond of. Jerome Baptist then looked into Winnie's eyes, and explained further, saying that this is the third day and from what she and her sons can see, the rescue team are only recovering the dead, and not the living, even when the wish of the rescue team is to find victims alive.

It's quite obvious that Jerome Baptist isn't just telling this grieving family a cacophony of lies, and perhaps he's rather preparing them for the reality of the situation on the ground.

Jordan then walked into the conversation, "mum, what's he saying, and what about dad?" asked Jordan.

Winnie couldn't say much but replied to her son, saying she doesn't understand, and then began to sob, yet urged her boys to continue praying so their dad would return to them alive.

Peter then turned to Jerome and said they'll be hanging around, and urged him to just continue the search, and they hope their dad will be found.

"Mum, let's go somewhere and wait for them to find dad," said Jordan. They then moved some distance away and held hands as before and continued praying for the Evangelist's safe return. They needed somewhere to stay, away from the scorching sunshine, and decided to seek shade under a make-shift shed meant for families waiting to hear news concerning their loved ones.

The whole thing was a bit rickety compared to what a proper shed used to look like in Bucharest, unfortunately, they'd no choice but to make do with it.

# CHAPTER

## FIVE

### *The bliss Luciferian Camp*

Hundred kilometres away from Kaija, lies a private and secluded Luciferian Camp by the seaside, and this camp is a hive of activity that allow Luciferians the opportunity to indulge in their spiritual proclivities away from the prying eyes of the Romanian public. By the evening of the third day after the accident, and just before sunset, Rebecca and Stacy were by the seashore of the Bliss Luciferian Camp walking barefoot on the beach.

Rebecca saw a figure afloat in the water and rushed to Stacy pointing to the floating object, and asked Stacy what that could be, and even before Stacy could take a closer look, Rebecca muttered and said it looks like a person. Stacy wasn't too keen on what Rebecca was after, and dismissed Rebecca, saying that can't be, but on a second thought.

"I mean, you're right, it's a human being," said Stacy. Rebecca exclaimed and said this is strange and asked where this floating body could possibly come from, but didn't just stop at making suppositions, she then began inching into the sea.

"Who knows, he could be a fisherman or something, but where are you rushing to?" asked Stacy. Rebecca then rushed into the water to pull the body out of the sea, and said she of course, wants to save him. Stacy on the other hand tried stopping Rebecca from making the audacious move of rushing towards a possibly decaying and stinking corpse. She urged her not to waste her energy and that she doesn't think it will be necessary, because he's already dead, and that's why he's floating on water.

Rebecca wasn't backing down, as she urged Stacy that it's best, they pull him out of the sea first before the debate over whether he's alive or dead.

Stacy eventually accepted and they went into the water and pulled out the supposedly floating object that happens to be Evangelist Fredrick Douglas. Rebecca exclaimed, saying he's dead, asking herself where the body they just pulled out of water had come from and pointed to Stacy that the dead man had a bible on him.

"A bible?" asked Stacy.

"That's a pocket bible in the breast pocket of his shirt," said Rebecca.

"Ooh, he's a Christian, one of those saying horrible things about Luciferians, describing our lifestyle as abominable, they spew hate everywhere," said Stacy.

Rebecca quickly admonished Stacy, saying the man is dead and doesn't deserve Stacy's criticism, as she reminded her about the saying that 'a dead man does no wrong'. These two ladies are now left with a dead man on their hands, even though they remained confused about what to do with the corpse in front of them.

Stacy then suggested to Rebecca that one of them should rush back to the camp hall to get help, so others will know, and decide what to do with the body. Rebecca then said, that's ok, but urged Stacy to be fast about it, because she wouldn't want to be left alone for too long with a dead person. Stacy stopped, and turned to allay Rebecca of her fears and said the man is already dead and won't bite, yet promised to be back soon.

Minutes later, Stacy rushed into the camp office, to informed Jonathan who's in charge of managing the Luciferian camp, that there's a dead body by the seashore but finding Jonathan suddenly became an arduous task.

Stacy ran the nook and cranny of the Bliss Luciferian camp and couldn't find Jonathan. On a normal day, Jonathan pops up everywhere even when not needed, but finding Jonathan is suddenly looking like someone searching for a needle in a haystack. She suddenly stopped out of frustration and muttered saying, looking for someone in this camp has suddenly turned into hide and seek with the person you're looking for. Not long after muttering her frustration, she found Jonathan strolling towards her, and she then passed the news of a dead man by the seashore to him.

Jonathan was riled to hear of the news of a dead person at the shore of a camp that's secluded from the human society.

"Dead body, how did it get there, and where could it possibly come from?" asked Jonathan.

Stacy had to explain herself further and said they saw the body floating and pulled it to shore.

Jonathan quickly pointed out to Stacy that she used the word "we," and asked Stacy she and which other person pulled the body in question out of water. Stacy seemed to be tired of the third degree from Jonathan, and said it's she and Rebecca, though she's at the seashore waiting for them.

"Ok, let me get some help, so we can go immediately," said Jonathan. They both turned around to leave, but Jonathan's first point of call was to get Mario who is a medical doctor, and just arrived the camp waiting for Jonathan to allocate camp rooms for his family. Funnily, while Jonathan was going for Mario, Stacy's patience was beginning to grow thin, as she accused Jonathan of dawdling and asked where he was headed, reminding him that Rebecca is alone with the corpse and she's waiting for him.

"Sorry, Mario, I'll need your help right now, because there's a corpse by the seashore," said Jonathan.

"A corpse, how did it get there?" asked Mario.

Jonathan muttered and said that's what he intends to find out for himself, and said he needed some help to move the body, yet pleaded with Mario to please come with him. Mario turned to his wife, Grace, and said he will be back, he then followed Jonathan immediately.

It didn't take long before Jonathan and Mario arrived the scene where the corpse was, but the first question Jonathan asked Rebecca who stayed by the corpse, was how far the corpse was from the shore when she found it. Rebecca pointed to a spot in the sea, and said, just there, about ten metres away from the shore. She then went on to say, though he was already dead as at the time they discovered him.

Stacy continued to mutter and said she just can't get her head around where the body came from, Jonathan seemed to have a better idea and said this is a sea, and sea accidents happen every day and people die daily as well. Typical of a doctor, Mario knelt close to the corpse to check to see if there's any pulse, to confirm if the man is actually dead.

"Wait a minute," he said.

Stacy became quite curious, and asked Mario what the matter was.

"He's alive," said Mario.

Rebecca quickly knelt down to check for pulse as well, but felt nothing, "He's dead, Mario, this man is long gone," said Rebecca. Mario was needled by that fact that a man that has spent considerable time in the water should have died of hypothermia, but he was riled that this man even had a pulse and still hanging in there.

The new twist of this supposedly dead man being alive has caused some kind of euphoria among the residents of this camp. Jonathan quickly got on his knee in his attempt to confirm Mario's assertion that this man is still alive even though Stacy didn't find any pulse. He then tried to check for a pulse, and sadly, Jonathan equally felt nothing and said there wasn't any pulse, and then turned to Mario and said the man is dead.

"I'm a doctor, and this is my job, Jonathan. The man is still alive, I can feel his pulse, but it's very, very faint, and meaning, he's almost gone," said Mario.

"Ok, if you say so, let's take him to the hospital immediately," said Jonathan.

Mario is a doctor and understands that this man's life is hanging by a thread. He quickly interjected and said it might be too late by the time the emergency services will get here. He then suggested they take the dying man to the clinic within the camp.

Jonathan wasn't too keen to risk this man's life any further, if at all he's still alive, he then asked Mario if he's sure that the medical doctors in the camp clinic will be able to handle this case, stressing that they aren't as experienced as Mario.

"Don't worry, I'll assist them, and let me attend to him right away," said Mario.

"Ok," said Jonathan.

Stacy seemed to be observing Rebecca for a while now, and she couldn't get her head around Rebecca's' sudden change in mood, she then turned to Rebecca, and asked why she has been smiling uncontrollably.

Rebecca didn't divulge too much to Stacy but replied her saying, she's just excitingly happy that this man is alive. Evangelist Fredrick Douglas was then rushed to the clinic in the Luciferian camp where he was being attended to, and hours later, Jonathan walked into the clinic, and asked to know how this stranger is doing.

Mario responded, saying the man is still in a critical condition, and will take some days to come around. Jonathan wasn't keen to throw caution into the wind, and he's sadly being nagged by this needling feeling that the decision to treat this stranger in the camp wasn't a good one and might possibly come back to bite. He then asked Mario if he's sure the man will be fine, because he doesn't want anything to go wrong with this man inside this camp.

"He'll be fine, and I'm assuring you that I have a handle on this," said Mario.

Jonathan then turned to Rebecca, who has been hanging around to see how this stranger's treatment was progressing.

"Are you still here?" asked Jonathan.

"Yes, of course, and I'm still trying to get my head around where he came from, or whatever his story might be," said Rebecca. In life, we all have stories, while for some, their story seems ongoing and far from over, others can see their story nearing its end, but for this stranger, his story is far from over, because his has just begun. Bizarrely, Rebecca isn't just keen to hear this stranger's story, she'd somehow love to be a part of it.

Mario interjected and said whatever this man's story was, the truth is that he has a swelling in his head, and he's conducting an X-ray, and then a brain scan to be sure of the extent of his injuries. Rebecca who has been quite upfront and forth coming with her ideas, then suggested that the man may have been a victim of a brutal attack, but the question begging to be answered will be, who attacked him, and how.

Jonathan happened to be quite more precise about the story of this stranger, he refuted Rebecca's assertion and suggested that this man could be one of the cruise ship accident victims.

"No, I don't think so, that accident took place about hundred and twenty kilometres away and that's about three to four days ago," said Mario.

Rebecca then toed Mario's line of argument and said, this man must be from a separate incident that has no relationship with the cruise ship accident. She proceeded to suggest that this stranger can't be among the shipwreck victims because it's impossible for any man to stay in the water for days and still be alive.

Mario insisted that this man must've been hit by something, and there's a sign he suffered from a blunt force that resulted in a concoction, this assertion further suggests that this stranger must have been attacked. Marcus, a businessman who's a regular visitor to the camp, walked in.

"How is he?" asked Marcus.

"Mario said he'll be fine," replied Rebecca.

Marcus seemed to turn his focus on Rebecca and pointed to her that she seems to have latched onto this man strangely, and her particular interest in this man makes her an unassuming personality. Jonathan didn't hesitate to support Marcus's assertion about Rebecca's connection with this stranger, saying that strikes him as well. "I guess Rebecca is just being humane and nothing more," said Jonathan.

Stacy who went about her business after handing the case of this stranger to the camp's authority, later walked into the clinic's waiting room to see how this stranger was fairing, and was surprised to see Rebecca still hanging around. She didn't hold back but asked Rebecca what she's still doing in the clinic and urged Rebecca to allow the doctors to do their job.

Rebecca wasn't keen to be lectured about what she should and shouldn't do, as she reminded Stacy that the doctors aren't complaining.

"Aren't you returning to the beach?" asked Stacy.

Rebecca replied and said that's all for today, she then told Stacy that this stranger is now her assignment.

"Oh, that's strange," replied Stacy.

The fourth day after the Kaija incident, Winnie and her two sons continued to hang around and hoping for news concerning the Evangelist who hasn't been found, either alive or dead. Jordan walked up to Peter and said their mum has been crying all day, and he can't help it anymore, and sadly, Peter wasn't oblivious of the fact that their mum has been sobbing for days now.

Peter didn't mince words as he asked his brother what he expects from a woman whose husband is trapped under water for days. Jordan interjected and said he understands the situation but reminded his brother that they seemed not to be comforting their mum enough.

Peter took his brother's advice on board and walked back to their mum. "Mum, you've been crying, and I know this is hard, but please be strong," said Peter.

Winnie couldn't hold back her tears as she reminded her son that she's now feeling so empty and she's devastated and broken. She then asked Peter what could have happened to her husband and questioning why they aren't finding him. Jordan interjected and said it means what Simon said about their dad being unconscious was right.

Winnie isn't refuting Simon's claim, but she's rather insisting that Simon's claim doesn't explain why they haven't found her husband, and she's keen to see her husband. Rationalising her husband's whereabouts was something that left her quite perplexed. Winnie was nagged by this needling feeling that all the prayers for a smooth trip, that's meant to keep the devil at bay and behind bars seem not to have been effective.

"Dad can't just disappear from the ship," said Jordan.

Peter quickly interjected and urged his brother not to rush into a hasty conclusion, and that the recovery process is still on. "Recovery! What recovery are you talking about? After all, all they're bringing out is nothing but the dead," said Winnie.

Peter pleaded with his mum, and said they've got no choice but to keep hope alive, Winnie muttered and said, that's what they are doing, even as she sobs uncontrollably.

"Mum, you have to be strong, please try to be strong," said Peter who then turned to Jordan, and asked him to please stay with their mum. Funnily, as Peter walks away, Jordan retorted and reminded Peter, he should know he can't do this alone.

Peter walks back, he then asked Jordan who he expects should stay with their mum if not them, he then insisted that things are difficult and complicated as it is. "You know I need to be close to the search and rescue team in case they find dad," said Peter.

"Ok, go on, I'll stay with her," said Jordan.

A week after the wreckage and with no news about the Evangelist, Winnie and her sons remained by the seaside and refuse to leave until they find her husband. Jerome Baptist seemed to be drawing this operation to a close yet couldn't be happier if the search and rescue team miraculously find the Evangelist, he then walked up to Winnie, and said hello to her.

Winnie on her part wants to see results and didn't hesitate to remind Jerome Baptist that his endearments won't soothe her pain, and she doesn't need him patronizing her when he should be out there searching for her husband. She wasn't particularly a fan of a dawdling paramedic and urged him to pull his socks up, her unwillingness to engage Jerome in further conversation suggests to Jerome that there isn't a need for any tactless indulgence at this point.

Jerome Baptist understands Winnie's frustration, and took her criticism on the chin, he then said he does understand how she feels, just that he's unable to take her pain away.

"Good you know," said Winnie.

Despite the possible backlash from this broken woman and her two sons, Jerome Baptist went on to inform Winnie of his decision to call off the search. Winnie went ballistic, and asked Jerome what he meant by calling off the search, she insisted that Jerome Baptist can't do that because her husband is still beneath the water. She considered it a cold-hearted move to call off the recovery operation prematurely and she finds the idea of returning home empty handed while her husband remains on the seabed as something quite terrifying.

Jerome remained speechless for a while, even as Winnie proceeded to remind him that it isn't within his gift to end the search and rescue operation while all the passengers on board the ship haven't been accounted for. Jerome Baptist went on to explain to Winnie that they've accounted for all the passengers, except two. "Ooh, my husband, and one other?" asked Winnie.

"Yes, presumed to be trapped underneath the ship," said Jerome.

Winnie didn't hold back, as she's ready to move heaven and earth to get her husband back, whether dead or alive. She then asked Jerome Baptist why he isn't getting a crane to move the ship and recover her husband. Jerome Baptist seemed to add salt to injury when he said there isn't any plan to move the ship, for now.

Winnie holds no punches as she made it clear to Jerome that she isn't taking this lying down. She immediately accused Jerome of playing her like a fiddle all this while and making her think he cares about their loss. Jerome on the other hand is keen to let her know that he does care but this isn't a mere textbook operation, and that the intricacy of each operation is specific to the circumstances surrounding the wreck.

She pointed it out to him that his concern for her family is touching but his effort is not good enough. Realising that Winnie is now taking it out on him, Jerome Baptist was lost for words, and insisted he does care but the decision to move the ship lies with the authority. Peter walked into the conversation and asked his mum what's it that she's angry about.

Winnie isn't holding back, and she's willing to tell anyone who cares that the man in charge of the operation is about to call off the search and rescue of her husband.

"Hell no, he can't do that," said Peter.

He then turned to Jerome and said for God's sake his dad is still in there. Jerome Baptist had to justify his decision, and said they dedicated the last two days searching for the Evangelist and the other victim yet found nothing. Peter's disposition is like using his body language as a means of communication and asking Jerome if he wanted a pat on the back from them when his dad's whereabouts is still in question.

He then suggested to Jerome that maybe he should do his job better, instead of calling off the search. "Ooh, despite working as hard as mongrel dogs to find your dad!" exclaimed Jerome.

Jordan who was sat some distance away, saw the drama between his mum and Jerome, he then drew closer to know what it was, and after having an ear full, Jordan then turned to his mum and urged her not to let them stop the search while their dad is still beneath the water.

Jerome Baptist then chuckled, and said they couldn't find the Evangelist, and he assumes that moving the ship is the only way out.

"Then what?" asked Jordan.

"Calm down, boy," said Jerome.

Jordan referred to his family and said family members of victims of this accident have thronged to this site, expecting to get answers, yet nothing. Jordan wasn't explicit, yet it's general knowledge to those around that he's implicitly casting Jerome as ice cold.

Peter had to calm his brother down, as he reminded Jordan that they've been on this conversation before he joined them. The tense situation is about to affect the relationship between these brothers.

"And what are you insinuating, are you suggesting we should let them call off the search?" asked Jordan.

Winnie had to make sure his children don't get at each other's throats, and requested they return to their tents, saying this has gotten more complicated, and doesn't seem to get any easier. Jerome Baptist then walks away as he returns to work, but stopped briskly and said, he'll fill them in on any new development. "Peter then thanked Jerome and then turned to Winnie.

"Mum, let's go," he said.

This incident that has supposedly caused aftershocks across Europe has eventually become what victims' families will have to deal with personally, and it's obvious to Jerome that this family is hollowed out, and their desperation is quite palpable. This whole thing has suddenly turned into a patchwork of search and rescue operation that does no one any good.

Days after the unfortunate cruise ship incident, the Evangelist's dad, Fin, his mum, Dorothy, and his immediate younger brother, Brett, flew into Romania, and from the airport in Bucharest, they headed straight to Kaija.

Just as they arrived the seaside, and was greeted by Winnie, Peter and Jordan, Dorothy froze, leaving everyone wondering what the matter could be. Things bizarrely took a new turn as Dorothy opened her mouth next, and said her son isn't dead and not underneath the sea. She immediately asked her son, Brett, to take her home, insisting her son isn't here and not dead.

"Why search for the living among the dead," was all Dorothy muttered.

She made it clear and in no uncertain terms, that not a cat in hells chance will she stay by this seaside in search of a son that isn't dead. This new twist by Dorothy left everyone aghast, with some reeling with anger, and others befuddled as they tried getting their heads around what she's getting at.

"The twist and turns of life can weigh so much on us, but should not translate into an unacceptable drama," Simon muttered.

Some family members of victims present at the scene empathised with Dorothy, yet consider her showy display of emotion to be utterly indefensible. Dorothy on the other hand, didn't consider her action to be anything overly, like someone naval gazing or attempting to use a sledge hammer to break a walnut. And as far as she's concerned, this has nothing to do with falsity, but everything to do with altruism.

Dorothy was obviously delighted to see her grandchildren, more so, is she delighted for the warm embrace from her grandchildren.

Yet, her grandchildren, Peter, and Jordan, aren't spared the confusion precipitated by Dorothy. They obviously love their nan, and was quite pleased to see her, but this new twist isn't something they find to be funny.

Jordan who has always loved his nan's company was unequivocal in his push back against what he perceived as his nan being awfully insensitive. Even as Jordan was giving his nan a piece of his mind, Winnie seems to be cutting her some slack. She seems to nod her head by way of affirmation each time Dorothy speaks of her exception to the situation on ground. Winnie herself doesn't have answers to the matter at hand, she's equally lost and she wasn't doubly sure of what her mother-inlaw was about, yet she connected with Dorothy in a way.

Her presence is now untenable but her intuitive display isn't atypical for a person with a strong hunch. Unfortunately, she hastily made a trip across the pond in search of her son, only to be faced with an accident scene that made her skin crawl. Dorothy's showy display of emotion left some members of the search and rescue team on the edge, and despite being down in the weeds, Jerome had to get on with the task at hand.

Fin, the Evangelist's dad, stood confused for a while but soon realised Dorothy is never flippant and always scrupulous particularly when her hunch is at play.

Brett tried constraining his mum from going ahead with her request of taking her back home, but his dad urged him not discourage his mum from following her hunch.

Brett is the Evangelist's brother, he'd loved to be active in the search for his brother, but attending to Dorothy's request would mean, he has to let others get on with it, while he takes his mum back to Bucharest.

Dorothy isn't necessarily requesting to be taken back to the United States, she just wanted her son to either take her to the Evangelist's home or to an hotel in Bucharest, where she would stay and wait for her husband to return. Bizarrely, Brett was enjoying a day out with his family where they attended the premiere of a

Christian Movie at the Madison Square Garden when he received the news of his brother's mishap. The feeling that he didn't do much in the search of his brother, was something that left him in a pickle.

Back in the Luciferian camp, Prophet Gregory who knows about the nitty gritty of what goes on in his camp but doesn't get involved directly in the day-to-day administration decided to pay this stranger who strayed into his camp a visit. "Rebecca, how is he doing, and I learnt you have been taking care of him?" Asked Prophet Gregory.

"Yes Prophet, I'm glad he's coming around," replied Rebecca.

She bowed her head in reverence to the prophet who then blessed her and she kissed his ring. He then proceeded to have words with Doctor Van as he inquired about the patient's condition and welfare. "I will love to keep him here, but if his situation deteriorates let me know because I wouldn't want this man to die here," said the prophet.

The doctor concurs and moves the conversion to other areas he wants the prophet's attention, and minutes later the prophet then turned around and walks away.

A week after he was found floating in the sea, and rushed to the camp clinic inside the Luciferian camp, the Evangelist seems to be coming around nicely. Rebecca who has stayed by his bedside and kept constant watch over the Evangelist, noticed he opened his eyes, and out of excitement, she rushed to him. "Hey, you're awake!" she exclaimed. Funnily, the man that just regained consciousness wasn't speaking to Rebecca who was filled with excitement that this stranger that was supposedly dead, has come back. She sounded surprise that he isn't responding to her.

"Hello, hello, are you ok?" asked Rebecca.

The Evangelist opened his eyes, and looking lost, and though, still very frail.

Rebecca continued speaking to him and asking if he's ok, she went on to introduce herself as Rebecca, then ask how he's doing. While the Evangelist tried responding by mumbling back to Rebecca, he slipped back into unconsciousness. Rebecca was absolutely thrilled to be the first person to get a glimpse of this stranger's recovery process, she was incredibly grateful that her labour of love wasn't a waste.

Rebecca rushed to Doctor Van, the doctor managing the camp clinic, and said the stranger is awake, this news was received with joy, Rebecca went on to say the stranger opened his eyes for a few minutes and returned to sleep. Van left everything behind and rushed to the Evangelist's bedside to confirm Rebecca's news, but realised he had actually slipped back into unconsciousness, he then asked Rebecca if she meant the stranger went back to sleep.

"Yes, after a few minutes, he closed his eyes," said Rebecca.

Doctor Van was excited and said that's good news, yet said he hoped he hasn't returned to unconsciousness. Obviously, the doctor wasn't in a hurry to leave the stranger's bedside, as he began performing some checks on him, but first requested the nurse to take his vitals.

Rebecca quickly asked if she should call Mario and said he's at the tennis court.

"No, not now, let's continue to watch him," replied Doc. Van. But as the doctor attempts to leave after conducting a series of checks, Rebecca asked if he's leaving. Van confirmed with a nod, and said he's leaving and will be back, he then said the patient is still under observation, but his condition has improved greatly.

"Can I stay with him?" she asked.

"Yes, of course, if you wish," said Van.

Later that evening, Eric who is based in Bucharest arrived the Luciferian camp. "Hey, Orla, how are you?" asked Eric. Orla replied to Eric, saying she's fine and asked Eric when he arrived. Eric was all smiles and said he just arrived, but he then went on to ask Orla about Rebecca's whereabouts.

Orla laughed, "hmm, she's babysitting," said Orla, in quite an ingenious manner.

Orla will never acquiesce staying quiet, and regardless of the circumstances she will always throw in her two pennies because staying neutral is her Achilles heel.

"Babysitting you said, whose baby?" asked Eric.

"On the contrary, she's babysitting an adult," said Orla.

Eric smiled and said he understands that Orla is now being cheeky and urged her not to bluff the bluffer because it will do no one any good. He then reminded her she has got jokes, but then pleaded with Orla to please be serious and tell him where to find Rebecca.

Orla insisted she wasn't joking, and had to cut the chase, and she then urged Eric to visit the camp clinic, he'll find her there. Eric became worried about Rebecca and asked what she's doing in the hospital, and if she's sick. Orla urged Eric to stop being critical as she informed him that Rebecca is attending to the sick. Eric thinks Orla was speaking in riddles or just having a laugh, and to avoid trading barbs at each other, he decided to visit the clinic to see what it was about Rebecca.

Moments later, Rebecca sighted Eric as he approaches, she then came out of the ward to say hello to Eric. "Thank goodness, here you are, Rebecca," said Eric.

"Good to see you, Eric, how is it out there?" she asked.

Eric replied to Rebecca that it's beautiful out there, and asked to know how Rebecca is doing, before proceeding to remind her he missed her company and her friendship while he was away. Rebecca laughed and teased Eric, saying she equally missed his humour, and the care he shows towards her.

Eric burst into laughter as this pair became quite jocular. He then said it is fine and beautiful out there, and suggested to Rebecca that maybe she'll go to town with him when he's due to leave. Rebecca smiled as though she liked the idea, but with a caveat and said that would've been nice.

Eric sensed Rebecca wasn't as upfront as she used to, he then asked to know why there's a reservation in her response. He then proceeded to ask, what it is about her babysitting the sick. He wasn't expecting to walk into a fire storm, but he has serendipitously come to realise that Rebecca has something cooking, and funnily, she didn't strike him as suspicious.

"Ooh, where did you get that?" asked Rebecca.

Eric had to spill the beans, and said Orla told him she's here in the clinic attending to the sick. Rebecca wasn't quite pleased to hear words about her swirling around the camp behind her back, she didn't hesitate to express her exception. He then asked Eric, why he didn't come straight to her instead of chitty chatting about her.

"I was at your door, and you weren't there, before Orla came to my aid," replied Eric.

Eric had to give it straight to her even as he pointed out to Rebecca, she doesn't seem happy seeing him, and asked if he has done something wrong. Rebecca was cold in a way but said she's happy seeing Eric that was why she rushed out to receive him, but maybe she has bigger fish to fry. Eric became a bit jocular in a bid to return the warm and unhurried ambience, he then informed Rebecca he got her something from the outside. Rebecca smiled at the news that there's some goodies waiting for her, she then whispered and said.

"That's good of you, thank you." Eric then suggested to Rebecca to come with him to the park, so he could get her entertained, he then pulled her along with him.

"Stop Eric, I can't!" she exclaimed.

Eric stopped and with some expression of frustration on his face, he then asked Rebecca what the problem was. Rebecca immediately suggested taking a rain check but then replied him saying she has to be with him.

"With him, and who is him? Hmm, what Orla said was actually true, isn't it?" asked Eric.

"I don't know what Orla told you, I'm only watching over a sick man, he's in a critical state?" said Rebecca.

"A wounded man, what about his family?" asked Eric.

Rebecca replied to Eric who has suddenly become apprehensive and said the sick man has got no family for now, until he's fully recovered. Eric didn't take lightly to the fact that Rebecca was giving him the run-around with her too many twists. He then asked Rebecca if Jonathan actually attached her to this sick man, or it's just her that chose to babysit him.

Eric's comment seemed to have left a bad taste in her mouth, and that got her kicking off at him. Before now, none of his questions got her kicking off, but things have unwittingly changed, even if they don't know it. She now felt Eric is giving her the third degree, and his questions are now too close for comfort. Rebecca had to stop Eric from continuing on the subject.

"Enough of this, Eric," she said, then urged him to stay here in the clinic with her.

Eric accepted to go along with Rebecca's request in a bid to calm things down, they immediately walked into the waiting room and continued their conversation. This little tiff between them brought Eric to the realisation that he and Rebecca are no longer singing from the same song sheet. After their awkward moments at the camp clinic, Eric spent most of his time in the camp doing botanical walking with some residents who find walking closer to nature more comforting. Eric tried as much as he could to stay away from Rebecca, to avoid provoking Rebecca further.

Three days after his arrival at the camp, and finding the woman he's hoping to befriend suddenly becoming elusive, Eric walked up to Rebecca at the clinic, and said it's time he returns to Bucharest. Rebecca exclaimed and asked Eric, why he is leaving so soon, and after all, he came in just three days ago. Eric didn't say much but reiterated that the woman he'd hoped will keep him company during his visit to the camp, seemed too busy attending to some sick man found drifting away in the sea, and said it's time to go because he has businesses to attend to.

Rebecca now realised she had left this man that has always made her laugh quite disappointed, and she then apologised for being a bit nerdy. She thought Eric still has some time with them in the camp. Eric on the other hand reminded Rebecca that she never asked and never cared, saying this is unlike her, because it's obvious to all around the camp that she has casually but cruelly given him the elbow.

Rebecca understands that she has just lost the one friend that values her, she then held Eric by the hand and begged him to pardon her indiscretion, saying she's only eager to see the sick man back on his feet. After a while, it's now time for Eric to leave, he stopped speaking for a moment, and asked Rebecca if she knows that his regular visit to this camp isn't just for the sunshine or the religious rites, but it's because of her. Rebecca concurred and said she understands they're good friends and she enjoys Eric's company. She confessed that it's Eric sense of humour that kept her hooked on him, but visiting the camp more regularly for her sake isn't something she's aware of.

"Maybe we will elaborate on that in my next visit, but what is it about him?" asked Eric.

"What's it about whom?" replied Rebecca.

"The guy you're babysitting, and why has he taken all the attention I seek from you," asked Eric.

Rebecca had to inform Eric that the sick man has no known relatives, and nobody to care for him, so she volunteered, but reminded Eric that displaying fits of jealousy wouldn't be helpful in this circumstance. Eric still thinks Rebecca is holding something back and isn't telling him everything that kept her glued to this sick man, he then asked Rebecca if she unwittingly assumed the role of caring for this man or it was a purposeful act.

Eric was left reeling from within, as Rebecca remained unable to shed more light on the sudden epiphany that left her clinging on to this stranger. Sadly, Rebecca sensed that there is an air of suspicion around her interest in this man, but she isn't backing down, as she asked Eric how else she should assist a dying man.

Eric poured out his mind as succinctly as he could and said the three days he came to spend with her in this camp seems to mean nothing to her. Rebecca had to blame Eric and said all this while he never said anything about his interest in her, and that Eric has only presented himself as a friend with nothing else in mind.

Rebecca's twist seems to arouse Eric's indignation, and he wasn't flattered, as he asked Rebecca in what other ways do people show how much they care, if not first being a true friend. Funnily, she just couldn't bring herself to look at this through a different prism, and her reason for taking up this babysitting task wasn't well received. Eric muttered, reminding Rebecca that her stories are riddled with holes like Swiss cheese, but she laughed it off without giving much thought to it. She then turned it around into a joke and said a trampled vest was more suiting than Swiss cheese.

Rebecca yielded to Eric's prodding, and she then opened up to Eric that she has been lonely since the passing away of her husband, and all these while she wanted much more than a friend, but Eric stopped at being just a friend. Eric seemed to understand that Rebecca expected him to have been more upfront with his intentions, he then promised they'll talk about this on his next visit, and asked if that will be ok.

"It's ok," replied Rebecca.

He felt Rebecca is chipping away his ego, little by little until there's none left, after a moment of reflection and pouring their hearts out, Eric then said he has to get going, but asked Rebecca if he can have a hug.

"Yes, of course," she said. She gives him a hug, but Eric seemed not to be letting go, she then urged him to go easy, after all, they are just friends. Eric then loosened his grip on her and said it's time he hit the road.

"Bye, stay safe," said Rebecca.

Eric nodded and said he will, he then turned and left, while Rebecca returned to stay with the sick Evangelist.

By the evening of the same day Rebecca realised the Evangelist had returned to consciousness for a second time. "Hey, you're awake!" she exclaimed. The Evangelist was just looking lost, and aloof, yet Rebecca continued to engage him in a conversation saying hello, hello, and welcome back, to this man who remained oblivious of the happenings around him.

"Nice to meet you, I'm Rebecca, and what's your name?" she asked.

"Name, what name?" replied Evangelist Fredrick.

"My name is Rebecca, what's yours?" she repeated.

"What name?" he replied.

Rebecca soon realised that the Evangelist's words don't seem coordinated, she quickly rushed to get the nurse to come over but the doctor seemed to be just passing by, and asked Rebecca what's up with her friend. Rebecca didn't hesitate to ask the doctor to come with her, as she said her friend woke up, though, his words are disoriented. Doctor Van then followed her immediately to see the Evangelist who has been in a prolonged state of unconsciousness. A moment later, Doctor Van was by the patient's bed side and said hello, welcome back, he then introduced himself as Doctor Van.

"Name, what name?" asked Evangelist Fredrick. Rebecca turned to the doctor and said that's all the patient has been saying since he returned to consciousness. Doctor Van muttered and said that shouldn't be, he then turned to the Evangelist, and said hello to him, before asking how he's feeling. "Name, what name?" replied the Evangelist.

This seemed to be a rude awakening for Rebecca who's now quivering and asking the doctor what could be wrong with this man, and questioned if he's going to be ok. "Oh, I don't like this," Doc. Van retorted. Rebecca then asked the doctor what he meant by him not liking this as she couldn't get her head around the drama playing out before her eyes. She's now a victim of her own success and her first hunch was that this could be a mad man who ran out of the psychiatric unit and jumped into the sea, and now spouting gibberish.

Immediately, Doctor Van decided he'll need to run some tests to be sure it isn't what he's thinking. "Let me excuse you, while you run your tests," said Rebecca.

The new state of this patient left her quite devastated, because she's now presented a man that's so poorly and disoriented, and then decided to go for a walk in the park within the camp. Jonathan walked past Rebecca and walked back to her, and asked why she isn't by her friend's bedside. Rebecca informed Jonathan the patient is awake.

"Wow, that's good news, and how's he?" asked Jonathan.

Rebecca replied to Jonathan saying the patient is fine, though, not too fine because his words are disoriented and Doctor Van is running some test on him.

Jonathan then suggested to Rebecca to get Mario to attend to the Evangelist. Rebecca wouldn't want to cause any offence, and quickly informed Jonathan that Doctor Van is already attending to him. Jonathan had to remind Rebecca that Mario is more experienced, and this is his call, he then urged her to involve him.

"Ok, let me give him a call," said Rebecca. She then dialled Mario's phone, to see if she could get him to help. "Hello Rebecca, is everything ok?" asked Mario.

"I Suppose so, but we will still need your help," said Rebecca.

"Help, I believe you need help with your friend, any new development?" asked Mario.

Rebecca had to inform Mario that her friend had just regained consciousness, but he seems to be lost. Mario exclaimed and said that's strange, and promised to join her in a moment.

Moments later, Mario walked into the clinic, and said he was at the tennis court when Rebecca called, and then asked how the stranger is doing. Van interjected and said the Evangelist is actually conscious but doesn't seem to know himself.

Rebecca is now struggling to deal with the current happenings with this patient, she then asked to excuse herself while the doctors check him out. It was obvious that she has mixed feeling about all this, because the man assumed to be dead is back to life, but seemed to have lost his mind, she then left the doctors as they perform some checks.

"Ok, he seems to be displaying signs of memory loss," said Rebecca.

"I thought as much, but just wanted to run some more test to be sure," said Doc. Van.

Mario agreed with Van and said the tests are necessary to validate this assertion. They went ahead with performing some tests, and moments later, Mario had to seek Jonathan out, to brief him on the state of this patient.

While Jonathan was out and about the camp, Mario walked up to him, and informed him the patient is awake and fine.

Jonathan thanked Mario for filling the gap, in times of need.

Mario had to move the conversation to other needling matters of concern, he then said they seem to have a little problem, implying he's still a cause for concern. Jonathan was glad to hear this man is now doing fine, but the mention of a concern meant this patient isn't out of the woods yet, he then interjected and asked Mario what the concern is.

Mario subtly informed Jonathan that the man has lost his memory and remembers nothing of his past. Jonathan first breathes a sigh of relief at this news, but then muttered saying this man's case is becoming more difficult by the day. Mario didn't expect to perceive any fear in Jonathan, and asked why the trepidation, he went on to inform Jonathan that this is his call, and he'll help the patient pull through this.

"I hope we aren't biting more than we can chew, because this has suddenly turned into a mission creep," Jonathan retorted. Mario thinks Jonathan's fear is misplaced as he reminded him that bringing a man back from the dead, is the humane thing to do. Jonathan isn't debating this matter out of ignorance, he's just following his hunch and insisted that his hunch tells him this won't go down well. Mario pressed on Jonathan and said there is no contesting of the fact that the patient is now better than when they found him.

"Please indulge my curiosity on how this won't blow up on our faces?" Jonathan retorted.

"But he's better than we found him," replied Mario.

Jonathan agreed with Mario that the man is obviously much better than he was days back, and he isn't suggesting this to be an open wound, yet insisted that it might be quite difficult for them to tell this man's story to the world. Mario didn't think they've done anything wrong and suggested to Jonathan not to mask anything but tell the world they rescued a dying man, gave him life, and they're now helping him regain his memory.

Rebecca later returned to see how this man is doing, and walked into the conversation, she then inquired from Mario to know how the Evangelist is doing and asked if she can be by his side.

Jonathan had no choice but to reiterate the obvious and said Rebecca's interest in this man without a name leaves him amazed. Rebecca interjected and reminded Jonathan that she found him, which implies, this man is her trophy. The saying that 'nobody kicks a dead dog' doesn't seem overly overrated but in this circumstance, the fight to keep Ambrose despite his obvious shortcomings meant he's much more than a dead dog to Rebecca, who seems hell bent on keeping him stringed to her apron of mischief.

Sadly, Rebecca's interest in this man isn't just about caring for him, it's a rather selfish one, and her intent is now beginning to come to light. It's blatant that her push to care for this stranger is a mere smokescreen, as she interrupted their conversation rudely in a manner that shows she's unapologetically a rebel. Jonathan was lost with Rebecca's description of this man as her trophy yet went on to give her the shocker by reminding her that her trophy has lost his memory.

"How do you mean he lost his memory?" asked Rebecca.

Mario replied her saying, the man doesn't remember anything about his past, and not even his name. Jonathan then interjected and said its best they return the man to the society for the government to identify him and find his family, at least, there must be someone out there who is related to this man.

Rebecca seems to see an opportunity in this hopeless situation and suggested that if the man has lost his past, she will help him get a grip on his present.

"What gives you the impetus to think you can help him, you aren't family to him," said Jonathan. Mario unknowingly seemed to be under Rebecca's spell as he toed the same line with Rebecca, in a manner that left Jonathan in the minority in this matter. He then turned to Jonathan and said if Rebecca is willing to assist the man regain his memory, why not.

Jonathan didn't stay silent as he insists, he doesn't subscribe to this, before asking what skill Rebecca has, that makes her the most suitable person to assume this role. Mario agreed to help stabilise the sick man yet said he will do this with Rebecca's help.

Jonathan eventually caved in and said this whole thing has taken a new turn, and he doesn't like it. "Let's help the man, because it's the humane thing to do, and I'll work with Rebecca to see this through," said Mario.

Days later, Mario walked in on Rebecca and the sick Evangelist, and asked to know how he's doing. Rebecca replied and said she can see a great improvement and then suggested to Mario that Doctor Van has equally been helpful. Mario went on to ask if the patient is beginning to engage in meaningful conversations, Rebecca nodded in affirmation, yet said the process is monotonous and tiresome.

Mario understands what it meant to get a man without memory of his past come around and said Rebecca's remark isn't misplaced.

"But I don't know his name and sometimes I find it difficult to relate with him," said Rebecca.

"Oh, yeah, that's insightful, why don't you suggest a name, but the name should be temporary, so it doesn't stick," said Mario. Rebecca had to consider her options and asked what if the name she suggests for him sticks.

Mario insists it shouldn't because the man has a name already, just that they don't know what it is. He reiterated that the man's family won't appreciate him bearing a different name by the time he's reunited to them.

She then asked Mario what if she calls him Ambrose. Mario laughed and quickly asked Rebecca where she got the name from, but then guessed she must have been attached to that name in a way. "Hmm, yes actually, that's the name of my first love, and I like him a lot," said Rebecca.

"Do you think naming him after your ex-partner is a good idea, because I don't think so," replied Mario.

Rebecca didn't think extending the care for someone she likes to this man is a bad idea. It is a just infatuation that made her stick to him, but Mario quickly urged caution and reminded Rebecca that this isn't a free pass to a love relationship. He proceeded to suggest that this man's care shouldn't be mistaken as a love relationship, and then reminded Rebecca for a second time that he wouldn't want anything sharp-witted.

"Let's help him stand on his feet, before engaging in a discourse laced in rhetoric," replied Rebecca.

Unfortunately, Rebecca realised her intentions for this sick man will be faced with strong opposition and she's now trying to tread carefully by looking for the best way of making this man hers without causing a stir, because she's bent on keeping him for herself. She then walks away before things turn sour.

Fin has remained speechless since he arrived Kaija, he's lost for words over what fate may have befallen his son, and why his whereabouts remain unexplained. Even as eyes focused comprehensively in the manner in which this search and rescue operation is being prosecuted, Fin spent the last two days taking cover under a rickety shade that lies by the sea side.

The scene by this seaside that was left awash with too many dead bodies represents nothing but moral ambiguity for Fin who felt some ambivalence, as he's faced with two contrasting moral issues. Just as victims' relatives are mourning their loss, the search and rescue team, steadily and tireless continues working hard to recover victims from the wreckage and that to Fin, meant hope.

He's now that voice of hope that Winnie returns to, each time she finishes having words with Jerome, particularly now that Jerome has nothing but negative feedback for her.

The company of her father in-law came handy for Winnie, as this eighty-three years old man is now a place, she draws strength. Even in the mist of his gripping emotional distress, Peter still finds time to always walk to his grandad to check on him.

Unsurprisingly, the moment Dorothy stepped into their hotel room, she reached for her bible and began praying for her son's safe return.

After Brett took his mum back to Bucharest and returned a day later, which unfortunately, is the last day of this search and rescue operation. He didn't stop kicking himself for not being there, for most part of the search for his brother.

Dorothy didn't return to Kaija, she spent the next two days in Bucharest but remained on the phone with her husband who stayed back to see this through. Dorothy didn't travel all the way from the United States with the intention of stomping and snorting at those working tirelessly to find her son, she just couldn't go against her hunch at this point.

After ten days of intense search and rescue, the rescue team was unable to find the Evangelist, the operation was then called off. Despite their opposition to Jerome Baptist's decision to call off the search and rescue operation, Winnie and her sons had no choice but to go home empty handed, amidst their grief. Peter had remained in the same clothes since he left home, he now practically lives in the Jeans and T-Shirt he wore when he left home about ten days ago, but his looks is the least of his concern. During their ten days tortuous stay at the site of the shipwreck at Kaija, Doctor Saul and Alisabel joined Winnie and her sons and spent two days with them, doing all they could in a bid to give some moral support and comfort as they await news concerning the Evangelist. They returned to Bucharest after spending two days with this grieving family.

On return from Kaija, Fin, Dorothy and Brett spent two days with the Evangelist's family as they grieved together. They then returned to the United States, even as the whereabouts of the Evangelist remains unknown.

Two weeks after returning from the site of the Wreckage Rita paid Winnie a visit, and as she stood by the door and knocked, "knock, knock, is anybody home, Winnie, are you home?"

Jordan walks to the door and opens the door, and then said hello to Rita. Rita exchanged pleasantries with Jordan and asked if his mum is at home.

"Yes of course, come in," said Jordan.

Winnie walks to the living room to receive Rita, and the moment she walks in, she said she heard that voice and immediately knew it was her. "Sad to hear about your husband, Winnie, it's a shame this is happening," said Rita. Winnie began sobbing, and said she doesn't know why they called off the search, and informed Rita that her husband is still beneath the water.

"It's a shame this is happening, why didn't you protest to prevent them from calling off the search?" asked Rita. Winnie stopped sobbing as she narrated to Rita how hard she tried to keep the search going but failed, and asked, what else can she do. She then proceeded to say she just needed her husband back, and that is all that matters to her. Rita insisted the search and rescue team aren't supposed to call off the search when the entire passenger hasn't been accounted for.

Winnie was curious as she expressed her disappointment, but said they accounted for all the passengers except her husband and one other. Rita went on to asked Winnie if she was given any possible reason why they couldn't locate her husband. Winnie had to repeat what she was told, and said Jerome Baptist, the head of the rescue team, felt the ship may be resting on top of her husband. "Oh my God, you mean the ship could be resting on him, what a shame?" said Rita. Reliving her husband's experience was quite difficult for Winnie, yet she went on to tell Rita that there are indications that Fredrick was unconscious and fell off the ship before it went down.

"Why can't they move the ship, so we can recover his body?" asked Rita.

Winnie was still sobbing even as they spoke of her heartache, she then opened up to Rita that there isn't any plan to move the ship in the near future, and she remained terrified by how long she would have to live with this nightmare. Considering the role she played in making Winnie stay back and not join her husband in this trip, Rita is still plagued by guilt, and that guilt kept her away from coming to see Winnie when other work colleagues were coming to comfort her.

She was needled by the presupposition that if Winnie had gone with her husband, maybe he wouldn't have been with the captain where he suffered concussion that resulted in his being unconscious in the first place, and the subsequent setbacks that followed wouldn't have happened. Rita obviously didn't see God walking through all these chaos, and she was awfully damming in the manner she expressed her feelings about this to this Christian family.

It was quite poignant for Rita to hear of the trauma this Christian family has suffered, she though finds it difficult to believe that sincere devotion to God and heartbreak exists side by side, but that's just this family's present experience.

"We will need to press the government on this, and I was to come earlier but felt you weren't ready to see my face," said Rita.

"Saul, Alisabel, and the others have come, and why do you presume I wouldn't want to see your face?" asked Winnie.

"For messing your holiday, and I've this hunch that if you were with Fredrick maybe things would've been different," said Rita. Winnie on the other hand was awfully glad that Thomas's ill-health prevented her from embarking on this ill-fated trip, that may have consumed her and her husband.

"How, really, it's you that deserves a thank you," said Winnie.

Rita wasn't following, she then asked Winnie, "the thank you will be for what?"

Winnie then shed more light, and said she's now convinced that God used Thomas's accident to stop her from embarking on this trip because she should've been in that ship, and may be among the dead. She was equally glad that she didn't make a fuss when asked to stay back after Thomas's accident. "Hmm, Winnie, you've got strange ways of looking at things," replied Rita.

Winnie then went on to say it would've been worst for her sons, if both her and her husband were in that ill-fated ship, yet went on to hint Rita that she still has this strange feeling.

"What feeling are you talking about, Winnie?" asked Rita.

Winnie subtly said it might seem crazy, but she has this feeling that Fredrick is still alive, and she can feel him reaching out to her. Rita doesn't want to be too dismissive, yet said Winnie's perception is weird, and reminded her that Fredrick has been under water for twenty-four days since the accident and urged her not to raise their hopes falsely.

"Yeah, I get that, it's actually weird but please pardon my manners, and what do I offer you?" asked Winnie. Rita settled for a cup of tea, moments after Winnie put the kettle on and they soon continued their conversation after Rita's cup of tea was served.

# CHAPTER
## SIX

## *The Grim Realities*

Back in the Bliss Luciferian Camp, Mario walked into the gym centre and saw Rebecca doing her routine fitness exercise and joked with her, saying she seem to like spending some of her time keeping fit. Rebecca smiled and said as a resident in the camp this is her primary hobby, yet this also helps to keep her mind in check.

"In check, how do you mean?" asked Mario.

"From wandering wrongly, my whole life has been laced with too many troubles, this helps me keep my mind in check," said Rebecca.

"I guess you're right, my holiday is over, Rebecca, and I'm going back to work," he said.

"Oh, it's all happening so fast, what about your patient?" asked Rebecca.

Mario reminded Rebecca that it's been more than a month since they found her friend, and they left him with her three weeks ago after he regained consciousness.

"He's on his feet now and it's time for me to go," said Mario.

Rebecca thanked Mario for putting his expertise to use when it mattered most and thanked him for saving her friend.

Mario interjected again and suggested to Rebecca that she knows what to do, as he urged her to help them return the patient to himself, and then return him back to the society. Rebecca sees Mario's suggestion as a big ask, she then muttered and said if she does all that Mario has just suggested, then she will be the loser in all of this.

"A loser, how, do you have a stake in his affairs?" asked Mario.

Rebecca had no choice but to cut to the chase and said Mario should know she does have a stake in this stranger's affair because he seems to like her, and she likes him too.

Mario was gutted by the words coming out of Rebecca's mouth, he quickly reminded her that her ideas seem to make him squirm and asked her where this her new narrative leads.

Rebecca didn't mince her words, as she sounded as if Lucifer gave her this man as a gift in compensation for her too many woes. She then told Mario that she has lived a life devoid of humour, in which having a laugh and tickling has regrettably been scarce.

Mario had no choice but to inform Rebecca that accepting this swirl of madness will be difficult for him and suggested to her to have a rethink. It now dawned on Mario that Rebecca is no longer speaking reassuringly, but has rather become assertive on this matter.

Rebecca stopped what she was doing, as she hurried up in her bid to leave the gym centre because of Mario's stern criticism yet stopped to accuse Mario of being a bit of a contrarian, insisting she would manage any fall-out arising from this. Mario muttered, saying Rebecca couldn't wait to get her feet under the table, and subtly reminding Rebecca that he isn't just trying to be spiteful, but made it clear to her that this act will paint her to be a blurry character with trust issues.

Mario knows too well that as a religious group that venerates Lucifer, they are seen by the society as anti-God, and Christians would use any opportunity to cast a dark shadow over their belief.

He sure doesn't want Rebecca taking everyone to the gutter because her unscrupulous posturing was quite polarising and didn't help either.

"Do you prefer I pathologically commit to acting the loser?" asked Rebecca. Mario looked on, and tried toning down the heated conversation, yet subtly said he likes her modesty, but she's sarcastically going overboard this time.

"Do you consider me as going into an overreach mode?" asked Rebecca.

"But you refuted Jonathan's assertions, the other day," he retorted.

"Tell me about it, but of a truth, there's something in him that strikes a chord in me," replied Rebecca.

Mario continued to insist that Ambrose should return to the society where he belongs because his family wants him, and might be looking everywhere for him.

Rebecca was quite ingenious as she twisted the conversation to absolve herself of any wrongdoing in this matter, as she now insisted that the decision to stay or leave should be up to this stranger to make. Common sense suggests to Mario that time spent by Rebecca in helping this stranger to get back on his feet may have created some kind of bond between the pair. Mario then pushed back against this deceitful suggestion, knowing full well that Rebecca is now playing to the gallery, and he then insisted that such a decision shouldn't be left to the man to make because people don't make sound choices when overtaken by love.

Rebecca bluntly asked Mario if he thinks Ambrose wants to return to the society, she then urged him to go and find out for himself. Mario started walking away again, he stopped a second time, then suddenly walked back.

"Wait a minute, I thought you and Eric have something going?" he asked.

Rebecca didn't hesitate to distance herself from Eric, as she reluctantly replied to Mario, saying stories of her and Eric swirling around the camp is nothing but a litany of tales, and stressed that there's nothing between Eric and her. Mario wasn't pleased with the manner with which she quickly dismissed her relationship with Eric and said she doesn't have to lie about Eric. He went on to say Eric is a nice guy with a good heart.

"You have a thing going, don't you?" asked Mario.

Rebecca insisted she likes Eric, but he hasn't made any advances towards her, and therefore he's just a friend with no strings attached. Mario became upset and said this is a travesty which he intends to fix even if this is the last thing he does before he leaves this camp as he plans to return to the city, saying he wouldn't want to be associated with any complacency.

Rebecca felt slighted by Mario who seemed ready to butt heads with her, and said she had no idea he wants to join in the fray. She then promised as she urged him not to worry because she won't be scarred by his actions.

Mario is now trying not to be overly involved in Rebecca's game yet reminded her that her life was a mess when she lost her husband and he understands she's now trying to pick her pieces together, but Ambrose belongs to somebody.

"No worries, Mario, everything will be just fine," she retorted.

Mario then decided that he has said enough, and excused himself, yet reminded her he will leave her to it but she will have to deal with Jonathan. He then walks out from the gym, leaving Rebecca behind. Moments later, Mario walked into Jonathan's office, and even before saying a word, Jonathan joked saying Mario has come to tell him good bye.

"Yeah Jonathan, it has been a refreshing time for me," said Mario.

Jonathan turned around laughing, and asked Mario to tell him all about the fun he has had in the last one month. Mario smiled and said that wouldn't be necessary and insisted that Jonathan should know that most times, he withdraws from the society whenever he feels like he's running out of steam.

"Meaning?" asked Jonathan.

"I am fully charged now," Mario said, then burst into laughter.

Jonathan then asked about Grace and the kids, Mario's family, and then suggested they stay behind a little longer, Mario laughed at the suggestion and accused Jonathan of wanting him to experience bachelorhood for a while. Jonathan nudged him with his elbow, saying it doesn't matter, and that it's sometimes fun having the opportunity to relive some sense of bachelorhood.

Mario had to steer this conversation to a more needling matter of concern, and said he just finished speaking with Rebecca, moments ago.

"Rebecca, what about her?" asked Jonathan.

"It's about Ambrose, they're in love," said Mario.

"I said it the other day, but you guys didn't seem to believe me," said Jonathan then chuckles, and said he saw it in her eyes. Mario then asked Jonathan what he suggests they do.

Jonathan didn't hesitate to find a way around this situation that's fast becoming a mess, he then suggested to Mario that they should hand this man over to the police to allow the police take it up from there. Mario concurred and said getting the Police involved is the best way forward and said the police will help locate the man's family since he lost memory and remembers nothing of his past.

"That's what I would do, and soon, since he's already being entangled with Rebecca," said Jonathan.

"Ok, that won't be a bad idea," said Mario.

Jonathan then said he had to act fast because he doesn't want this camp going belly up, under his watch. Funnily, while a conversation about her conduct was on the table, Rebecca serendipitously strolled into Jonathan's office and into the conversation, and said she saw Mario walked into the office.

"And you decided to follow me, to conclude on our last conversation?" asked Mario.

Rebecca then said she doesn't want Ambrose's matter discussed behind her back, because it would be like a joke that's beneath them, she then insisted that she and Ambrose has something real. Jonathan stood up from his seat in anger and said Ambrose is no joke, and that he's handing Ambrose over to the police, but will discuss his decision with the Prophet before taking that action.

Rebecca's action has brought a dissonance of conflict in this camp, as she stood against this army of opposition against her. She interjected and urged Jonathan not to do a thing like that and asked. "What about Ambrose, is that's what Ambrose would want?"

Mario insisted that this isn't about what Ambrose wanted, and it's perhaps about doing the right thing. Rebecca had to make her case before the camp manager whose say-so matters a lot in this matter, and said Ambrose has already settled in, she then suggested to them to ask Ambrose and find out if he wants to return. She looked glum and feigned ignorance, even though it's obvious to all that something is in the offing.

Armed with the understanding that Ambrose has lost his memory and remembers nothing about his past except for the present, there's a possibility he wouldn't want to return to a society he'd no knowledge about, Jonathan isn't buying any of Rebecca's suggestions. He then asked why it is that she's requesting they find out from Ambrose, a man with no memory of his past. "What would he settle for, if not his present?" asked Jonathan.

"Have you asked yourself what happened to Ambrose, and how he ended up the way we found him?" asked Rebecca.

"How he ended up in the sea half dead is for the police to unravel," replied Mario.

Rebecca shifted her focus away from Jonathan to Mario and reminded him about his diagnosis of a swelling on Ambrose's head, which Mario himself suggested was the result of a blunt force which could be the result of a possible attack. She went on to say that their present concern should be about Ambrose's safety and focus on the question of who is responsible for the attack on this man.

Jonathan interjected. "What question, Rebecca? the picture you painted is just to make you feel comfortable with yourself," said Jonathan.

Rebecca unwittingly assumed the moral high ground as she accused this pair of sending Ambrose back to the very people that wants him dead. Jonathan walked out of his office and stood in the foyer for a while as the drama suddenly became too heated. He then left Mario and Rebecca in the office, and funnily, there was utter silence in the office while Jonathan was out. Jonathan returned to the office minutes later, and said they're only turning him over to the police, and not to any bloody killer.

Rebecca now realised she isn't winning, she then toned down the ferocity of her argument as she moved away from her combative posture to one of reason. She reminded them that Ambrose remembers nothing of his past, even when his attackers come around pretending to be family members, he wouldn't know they want him dead.

"Hmm, you have a point, but our hands are tied," said Mario.

"I seem to have made a mistake with you, Rebecca," replied Jonathan. She is now perceived as a snake in the garden. Without minimising the awfulness of her action, he urged her to watch her steps, saying, even vampires don't cast their fortunes in the mirror but Rebecca erroneously think this doesn't apply to her.

"Mistake, how?" asked Rebecca.

Jonathan had to remind her he shouldn't have allowed her watch over Ambrose, he then accused Rebecca of using the time of watching over Ambrose as an opportunity to creep into Ambrose's head. Rebecca frowned at Jonathan's description of her action and said that isn't a good thing to say, but then suggested they should all allow Ambrose to answer for himself.

Jonathan didn't bat an eye lid and said he knows his comments are unsettling, but she actually crept into this man's head, and stole his emotions.

"I'll leave you to use your discretion," Rebecca said and walks away.

Immediately Rebecca left, Mario pointed out to Jonathan and suggested to him to reflect on Rebecca's point, because if Ambrose had no memory of the past, he might walk right into the hands of those who possibly attacked him.

He emphasised the possibility that Ambrose may have come into contact with some very unpleasant people, who may have attacked him, and sending him back into society without due care, might mean they're inadvertently giving his attackers the licence to finish the job.

Faced with the grim realities of widowhood, Winnie and her boys have to accept the fact that her husband is dead and isn't coming back, and the reality of a life without her husband going forward.

Peter on the other hand couldn't stop imagining what the Octal Flamingo crash site would look like by now. The crash site must have been deserted and the atmosphere in the area must have become as quiet as a tomb, with just his dad and a fellow passenger resting beneath the sea. He'd this bizarrely awkward feeling inside him that his dad must be quite lonely, staying alone in a deserted crash site.

This grieving family have accepted their fate, and it's now obvious to them that the Evangelist isn't returning to them anymore, and just months after the accident they've come to take their own with them. Winnie walked into Jerome Baptist's office, flanked by her two sons, she was quite polite this time as she said hello to him, and asked how he's doing. Jerome Baptist stood up from his seat to receive Winnie and her sons, and immediately after their brief exchange of pleasantries, Jerome Baptist welcomed them and asked them to make themselves comfortable, before saying he knows that life must have been very hard for them.

Winnie was a bit distant, yet managed to smile, as she subtly told Jerome that as he can see, she isn't fine because if she is, she wouldn't be here. Jerome Baptist replied to Winnie saying she's right, and she isn't supposed to be fine considering her present circumstance.

Winnie then went on to say she wants her husband, and wants him retuned to them, whatever it takes, dead or alive. Jerome is good at what he does, rescue operation of this nature is his gifting and he's a dark horse, sort of, but locating the missing Evangelist has proved to be a bit more than a handful.

Jerome Baptist then inquisitively asked Winnie if she meant, whatever it takes. Winnie continued her weird theory and said she has a feeling that her husband is still alive.

Jerome Baptist didn't hesitate to dismiss Winnie's comment that her assertion is a long one. Despite the situation, he isn't in a position to put a dampener on her hopes for her husband's return to her alive.

"Yes, whatever it takes, I can't take it anymore, and I mean we can't take it anymore," she insists.

"I know your husband's whereabouts is an ongoing concern," said Jerome.

Winnie interjected and exclaimed, as she asked Jerome to do something about it then, she wasn't gaiety in her mannerism because she wants that ship moved and her husband removed from beneath.

Jerome had to dissuade this grieving family who thinks he holds that much sway over the decision to move the ship. He then turned to Peter and said the decision to move a ship isn't within his jurisdiction, that decision rest on the authorities and the cruise ship company. Peter understood that Jerome Baptist isn't just blowing smoke, he's telling the truth considering the bureaucracy of government ministries, yet he went on to suggest to Jerome that his recommendations could speed things up.

This isn't the most audacious request ever presented to Jerome Baptist since he became the head of the search and rescue team, but the nature of this assignment meant he had to go above and beyond, and possibly pull some strings to get this done. He cautiously avoided portentous promises that might put him in a pickle but determined to do his best for this family. She's convinced that if she keeps pushing, something is bound to give, at least those in authority will cave in to her demands and do something about the ship.

Jerome Baptist then turned to Winnie and assured her that her look of disdain isn't misplaced, he then promised he'll do his best to speed things up. Winnie thanked Jerome Baptist and said she looks forward to his assistance. She then began to sob, saying this whole thing has left a hole in her heart and has taken a toll on her.

"Mum, it's ok, you don't have to start," said Jordan.

Peter understands too well that emotion isn't meant to be bottled up, he then asked his brother to allow their mum some time to sob because that's her way of coping and reducing the tension inside her.

Jerome Baptist was touched by the raw emotion displayed by this grieving family as they struggled to come to terms with their loss. It's more like life serving them its cruellest. He then promised this family he will do all within his power to get this ship moved, so this family could find the closure they need.

After getting the assurances they need, Peter thanked Jerome and said they'll take their leave because his mum is now sobbing uncontrollably, he then urged Jerome to keep them in the know the moment something comes up.

Jerome Baptist thanked them for coming and he then turned to Winnie, and urged her to please be strong, saying he knows she's going through a difficult time.

"This is a difficult time for us, your inability to recover my husband's body leaves us in limbo," she retorted. Jerome Baptist yet assured her he understands her feelings of despair, which explains her tears, but urged her to please be strong, "please, I beg you," said Jerome.

As they walked to their car, Jordan stopped and comforted his mum, saying it's ok, and urged her to stop crying, as he reminded her, she's creating a scene.

Winnie dismissed Jordan's concern, and said who cares about making a scene, and that she doesn't mind crying much more, just to get her husband returned to her.

Jordan then tried hurrying his mum into the car, even as he reminded his mum that her crying much more won't bring their dad back, and that he understands she feels terrible. It didn't take long before Winnie pulls herself together and they drove off.

Just days after the Octa Flamingo incident at Kaija, Prophet Gregory who is a news addict, was inadvertently surfing the internet and reading about the Kaija incident. He spent some time going through the cacophony of images from the crash site, including information relating to the victims of the accident.

It didn't come as a surprise when he saw Evangelist Fredrick Douglas photograph as one of the victims of the incident at Kaija. He was smart enough to match the face in the photograph with that of the stranger he visited at the camp clinic just days ago. He suddenly stood up from his seat as he told himself that his gut feeling is right about this stranger that strayed to the seashore of the Bliss Luciferian Camp just weeks ago.

Realising that Fredrick Douglas is an Evangelist which supports the narrative that residents of the camp found a bible on the Evangelist, reinforces the prophet's determination snatch the Evangelist from God.

He however didn't say a word of it to anyone, and left Jonathan and others to continue belabouring themselves with too many suppositions about how this supposed stranger found himself by the seashore. This is now a secret he alone knew about, Gregory Helsing is never bombastic in his public demeanour, and has this reassuringly harmless posture of a dove, but he's such a wolf in sheep's clothing. Though perceptions of Gregory Helsing as a nice guy, was loosely based on facts and dealing with him will require some unique wisdom. This prophet can do anything, he could go as far as donating his blood to a vampire, just to achieve his aim.

Jonathan isn't sitting on his hands until he sorts the unravelling situation out, and the next morning he walked into Ambrose's room to check on him. Jonathan's stance in this matter was already driving Rebecca around the bend, and this was his opportunity to see the swan's leg under the water kicking.

"Hello Ambrose, where's Rebecca?" asked Jonathan.

Ambrose replied to Jonathan and said Rebecca just left for the gym, it's now obvious that Ambrose is now back on his feet and remembers everything about his present except his memory before the accident. While they exchanged pleasantries and got chatting, it didn't take long before Jonathan exclaimed and said he can see Rebecca's things all over the place.

"Implying?" asked Ambrose.

"Are you guys now living together? And I know the two of you have separate rooms, except the fact that you live next to each other," said Jonathan. The new Ambrose seems to be more than a handful for Jonathan, and he didn't hesitate to ask if there's any law preventing people from sharing a room within the camp. Jonathan wasn't expecting Ambrose to suddenly be a lawyer, a pocket one for that matter. Jonathan quickly stepped back and said, not at all, but reminded Ambrose that the circumstance surrounding how he got to the camp is still shrouded in a mystery.

It seems as if Rebecca got into Ambrose's head prior to Jonathan's arrival, and Ambrose seemed to be battle ready as he urged Jonathan not to dwell on petty issues in such a meddlesome manner.

He insisted that Rebecca is just a friend who nursed him back to health. Jonathan dismissed Ambrose assertion, as he pointed out to Ambrose that Rebecca seems to have gone a bit further from nursing him back health to nursing Ambrose's emotions.

"Yeah, you seem right about that," Ambrose chuckled.

"I've a question for you," said Jonathan.

"Question, what question, in particular?" asked Ambrose.

Jonathan then steered this conversation into a thornier area, and asked Ambrose what about if they return him to society for the police to help him with his identity.

Ambrose became quite furious and accused Jonathan of trying to send him away, and he didn't stop at that, but characterized such move to be cruel and heartless.

"Cruel, you said, what about your wife, your children, your brothers, your sisters, and even your parents, if any?" asked Jonathan.

"What about them, do you think I have any of what you've just mentioned? I don't know, and maybe I don't," replied Ambrose.

"Do you care about meeting them, we can help you?" asked Jonathan.

Ambrose insisted he doesn't remember anything, and he has tried to reconnect with his past, but nothing is panning out, it's all blank. Jonathan interjected and asked if he meant nothing, and then pressed further by asking if he's not able to recollect anything at all.

"Yes, of course, why won't I want to recollect?" asked Ambrose.

"But the police can help you," said Jonathan.

Ambrose seemed to be happy with his present, and not quite interested in the past, and said he doesn't need anyone helping him to recollect, and that his life will return to normal with time.

"Meaning?" asked Jonathan.

While Ambrose and Jonathan were at it, Rebecca walks in, and without mincing words she told Jonathan that Ambrose wants her to stay here with him. Jonathan hushed Rebecca and asked her to stay out of it and allow Ambrose to speak for himself because the decision to remain here should be his to make.

Rebecca made Ambrose to believe that his stay in the camp is borne out of necessity, and the staggering dose of fear she put into Ambrose was that there's someone out there who wants him dead. She inadvertently made him to belief that his stay in the camp is punctuated on the premise that he was attacked and left to die and the attackers are still lying in wait and waiting for his return, if perhaps he makes it alive. Rebecca is now a reliable shoulder to lean on, particularly for a man who has no idea of the family he left behind.

Rebecca turned to Ambrose, "Stay with me, let's stay together," she said.

"Oh, you're playing him now, and he's now your toy isn't it, your fiddle?" Jonathan retorted.

Ambrose unblinkingly, told Jonathan to his face that he will do whatever Rebecca says, and pointed out to Jonathan that there isn't any need for disagreement. Without the likes of Mario, and other sane members of the camp in this conversation, this pair seemed to be running rings around Jonathan.

Rebecca then went and sat next to Ambrose with her hand around Ambrose's shoulder and threatened that she'll go with Ambrose if Jonathan sends him out. She then left Ambrose and walked up-close, face to face with Jonathan, and asked if he will follow them back to the society to tear them apart if they leave the camp together. "Your feigned politeness gives me a deep sense of concern, since it is laced in deceit," said Jonathan.

Rebecca seemed to have had enough of Jonathan's insistence, and then reminded him that her stay in this camp is of her own accord, and she isn't in servitude. Her new line of conversation seems to be painting Jonathan as a bully of some sort, who cared less about others. She reminded him they're Luciferians and morality isn't the basis of their belief, but a feeling and the pursuit of happiness, in a manner a person deems fit.

Goffman came in search of Jonathan. He interrupted the long-heated argument between Rebecca and Jonathan as he walked up to Jonathan and handed him a piece of paper with some numbers scribbled on it.

"I promised I will make it up to you," said Goffman.

Jonathan didn't like the manner Goffman interrupted his conversations, yet stopped and unwrapped the paper.

"What's this, Goffman?" Asked Jonathan.

"That's me keeping my promise," replied Goffman.

What are these numbers, your bank account number, the combination to your safe or girlfriend telephone number, which is it?" Asked Jonathan.

Those are lottery winning numbers, just play those numbers and you will win something big, and this is my own way of making it up to you," replied Goffman.

"Are you having a laugh or what?" Asked Jonathan.

"Of course not, the prophet blessed me yesterday, and when I went to bed, I came about these numbers," said Goffman, as he explained further.

Jonathan thanked him but then returned the piece of paper to him, and said he isn't interested. Goffman didn't say much as he collected the paper and began singing in his native Tatar language, then walked away to allow Jonathan and Rebecca to continue with their contentious conversation.

She then accused Jonathan of pursuing the ideals of Luciferianism based on his own subjective definition of what is good and what is wrong. Jonathan on the other hand wouldn't want to be seen as setting his own rules outside the ideals of the Luciferians, something Prophet Gregory might not approve of. Jonathan then attempted to walk away after Rebecca's stern rebuke, but then stopped by the door, and said his silence should mean a thousand words to her, and her assertion leaves him numb.

"Fittingly, the absurdity of considering me as a discarded lump of clay, as a result of my stay in this camp would result in an interesting turn," Rebecca threatened.

Jonathan's indignation as reflected in his hand gestures shows he's already angry and worked up by this pair, he didn't mince words as he reminded them that they're a flourishing community. He then asked Ambrose why he has come to strip them of their vestige and dignity. Jonathan then walked out of the room angrily and realising that she might be the loser at the end of this, she rushed after Jonathan to see how she could persuade him to resolve this without drawing their swords. She then toned down her voice to avoid further tiffs and said she has helped to nurse Ambrose back to health.

"Stacy brought you to this camp when things around you were in tatters, we received you, didn't we?" asked Jonathan.

Rebecca took exception to Jonathan's comment and said she will be eternally grateful for their help in getting her back on feet. Yet stressed that his reminding her of her past in every conversation isn't right. She then urged him to stop rubbing her past in her face.

Jonathan apologised and said there isn't any intention to spite her, but he just doesn't want her taking advantage of a vulnerable man.

Rebecca followed Jonathan and reminded him that she feels bubbled up by his utterances, even when they aren't audibly loud, but then concurred with Jonathan that his concern isn't misplaced, after all, he cared for her when she was vulnerable. She then pleaded with Jonathan to allow her care for Ambrose now that he's vulnerable.

Jonathan continued walking even as Rebecca continued to follow him and making her case, he then entreated her to allow Ambrose to make that choice himself. Rebecca interjected and reminded Jonathan that Ambrose has already made his choice, but it's just that Jonathan has refused to acknowledge Ambrose's choice. He then stopped again and said if she insists, he remains here, then Ambrose can't go about the camp like a visitor, this is a Luciferian camp, and she knows it.

"No worries, he will be dressed just as every other person in this camp," said Rebecca.

"I still had to discuss this with the prophet, and this decision isn't from malice or hate," said Jonathan.

"I know, but Ambrose's presence lights me up," said Rebecca.

"Ooh, like a Christmas tree, I suppose?" asked Jonathan.

"Yes, of course, not minding the vile from naysayers," she said and smiled.

Jonathan left with a disposition that's reflects nothing but indifference. Rebecca seems to have managed to ride out the storm after Jonathan's attempt to strong-arm her failed. Jonathan decided to tell Prophet Gregory of the budding relationship between Rebecca and Ambrose. While Jonathan considers Rebecca's action to be shameful and reprehensible, she perceived him to be some kind of glove puppet being manipulated by the leadership of the camp.

It was a menacingly tumultuous slog as this family strive to get their loved one returned, and arguably, their emotions were nothing but humane. It was a foggy Sunday afternoon and nothing bizarrely out of the blue that might remind her of her loss. Just few weeks after her visit to Jerome Baptist's office, Winnie was having her lunch, and her son, Jordan, was in the living room watching the television. Her thought ran to-and-fro as she imagined what might be left of her husband, possibly the fishes might have wiped his bones clean after feasting on his flesh. With the media tinkering on how this missionary assignment with seemingly divinest of purpose suddenly became horrid, she inadvertently finds herself relieving her loss over and over again.

The thought of her husband suddenly got hold of her, in a manner that made her shudder and the spoon in her hand dropped to the floor. The clattering noise that followed unwittingly attracted Jordan's attention who immediately turned around and saw his mum in tears.

"Mum, what's it? This is about dad, I suppose," asked Jordan.

Whimpering as she expressed her deep emotional trauma, she hinted her son that her husband's whereabouts worries her. The sustained media involvement was the monkey wrench that has perpetually left her oscillating between healing and pain over her loss.

Jordan had to stay with his mum, as he spent most of the afternoon consoling and reassuring her that his dad will be returned to them once the ship is moved.

Back in the Luciferian camp Jonathan had to schedule a meeting with Prophet Gregory, and not long after his meeting with the prophet began, Jonathan told Prophet Gregory that he sensed Rebecca and Ambrose are seeing each other. He unfortunately didn't get the kind of surprise he expected from Prophet Gregory whose immediate response was that he's already aware there's something between those two, but they aren't romantically involved yet.

'I'm not in support of it but let them be," replied Prophet Gregory.

Romantic relationship between members isn't uncommon, yet Jonathan muttered and said the prophet's decision this time is a break with solidarity for this stranger. To avoid making Jonathan feel like a barking dog without a bite, he advised Jonathan he's already aware of the verbal exchanges between Rebecca and him, then pointed out that Rebecca has suddenly become a polarizing figure. He urged Jonathan to let Rebecca and Ambrose carry on, to avoid allowing ill-feelings fester in the camp. Unbeknownst to Jonathan, Prophet Gregory is happy Rebecca and Ambrose have unwittingly entangled in a manner that will keep him hitched to the Bliss Luciferian Camp.

# CHAPTER

## SEVEN

### *Rebecca's heart*

Few months after his previous visit, Eric returned to the Bliss Luciferian camp on a return visit, and as he drove into the camp, he spotted Rebecca and Ambrose holding hands from a distance and looking so much like a couple as they walked in locked step.

Rebecca saw Eric and turned to Ambrose and said 'that's Eric,' she then stopped as Eric drove in and parked his car in the designated parking area, and while Ambrose was itching to continue, Rebecca urged him to wait so she could exchange pleasantries with Eric.

"Eric, are you just arriving?" asked Rebecca. This exchange of pleasantries didn't go down quite well, and suddenly took a bizarre turn, as things quickly became sour even before it started.

"Yes, of course, Rebecca, are you for real?" asked Eric.

Rebecca was taken aback and asked Eric what it was that he's going on and on about, she quickly asked Eric if he isn't happy seeing her again. Eric has suddenly become highly opinionated even at the least mundane things, he then exclaimed at Rebecca's showy display of affection towards Ambrose.

"The two of you holding hands now, you now walk around the camp openly holding hands with him?" asked Eric.

Rebecca didn't hesitate to bemoan Eric's passive aggression towards her newly found happiness and asked if her open display of affection towards Ambrose should warrant any form of yelling or passive aggression from Eric. "I wasn't yelling, Rebecca, I was only calling out. It's just about four months now," said Eric.

Rebecca had to tone things down, particularly now that accusations and counter accusations are flying here and there. She then asked what he meant precisely by his mention of months. Eric seemed to have issues with Ambrose who knew little about him and Rebecca, except for what Rebecca had told him about their friendship. Instead of sorting things out with Rebecca he seemed to be taking his frustrations out on Ambrose for being the stooge in his way. He however made himself clearer and said it's now about four months since Rebecca found this witless worm.

"Why the burst up then, what's it with you, and why can't I hold hands with a man I claim to be in love with?" asked Rebecca.

Eric had to take Rebecca down the memory lane, in his bid to bring to the fore of how deceitful she'd been all along with the Ambrose's story. He reminded Rebecca of her telling him she was only helping to nurse Ambrose back to health and also helping with his memory.

Rebecca smiled and said that's what she's still doing, and though, differently this time, as a couple.

"What about me, Rebecca, does it mean the time and emotion I spent on you meant nothing?" asked Eric. Rebecca understands that Eric's ego was hurt and he's now feeling like a loser in this whole situation. Yet didn't do much to sooth his feelings as she interjected, asking Eric where this rhetoric will lead him. She then urged him to stop playing the loser, and after all, they're still friends.

Eric muttered, and said it doesn't matter anymore, and if it had mattered, Rebecca wouldn't have disappointed him, he then told Rebecca point blank that she disappointed him.

"I asked you earlier, where were you before Ambrose came along?" asked Rebecca.

Eric didn't really like Rebecca's posture on this matter, he quickly reminded Rebecca he was with her before Ambrose came along, and Rebecca never gave him any indication they weren't seeing each other. Rebecca had to absolve herself of any blame, and said yes, they were together, but Eric didn't make any advances towards her, and accused Eric of not embracing the bubble.

"I thought we'd something going, but you just made me look cheap," said Eric.

Ambrose is now back to himself and didn't like the fact that he's the subject of this kerfuffle. He then turned to Eric and asked what the problem is with him.

"Can't people be in love and enjoy some peace?" asked Ambrose.

Now that Ambrose decided to break his silence, he now seems to have opened up the opportunity Eric seeks to give Ambrose the dressing down. He accused him of pretending to be sick, wormed his way into this camp, and then crept into his fiancée's head and snatched her. Eric didn't hold back as he called Ambrose a man of diminished capacity and said he wouldn't want to waste his time by going the extra mile to press Ambrose's buttons just to see which one lights up.

Ambrose wasn't too keen to pick a fight with Eric, he dismissed Eric's accusation and said he has no idea of what Eric was going on and on about, yet reminded Eric that he isn't a worm, and neither was he being creepy in his character.

"If you aren't a worm, then it would be right to conclude that Rebecca steadily and obtrusively crept into your head," said Eric. Ambrose wasn't quite pleased with this passive aggression by Eric. He sensed his position in this matter is sort of tricky, because there's no way he will win with Eric, if he keeps quiet Eric will take him for a fool and contemptuously walk all over him with abusive words. If on the other hand he decides to speak up for Rebecca, Eric will be more abusive and accused him of taking his woman.

This conversation seemed to hold this couple bound, but Rebecca in a way felt indebted to Eric, and thinks that an amicable resolution of this misunderstanding is the best way to go. Yet she'd to make it clear to Eric in no uncertain terms that she might lose no sleep losing him as a friend, if he continues in this path.

"You craftily sidestepped me for Ambrose, didn't you?" said Eric.

These residents aren't fighting over who enjoys the great outdoors, and this isn't a domestic squabble either. He tried screaming as much as he can just enough to make her ears bleed but it will do Eric no good if he continues to treat Rebecca like a woman with a belly full of trouble. Kind words and a pack of chocolates would have done the trick of calming frayed nerves, but Eric seem to be going about this matter over and over, like a mouse on a wheel.

Tabitha walked past them but stopped and asked why it is that they're at each other's throats, Eric on the other hand didn't even hold back, he seemed quite ready to tell as many that cares to listen that Rebecca left him for Ambrose. After all, rumour mill on Rebecca's dumping of Eric and hooking onto Ambrose despite efforts to return the stranger back to society where he belongs went wild in this camp. Ambrose who now seemed to have made a few friends in the camp, had to tell Eric off, and asked why it is that Eric looks at him like a thing and not as a person deserving of love.

Tabitha suddenly finds herself caught in the middle of this supposed tiff that started from a mere exchange of pleasantry to a squabble between old friends. Tabitha stood speechless and watched as they tongue-lashed each other. These obviously, aren't people doing a panto, it's more like a domestic squabble with Rebecca at the centre of it, as she allowed these two camp residents jostling and jockeying to win her heart.

"What do you expect I do? Pretend I wasn't hurt," asked Eric.

Serendipitously, one among the hawks kittling overhead dropped the dead prey clinched to its claws and the prey dropped on Tabitha who cared to stop and calm the nerves of these squabbling ex's.

"Ooh my goodness, that's a dead bird, and where did that come from!" Exclaimed Rebecca.

"Are you ok, Tabitha?" asked Eric.

Tabitha was left seething over a dead bird dropping from the sky on her head, because she considered it a bad omen and blamed Rebecca and Eric for this. She then walked briskly and was soon out of sight, leaving the pair to continue with their squabble.

"The short time spent with Ambrose has been refreshing," said Rebecca.

"Refreshing, you say?" asked Eric.

"Yes, of course, here is a little something for you," said Rebecca.

"What?" asked Eric.

"Turf," said Rebecca.

Now that Rebecca has resorted to giving Eric the middle finger and asking him to turf, Eric couldn't say much but emphasised that Rebecca's' apathy and vengeful posturing towards him, leaves him speechless.

Ambrose seemed to have had an earful, he then turned around pulling Rebecca along, and suggested to Rebecca that's it's best they continue with their stroll because this guy seems to be living in the past.

"Ooh, I'm glad I have got a past, but you haven't got any, and soon I will open you to the world, you're nothing but a can of worms," said Eric.

Rebecca then made jokes out of the situation, saying she and Ambrose are two peas in a pod, two people with strange pasts in love.

"Hmm, shame," said Eric.

Instead of walking away with Ambrose and saving herself the heartache of this conversation, Rebecca gave Eric a parting word, as she asked him to stop being a cynic because he's almost making her a single-minded woman with this tasteless debate. Eric realised Rebecca is about walking out on him, he then quickly apologised for taking much of her time, and said he also needs to retire to his room.

News of the tiff between Eric and Rebecca seemed to have serendipitously spread through the length and breadth of the camp, and by the evening of the same day. Stacy, who is Rebecca's closest acquaintance in the camp, walked into Rebecca's room and without further ado, inquired about the bust-up between her and Eric, reminding Rebecca that the disagreement between the pair seemed to have suddenly morphed into what you see between arch enemies.

"What about him, I hope he didn't engage you in some chitty chatty," asked Rebecca.

"I just walked past Eric, looking gloomy, with his head drooping like bulrushes," said Stacy.

Rebecca had to explain her present situation to Stacy, and said that her matter with Eric has turned into a case of delusional fixation, and her subtle attempt to keep their friendship on a platonic level seemed not be getting through to Eric. Stacy wasn't helpful either, saying she felt it's best to call it what it is, and suggested it's best to label the situation as erotic fixation, yet she'd to express her confusion on why Rebecca chose Ambrose over Eric.

Rebecca's idea of a bird at hand worth two in the bush, meant Ambrose came handy at a time she was worried about Eric's intentions towards her. Stacy on the other hand suggested to Rebecca that Eric isn't some kind of petulant misbehaving child to be kicked around, and said Eric deserves better. Stacy is a bit of a mixed bag, with the capability of playing both the good and the ugly at the same time, and this makes her the right candidate to play along with Rebecca. Rebecca didn't mince words as she poured out her heart to Stacy that her heart and emotions were lying fallow all this while, until Ambrose showed up. She was however frank with Stacy, as she insisted that before now Eric didn't make any advances. Stacy then made herself comfortable as she sat next to Rebecca. She then urged Rebecca to manage this situation properly, and not allow this whole drama to become more contentious.

"Why don't you ask him to let me be? He should stop displaying the countenance that best describes a person suffering conversion disorder," said Rebecca.

"Conversion disorder, how do you mean?" asked Stacy.

"When a person can't talk or speak due to intense trauma," said Rebecca.

Stacy wasn't quite pleased to hear of Rebecca's characterization of a man who has showed her so much care in no distant past, a man whose shoulder she has always leaned on, and found solace. With Ambrose around while the friends discuss their perceptions about Eric, Stacy thought it wise to remind Rebecca that her characterization is a weird way of describing a man she was running around this camp with, not too long ago. Rebecca replied saying she's trying to manage the situation with respect, but Eric's feeling of despondency is resonating this craze, and it's a shame.

It didn't take long before Stacy stood up to leave, but Rebecca decided to walk her, and as they walked some distance away from Ambrose, Stacy then reminded Rebecca that Eric is a nice guy, and she shouldn't make him look like a man saying nothing but gibberish.

"I will try empathizing with him, and I hope he appreciates the gesture," said Rebecca.

"You seem crazy over Ambrose, don't be quick to get romantic with him," said Stacy.

Rebecca scoffed as she tried making less of the situation, after all she didn't hide her feelings towards this man to Jonathan, the man managing the affairs of this camp.

Days after Eric's visceral reaction towards Rebecca, she attempted to get romantic with Ambrose but he seems to be dawdling and wasn't forthcoming. She really didn't like the fact that he isn't reciprocating her overtures. She then stopped after sensing that Ambrose isn't ready for such full-blown romance.

This relationship wasn't consummated, and subsequent attempts to progress this relationship to something more scintillating seem not to have work out as Rebecca had expected.

She had to limit her affection to mere hugging, tickling and holding of hands but nothing heavy, and returning to Eric whom of late was asking for more, doesn't seem a good idea at this point, particularly in the manner she publicly tongue-lashed Eric. She then decided to leave things the way they are, and even at that, she remained chuffed to have Ambrose by her side.

Prophet Gregory had to practically get involved his bid to end the feud between these squabbling ex's. Rebecca was the first to be seated in the visitor's lounge of Prophet Gregory's residence. Eric walked in minutes later, he was stern looking at first, but his disposition changed moments after, and softened up as he took his seat opposite Rebecca.

It was kind of awkward with the intermittent eye contact that made them both uncomfortable until Eric had to look away. Obviously, these two aren't here for candy floss and lucky dips, they're here because the prophet wants calm in his camp.

Minutes later, the prophet walked in and took his seat. He began by first thanking Rebecca and Eric for honouring his invitation, he then informed the pair that news of their feud got to him. It was obvious to the prophet that Eric was eager to speak, at least to get his concerns off his chest. Prophet Gregory had wanted to let Rebecca speak first but on a second thought, allowed Eric who seems to be chocking on his concerns to be the first person to have a go.

"Prophet, I don't know why, but Rebecca betrayed me," Eric muttered.

Eric didn't speak further, Prophet Gregory then interjected and asked if he still has something to say. From Eric's brief submission, the prophet realised that Eric was pained by whatever it was that happened between the pair. Instead of asking Rebecca to tell her side of the story, the prophet immediately admonished them by reminding them of his standing instructions that Luciferians mustn't engage in prolonged feud among themselves. He made them understand that they were once good friends and its' not the end of the world, even though they didn't get their expectations from the friendship.

Prophet Gregory then turned to Rebecca, to hear her side of the story, but instead of justifying her decision to dish Eric, she turned to him and apologised to him, but then urged him to move on and put the past behind him, so they can remain friends. The prophet didn't speak, he only shifted his attention to Eric to hear his reaction to Rebecca's comments.

With eyes now on Eric, he accepted, to avoid being perceived as some kind of mischief maker.

The prophet then encouraged them to find ways of mending their friendship if they want to remain Luciferians. They both thanked him, after promising to repair their friendship and then left as they went their separate ways.

With the passing of time, Winnie and her sons are beginning to come to terms with their loss. Jerome Baptist was at Winnie's residence, months after the wreckage, and while at the door of Winnie's residence, he knocked the door asking if there's anyone at home.

It didn't take long before Peter opened the door.

"Hmm, it's you," he exclaimed.

"Yes, of course, it's me, the least person you expect to see, isn't it?" asked Jerome.

"I guess you're right, though, come in," said Peter.

"How's your mum, how's she holding up, and is she at home?" asked Jerome.

Peter nodded and said his mum is at home but was quick to ask Jerome Baptist if there's any news about moving the ship for them to recover their dad because that should be the only reason that should bring this man to their home. Jerome Baptist was in the process of sitting down in his bid to make himself comfortable in the sofa in the conservatory, before Peter asked to know if there's any news about moving the ship. He then stopped and said he's sorry to disappoint them, that there's no news yet, but something could come up sooner than expected.

"Then, how do we title your visit?" asked Peter.

"Give it any title, solidarity, condolence, or whatever, but not a follow up," said Jerome.

Instead of sitting in the conservatory where he'd wanted to make himself comfortable, Peter took Jerome Baptist to the living room where his mum was seated with her work colleague who came visiting. Interestingly, when Jerome walked in, Winnie and her colleague, Alisabel, were in the living room.

"Oh, Jerome, how are you?" asked Winnie.

"I am fine, Winnie, and glad to see that you're returning to your normal life," said Jerome.

Winnie interjected and didn't hesitate to remind Jerome not to make assertions, just to make himself feel comfortable in his skin.

"You seem to think differently of me, but I only intend to say letting your hair down after months of grieving isn't a bad idea," said Jerome.

Winnie had no idea her son has already given their guest the third degree, she went on to admonish their guest for his insensitive comment for suggesting she should let her hair down while her husband's body is still trapped beneath the sea. This obviously isn't the first time Jerome is meeting Alisabel, they first ran into each other when Alisabel and Doctor Saul visited Kaija, the scene of Octa Flamingo crash site. Jerome Baptist needed to manage the reverberations in the wake of his comment, and he then turned to Alisabel and asked if she's a friend of Winnie, then urged her to please help Winnie find a reason to move on.

Alisabel seemed to toe the same line as Winnie, as she suggested to Jerome that Winnie can't let go until she recovers her husband from the wreckage. Winnie seemed suspicious of Jerome's visit and asked him if the lofty idea of paying victims family a visit, and asking them to move on while the whereabouts of their family member remains unaccounted for, is his usual tenets. Jerome Baptist understands the wisdom in Winnie's question and quickly said it isn't, yet reiterated that he's moved by her difficulty in finding closure to this accident.

"Ooh, good to hear that, Jerome, but closure isn't something that's easy to come by," replied Winnie.

Jerome then moved the goal post further to an uncomfortable subject as he suggested that holding a funeral for her husband will help her find the closure she seeks.

Winnie went kicking off, though still trying to keep things civil not to embarrass his guest, as she asked to know what his postulation is hinged on.

Jerome couldn't say much, as he said it's nothing, but then suggested to her that a funeral might help her find closure.

"I'm still at sea as to why you think conducting a funeral for my husband will bring us the closure we seek, even when his body hasn't been recovered," Winnie retorted.

Jerome smiled in his attempt to address the elephant in the room as he tried to disabuse Winnie's mind of any creepy intention behind his visit. He then looked away, and said there isn't any overt or covert attempt in his suggestions, insisting it's from the sincerity of his heart.

Alisabel and Winnie seemed not too convinced by Jerome as they gave each other this kind of suspicious side-long glance. These ladies have been around the block, and even as Jerome tried to disabuse her mind, Winnie urged Jerome to come out straight if he knows something about her husband. She smiled and urged him not to confuse her family with those of other victims of the Kaija incident, saying those other families have bodies to bury, but hers doesn't.

"These are perilous times, and I don't want cynics making this more emotional than it already is," said Winnie.

Winnie pointed to Jerome that he most likely might be familiar with the nuances of the media, but how they manage their emotion should be their concern. Jerome Baptist stood up from his seat, saying he just come to condole with her family, yet hinted that his visit seemed to have been misplaced or misconceived.

"Of course not, please sit. Your visit is well received even where we manage matters of the heart differently, I appreciate your interest in seeing us pull through this. This pastoral care from Jerome has ambiguity written all over it, and this is the sort of thing Winnie seem not to like. Jerome Baptist stood for a while, and then returns to his seat after a moment of rethink.

"What can I offer you? Everything soft, no alcohol, make your choice," said Winnie.

"Ok, a cup of tea will do," he said, then laughed.

Funnily, his concerted effort to help this family move on seemed to have been misconstrued as slightly offensive, and the ambience in the home became a bit humid. Jerome has a great deal of talent so reminiscent of search and rescue but giving unsolicited advice to victims seems not to be within his gifting. Jerome is now cut adrift, and struggling to keep up the conversation, and it didn't take long before Winnie found a way of making him feel more welcome. After all, there's nothing lurid about a paramedic chief masquerading as a family friend and giving the kind of suggestions expected from priests and counsellors.

Winnie then muttered her earlier hunch as she hinted her guests that she still has a feeling that her husband will walk through that door one day. Jerome interjected and urged Winnie not to toe Dorothy's line of thought, but accepted that he perceives Dorothy as someone who is scarcely sarcastic, even though some described her action as some sort of satirical propaganda. Jerome hadn't the slightest inkling that Dorothy is obviously a Christian woman whose spiritual gift is perfectly connected to a hunch, that has always led her right into the bull's eye.

For all it's worth, this visit increased Jerome's determination to see to it that the ill-fated ship is moved to allow this family to retrieve the body of the late Evangelist. Two months after his visit to Winnie's residence, Jerome Baptist gave Winnie a phone call.

"Hello Winnie, how are you doing?" asked Jerome.

"I'm fine, Jerome. Please, I'm attending to a patient," said Winnie.

"Ooh, you're at work!" exclaimed Jerome.

Winnie replied to him, saying of course she's fine, and then asked Jerome if anything came up. Jerome Baptist didn't hesitate to break the good news to Winnie, as he informed her that the removal of Octal Flamingo from beneath the sea will commence on Tuesday of the coming week.

Winnie doesn't want to be on the back foot by the time she will arrive at the seaside in Kaija. She immediately asked Jerome if his team will be there to recover her husband's body.

"Oh, sure, I thought you'd like to be there as well?" replied Jerome.

"I surely will be there with my boys, and thank you for your kindness," said Winnie.

Jerome Baptist went on to reiterate that he hopes that this move will help Winnie and her sons find the closure they seek. Winnie nodded her head in affirmation even as she held the phone to her ear, and said she knows for sure that it won't get any easier, suggesting it's best they start from somewhere. After speaking for a while, Jerome Baptist had to let Winnie return to work, and said he has to go, saying he hopes to see her in Kaija.

"Ok, thank you," said Winnie.

A week later Reverend Fitzgerald joined Winnie and her sons this time, as they arrived the scene of the accident at Kaija. Jordan suddenly realised something is amiss, and decided to bring it to his mum's attention, he then drew closer to his mum who was having a chat with the reverend. "Mum, we seem to miss something," he said.

Winnie turned around "What's it my dear?" she asked.

Jordan didn't hesitate to remind his mum that the coffin they've arranged to convey his dad's remains seems not to have arrived. Unbeknownst to Jordan, his mum seemed to have all that sorted, as she informed him, she has made arrangements with the paramedics, and they came with one for their dad. Jordan has a lot more in his mind, as he went on to inquire of the family of other person trapped beneath the water alongside his dad. "They should be here as well, and I watched them on the news the other day expressing their grief," replied Winnie.

While Jordan engaged his mum in a conversation, Reverend Fitzgerald walked up to Jerome Baptist, and said hello to him. "Hello Reverend, you're here for Fredrick Douglas, I guess?" asked Jerome.

Reverend Fitzgerald nodded in affirmation, saying of course he's here with Fredrick Douglas family to take Fredrick's body home. Jerome Baptist smiled and said he hopes this will give Fredrick's family the closure they seek.

Reverend Fitzgerald tried not to rationalise the situation as he put a touch of reality to it, and reminded Jerome that in actual sense, there isn't any closure because sense of loss like this one doesn't ever go away. Winnie finished with her son, Jordan, and then walked into the conversation between the reverend and Jerome. She immediately said hello to Jerome, then proceeded to asked how things are going.

Jerome was quite upfront and said it's all on course, but the search for Fredrick will commence from the next day. Winnie wasn't quite pleased to hear of this procrastination, it seems to her that Jerome had preoccupied himself with needless administrative duties, and she quickly interjected and asked.

"Why tomorrow, and why not now?"

Jerome on the other hand reminded her that the search can only start when the ship has been moved to enable a search team do a thorough search. Reverend Fitzgerald then suggested they don't mind hanging around until Fredrick's body is recovered.

Jerome had to put the reverend's mind to rest as he asked him not to worry, that before this rummaging is over, they'll recover his friend and return him back to them. Now that there's a possibility that they might be spending some days in Kaija until the search and recovery operation is over, Peter then suggested arranging for accommodation, while they wait for the search team to recover his dad's body.

"Let's find some place to rest," said Reverend Fitzgerald. They then walked some distance away and picked a spot where they can watch as the operation to move the ship progresses.

Two days later, after the ship has been moved and the search team carried out their search of the area, Fredrick Douglas's family remained disappointed that the team in charge of this search and recovery operation have failed to recover the Evangelists' remains. Peter had to press Jerome further, as he reminded Jerome that he has been able to recover the other victim trapped alongside his dad, and then asked, about his dad's whereabouts.

Jerome had no choice but to continue giving this bereaved family hope, saying he hope to find Fredrick's body before the close of the day. "Let's hope that would be plausible," said Peter.

Winnie's confusion didn't abate, as more questions than answers ran through her mind, and the only person to assuage her fears is Jerome, she then walked into the conversation between her son and Jerome, and asked Jerome what's happening, and why hasn't the search team recovered her husband's body. Jerome on the other hand could feel the concerns of this family, it was quite palpable, and all he could do is to continue giving them hope even as he told them, nothing yet, but they're doing all they could, and nothing is panning out.

"I want you to do more, you've been searching since yesterday, just find my husband," Winnie insists. Jerome finds Winnie's comment to be quite cantankerous, and it's like Winnie's continuous nagging got to Jerome, he then pushed back. "Enough of the drubbing, Winnie, be patient, and it's my desire to help you find closure and some peace," said Jerome.

"Then why doesn't your team do things differently?" Winnie retorted.

"We have done all we can, and we're still doing but couldn't find your husband," Jerome retorted.

Peter interjected with accusation against Jerome as he pointed out that Jerome's body language seems to suggest he's planning on calling off the search despite his earlier comments that he hopes to find the Evangelist before the close of the day.

"Yes, of course, the search would be called off at the close of today," said Jerome.

Peter couldn't help it but ask Jerome if he considers the recovery of one of the two bodies trapped under water as success. "Even when you haven't found my husband, you intend calling off the search?" asked Winnie.

"Your husband whereabouts baffles me, and I don't think he's within the perimeter of this ship," said Jerome.

Jordan became quite furious as he asked Jerome if truly, he's planning to call off the search while others are grieving.

"I know you're enjoying this, you are gobsmacked, aren't you?" asked Jordan.

Jerome Baptist is faced with raw emotion from this grieving family, and it now dawned on him that they seem to be taking out their frustration on him. He then turned to Jordan and said he understands his repressed hostility but making him look like a whack and creepy personality shouldn't be the best way out.

"Then this whole search effort is nothing but a disappointment," said Winnie. "Painful enough that I lost my dad, but most calamitous is the fact that I couldn't recover his body," said Peter. Jerome became momentarily silent as he allowed this family to vent, he then reminded Peter that they're trying, and urged him not to lose heart.

Reverend Fitzgerald, who stood as this family expressed their frustration didn't really join in the frenzy, when calm was restored, all he could say to Jerome was that they're still hoping and still waiting. He then urged him to please put a little more effort.

The search team returned to work, and after intensifying the search and recovery operation, the search team couldn't find Evangelist Fredrick Douglas, and the search was eventually called off at the close of the day. Immediately the news that the search has been called off got to Peter, he walked to his mum, and suggested they return home since they couldn't find his dad.

"You mean Jerome called off the search?" asked Winnie.

"He just did, as he mentioned earlier," said Peter.

"What do we do, how do you expect me to leave while my husband is still beneath the sea?" asked Winnie. Peter had no choice but to encourage his mum to face the obvious, as he told her that Jerome tried his best and it isn't within Jerome's gift to continue the search indefinitely.

The word "best" used by Peter to describe Jerome's effort in this circumstance seems overrated as Winnie muttered saying, Jerome's best isn't good enough because he didn't find her husband.

"Reverend Fitzgerald and Jordan are there and they are waiting for you, we have to get going," said Peter.

Winnie began sobbing, saying her spirit is low, and she just can't imagine leaving her husband behind. Peter then held his mum by the hand and urged her to come so they could go with the helicopter because they're waiting for them, she then stood up and followed Peter as they walked towards the helicopter crew.

"Winnie, I know how you feel," said Jerome.

"No, you don't, on a sweltering day like this; the last thing I expected is my trying to recover my husband from beneath the sea, yet I have failed again," replied Winnie. This isn't some kind of innuendo, but Winnie is establishing fact and Jerome knows it.

Winnie was speechless and burning with anger inside of her as she stood and listened to Jerome's "we did all we could" excuse. The news deafened her, because her mind seemed to have blanked out, and was unable to differentiate Jerome's voice from the audible noise of birds flying around and whistling, noise from their fluttering wings and even the distinct sound of sea water beating against itself.

She suddenly opened her mouth and accused Jerome of sounding as if her husband fell into some fathomless moat where he can't be reached. She proceeded to ask him if there's a back door to the seabed through which her husband will disappear from. Her anger isn't particularly directed at Jerome, but the fact that she failed again, but Jerome seems to be bearing the brunt of her frustration.

Jerome Baptist tried to assuage Winnie's mindset about him, and in his attempt to disabuse her mind that he isn't some kind of bogyman in the basement who just enjoy seeing others hurt. He frankly told Winnie that his inability to recover Fredrick's body shouldn't leave her numb, because he did his best.

Winnie on the other hand isn't satisfied with Jerome's excuses, as she asked if he really understands that his failure to recover her husband's body will put her and her sons in a state of crippling grief. Jerome joined this family to share in their collective sense of loss, but they don't seem to notice it because they're at the moment, grief-stricken and overwhelmed by their grief.

"We did our best, but our best wasn't good enough, I know," said Jerome.

"You need to be strong, and it's time to go, Winnie," said Rev. Fitzgerald.

The idea of returning home empty handed after Jerome called off the recovery operation hit a raw nerve in her, she stood motionless, gazing at Jerome's' face from a distance. She didn't even hear the reverend's call, all she heard was faint recurring echoes from a distant past.

The priest stood for a while looking at what used to be a breath-taking and quite fascinating seascape from the shore of Kaija that has now suddenly turned into a final resting place for his beloved Evangelist. Unfortunately, Jerome ended this operation feeling sort of hollow, after sweating his socks off and having this family giving him the treatment of a clown.

Winnie soon came to her senses and acknowledged she is taking out her frustrations on the wrong person. She stopped for a moment, then apologised to Jerome and thanked him and his team for going above and beyond in their bid to recover her husband. She was tellingly sincere in her apology as she hugged and apologised to Jerome and his team.  Her sudden appreciation calmed frayed nerves and gave Jerome and his team some sense of fulfilment.

# CHAPTER

## EIGHT

### *The Closed Chapter*

Days after the search was called off, Reverend Fitzgerald gave Winnie a call in his bid to find a way of helping this bereaved family to which he's closely knitted move on. Reverend Fitzgerald himself is equally grieving the loss of his beloved friend, but he has unwittingly suppressed his emotions concerning Fredrick Douglas, so as to focus his attention on the Evangelist's immediate family.

"Reverend, how are you doing?" asked Winnie.

"I'm fine, Winnie, and I think you and I need to talk," said Rev. Fitzgerald.

"Now?" asked Winnie.

"Maybe now, that's if you're free," said the reverend.

Winnie didn't hesitate to let the reverend know that she's free and urged him to go ahead.

Reverend Fitzgerald then started by stating that he's quite aware that it's been difficult, not being able to account for Fredrick's whereabouts. Winnie interjected even when the reverend was still speaking and said she use to be hopeful that the search team will find her husband, once the ship is moved.

"I was hopeful too, the whole situation now looks worrisome, I share your frustrations," said Rev. Fitzgerald.

Winnie muttered, saying it's quite confusing, and that the current circumstance meant she can't give her husband a decent burial.

"Yes, we will give Fredrick a decent burial, that's why I'm calling, to discuss funeral arrangements," said Rev. Fitzgerald.

Winnie chuckled, and then exclaimed as she pointed out that funeral arrangements without a body is an embarrassingly obvious situation she would want to avoid. She wasn't adrift but obviously thinks no one deserves an empty coffin. She then suggested to the reverend that she doesn't think the idea of a funeral will be a good one.

"What do you think, Winnie? This is the best way out of this quagmire, because we need to help you find closure in all of these," said Rev. Fitzgerald.

"There isn't any way out, Reverend, and nothing hurts like a funeral without a body to bury," said Winnie.

Reverend Fitzgerald insists he knows how bizarrely awkward it is to organise a funeral without a body and said it's still the best way to try to put a lid on this tragedy, for her and for the boys.

"If you say so, Reverend," said Winnie.

"I know this funeral won't give you the closure you need, but it will put a lid on this matter," said Rev. Fitzgerald.

"Ok, just let me know what the plans will be like," said Winnie.

After the conversation with the reverend, Winnie was able to convey and even convince her sons on the idea of organising a funeral for the Evangelist even when there isn't a body to bury.

The strongest opposition to the idea of a funeral without a body came from Dorothy, the Evangelist's mum, she's yet to come to terms with her loss. Her insistence that her son isn't dead and will walk through the door one day left other grieving relatives concerned. Talk of a funeral without a body is more like having an abortion before pregnancy, so there's no need jumping the gun.

She'd to be doubly sure about going along with this, particularly where her hunch tells her otherwise.

It took Reverend Fitzgerald's intervention to bring her around, and allow the funeral service to go ahead.

A funeral mass was then planned by Reverend Fitzgerald, and a month later, the funeral mass is in progress. Jerome Baptist walked into the church and sat right behind Winnie who was seated between her two sons.

"Hello, Winnie," said Jerome.

"Ooh, Jerome, you're here," replied Winnie.

"Yes, of course, I'm here, to pay my respects to your husband, and to comfort you and the boys," said Jerome.

Winnie spoke in quite a low tone, as she asked Jerome how he knew the funeral is fixed for today.

"I saw your friend, the one I met at your place the other day," said Jerome.

"You mean, Alisabel, the blonde lady?" asked Winnie.

Jerome concurred and nodded in the affirmation, then said she told him of the funeral, he then proceeded to inquire about how she and her boys are holding up.

"God has been merciful, even though this is a difficult time for me and my sons, but thank you for coming," she said. Jerome muttered and said he knew what it's like to lose a spouse, and said he was there, and it hurts.

Winnie muttered and said the grim realities of widowhood, has remorselessly caught up with her. While Jerome and Winnie exchanged pleasantries, the Priest walks in and was about to begin the funeral mass.

*Rest in Peace, Evangelist*

**Rev. Fitzgerald**: Today we are gathered here to celebrate the life of Fredrick Douglas, as death laid its icy hand on our brother, Fredrick. I must say that we were awe-stricken, pained and stultified by Fredrick's unannounced departure. Fredrick was one of us, and he's a man who has drawn us to see the world through the mirror of his lifestyle. The gash of this incident on our psych is hard to bear but with time our memory will relieve itself of this burden.

Jerome whispered to Winnie and told her that a lot of quality people graced her husband's funeral, and said he never knew Fredrick was this popular.

Winnie subtly urged Jerome to stop talking, and that the priest is still speaking, she then urged him to allow her to hear what the priest is saying. Jerome isn't some kind of nuisance, he's just a man who would relish every opportunity to engage Winnie in a conversation.

**Rev. Fitzgerald:** Six months on, Fredrick's memory remains fresh and still shines bright. Though, this tragedy shows us the ambivalence of life in itself, just as we pray for the soul of our brother to rest in peace, I call on Peter Douglas to give a Eulogy.

**Peter:** Seven years ago, when I was nineteen, I recalled wanting to travel to the United States on holiday, then my cousin, Tony, who was twenty and was living with us at the time wanted to travel to London on holiday. All the money my dad had on him could barely cover for one person's holiday expenses, can you imagine my dad gave the money to Tony because he's the eldest and I had to stay back. This is because he's a man that put others first. My brother and I remind ourselves daily, if only we can be as good as our dad heaven will be our sure destination, and I promise you, dad, we will be as good as you and even better. We love you dad, and just to remind you, mum still keep imagining you will walk through the door one day, while my brother and I will keep working hard to be like you.

Immediately after the funeral service, the procession began with the hearse which typically was leading the procession. This is followed by the chauffeur driven limousines, with the priest right behind. Winnie and her sons, and even her parents were obviously right behind the priest. This is then followed by Fredrick Douglas' brother, Brett, and his parents walking right behind Winnie and her boys. While friends and other relatives followed. The most traumatising for Fredrick's family members was the fact that they are burying an empty casket. This whole thing is just a make-belief, and rationalising what went wrong is beyond imagination for this family, particularly, for Fredrick's mum, who have passed out twice since she arrived Bucharest for her son's funeral.

Dorothy remains convinced that her son isn't dead, and when the idea of a funeral was first presented to her, she asked repeatedly. "If it isn't broken, why fix it with a burial without a body?"

It didn't take long before the procession arrived the cemetery, where the evangelists will be laid to rest and final goodbye said.

It didn't take long after they arrived the graveside, Reverend Fitzgerald performed a short service by the graveside, then the coffin was then lowered into the ground in what was quite an emotional moment for all present. The fact that they're burying an empty casket didn't make the emotional trauma any lesser. It was another opportunity for the mourners to say their final goodbye.

There was raw display of emotion, as the coffin was being covered with sand, and it didn't take long before the activities by the graveside were over, and families and friends present, returned to the Church for refreshments.

Just a day after Evangelist Fredrick Douglas's funeral service, Stacy inadvertently stumbled into something she would want to share with her friend. While in the camp, Stacy walked to the room Rebecca now shares with Ambrose and stood by the door for a moment before knocking. "Knock, knock, Rebecca, are you inside?" asked Stacy.

"Yes, of course, and that must be Stacy, I guess?" replied Rebecca.

Stacy opened the door with a smile, and said who else, if not Stacy Silaots.

Rebecca welcomed Stacy and asked how her morning went. Immediately, after confirming to Rebecca that her morning went well, Stacy quickly asked Rebecca to come with her. Ambrose was also in the room, as he lay on the bed but facing the wall, he then turned around.

"Hello Stacy, you seem to be up early?" he asked.

Stacy smiled and subtly reminded Ambrose, it's 10.am already, and as they both seem to still be cosying up in each other's arms, how then would they know the day is far gone.

Ambrose smiled and became jocular, saying time with Rebecca is always rewarding.

"Ooh, good to hear that, Rebecca please come with me," said Stacy.

"Hey, now?" asked Rebecca.

"Yes, now! Something came up," exclaimed Stacy.

Rebecca then got up from bed, "I am all yours," she said. She then followed Stacy to her room.

Immediately they entered Stacy's room, she informed Rebecca she has a little something for her. Rebecca on the other hand, was surprised as to what Stacy's little surprise might be. It was as if Stacy was about to pull some tricks out of the sky. She then asked Stacy what's it she has for her.

Stacy went straight and quickly turned her laptop on, and showed her online news. "Take a look at this," said Stacy. "Oh my God, this is Ambrose, and where did you get this?" asked Rebecca.

Stacy replied to Rebecca, saying she stumbled on the news online, and decided Rebecca needs to see this for herself. Rebecca's reaction seems to add to the confusion.

"You mean his name isn't really Ambrose but Fredrick!" exclaimed Rebecca.

Stacy has been around the block and could read between the lines, she went on to ask Rebecca if she's merely having a laugh or genuinely surprise that her partner's name isn't really Ambrose. She reminded her she named him Ambrose herself, because the man remembered nothing about himself.

Rebecca was open-mouthed and distraught at the same time, yet she quickly asked Stacy if any other person has seen this. Stacy doesn't seem to like Rebecca's ingenuity, and then became quite critical as she asked Rebecca if her being the only person who has seen this her only concern. She stressed that Ambrose's family just held a funeral for him thinking he died in that Kaija shipwreck.

Rebecca continued her line in this conversation as she pleaded with Stacy to please assure her that no other person has seen this, insisting that Ambrose is now in her life and he's already a part of her. Stacy realised this thing is about to metamorphose into a quicksand and will never acquiesce being a part of this thick conspiracy, she then suggested they inform the camp authorities of this discovery because this is getting weirder as it is.

Rebecca was left with too many thoughts swirling round her mind and that leaves her quite exasperated. Stacy may have sat on the fence all this while but this time, she just doesn't want Rebecca to railroad her into playing along with this dark secret as she feared that this convoluted arrangement will definitely come back to bite someday. Yet, Rebecca held on to the supposition that led to the funeral and insists, Ambrose's relatives think he's dead, held a funeral to that effect and they've moved on. She then asked Stacy why she would want to make a mountain out of a mole hill.

"Ambrose knows nothing of his past, but you and I know now that Ambrose has a family that cares dearly about him, and I suggest we do the right thing," said Stacy. Arguably, Stacy just found out her friend, Rebecca, is such an accomplished liar, who's trying to minimise the fall-out from her romp with another woman's man. Rebecca became quite exasperated, she quickly knelt down and pleaded with Stacy to keep this under wraps saying she can't return to those lonely tortuous days, and then acknowledged that Ambrose is the best thing that happened to her since she came to this camp.

The information on the internet about Ambrose as a Christian Evangelist kind of gave them an idea that this man has been living a life of piety before whatever happened to him happened. Rebecca needed to justify her action which Stacy already characterised as a travesty, she then muttered and said she thinks Ambrose might be a missionary who went AWOL, particularly when the opportunity for a breather from his Evangelistic missions presented itself.

Rebeca's description of Ambrose as some kind of man whose wife ran off with the Milk man and needed comfort from the warm embrace of a lonely woman in the Luciferian Camp wasn't well received by Stacy.

Stacy remained miffed at her friend's ambivalence, she immediately withdrew herself from Rebecca, and reminded her to stop sounding as if she can't move on without Ambrose, and then asked what about Eric, before suggesting to Rebecca to return to Eric.

"You know I can't do that, after his feeling of being jilted," said Rebecca.

"Bad blood I guess, but this is the best time to return to Eric, before you lose on both sides," said Stacy.

Rebecca muttered to Stacy that it isn't ideal to burn a candle from ends, and urged Stacy to please tell this to no one, and let this be their little secret. Stacy walked to the door and opened the door as a way of asking Rebecca to leave her house, without audibly asking her to leave her house, she urged Rebecca not to make her a part of this dark secret. Then reminded her that this will get ugly someday, and making her a part of something this ugly, isn't right.

Rebecca tried making her defence as water-tight as possible, saying she's glad Ambrose's funeral wasn't aired on the television, neither was it reported on the regular online news channels.

"Let's keep this between us," said Rebecca.

"What if some other person visits this site for news and discover this just as I have, I hope this won't blow up on our faces?" asked Stacy.

Rebecca steered the conversation as she told Stacy that Ambrose enthusiastically responded to her advances.

"You're already in a wild romance, and I can see it in your eyes," said Stacy.

"Of course not, but I intend to and I'm in for a long ride, and who said romance is dead?" replied Rebecca with a smile.

Stacy looked at Rebecca and gave a subtle word of caution, saying her burgeoning relationship is rapidly becoming more bizarre or perhaps dangerous, as she's dealing with a man who's past, she knows nothing about.

Rebecca seems to enjoy the weirdness of her metamorphosing relationship with this stranger, as she urged Stacy to let things be the way they are, and that no one will discover this. "Let's pretend we never saw this," said Rebecca. Stacy's hard stance on this matter began to thaw, as she insists there's no honour in this, but agreed to keep Rebecca's secret, a secret.

"Thank you, Stacy, you're a true friend," said Rebecca.

Unbeknown to these two ladies Prophet Gregory beat them to this secret but kept it to himself.

As time passes by, with days becoming weeks, and weeks becoming months, and months becoming years, the Evangelist soon acclimatised himself with life in this camp. The idea of him as a man of diminished capacity isn't something anyone talks about. They may have characterised him in that manner, but that's now in the past, because he's now one of them, a full-fledged member of the Bliss Luciferian camp, with so much to offer, and so much to benefit.

After an emotional break up with Rebecca, Eric needed to move on, and somehow, the opportunity to do just that presented itself when Loana who visits Eric's place of business weekly for her office-related assignment kind of like his company. The organisation Loana works for was into some kind of contractual arrangements with Eric's firm, Loana's firm outsourced some of their services to Erics' firm. Loana works directly under the key person overseeing how Eric's firm performs the services for which they've been contracted to perform.

Things took an interesting turn when Loana will always stay back for a chat with Eric, and in occasions where Eric was out of sight, she seeks him out for a conversion about the service her organisation received from Erics' firm. "Hello Eric, I just stopped to say hi to you, and to as well catch a glimpse of your face," said Loana, in one occasion.

It didn't take long their conversion morphed from the services her firm received for the day to everything, and interestingly, they both graduated from the same alma mater, and that sort of gave them more to talk about. One truth about Loana's presence is that she seems to make Eric's day look brighter.

Somehow, Eric took an interest in Loana, and somehow, they seem to enjoy each other's company, and things kind of moved from saying hello to each other, to having coffee and grabbing breakfast together, and eventually to dinner dates.

Their relationship blossomed but they are yet to consummate their relationship, Eric on the other hand felt the need to introduce Loana to his Luciferian lifestyle, as well as introduce her to his friends in the Bliss camp.

Eric was caught up in a romantic blues with Loana, and couldn't wait to show how much he cares about her. In one of their evening outings, Eric hinted Loana he has a surprise for her, this treat is more like the cherry on a Sunday for Eric.

A week later, Eric decided to take Loana to the Bliss Camp in what looks like a surprise treat, Loana was doubly excited with Eric's gesture of a surprise treat, she was quite up for it.

While in the car, with Loana sitting by his side, they chatted, cracked jokes, laughed and giggled, as they headed to the camp.

Eric was all smiles the moment his car negotiated the last bend before approaching the gate of the Bliss Camp, but had no idea he's in for a rude shock. He drove through the gate and travelled some distance into the camp, and then a large billboard of Lucifer was the first to capture Loana's attention, and amidst the shock and awe, she was suddenly faced with Luciferians parading the camp, with witchy pendants around their necks.

"What's this, and where are we?" asked Loana.

"These are my friends, Loana," replied Eric.

Loana's shock was quite palpable, and Eric could see that she seems not to like this surprise treat, and his effort to calm her seem not to have worked.

"Your friends, you said, and you mean, you're one of them?" she curiously asked.

"Of course, these are my friends and I want you to meet them," Eric replied in quite a reassuring tone.

"Oh my God, you're a Satanist!" She exclaimed.

"No, of course not, we are Luciferians, we venerate Lucifer, we serve Lucifer, we aren't Satanists," replied Eric.

"Stop trying to pull the wool over my eyes, you guys are Satanists," she retorted.

Eric soon realised he's in for a surprise as Loana reminded him that there are always news making the rounds of unexplained accidents happening close to where the Bliss camp is located, and fingers of accusations has been pointed at the residents of the camp for their use of magic to hex innocent Romanians, causing accidents that take innocent lives. She began prodding Eric with more accusations that he wants to marry her for ritual purposes, and that Eric might be planning to strike her with a strange illness after he marries her.

"No, no, stop, and take me back," she retorted in anger.

Eric hesitated, and his effort to calm her down failed, and in a highly spirited agitation, Loana immediately opened the door to her side of the moving car, and wanted to jump out. Eric then interjected "Ok, ok," he then immediately turned the car around in his bid to take her back.

There was a sudden dead silence in the car, that lasted about two minutes and the stillness in the car was quite palpable and such that could be cut through with a knife. While Eric was worried that he seems to have erroneously presented himself as some kind of evil man, who could possibly eat his wife for breakfast, Loana just couldn't wait to get out of Eric's car.

The moment they drove through the gate and out of the camp, Loana asked him to stop the car immediately, and while Eric was still trying to calm her down and suggests taking her back to town. She insisted he let her out of his car immediately.

"I've had enough for one day, Eric, just stop this car now," she retorted.

"Ok, ok," replied Eric.

Immediately, Eric stopped the car, Loana alighted and walked behind an old jalopy car parked by the side of the road, and began walking away, and all plea from Eric to get her back into the car failed. Eric watched as she walked away, until she was out of sight.

Unfortunately, Eric returned home without Loana, but he finds himself lucky that his Luciferian friends in the camp some of whom he fell out with lately, had no knowledge of this drama between Loana and him, and he intends to keep things that way. Eric could only imagine how Loana returned to the heart of Bucharest where she lives. Arguably, this visit that started on a bubbly note, has become an experience that left a bad taste in their mouth as they both had their expectations shattered.

Weeks later, Jonathan received a phone call from his ex-wife, Penelope, with whom he's estranged. "Hello, Jonathan," said Penelope. Jonathan seems not to understand that this isn't a social call from his ex.

"Hello Penelope, it's been quite a while, and how's Denton?" asked Jonathan.

"You're asking me of Denton because I called you, what sort of a father are you?" asked Penelope.

"But he's still my son, and asking after him isn't out of place," Jonathan protested.

Penelope turned the conversation around as she reminded Jonathan that the phone works both ways, and she also wouldn't consider it out of place if he picks up his phone and call to inquire about his son, without asking of him only when she calls.

Jonathan seems to find Penelope to be too contentious, as he asked if she woke up from the wrong side of her bed. "You seem not to be in a good mood today," he muttered.

Penelope seems not to want to join issues as she insists on putting this conversation back into perspective, asking Jonathan how he would know about the happenings in his son's life, while he's living in a Luciferian camp working for Lucifer and wreaking havoc in people's lives.

"You're at it again, why can't we just talk without you bringing up issues to stall our conversation?" asked Jonathan.

Penelope's frustration seems to be deep seated, as she reminded Jonathan that each time she remembers the fact that her son's dad is working for Lucifer, it gets her thinking. Jonathan muttered saying it's unfortunate that he and Penelope are world apart, and that Penelope has a conservative perspective towards life, while himself is liberal at heart and flows with the changes of modernity.

"Thank you for the enlightenment, for your information, your son is sick," said Penelope, she then began to sob.

"What! Denton is sick, what's wrong with him?" asked Jonathan.

Penelope chuckled and accused Jonathan of leaving his son, and running off, but to avoid joining issues she had to let the cat out of the bag. "Denton was diagnosed with leukaemia," she muttered.

"Ooh my goodness, what's going on!" exclaimed Jonathan.

"I have a question for you, are you behind Denton's illness?" Asked Penelope.

"What, are you out of your mind? Denton is my son!" he retorted.

Penelope wasn't mincing words as she reminded her ex that satanists are known for inflicting people with mysterious illness, and she needed to be sure that Jonathan isn't planning on using his son for his satanist rituals. This is too much for Jonathan to take, the accusation of being behind his son's illness, plus the shocking news of his son being diagnosed with leukaemia is more than he'd bargained for that day. Penelope also informed Jonathan that she has done some internet searches about the Bliss Luciferian Camp, and the horrible and mysterious things happening to people around Europe were mostly attributed to this camp. Jonathan knows his ex-wife was establishing value and decided not to engage her further about the substance of her accusations. Penelope suddenly became momentarily silent, and then opened her mouth and said she just think he should know, and she has to go now. Jonathan knows for sure that he's skating on thin ice as far as his business with Penelope is concerned, and there's no need exacerbating this brouhaha.

Jonathan then pleaded with her, saying no, no, and begging her not to end the phone conversation as if his life depended on it, before proceeding to ask what treatment his son is receiving. "When does Denton suddenly become so important to you, and I'm pretty sure that your Luciferian wife must have given you a child," said Penelope.

Jonathan tried keeping the conversation within the boundaries of what can best be described as civil, as he insisted that he has told her repeatedly that he has no wife here, and he's just in the camp because it brings him closer to nature.

Penelope on the other hand continued winding him up and muttering that he should tell that to the birds. Jonathan needed to play an active part in his son's treatment, but it's now blindingly obvious that he must win Penelope's heart to be able to do that, he then promised to take her and Denton for a night out when he comes over to see them. Penelope chuckled repeatedly, and spoke in quite a sarcastically low tone, saying she'd rather stay at home and eat her own eyes than go out with Jonathan.

Penelope was once head over heels in love with Jonathan until he suddenly turned into a Luciferian and abandoned his wife and kid to live in a Luciferian camp, she's now a scorned woman who hates Jonathan with a passion. Serendipitously, her resolve to punish Jonathan seems to break as she suddenly reminded Jonathan that it's now up to him, if he wishes to be a part of his son's life.

"Ok, I will inform the Camp leadership of my departure, so they can find a replacement for me," said Jonathan.

"And then what?" she asked sarcastically.

Jonathan quickly replied to her, and said he'll join her to take care of Denton.

"Ooh, you're wagging your tail back to us, why, because posterity won't forgive you?" asked Penelope.

"I don't have a tail, Penelope, and I'm coming back to you and Denton because we are family," said Jonathan.

Penelope quickly interjected and said she hopes he's aware he isn't crawling back into her life because the relationship between them no longer exists. Jonathan acknowledged that things aren't the way they used to be and he obviously didn't see himself running to Penelope's open arms, yet pleaded with Penelope to pursue peace for the sake of Denton.

"I hold nothing against you, just that you make me sick, and I'm disgusted at you," said Penelope. Jonathan seems to have had an earful of Penelope treating him shabbily as some creature at the bottom of the social food chain, he then hushed Penelope urging her to stop the tongue lashing.

"Hmm, I have to go, I will get back to you soon," said Jonathan.

"Whatever," she muttered.

Moments later, Jonathan ran into Goffman, but Goffman seem keen on having a conversation with Jonathan, as he informed

Jonathan that he was coming to see him in his office and asked where he's off to.

"Not now, Goffman, I've got a lot on my plate right now," replied Jonathan.

Goffman seem not to be letting Jonathan off easily, as he pestered him further, asking Jonathan about the job he told him about. Jonathan subtly intimated Goffman that his worry goes beyond giving him a job because his son is sick.

"Your son! You have a son? But you never told us you have got a son," replied Goffman.

Jonathan concurred, saying of course he has a son and told Goffman that he never asked, so won't know about him. Goffman steered the conversation away from who knows what.

"You just said he's sick, what's wrong with him?" asked Goffman.

Jonathan suddenly became emotional as he told Goffman that his son has leukaemia, and asked why this should happen to his little boy. "Oh shame, innocent boy, why should he suffer a thing like leukaemia?" asked Goffman.

Jonathan was obviously itching to continue, yet reminded Goffman that now he knows how much his worries are, and he needed to be with his boy. Goffman seems wrapped up in this conversation and he seems to be using his queries to hold Jonathan back, as he asked about the boy's mum, and if she's also a Luciferian, and resident in this camp.

Jonathan kept walking away even as Goffman whom he suddenly finds to be unwittingly menacing in a manner of clinginess followed him around. Yet, Jonathan stopped in a bid to set the record straight and said he doesn't have anything going with any woman in this camp, so his ex-wife can't be here.

"You should have made her one of us, by so doing your son would have been with us," said Goffman.

Jonathan became quite uncomfortable and then hushed Goffman, urging him to stop asking him questions that makes his toes curl. Goffman seemed not to realise that he's becoming an irritant until Jonathan stopped for a second time and told Goffman he's actually making him to want to punch something.

"Oh sorry, I am just being a friend, don't punch my face," said Goffman.

"Ha-ha, that's just a figure of speech, you know I won't do a thing like that," said Jonathan.

Goffman sincerely sympathised with Jonathan, as he told him to please let him know if there's anything he can do to help. Jonathan was hurrying on, and all he could say was that he needed to speak to the camp leadership, because he'd to leave this camp immediately and be with his son.

"Please do, Jonathan," replied Goffman.

Jonathan got to Noel Zeppelin's office within the camp and unfortunately, he isn't on seat, he then reached for his phone and gave Zeppelin a call. "Hello Zeppelin," said Jonathan.

"Jonathan, how are you?" asked Zeppelin.

Jonathan replied saying he's fine, but he isn't feeling great.

"You said you aren't feeling great, what's happening, Jonathan, are you ok?" asked Zeppelin who's keen to know what it was that troubles the manager of this Luciferian camp.

Jonathan muttered saying he doesn't think he's ok, because his son is sick. "Your son is sick, what's wrong with him?" asked Zeppelin.

Jonathan opened up to Zeppelin that his ex-wife just called to inform him his son is diagnosed with leukaemia. "Ooh my goodness, and how long has he been sick?" asked Zeppelin.

Jonathan hesitated, as he said he sincerely don't know, because he was only made aware of his illness today. Zeppelin immediately apologised to Jonathan in a manner of sympathy, and then proceeded to ask what he intends to do now.

"I'm thinking of joining them, I need to be with my son, Zeppelin," replied Jonathan.

Zeppelin quickly steered the conversation into the obvious matter of concern, as he asked Jonathan if he has discussed his situation with Prophet Gregory Helsing, and who he intends to hand over the management of the camp to, since he'd to be with his son. Jonathan on the other hand, told Zeppelin that who takes over as the manager of camp is the reason he has come to see him.

This whole thing is just so sudden and picking a replacement in a whim isn't the most idyllic thing to do either. More so, Jonathan's pick will only be approved once the spiritual head of this Luciferian Camp, Prophet Gregory Helsing, gives his assent.

Jonathan is the go-to person as far as this camp is concerned, and Zeppelin would need someone with similar social attraction as best suited to replace Jonathan. There's no need pressing on Jonathan who seem already distraught to stay a little longer, Zeppelin then proceeded to ask Jonathan who he thinks can manage the camp as efficiently as he has done all these years.

"There are fifty members who reside permanently in the camp, do you intend to choose from them?" asked Jonathan.

Zeppelin thinks of the Bliss Luciferian Camp as a community that has wealth of experienced members scattered across cities and suggested it would be wise choosing from the over ten thousand members who live in and outside the camp. Jonathan isn't keen to spend another week in the camp over who becomes the next manager of the camp, and as far as he's concerned this isn't something he would lose sleep over because he urgently needs to be by his son's side, and as such, he would love to be replaced immediately.

"Get somebody to replace you, somebody efficient and maybe from the camp," said Zeppelin. Jonathan immediately promised Zeppelin, he will get him a committed Luciferian.

"Please do and get back to me," said Zeppelin.

"Ok, thank you," said Jonathan, as he turned around and left.

Jonathan couldn't wait any longer but to inform Prophet Gregory about Denton but saw him watering the rose bed in front of his office. Immediately Jonathan approached, Prophet Gregory turned to him and asked what troubles him.

"Prophet, you seem to know that I am troubled even when I have said nothing to you," said Jonathan.

"Lucifer is the great revealer, nothing in this camp is hidden from me," replied Prophet Gregory.

"You're right, Denton is sick, he has Leukaemia, and Penelope just informed me about it today," said Jonathan.

Prophet Gregory interjected and said news of Denton's health isn't good news, even as he assured Jonathan that he will bring Denton's case before Lucifer, the guardian and the bringer of light. He then hinted the prophet that this news seemed to have suddenly pulled the rug off under his feet, and he just don't know where to start.

Prophet Gregory interjected and urged Jonathan to begin with the purpose of his visit, as he went straight to inform Jonathan.

"You have come to request a replacement, so you can attend to your son, I suppose," said prophet Gregory.

"Yeah, please I need to be with my son," replied Jonathan.

After sympathizing with Jonathan, the prophet gave him the green light to shop for someone to take his place as the manager of the Bliss Luciferian Camp.

Jonathan thanked the prophet, turned around and left, with a shopping list that has only one item on it, which is to shop for his replacement.

Moments later Doctor Van walked up to Jonathan who seemed distracted and reported to him that they just received delivery of stocks of syringes, injections and medicines. The doctor then urged Jonathan to please approve the invoice for payment.

Jonathan immediately reviewed the documents and approved the payment, but then muttered and said soonest it wouldn't be him doing this.

"What do you mean? I don't get you," asked Doc. Van.

"I'm leaving, my son is sick and will need me by his side," said Jonathan.

Doctor Van interjected and asked Jonathan if he leaves, who then will be managing this camp. Jonathan told the doctor that he has spoken with the chairman and just finished speaking with the prophet about it, and Zeppelin has authorised him to get a replacement. Doctor Van was keen to know who the next manager of the camp would be because it matters a lot to him, for the smooth running of the camp clinic as he asked Jonathan if he has chosen a replacement.

Jonathan on the other hand thinks there's no need for a premature guess work, and since the doctor is this interested, he muttered and told him he hasn't actually picked anyone. He suddenly turned to the doctor whose ears he has for advice with regards who he thinks should be picked to manage this camp efficiently. Doctor Van's interest meant he couldn't keep his opinion to himself and had to throw in his two pennies.

"I don't know actually, but I think the best person for this job should be Ambrose," said Doc. Van.

Jonathan nodded as a way of saying the doctor is making sense, yet was needled by the fact that Ambrose was just about a year and six months in this camp, and worries about a possible squawky reaction from residents who might think they've been in this camp forever and deserve to be at the helm of affairs. Doctor Van didn't hold back as he stressed that Ambrose is so far the best person for the job because he's popular and respected by members far and near, and most people love him.

Jonathan concurred with the doctor and said it's of a truth that Ambrose is a mature guy, with good people skills and has the wisdom of managing people, but then said his concern is whether the chairman will accept him as his potential replacement. While the conversation persisted, Jarrod and Orla walked past them but somehow found themselves in the conversation.

"What's it about Ambrose?" asked Orla.

"We're considering him a possible replacement to Jonathan," said Doc. Van.

"Ooh no, Jonathan, are you leaving!" exclaimed Orla.

Jonathan muttered with a cheeky grin on his face, and said it has become necessary, and that he has to leave to attend to urgent family matters. Orla has an axe to grind with Rebecca, she didn't hesitate to join issues as she gives her unsolicited advice urging Jonathan to get someone else and asked why he should even imagine handing the management of this camp to Rebecca and Ambrose.

"Hmm, no, no Orla, I understand your bad blood towards Rebecca, but for Ambrose, I don't," said Jarrod.

Orla isn't veiling her animosity towards Rebecca as the thought of having Rebecca and her supposed partner in charge of this camp was now the only thought swirling in her mind, and this sort of left her exasperated. She then insisted that Ambrose and Rebecca are one and the same, and who would want to take instructions from them. Jarrod immediately took exception to Orla's comment and said Ambrose is the best man for this job as far as this camp is concerned, except she intends to suggest a pick from off camp members.

Jonathan who seems to be dawdling minutes earlier about his possible replacement, suddenly interjected and said he can't pick an off-camp member, then insists he need a member who is resident in this camp, and Ambrose has been highly recommended.

"You mean your mind is made up about Ambrose?" asked Orla.

"Yes, of course, Orla, most people in this camp speak highly of him," said Jonathan. It's arguably embarrassing that Orla doesn't do nice, a tooth for a tooth, an eye for an eye. She tells it as it is, and funnily, Orla didn't have her way this time. She then walked away angrily after muttering under her breath that it would be weird to see Ambrose at the helm of affairs of things in this camp.

Jonathan kept a straight face and seemed unperturbed by Orla's concerns as he concludes in his mind that Ambrose is the right person for this role. There's something particular about Ambrose that makes people gravitate towards him, despite being a man without a past, whose baggage is embarrassingly obvious. Yet, people kind of find him to be quite an assuming man. He has this nurturing spirit that seem to give people a sneak peak of his past, as someone with some leadership qualities that make people to want to associate with him.

# CHAPTER

## NINE

*Ambrose is the man*

The next day Jonathan walked up to Ambrose and Rebecca as the pair enjoyed a walk by the beach, and jocularly said the pair seems to be enjoying each other's company by the seaside. Ambrose turned around facing Jonathan who was still approaching, and said the sound of the waves, the songs of the birds, and the cool breeze out here is very comforting to the soul. He then asked Rebecca what she thinks about what he just said.

"Of course, Ambrose, and it's fascinating," said Jonathan.

Rebecca continued and asked Jonathan what it was that fascinates him, because she thinks Jonathan's comment is more of banter than a mere complement. Jonathan smiled because he isn't here to trade barbs with this couple and said the desire of the pair to stay close to nature is the one thing that makes Ambrose a unique Luciferian.

"Well said, your compliment is soothing for one's emotions," said Rebecca.

"Though, I've something else for you, Ambrose," said Jonathan. Ambrose smiled and was all ears to know what it is, as he asked and said he hopes it will be something he loves.

"You will definitely love this, I guess, I want you to replace me as the manager of this camp," said Jonathan.

Ambrose suddenly became jocular as he turned to Rebecca and exclaimed, before asking her if she just heard Jonathan's new prank. Rebecca interjected and said Jonathan isn't known for playing pranks, and then urged Ambrose to hear him out.

"Ok Jonathan, I'm all ears," said Ambrose.

Jonathan toned his voice down, and said he's leaving the camp to join his family, and wants Ambrose to replace him. "What makes you think I can run this camp as efficient as you do?" asked Ambrose.

Jonathan had to allay Ambrose's concerns over his ability to run the camp effectively, as he told Ambrose that lots of people have recommended him as the best person for the job, and they seem to like his candour. He then urged him to consider it an honour.

Rebecca kind of liked the offer on the table, and she quickly urged Ambrose to grab the offer, because he can do this. Now that Rebecca is pressing on Ambrose to take up the offer, Jonathan smiled and said he's seeking Ambrose's support on this matter, and possibly through a casual discourse, since he alone cannot approbate and reprobate.

"Ok, I will give it thought and get back to you," said Ambrose.

"I don't have time, Ambrose, all I need is a, yes," said Jonathan.

Ambrose shockingly asked Jonathan if he truly wants him to say yes right away, after all, he predicated his decision to pick him for the role based on the recommendations of others.

"Yes, of course, just say, yes," said Jonathan.

Rebecca immediately nudged Ambrose with her elbow as a way of urging him to say yes.

"Ok, yes," said Ambrose.

Jonathan smiled as he heaved a sigh of relief and thanked Ambrose repeatedly for stepping in. He then turned around and walked back to the camp, leaving the pair by the seaside to continue their seaside experience.

It's now two weeks since Loana walked out on Eric and turned her back on him, she had refused to speak to him or return Eric's phone call. Eric on the other hand feared the treatment he might get from her if he braves it to her office in his attempt to win her back. Funny enough, Loana's boss now sends a different staff to do business with Eric's firm.

Loana's decision to turn her back on Eric weighed heavily on him, his emotion was bruised, and days later Eric walked into his office looking quite downcast. He walked in, facing down as someone who lost his index finger and couldn't find it on the floor.

After making himself comfortable he turned on his system but couldn't concentrate, with his fist on his chin for a while, he picked up the phone and called Anca, his secretary.

Anca walked in, but Eric didn't say a word or the reason he called her in the first place, she stood for a while then asked if everything is alright.

"I blew it, didn't I?" Asked Eric. Anca didn't at first fathom what he was droning about and asked if he's ok.

"I'm talking about Loana, I shouldn't have taken her to the camp," he retorted.

Anca encouraged him to reach out and possibly pay Loana a visit at her work. Eric interjected and said visiting Loana at work will be a very bad idea, as he reiterated the fact that he's trying to avoid making another ill-thought decision on top of another.

Anca is Eric's receptionist, she knows Eric is a Luciferian and lives the lifestyle, but has no qualms about Eric's religious inclinations, his proclivities, and even his social disposition, but this isn't the case for most of Eric's acquaintances.

Eric realised Anca seems not to understand his reasons, and this may be the reason they are singing from different song sheet. Before now Eric only told Anca that he and Loana broke up after visiting the Luciferian camp, but he didn't really narrate to Anca in granular details of the manner in which Loana treated him like some kind bacterium the moment she realised he's into the service of Lucifer. Eric then took his time to narrate the treatment he got from Loana and obviously she didn't hesitate to support his decision not to go anywhere near her office.

After putting heads together, they decided it's best to let Loana be, to avoid the already weird situation becoming uncanny. Eric couldn't stop beating himself up, as he muttered repeatedly that he took Loana to the Luciferian camp because he loves her so much and wants her to know more about his religious inclinations but had no idea that the surprise will be a shocking one for her.

Now that Jonathan has found a good pick to replace him as the manager of the Bliss Camp, he immediately dashed to Prophet Gregory to discuss his pick for the camp manager's position.

Immediately Jonathan opened his mouth to inform Prophet Gregory that he has found a reliable replacement. The prophet interjected "Jonathan, I know you picked Ambrose," said Prophet Gregory. "Did you by any chance come across Ambrose? Perhaps Rebecca must have told you about my pick," replied Jonathan.

Prophet Gregory became jocular as he reminded Jonathan that he hasn't spoken to anyone, but then laughed as he encouraged Jonathan to do away with the suppositions, before opening up to him.

"Ambrose is my choice and I helped you pick him, he's the choice of the great Lucifer," replied Prophet Gregory.

Jonathan on the other hand didn't know what transpired behind the scenes, all he knew was that he was given a free hand to pick a replacement and was glad after all, that he picked Lucifers' choice.

A day later, Jonathan reported back to Zeppelin, who immediately asked him if he has been able to get a replacement. "Yes, I have, and I've just scheduled a handed over meeting for this evening, and I felt I should let you know," said Jonathan. Zeppelin became quite interested in this conversation as he closed the file on his desk and asked if he knows who the new manager of the camp is.

Jonathan was upfront and said of course, Ambrose is his replacement, and he just finished informing the prophet about his pick.

"Ambrose, is it the same Ambrose that was recovered from the sea?" asked Zeppelin.

"Yes, of course, you guessed right, and he's a well-respected member," said Jonathan.

Zeppelin applauded Jonathan for his pick, saying he knew Ambrose, he's a charismatic character, and Jonathan is right in his assertion about Ambrose.

"Right about him, in what sense, if I may ask?" asked Jonathan. Zeppelin now took his time to narrate his first-hand account of his experience with Ambrose and said he has in many occasions witnessed Ambrose in the middle of a conversation and his input seems to arouse the interest of his listeners, and funnily, he has a certain affinity that makes him likeable.

Jonathan suddenly realised he doesn't have to do much convincing since Zeppelin is happy with his choice and said he's glad Zeppelin knew Ambrose this much. Zeppelin smiled and said a man who's much loved by members hardly goes unnoticed in the crowd.

"I'm glad you approve of my pick, and I will update our website, informing members of the change," said Jonathan.

Zeppelin muttered saying, not a bad idea, and urged Jonathan to inform all those residing in the camp of the change.

"Thank you, Zeppelin, thank you for all the support I got from you, please give the same support to Ambrose," said Jonathan.

In return, Zeppelin wished Jonathan all the best, and wished his son a quick recovery.

"Please keep me updated about your son," he said.

"I will, and thank you for your support," said Jonathan.

Unsurprisingly, Zeppelin didn't bid Jonathan goodbye without giving him some financial assistance towards Denton's care.

A day before Jonathan's departure, Prophet Gregory Helsing and Zeppelin stood side by side as they addressed the residents of the Bliss Luciferian Camp about the change.

"Fellow Luciferians, I want to thank you for your continued membership, and particularly because you have all ensured our primordial identity is sustained. You're all aware of Jonathan's planned departure, and the need for this camp to appoint a new manager," said Gregory Helsing. Rebecca screamed out loud from the crowd, "Ambrose," she said. Zeppelin smiled and then muttered, as he said someone from the crowd just let the cat out of the bag, and yes, the new manager is Ambrose. He proceeded to say that it's no secret to all residents that Ambrose has proved himself worthy of this position, and the prophet equally finds Ambrose a worthy replacement for Jonathan.

The crowd cheered, Ambrose, Ambrose, with applauds.

Zeppelin then called Ambrose to the front so he could say a few words to residents of the camp. Ambrose hurriedly came forward and stood beside Zeppelin.

"Thank you, thank you for choosing me, and I will try my best to serve you to the best of my ability. I will also try to listen more and talk less," said Ambrose who then turned to Prophet Gregory Helsing and thanked him. The prophet then laid his hands on Ambrose to pronounce a Blessing on him, he then removed one of the rings in his finger and gave it to Ambrose. After addressing residents, Ambrose turned to Zeppelin and thanked him for giving him the opportunity to serve.

"Thank you, Ambrose," said Zeppelin.

Months and years have passed since the failed search and rescue operation, Jerome Baptist paid Winnie a visit in the cool of one of the Saturday evenings. He leaned on his car in front of the hospital, and waited for Winnie until she leaves the ward.

"Hello Winnie, it's been a while," he said. Winnie had a cup of tea in one hand and her handbag on the other as she walks through the main entrance door of the hospital.

"Yeah, it's actually been a while, and you aren't supposed to park here if you're waiting for a patient. This parking spot is for hospital staff," she replied.

Jerome immediately said he's here to see her, and there won't be any need parking in the visitor's parking space because he's here to see her briefly.

"Ooh, you're here to see me, any news about my husband, and have you been able to recover his body?" Winnie asked curiously. Jerome replied her saying, no, he then walked closer to Winnie, but then used the usual filler in his words as he struggled to say what's in his mind, but eventually said he doesn't know how to start this conversation. Winnie smiled and urged him to start somewhere, or anywhere, and she then became jocular, pointing to him that he seems to have pinched hospital staff parking space.

"It's been close to two years since your husband passed, and I felt you may have finished mourning and considered moving on," said Jerome.

Winnie looked on, as Jerome tried getting off the content of his chest, funnily, she couldn't ferret out what he's about. She then asked if he has come to advise her to move on or he came just to see if she has finished mourning her husband.

"Hmm, Winnie, don't make this visit difficult for me," Jerome muttered under his breath.

"Is this some sort of after sales service, like after rescue service, or what? Your rhetoric is getting weird and weirder by the day," said Winnie.

"Winnie, I like you, if there's any slightest chance you intend to love again, please let me be the man that would share your happy and sad moments with you," he said.

Winnie suddenly finds Jerome to be overly patronising, and said she now knows why he has been lurking around since he realised her husband isn't coming back. She immediately reached inside her pause and brought out her Bible, the subtlety and nuance in her voice reflects someone who is indifferent irrespective of what Jerome had to say.

Jerome now began to struggle in keeping up with this new line of conversation as he mumbled saying he's a decent man and not some kind of creep, and she knows that for sure, just that since his wife passed, he hasn't seen a perfect replacement until he met her.

"You call me a perfect replacement to your wife? I love to hear your narrative," said Winnie.

Jerome Baptist chuckled and subtly told Winnie she shares some features with his late wife, which kept him attached to her. It dawned on Winnie that Jerome is just a man pursuing happiness by following the pulse of his heart. She then toned things down a bit and said she appreciates his courage, but she isn't ready for any relationship for now.

Arguably, Winnie hated having this kind of conversation just less than two years after her husband's demise, because it's way, way too early, for any sane person to start a relationship. Yet, Winnie didn't eviscerate him with some harsh rebuke for coming to her with matters of schoolboy romance.

Understandably, this isn't a throwback of some kind of antiquated romantic interest. Jerome is a widower trying to move on with life in a world where people are trying to make the best of the time they've left, but things got awkward because romance is the least of Winnie's concerns. She's an Evangelist, and that takes priority.

"I'm not suggesting a relationship immediately, though," he said.

Winnie loosened up, while sipping from her cup of tea as she speaks, yet thought it wise not to be passive and said even in the foreseeable future, she doesn't see herself in a relationship.

Jerome Baptist isn't just giving up, and said if there's the slightest chance for her to start again, he would be the happiest man, if she starts with him.

Winnie became jocular as she made it clear to Jerome that she doesn't have any animosity towards him for this brave move. Yet, buttressed her earlier position that her late husband isn't a man any woman can get over easily, and there's more to him than being just a husband.

"I've known no finer man than Fredrick Douglas, and his memory is one I'll treasure all my life," she retorted. Jerome nodded in the affirmation and said he knew, at least he was present in his funeral service. Yet he remained in the hypothetical as he dissuaded Winnie from holding onto the past this much because that wouldn't help her. Jerome thought it wise not to embellish his words with memes of teenage romance because it wouldn't' be helpful at this point, all he could do was to plead with her to let him help her move on.

Winnie was all smiles as she made it clear and in no uncertain terms that she wants to hold on to the past at least in the foreseeable future before letting it go, and that won't be anytime soon. Even as Jerome turned on his charm in his attempt to patronise Winnie with sweet words like "we never can tell where life will take us." Winnie reminded him she's an Evangelist and romance is the last thing in her bucket list and continuing in her husband's legacy is her only priority. She proceeded to ask Jerome about his Christian faith but went about it benignly. While the conversation persists, Jerome observed that Winnie has been looking at her wristwatch intermittently, he then muttered and said he can see that she's itching to return to work.

"Yes, of course, my break time is over, and I just came outside for some fresh air," said Winnie.

"Maybe some other time?" said Jerome.

"Ok, but when that other time comes, please let it not be this topic, please," said Winnie.

Jerome smiled and said he would only let this topic go, when they've exhausted this conversation.

Winnie turned around to leave but left Jerome a parting word as she said this conversation is exhausted and she now must go back to work. Jerome on the other hand told Winnie to have a nice day as he opened the door to his car, entered his car and turned on the ignition.

"I wish you the same," said Winnie, as she waves goodbye one last time, and returns to the ward, while he drove off.

Interestingly, Jerome drove off feeling better with himself as he's no longer hiding behind his feelings for Winnie. After all, his interest in her is now in the open. It's obvious that Winnie is a very discerning woman who will never acquiesce making life decisions in a whim. The thinking that her husband is dead, forgotten and belongs to the distant past isn't something to associate with Winnie. Her head is nothing but a book of memories, good ones, sort of, and letting go of those memories was a big ask, and her perception of her husband is in the present tense and not in the past tense.

Weirdly, her epiphany about her husband being alive and reaching out to her is something her friends and relatives find to be utterly ludicrous. The brilliance of her imagination that her husband is yet to stroll the streets of heaven's yonder for which he has worked tirelessly for, is one thing that made her acquaintances to consider her illusory. Funnily, this is a hunch she has in common with her mother in-law.

Months later, the Bliss Camp summer celebrations are set to begin. This summer event reminds members of the rebirth of modern renaissance in Europe, with the sole mission of kicking Christ out of every life, every home, and out of every nation in Europe. Luciferians in their numbers have continued to swell because they have maintained their primordial belief of the veneration of Lucifer through occult infused into esoterism.

Ambrose stood in the middle addressing a gathering of about one thousand two hundred Luciferians, at the behest of Prophet Gregory Helsing, and the chairman of this camp, Noel Zeppelin.

"Before we declare this celebration open, lets allow Prophet Gregory some time to remind us of our commitment to Lucifer," he said.

**Prophet Gregory**: "The summer festival is an opportunity for us to venerate Lucifer, share in the light and use our liberated lifestyle to explore the freedom of our bodies and nature.

Fellow Luciferians, it is with great joy that I welcome you all to our annual summer festival, a time for us to give account of our stewardship to Lucifer.

Many of you have come from far and near, but those of you with specific assignments and missions abroad should come forward and let us know what you have achieved so far. In so doing, we will be able to assess our collective achievements and discover areas we can make ourselves more useful in the service of Lucifer." Even as he makes his speech, more members are pouring into the camp for the celebrations and the count soon rose to two thousand people in attendance.

The first set of Luciferians to tell members of their achievements are those Prophet Gregory refers to as influencers for Lucifer. They are fifty in number, dressed in priestly robes and scattered across Europe. These Luciferians are pastors of Christian Churches. They're quite charismatic, good with motivational speeches, and quite convincing, sort of, to make followers remain loyal despite their farcical ideology.

These priests openly doubt the deity of Christ. They are proud to refer to themselves as priests who don't believe in Christ but are shepherds of Christian congregations. Unfortunately, their congregations have been unable to spot them out as wolves in sheep clothing because their loyalty is to Lucifer.

So far, influencers from Russia have recorded the least success, as they complained that the Russian society is quite orthodox, too family oriented, and they have obviously refused to embrace the rebirth of modern reinsurance which Europe offers. The news of Russia's reluctance to accept liberal values didn't come as a surprise to Prophet Gregory, he was well briefed about that even before this summer event, but he has to make it something of common knowledge to every member of the Bliss Camp, to rally them further.

"Russia will get more of us, more protests, more global condemnation, until they accept our kind of liberal values," said

Prophet Gregory. He promised more resources to the influencers in Russia and requested a private meeting with them later in the day.

The next group of Luciferians to speak of their assignment are referred to as the brains. This group spend their time surfing the internet for any bit of information that casts the church in a bad light. The brains have just one job, which is to encourage people to resign the church, and they do this by amplifying any negative news about Christians. It doesn't matter what continent the news emanated from, what matters is that they are able to amplify it enough to generate global condemnation against Christians. And so far, this group have recorded the greatest result in Europe. Many Christians who left the faith over controversial issues, had no knowledge they're dancing to the tune of these group of Luciferians.

The last of these groups are the foot soldiers, whose job is to plague the church with protests, to increase the prejudices against Christians, they always look for something to protest about. There are some among these groups who engage in covert operations at the behest of Prophet Gregory, covert operations could be, causing accidents that could be blamed on the church, taking compromising videos of priest's and Christians, and other stuff, at the service of Prophet Gregory.

Prophet Gregory is a lone wolf himself, and all he does is, hex conservative priests who he considers a stumbling block, and where hexing didn't work, the foot soldiers might undertake one of those covert operations to silence the priest.

Immediately Prophet Gregory finished encouraging his members to do more in their service to Lucifer, he then turned to Ambrose and asked him to declare the summer event open. Rebecca was standing beside Ambrose as he declares the summer event open, and immediately after making his speech, Rebecca turned to him and asked.

"This is beautiful, isn't it?"

"Is it about the large crowd or what?" asked Ambrose.

"Yes, you're blessed, the gathering for this summer celebrations is much more than previous years," she said excitingly.

Ambrose smiled and said thanks to Jonathan, but then turned to Rebecca and said all these have been possible because he had her by his side. Rebecca smiled, but then sighted Stacy in the crowd, and nudged Ambrose with her elbow before saying she'll be back, that she'll like to have a moment with Stacy. Ambrose concurred and said she should go and have her fun, she then left him to continue with administrative work while she walks into the crowd.

Funny enough as she makes her way towards Stacy, Rebecca stopped for a chat with Eric, and asked how he's doing. Eric overheard her but didn't respond because he pretended not hear her.

"Hey Eric, good to see you," she said.

"Did you just say good to see me, and you're walking past me?" Eric retorted.

Rebecca continued walking, and that made Eric to feel like her hello was just a passive gesture she just muttered, but then stopped in reaction to Eric's prodding remark, and said she needed to catch up with Stacy because they're taking part in the body art show.

"You're enjoying this, aren't you?" Eric muttered.

"Enjoying what? I don't get you," replied Rebecca.

"This thing between you and Ambrose," Eric said, and chuckled.

"Ambrose and I are real, why don't you get over this delusion?" Rebecca muttered.

Orla walked into the conversation, this time she didn't say much other than ask Eric to come with her, yet asked Eric why he remained in the company of this opportunist.

Rebecca reminded Eric that they've settled this matter and urged him not to allow this rabble rouser to get into his head. She then accused Orla of having an attitude, but then pointed out to her that her ignorance is sickening. Eric couldn't help but try diffusing this brewing quarrel and urged Rebecca to continue because Stacy should be waiting for her.

"Go, go, go, we've had enough of you," said Orla.

Rebecca muttered as she decided it's best to leave but apologised to Eric saying Orla's presence makes his company stale, she leaves them and joined Stacy.

The moment Rebecca got to where Stacy was, she held Rebecca by the hand and asked which of the activities she intends to participate in. Rebecca told to her she's interested in the body art show and said she's going for it.

"Hmm, I hope you won't change your mind?" asked Stacy.

"Why would I, is there something you aren't telling me, Stacy?" Rebecca retorted.

Stacy nibbled into her ears that Eric is one of the painters, and he's to paint members whose names starts with alphabet "R." On learning this, Rebecca exclaimed asking Stacy if she meant Eric would be painting her.

Stacy nodded in affirmation, and said of course, except she wants to stay away and be grouped with tomorrow's participants. Funny enough, even after she decided to postpone her participation in the body art show in her bid to avoid Eric, Rebecca has come to realise she still has to deal with Eric.

By noon the next day, with the summer celebration still on, Rebecca was in the queue waiting to be painted, and realised Eric was dawdling and then urged him to get on with it because it's her turn to be painted. Eric jocularly asked if she came to him as he jogged her memory and reminding her, she once said she never wanted anything to do with him.

"We have been grouped, and it's you who is to paint my face, won't you do it?" asked Rebecca.

"I will do just that, this is summer festival and it's your right to have all the fun you desire," he replied.

Eric immediately began painting Rebecca's face, and they soon got chatty, she then took advantage of the friendly ambience to ask Eric what the problem is with Orla, saying she just can't fathom how she has wronged her. Eric didn't say much, he only muttered under his breath that Orla is just disappointed, that's all. Orla wasn't obliging of Rebecca who thinks Orla begrudges her found happiness with Ambrose. Rebecca on the other hand thinks Orla's anger was misplaced because she doesn't have a dog in this fight, yet said Orla is doing all this at Eric's behest and asked Eric if he did put her up to this.

Eric asked why he would do a thing like that, after all, everyone in this camp knew she played him like a fiddle, and that's actually a betrayal.

Rebecca interjected as she pours out her heart, saying even when Eric doesn't stay in this camp, he left quite an impression that left her feeling haunted.

Eric avoided a steady facial contact with Rebecca even as he smiled and asked her not to worry, saying he's painting her into a beautiful artwork, and maybe as a token of his gratitude for the friendship they shared.

"Gratitude for the love that never was, or the love that was never meant to be?" Rebecca retorted.

"No, for love that was betrayed," Eric muttered.

"You're enjoying this aren't you?" asked Rebecca.

"What?" asked Eric.

Rebecca proceeded to say he must be having a laugh to be the one painting on her after their falling out. Eric smiled and said painting is fun for him, and it has got nothing to do with her.

"Easy, your paint brush tickles, and it's tickling me," she said, and minutes later, the painting was over and Rebecca leaves, and while Rebecca walks away, Eric whispered, saying he would have relished her being by his side, particularly in days like this when Luciferians celebrate the summer festival.

Rebecca stopped and said she's flattered, but she would consider it a mild aggravation rather than insidious, if he continues to relish that which is impossible.

"Ok, go have your fun," said Eric.

Rebecca then said, thank you, before walking away.

Jonathan has since reunited with his son, but seems to be reminiscing his time as the man in charge of the Bliss Luciferian camp, particularly during the summer festival when Luciferians from the length and breadth of Europe attend the Bliss Camp Summer Festival. He reached for his phone and dialled Ambrose to know how he's coping with his new role. Ambrose picked the call and immediately asked Jonathan about Denton, as he inquired from Jonathan about his son's welfare after their brief exchange of pleasantries.

Jonathan wasn't sounding too ecstatic as he told Ambrose that Denton is undergoing chemotherapy, but he's quite glad to be by his son's side during this difficult moment.

"What about your ex-wife, how are you guys' patching things up?" asked Ambrose.

Conversation about his ex-wife is one that make Jonathan feel vulnerable, yet said Penelope is fine. Jonathan didn't hold back as he told Ambrose that he should understand that patching things up with Penelope, means saying goodbye to being a Luciferian.

Ambrose went silent for a while and said, "I get it, and that's like choosing between a rock and a hard place".

Jonathan had to open up to Ambrose that his wife welcomed him with the accusation that he's behind the strange illness that struck their son, because that's the kind of thing Satanists do, and she hasn't stopped muttering, he's a Satanist.

Even as Ambrose listened keenly, Jonathan proceeded to inform him that he has compromised on some of his beliefs just to make Penelope comfortable enough to allow him stay around his son.

Ambrose reasoned Jonathan's quagmire and suggested to him that a compromise isn't a bad choice, sometimes, particularly when we knowingly become foolish just to please those we love. After discussing personal stuff for a while, Jonathan steered the conversation away and asked Ambrose about the summer week celebration going on in the Bliss Camp.

"Ooh, it's all fun, this is my first time of managing it, and members from far and near are in attendance," said Ambrose.

Jonathan was glad to hear of the success of the summer festival and said it's during festive times such as this that camp managers realise how far reaching the membership of the Bliss Luciferian Camp is.

Ambrose went on to inform Jonathan that over two thousand members are in attendance, people from various works of life. Jonathan's interest in Luciferianism hasn't waned, as he's keen on hearing from Ambrose if there are first timers, in this years' summer festival. He then asked if he observed how those visiting this camp for the first time find it odd seeing people openly showing their devotion to Lucifer.

Ambrose laughed and said he empathised with these first timers, saying they find it very weird though, but after a while they see it as nothing. Jonathan didn't end the conversation without reminding Ambrose on the need to sustain the camp rules that members aren't allowed to discuss other religious beliefs in the camp, except new members who require a bit of time to come to terms with reality in the camp.

"All camp rules are being enforced," said Ambrose.

"Ok, maybe we talk some other time, and I need to attend to my son," said Jonathan.

"Ok, pass my love to Denton," said Ambrose.

The summer festival turned out to be a big success, and this made Ambrose quite popular among the Luciferian community in Romania and across Europe. His leadership qualities were portrayed in his people management skill, and he suddenly became the go-to person, as far as the liberated Luciferian community is concerned.

After expressing his concerns about Shawn Tristan commitment to the Bliss Luciferian Camp, Prophet Gregory told Zeppelin of his desire to get other directors to kick Shawn Tristan out of the board. Shawn Tristan is one of the directors of the Bliss camp, but of late he has been scarcely involved in what goes on in the camp. The prophet summoned Shawn Tristan to a meeting before taking a decision on how to deal with this elusive director whose commitment to Lucifer is visibly absent and now in doubt.

"Shawn, I have been patient with you, are you still in the service of Lucifer?" asked Prophet Gregory.

"Prophet, I understand your animosity, I just have a lot on my plate," replied Tristan.

"Sort out whatever it is that troubles you, I want to see your commitment to this camp," the prophet retorted.

Though, not convinced by Shawn's excuses, the prophet expressed his disappointment in Shawn Tristan's sloppy commitment to the camp, but then held back on the decision to vote Shawn Tristan out of the board of directors.

It was dawn, and exactly a week after the summer festival came to a close, Ambrose woke up from a dream that seems quite real to him, he sat down, thinking about the dream he had. Funnily, he finds the dream needling because this same dream is reoccurring for the second time. Rebecca turned around and asked him why he isn't sleeping. He replied her saying he'd the very same dream he had narrated to her days back.

She then inquired if it is the same dream in which he said, he saw a bright light accompanied by a voice, saying, it is time, and by the time he got to where the bright light was, he was met by two young men and a woman, who led him by the hand as they followed the light that kept moving further, and farther as they approached it.

Ambrose couldn't shake off this needling feeling and was over-whelmed by the reoccurrence of the same dream, as he nodded in affirmation to Rebecca's question, saying he just had exactly the same dream. He doesn't know what the dream meant, and strangely the rarity of people having exactly the same dream twice is what makes this dream quite puzzling for him.

Rebecca reasoned with him for a while and since they're unable to make sense out of these dreams, she urged him to go back to bed, saying the dreams might be the result of stress from a week-long festival activity. She then suggested he should slow down on how he goes about managing the affairs of the camp.

Ambrose wasn't being looked for by his relatives as it's now concluded that he's dead and gone, and there wasn't any appeal for a missing person out there requesting members of the public to help either. He's presumed to be dead, and his family now finds solace from the funeral service that was held and now intends to move on. It was Sunday, and immediately after the service Winnie and Peter stayed behind to see Reverend Fitzgerald. The reverend was having a word with a member of the congregation, when his eyes caught Winnie and Peter. Immediately the reverend saw them hanging around, and sensed they might want to speak with him, he walked up to them, and they were soon seated.

"Winnie, you want to see me, I suppose?" asked Reverend Fitz-gerald. Peter turned to the reverend and muttered. "It's summer," he said, then informed the reverend of their intention to go on missionary work that summer.

"Missionary work! Where do you have in mind?" asked the reverend. Winnie interjected and said they intend to visit Ukraine to conclude her husband's failed trip. The reverend saw this as something out of the blue and asked Winnie if she thinks mis-sionary work is something she can continue doing, considering the fact that her husband died on a missionary assignment. Peter interjected and said he's going with his mum, and reminded the reverend that his parents are missionaries, and unfortunately his dad died on a missionary assignment, but his mum intends to continue her ordained work with God.

The reverend was touched and encouraged by the faith of this family that wasn't deterred by their unfortunate loss. Yet, he remained cautious as he's keen on making sure this desire to continue with their missionary work wasn't born out of obligation to complete her husband's failed missionary work, but a desire to bring lost souls to God by taking Christ to the people.

"Why are you particular about making Ukraine your first missionary assignment?" asked Rev. Fitzgerald.

Winnie became a bit sober but said their first mission to Ukraine was to complete her husband's assignment. She insisted that she and her late husband began this work and Fredrick has left a legacy, and she'd to see to it that the work is maintained. Reverend Fitzgerald then became jocular as he told Peter that Fredrick left a big shoe, which might require a lot of commitment and dedication from Peter to step into his dad's shoes. He assured Peter that with God's grace he will not only fit into his dad's shoe properly but surpass his dad's achievement if he put his mind to it. After spending some time with Peter and his mum, Reverend Fitzgerald prayed with them as he presented the mission before God. He then promised to put a phone call across to Reverend Boguslaw, and his wife, Olga, in Ukraine, so they could put plans in place for their visit.

When Sunday came, Reverend Fitzgerald had to announce to church members that Winnie and her son, Peter, will be going on missionary assignment to Ukraine in two months' time. He spent some time explaining to church members the symbolism of this particular missionary assignment and reminded members that this trip is as much important to God as it is to late Fredrick Douglas and his family. He emphasised that this family has a lot of missionary assignments to undertake in the future, but this particular assignment is of sentimental importance.

He then proceeded to encourage members to contribute financially, and in items, which should include clothing to support this assignment. Days later the reverend put a phone call to Reverend Boguslaw, and his wife, Olga, to keep them abreast of Winnie's visit, and encouraged them to make arrangements to receive the late Evangelists' wife and son.

Two months on, Winnie was working her last shift before she and her son set off for Ukraine, and just as she concluded her shift, she rushed to the office to say goodbye to Doctor Saul. The doctor hastily stopped Winnie for a little chat before she ran off. He immediately asked her if they're going to Ukraine by flight or they're travelling with the cruise ship. Winnie was upbeat about the trip and didn't hold back as she said she would have loved to travel to Ukraine by cruise ship, and most particular the Octa Flamingo that took her husband, but the ship no longer exists. She then said she would have found it terribly exciting to travel to Ukraine with the same cruise ship for her husband's sake.

Doctor Saul urged Winnie not to be overly obsessed about the past, reminding her that a trip in the Octa Flamingo would bring back some memories that would've better be forgotten. Winnie on the other hand, suggested to the doctor not to consider her desire concerning this trip petty.

This trip is a representation of a kaleidoscope of emotions that seeks to bring closure to the past, as well as chart a new path for the future. As far as Winnie is concerned this trip to Ukraine isn't something vain but an expression of her faith in God that death is conquered and telling the devil that their loss won't keep them away from serving God.

There is this subtle and unspoken concern for Winnie that's undoubtedly the result of the quiziness among colleagues about this trip that might do nothing but bring back bad memories. This trip isn't an irrational hilarity, its Winnie asserting her family's calling in the service of God, and she wasn't going about this trip as an emotional wreck but was going about it as someone doing what her late husband would have loved to see her do.

She made it clear to her colleagues who have in the past suggested she reconsider her decision to make Ukraine her first missionary assignment, by insisting that her desire to make Ukraine her first missionary assignment shouldn't pass off as a person in extreme naivety.

All that's required for the missionary assignment to Ukraine is now in place, and it is now time for Winnie and her son, Peter, to leave for Ukraine on their first missionary assignment since Evangelist Fredrick's demise. This trip isn't some kind of r and r, it's purely about God's work, and as it has always been the practice, Reverend Fitzgerald called Winnie and Peter out to come to the front of the church. He then asked church members to stretch forth their hands towards them and pray to God to go with them, and ahead of them in this missionary assignment.

The church members prayed as the reverend had requested, Reverend Fitzgerald then concluded by pronouncing words of blessings on them before wishing them a safe trip.

On arrival at Boryspil International Airport, Kiev, Reverend Boguslaw, his wife, Olga, and daughter, Bohdana, were already waiting to receive Winnie and Peter. After about thirty minutes of waiting, they were able to locate each other at the entrance of the arrival lounge, and they soon began formal introduction with the hugs that followed. They then loaded their luggage into the car then drove off as they head to the accommodation prepared for them. Reverend Boguslaw and his family were excited to show Winnie and her son around, but not without having them treated to a nice meal.

After about an hour of showing them to their accommodation and moving their luggage from the car to their rooms, they then drove them to their home where a table is already set to treat them to a sumptuous meal. By evening of the same day, Reverend Boguslaw and his wife drove to the church premises and introduced Winnie and Peter to choir members having their practice session.

Winnie though couldn't sing the song because the choir was singing in their native Ukrainian Tatar language, but she seems to have an idea of the song, and suddenly began humming the song along with the choir as they held their practice session. Her presence kind of lightens up the room, and Olga suddenly took a liking in Winnie. It was fun to see an American making an effort to sing in their native Tatar language even though she was quite terrible at it. Olga just couldn't wait to gain Winnie's attention, before saying she would really love it if Winnie could speak to a group widows, as she is a widow herself and not going about life like a car crash waiting to happen.

Winnie has lived vicariously through her husband, but this time, she has no need to bask in the glow of her late husband's glory, she's on an assignment for God, and Olga is already seeing the beauty of God at work. Olga pointed out that Winnie has refused to allow widowhood remain a frightener, embracing life, and working hard to see God's work and then her husband's legacy live on. Olga was keen to see Winnie pass that passion and her fire of enthusiasm on to these widows, some of whom have signed out of life.

Days following their arrival, Winnie gave several pep talks, some to widows, youths, particularly young girls, and to the church congregation, as well as donate items to those in need, as she brings her message of goodwill from church members in Romania to the Ukrainian church. While standing before the church congregation she became a bit emotional and with teary eyes, it was obvious to the congregation that she awfully missed her husband. She then made jokes and told the congregation that she didn't come bearing a handkerchief, as she urged them not to worry that she isn't going to cry, because she has cried herself a river already, and crying isn't what her late husband would expect from her.

Some of these widows are aware of Winnie's loss, because they're aware of the preparations made by their church awaiting Evangelist Fredrick's visit years back and the abrupt end of that missionary assignment. Her session with the widows was quite fruitful, being a fellow widow who has come terms with her loss. She was able to make inroads to help many of them come to terms with their loss as well, and also help them move on with life and trusting God with their future.

These widows think Winnie will be more bent out-of-shape than they are because of the circumstances surrounding her husband's death, particularly for a woman who held a funeral without a body, but they're are all mistaken. Olga was delighted to have Winnie around as God used her as an instrument of hope, and one of such beneficiaries was Olga's childhood friend, Oksana, who lost her husband recently and unwittingly began living life like the widow of the parish, as she goes about life like a broken record.

All of Olga's effort to help Oksana embrace hope failed until Winnie who shared something in common with Oksana spoke to her personally, and after hearing Winnie talk about embracing the future, Oksana smiled and jocularly said heaven must have felt bad releasing an angel like Winnie because she's in no doubt that Winnie is from heaven.

Her fear of fear itself, was very predictive, and unseemly predicated upon her recent experience of cold shoulder in the hands of her supposed friends, and she wasn't willing to let her guard down any time soon, until Winnie came along.

Winnie succeeded in getting through to a good number of the widows who seemed to have lost their mojo in life. Ania, in particular, was among some of the widows who did lose their mojo, after the untimely death of her loving husband. She now sees longevity to be of no-good use, because her life is now devoid of those moments of laughter and happiness she enjoyed from her husband.

Life happens to people, and it will always happen, but how they respond is what matters most, and Winnie seem to have responded well to her own life's surprises. The women were in awe of her, they held her in high esteem, and that was what made her trip a total success.

These women find Winnie incomparable, many of them admired her strength and faith in God that remained unshaken, despite the circumstance and manner of her husband's demise. While they all think of the Evangelist as dead and gone, and possibly pushing up daisies somewhere by now, they'd no idea he's somewhere, living amongst Luciferians in the person of Ambrose.

Peter on the other hand spent most of the time engaging the youths, Bohdana was instrumental to the success Peter recorded in most of the youth meetings he facilitated. Peter was at the foyer of the church building with Bohdana, after a youth meeting, when he puts a call to his brother, Jordan. After a brief exchange of pleasantries, Peter asked his brother to say hello to Bohdana.

"Hi Jordan," she said. Interestingly, Bohdana understands Balkan language, which is one of the major languages spoken in Romania, and that made her conversation with Peter and his brother possible. Jordan asked her how she's doing, funnily, Jordan hasn't met her in person but he obviously has seen a photograph of her and her parents. After the brief exchange, she handed the phone to Peter who concluded the conversation with Jordan.

After their previous phone conversation Prophet Lucian Gaia, decided to visit Prophet Gregory Helsing, who used to serve under him.

Prophet Gregory was having a conversation with one of the residents of the camp when he saw Prophet Lucian Gaia's car driving in. He immediately excused himself and went to welcome this special guest that came calling. Moments later, he approached

Prophet Lucian Gaia who stood beside his car to wait for Gregory Helsing.

"Prophet, you're welcome, and I'm blessed to have you," said Prophet Gregory, who proceeded to kiss Lucian Gaia' s ring.

They exchanged pleasantries, and moments later, Prophet Gregory welcomed his guest by treating him to sumptuous lunch. As they ate, they talked about everything but left the purpose of the visit out of their conversion.

After a refreshing time at the table, Prophet Gregory Helsing led the way and Prophet Lucian Gaia followed as they headed to the temple. They approached the alter, and Prophet Gregory stopped and stood to allow his guest take his seat first, after which he then sat opposite him.

"I suppose you know that what you're doing is outside the Luciferian order, and it isn't what I thought you," said Prophet Lucian Gaia. Prophet Gregory Helsing had a humble beginning, but then fell prey to gracelessness when power got into his head, yet he'd to humble himself before Prophet Lucian Gaia, who ordained him a Luciferian prophet. His humility didn't stop him from speaking up as he told his highly respected guest that he'd an encounter with Lucifer who reminded him that time is running out, and he must gather as much Christians to follow him because the judgement at Great White Throne is coming. He then reminded his highly respected guest that he once told him of this revelation.

'I know, you told me, but what you're practising is Satanism, and your antagonism of the Christian faith is too brazen, where is the subtilty of Lucifer?" Asked Prophet Lucian Gaia.

Prophet Gregory yet remained humble but reminded his guest that Luciferianism and Satanism is one and the same, and that Luciferianism is just a befitting name for the occasion because it is good for the ears.

Prophet Lucian looked at him, he chuckled but then said their duty is to portray Lucifer as the Liberator, guardian, and the giver of light, and they have no need butting heads with Christians in an open show of superiority. "Why not, Prophet, our job is to make Christians doubt their faith, isn't it?" Asked Prophet Gregory. Realising that it might not be easy talking Prophet Gregory out of his idea of a true service to Lucifer, Prophet Gaia had to pause and stop pushing him further. With each person trying to sell to the other, their cocktail of myth, and unable to make inroads, they soon reached a deadlock.

Yet, his highly respected guest pointed out to him that there are lots of social media posts, accusing the Bliss camp of being behind lots of unexplained accidents and illnesses suffered by Romanians, but then emphasised he's alluding to post by social media trolls.

Prophet Gregory didn't hold back but quickly reminded his spiritual father that the social media accusations isn't far from the truth, and that their job is to cause pain, hex people, strike people with strange illness, and most importantly portray Christianity as a religion of hate.

Prophet Lucian had to shift his position on the subject and said their role as Luciferians is to portray Lucifer as something good, even though their mode of worship is everything satanic and nothing benign. He though left a word of caution for Prophet Gregory as he reminded him of the fact that he might end up incurring the finger of Jesus Christ in the manner in which he's going after Christians, a cost he might have to pay.

Having given his guest a glimpse of the darkness within him, Lucian Gaia soon realised that this whole Luciferian thing has turned into a quicksand, as Gregory Helsing insists, he forgets about the vile that comes out of naysayers, suggesting he doesn't have to be cagey in the manner of his service to Lucifer. These two has forged a relationship that endures, and no love is lost even when difficult conversations of this nature happen, because the ambience is always one of mutual respect. In the spirit of respect for his guest, Prophet Gregory agreed to tone down on his bellicose rhetorical ideology of Satanism, Luciferianism and even his intentions of making an open show of Christians.

After spending some time, dishing out some father-to-son words of advice and wisdom, Prophet Lucian stood up to take his leave, his host then accompanied him to his car, kissed his ring and said goodbye to his guest. This visit was a watershed moment as it exposes the incorrigibility of Prophet Gregory Helsing.

# CHAPTER

## TEN

*Providence or Coincidence*

Nine months later, while Ambrose and Rebecca were asleep, Ambrose screamed out from his sleep, and Rebecca jumped out of her sleep, in shock, and turned to Ambrose and asked what it was and if anything is the matter. Ambrose didn't respond immediately as he continued to wriggle in pain, and began saying his tummy aches as he held tightly onto his tummy. His heartbeats were rapid, and irregular for that matter, and this got Rebecca feeling terrified.

"What, your tummy aches, and how is it?" asked Rebecca.

"I don't know, the pain is excruciating, and it's killing me?" said Ambrose.

"Oh my Goodness, what do I do, what do I do?" Rebecca muttered in confusion.

Ambrose continued to wriggle as the pain intensified by the minute, and he continued asking Rebecca to get him help, and urged her to do that fast. Rebecca stood up in a hurry and wanted to get help, but Ambrose beckoned on her, and asked her to take him to the camp clinic.

Rebecca looked at the clock, then said it's quite late and it's 2.am. Ambrose was overwhelmed by the pain as he said he doesn't care what time it is, before urging Rebecca who seemed quite confused to take him to the hospital immediately.

Rebecca needed an extra pair of hands to help take Ambrose who's now unable to walk to the camp clinic. She then urged Ambrose to give her a minute, so she could get Stacy to help out.

Rebecca then rushed to Stacy's place and knocked the door. Stacy on the other hand, heard Rebecca's voice and then opened the door. "Rebecca, oh my goodness, it's 2.am, are you ok?" asked Stacy.

"I'm, but Ambrose isn't," replied Rebecca.

"What's wrong with Ambrose, is he sick?" asked Stacy.

Rebecca immediately pleaded with Stacy to come with her and said she doesn't know what the matter is with Ambrose, he's suffering from intense stomach ache.

Minutes later, Rebecca and Stacy walked in, but Ambrose was still wriggling and moaning in pain, he then muttered asking Rebecca what kept her so long, and that he can't wait any longer. Rebecca immediately suggested that they take Ambrose to the camp clinic, she then turned to Stacy, and asked her to please give her a hand so they could help him up.

They immediately helped him up and then hurtled in the dark of the night to the camp clinic that's just a stone's throw away. Barbra was the nurse on duty, and immediately she saw Ambrose being brought in, she asked if he's ok. Ambrose was still wriggling, and said he isn't ok.

"Hmm, hmm, my tummy aches," Ambrose groans.

"Ok, bring him over here," said Barbara, as she showed them to a bed.

Rebecca looked around and didn't see Doctor Van, she then asked Barbara of Doctor Van's whereabouts. Barbara stopped for a moment and said Doctor Van isn't in camp at the moment and not in town either, but Doctor Barran Steel will be in by morning, then said she will be back in a minute to perform some checks on Ambrose.

Ambrose on the other hand, was in pain and couldn't wait any longer, he then muttered, urging Barbara to just do whatever she can to stop this pain.

Barbra returned moments later and began conducting some checks on Ambrose, she took his vitals, then proceeded to conduct other tests on him. After a while she informed Ambrose and the ladies with him that she can't find anything wrong with him, insisting his stats are okay.

Rebecca interjected and said something must be wrong with Ambrose, and if not, why then is he in pain. Barbra then informed them she will conduct a scan to find out what the problem could be, and meanwhile she will give him something to help relieve his pain.

"Ok, please just do whatever you can to ease his pain," said Stacy.

The scan result was out by morning, and Doctor Barran Steel was going through the scan result, and said he still can't find anything wrong with Ambrose.

Rebecca wasn't impressed with the doctors' pace and said the morphine isn't working, because the pain seems more intense than it was before they administered it. She muttered, saying the doctors' narrative doesn't fit the facts before them.

"What do you mean you can't find anything, then why is he sick?" asked Stacy.

Doctor Steel muttered in confusion, saying he'd no idea why Ambrose remains in intense pain even when the scan didn't reveal anything, and more baffling for the doctor was the inability of the morphine to ease Ambrose's pain. Why the pain killers aren't working remains another mystery for everyone, including Ambrose.

Stacy interjected again and asked the doctor what he suggests they do, insisting that Ambrose can't just remain in such intense pain. "Maybe we should get the paramedics; we need to get to the hospital," said Rebecca. Faced with a dilemma, Doctor Steel immediately reached for the phone and dialled Doctor Van for advice on how to proceed with this confusing situation.

Immediately after they exchanged pleasantries, Doctor Steel informed Doctor Van that Ambrose is sick, and he has done all he could, but nothing seems to be working.

Doctor Van hesitated for a while, but then reminded Doctor Steel he's a qualified doctor and should know what to do. Doctor Steel chuckled and told Doctor Van that his tone sounds like he doesn't know his job, but Van quickly interjected as he tried to disabuse Doctor Steel's mind of any misconception, and said, that's not what he's implying. He then said he's only trying to encourage him by boosting his ego. Doctor Steel then urged Doctor Van to set the rhetoric aside, that he has conducted some checks including the scan but found nothing, and have given him medications and injections but nothing, and the situation is just like beating a dead horse.

Doctor Van was upfront as he said a scan should be appropriate, and would pinpoint the problem. Doctor Steel reminded Doctor Van, he just informed him he has already conducted a scan, and the result of the scan is right before him as they speak, yet nothing.

"It's strange, isn't it?" asked Doctor Steel. These two doctors have worked together for quite a reasonable time, and despite being the head of this camp clinic, Doctor Van knows too well that Doctor Steel knows his onion when it comes to interpreting scan results.

"Strange is an understatement, the best bet is for you to refer him to the hospital outside the camp," Doc. Van suggested.

"That's what I intend doing, I just felt like contacting you, in case, one of those your low-tech ideas could help save the day," said Doc. Steel.

Doctor Van was undeniably aghast, he then cautioned saying there's no need taking further risk, as he urged Doctor Steel to just get the paramedics to take Ambrose. Doctor Steel immediately dialled the paramedics for them to take Ambrose to the hospital. It's now obvious to the ladies that they will be going with Ambrose to the hospital situated outside the camp. This obviously will be the first time Ambrose will be stepping out of the camp premises since he was pulled out of the sea, after the Octal Flamingo incident.

Stacy quickly asked for a few minutes so she could go and freshen up while they wait for the ambulance, but she then turned to Rebecca and urged her to do the same.

"I'll do that, but let me conclude arrangements with Doctor Steel," said Rebecca.

Stacy inched forward and then said, she will be back, yet urged Rebecca to put on something decent, reminding her they're going to town.

"I know, at least we don't have to advertise our beliefs on the streets of Romania," she replied. Minutes later the Paramedics arrived, and as they carried Ambrose into the ambulance, Jarrod rushed down to the Clinic to see Ambrose. He asked Rebecca what the matter was, as he said Stacy just told him Ambrose was rushed here.

"Yes, he is, and we invited the ambulance," said Rebecca.

Jarrod was shocked to see Ambrose in pain, and asked how bad it is.

Rebecca replied him saying she has no idea of the severity of Ambrose's health condition, and the clinic couldn't say, either.

Jarrod then turned to Ambrose, who's obviously in pain and asked how he's feeling.

Ambrose muttered, saying he has no Idea of what the problem could be, but his tummy is killing him. Rebecca interjected and pleaded with Jarrod to please stay with Ambrose, so she could freshen up and wear something decent. Jarrod immediately called Rebecca's attention and said he's going with them. Rebecca stopped to process what she's just heard, and said Stacy is going as well, then suggested that maybe he should stay back. "Just the two of you? Ambrose deserves more than that, and the space in the ambulance will take the three of us," said Jarrod.

"Ok then, I will be back in a moment," said Rebecca.

She then attempted to rush off so she could go and freshen up but Edmund, one of the paramedics beckoned on her and said she shouldn't expect he would spend an extra minute waiting for her. Doctor Steel interjected and asked to know why Edmund was in such a rush, and suggested he should finish with documentations before leaving.

Edmund on the other hand was quite irritated by the sight of Luciferians around him, with eerie looking pendants around their necks. He didn't even allow the doctor to finish speaking as he interjected again and said he'd rather do the documentation outside this camp.

"Just tell me all I need to know," he said. "Ooh, is it that your phobia for people scantily dressed, and going about their business in a camp, outweighs the life of a dying man?" asked Doc. Steel.

Edmund emphasised his thoughts this time and he said it in no uncertain terms that he just can't stand the sight of decadence in display. Doctor Steel urged Edmund to wait for Ambrose's partner to come before he leaves. "You guys should make yourselves useful, instead of moving in hoards around the camp half naked, displaying moral laxity in service to Satan," Edmund Chuckled.

Doctor Steel was quite tacky as he engaged Edmund and said he has been droning on and on since he arrived the camp, the doctor then threatened Edmund to do his job, else he would report him to the authorities. Liam, the second paramedic, stepped in and urged Edmund to calm down, and reminded him they're here to do their job. Minutes later, Rebecca rushed back to the clinic and the paramedics left the camp.

The ambience in the ambulance suddenly turned sour as the driver of the ambulance took a different turn and began heading the opposite direction away from the route that leads them to the hospital.

"What's happening, and where is he taking us?" asked Rebecca.

Liam interjected and said they're obviously taking the patient to the hospital, just that Hail Maria Hospital is their destination.

Stacy went ballistic and turned her attention to Liam with her face up-close to Liam's, and her finger pointing to the opposite direction. She insisted that Genesis Medical Centre is a stone throw from their current location and asked where the hell they're taking them.

"Why then are you taking us to Hail Maria Hospital, that's thirty miles away?" asked Stacy.

Rebecca immediately pointed out to Liam that Edmund is out to punish them because of the verbal exchanges they had earlier and promised to report Edmund to the authorities if anything happens to her partner. She described Edmund as the most obnoxious person ever, and accused Edmund of making unsubstantiated accusation, and with too many suppositions in his accusations.

Edmund on the other hand didn't speak much, he turned and reminded Rebecca, the black humour is unnecessary in this circumstance, and that her old and tired ideology about him wanting to punish her partner doesn't make any sense.

Liam immediately urged Rebecca to calm down, as he informed them there is RTA, and the Genesis Medical Centre isn't accepting new patients for now.

"I don't seem to get you, what's RTA?" asked Stacy.

"Road traffic accident," replied Liam.

The arguments stopped after Liam cleared the air. The ambulance made its way to the hospital, Rebecca remained apprehensive, and the paramedic couldn't help but urged Rebecca to calm down, saying they're doing their best.

"Yes, of course, you're doing your best, but your vehicle is just too slow for my liking," said Rebecca.

"Do you want your partner to make it through this?" Liam asked.

Stacy interjected and said, of course they want Ambrose to make it through, and then asked him what else he expects. Things almost went pear-shaped in the ambulance until Liam reassuringly explained himself in a much clearer term and calmed frayed nerves. The calm returned but the atmosphere remained sombrely as the ladies watched keenly as Liam attended to the sick Ambrose. Rebecca's attention has been focused on Ambrose, she then pleaded with the paramedics to please not make this harder than it already is.

The Paramedics tried to tone the tension down and said they are already in the hospital, and he then urged them to be positively calm and hopeful, everything will be just fine.

It didn't take long, the ambulance carrying Ambrose arrived the hospital, and he was then rushed to the acute assessment unit of the hospital. Rebecca followed the paramedics, asking them to be fast, even as she asked a doctor walking past her to help them.

Serendipitously, Ambrose fell into a deep sleep immediately they rushed him to the hospital, yet continued whimpering intermittently. Alisabel rushed to attend to Ambrose, she immediately asked the paramedics what the matter was with the patient.

"He's suffering from severe stomach ache and the pain seems not to be easing off," said the paramedic. Alisabel noticed some blood stains on Ambrose's face and asked to know how the blood came about on his face and said it can't be from stomach ache.

"Not at all, the blood is not his, it belongs to his partner who sustained a little cut while trying to help him," said the paramedic. Alisabel then muttered again, and asked. "All this blood from a little cut?"

"Yes, but the bleeding has been contained," said the paramedic. Alisabel then steered the conversation away and asked to know why Ambrose is asleep. The Paramedic responded saying the patient fell asleep as they approached the hospital, and said the sleep could be as a result of trauma.

Alisabel then stretched out her hand towards the paramedic and requested the documentation on the patient. The paramedic handed Alisabel the documentation on Ambrose, but Edmund who seem to have an appetite for gossip, nibbled into Alisabel's ear, saying he thinks she should know that these guys are Satanists, they worship Lucifer and cause mishaps for people, and they run around scantily dressed.

Alisabel twitched, then whispered in return. "Ooh, you mean they go about half-naked?" she retorted.

The paramedic became jocular and said, yes of course, but strangely though, he has to get going.

Immediately the paramedics left, Alisabel turned her attention to Rebecca and said she is about to start attending to her partner, but she then urged her to give them some time to take a look at him.

"How's he?" asked Rebecca.

Alisabel turned her attention to Rebecca for a second time and said she is about to start attending to her partner, but then urged her to give them some time to take a look at him.

"They said the blood on him is yours, lets clean the blood on his face," said Alisabel.

"Yes, it is, but the bleeding has stopped," said Rebecca.

Stacy stepped in and held Rebecca by the hand, she then gave her hand a slight squeeze to calm her down, as she urged her to give the doctors and nurses space to do their job.

Stacy then pulled Rebecca away to reduce her anxiety and exasperation, but while Alisabel cleans Ambrose's blood-stained face, Doctor Saul walked in and after spending a few minutes, he then asked Alisabel to inform him once she's done, so he could perform some checks before sending Ambrose upstairs for a scan.

"Ok, I will do that as soon as I am done cleaning him up, he's all covered in blood," replied Alisabel. Doctor Saul turned to leave but stopped and said he will want Winnie to give Alisabel a hand in attending to other patients needing attention.

"She's attending to an asthmatic patient," said Alisabel.

"Ok then, maybe I will give you a hand, let me know when you're done with cleaning him, and let's check him before sending him for a scan," said Doc. Saul, and then walks away.

Stacy and Rebecca stood aside as they watch the nurse clean Ambrose up, but Rebecca suddenly began to sob, and asking Stacy if she's sure Ambrose will be ok, she then muttered, saying she doesn't know what she will do to herself if anything happens to Ambrose.

Stacy squeezed Rebecca's hand once again urging her to calm down, that Ambrose will be alright, and that they should just be positive. Moments later, Rebecca seems to have come to the realisation that it's just three of them that's by Ambrose's side. She then asked how come it's just her, Stacy and Jarrod that came with the ambulance, "what about other residents, and why aren't they here?" asked Rebecca.

Stacy interjected and quickly put the conversation into perspective, and said the ambulance can't take everyone, it's just herself, Rebecca and Jarrod the paramedic made room for, and that others should be on their way.

"Are you sure? I saw Orla and the look on her face suggests otherwise," replied Rebecca.

Stacy tried to stop Rebecca from joining issues, as she cautioned her not to allow the bad blood between her and Orla cloud her judgement, and said no right-thinking person rejoices when others are in despair. Rebecca continued her line of conversation that Orla cares not about her travail.

"I know she hates me," she retorted. While Stacy and Rebecca were still having a conversation, Jarrod walks into the conversation, but before Jarrod could even say a word, Rebecca asked him of the whereabouts of other camp residents.

"They should be on their way," said Jarrod.

Rebecca tried getting her head around how things quickly became complicated, and muttered, asking why it should be a day like this when a more experienced doctor is needed to attend to Ambrose that Doctor Van decided to be absent.

"I know, of all days, why today?" replied Stacy.

Rebecca insisted that the delay means a lot, and she hopes it doesn't complicate Ambrose's situation. Jarrod tried to assuage Rebecca of her concerns and said they should stay positive because that's all Ambrose would require of them.

After cleaning Ambrose's bloodied face, Alisabel squirmed as she was confronted with the sudden realisation that the man in front of her is Evangelist Fredrick Douglas. It was quite an eerie moment for Alisabel as she almost jumped out of her skin from the shock of realising the true identity of the patient before him. Alisabel immediately exclaimed.

"Isn't this Fredrick Douglas!"

Rebecca was taken aback by Alisabel's sudden outburst of emotion, and she interjected. "Fredrick who? I don't get you, his name is Ambrose," replied Rebecca.

Alisabel continued with her emphasis, saying she knows this man, and she's certain about whom she thinks this man is.

Jarrod stood statue-still and was momentarily open-mouthed, but then asked the nurse what it was she's going on and on about this patient. He didn't hesitate to beat his chest as he pontificates on this thorny subject, saying he has known Ambrose for years, and he's like a brother and a friend to him.

Alisabel didn't hesitate to inform Rebecca and her friends that this patient, Ambrose, or whatever they call him, is someone she knows quite well because his wife works in this hospital. Alisabel insists that except her eyes are deceiving her, this patient isn't Ambrose but Fredrick, and his full name is Fredrick Douglas. With these new revelations coming out of the blue, Stacy and Rebecca eyed themselves, with this side-long glance that speaks volumes. Rebecca immediately urged the nurse to please stop these frivolities and do her job. Alisabel immediately stood up, excused herself, and hurried up to Winnie who's in a different end of the ward attending to an asthmatic patient. "Winnie, Winnie, you need to see this," said Alisabel.

"What, I'm attending to a patient, can't it wait?" Asked Winnie.

"This can't wait, follow me, you would need to see this, now," replied Alisabel.

"Ok, if you insist," said Winnie.

Alisabel smiled, saying she insists, because Winnie needs to see this, they then walked back to Ambrose's bed side. The moment Winnie set her eyes on Ambrose; it was as if she saw a ghost.

"What, what, oh my God, oh my God," exclaimed Winnie, as she screamed repeatedly.

Stacy became overwhelmed by this unravelling drama, and funnily she was able to recollect Winnie's face from the online news she read about Ambrose's funeral years back. Stacy had to find a way to keep Alisabel and Winnie on their feet, and asked what's going on, and reminded them that they're supposed to be treating this patient instead of orchestrating this drama.

"Where did you find him? Oh my God, oh, oh, what a day!" exclaimed Winnie. In Alisabel's attempt to erase any confusion, she turned to Stacy, and pointed to Winnie and said she's Ambrose's wife, and said this man was thought to be dead.

Rebecca looked on for a while and realised Ambrose is slipping out of her hands, and needed to take back control. She then screamed at Winnie and Alisabel, asking what nonsense it is they're talking about, then insists that Ambrose is her partner and enough of this drama.

"Ooh, it's you that's behind my peril all this while." Winnie retorted.

"What peril, and what are you talking about?" asked Rebecca.

"Damn it, this is my husband, what did you do to him to keep him away from us, did you take him hostage?" asked Winnie.

Stacy added her voice in support of Rebecca, and asked with some exasperation in her voice. "Who is this woman sounding like a tempest in a bottle?" Alisabel wanted the truth to sink into Rebecca's skull as she continued reminding them that this woman is this man's wife.

Stacy was a little ingenious with her tongue in cheek response, as she insisted that the patient's name is Ambrose. Alisabel then pointed to Winnie and told Stacy and her friend that this is Ambrose's wife.

Rebecca realised she's losing the plot, as it now dawned on her that her world is crashing down on her all of a sudden. She then muttered, saying all she cares about is the patient she brought to the hospital for treatment, and when he's back on his feet she's taking him with her.

"Hell no! You won't do that, he was involved in a cruise ship accident, where did you find him, and how did you meet him? Please tell me," Asked Winnie.

Rebecca stood her ground in the face of what she called an adversity, as she insisted, she won't tell Winnie anything of that sort, and reminded her that Ambrose is her partner.

Winnie is now torn between celebrating her husband's return and relinquishing her husband to this stranger who is laying a claim to him. She then fixed her gaze on Rebecca, saying she won't debate ownership of this patient with her, that she would rather get the police involved right away.

Jarrod was just aloof, and was confused as to what to say, but not dumb enough not to know that Rebecca coveted Ambrose. Funnily, he knew nothing about Ambrose's past, how they found him almost lifeless by the seaside was all he knew about this stranger.

Alisabel on the other hand wanted Winnie to be sure before unequivocally screaming blue murder to the world, she then whispered into Winnie's ear, urging her to hear from her husband before making this a police case.

Doctor Saul was on one of his ward rounds when he heard the noise from this kerfuffle, and walked into the argument. He then asked Winnie and Alisabel what the problem was as he reminded them that this is a hospital for God's sake. Alisabel didn't respond to Doctor Saul, rather, she pointed the doctor to the patient. Funnily, immediately Doctor Saul saw the patient he screamed out in shock, saying that's Fredrick, Winnie's husband.

"What! This can't be a joke, and I am not dreaming either, where did they find him?" asked Doc. Saul.

"Enough of this drama, he's my partner," said Rebecca.

Doctor Saul couldn't contain his emotion as he cautioned Rebecca, asking what she meant by the patient being her partner, he then pointed to Winnie, and said that is this man's wife. He then authoritatively said they all know this man very well. Rebecca muttered intermittently, asking Doctor Saul not to say what he knows nothing about, she then reminded the doctor that it's possible that Winnie used to be this man's wife but what if he has moved on.

Doctor Saul turned to Winnie, and said he's aware she's still in shock, and this is lot to take in, he then urged Winnie to go outside and get some fresh air so he could attend to the patient himself. He then promised her she will get the answers she seeks later.

Winnie was taken over by anxiety even as she tried so hard to keep her emotions intact. She interjected and reminded her boss that her nerves are a shudder, but she can't let her husband out of her sight, and that she once did, and this is where it got her.

"Ok, but I hope you'll be able to control your emotions," asked Doc. Saul.

"Yes, I would try, but do me a favour, send these impostors out of this ward," said Winnie.

Doctor Saul tried not to act on impulse, as such avoided taking any brash decision. He then urged caution, saying it wouldn't be right kicking them out of the ward, but when Fredrick is up and on his feet, they would hear his story.

"You can't steal him from me, that won't work," said Rebecca.

Doctor Saul immediately turned to Rebecca and urged her to give them time to attend to the patient, and that he isn't disputing her story, but the patient would speak for himself when he's well enough to do so.

"What a grim reality, the day is getting grimmer than I expected," said Jarrod, who seemed to have remained on the fence, as these new revelations came to light.

Sensing that this situation could become more contentious, Stacy held Rebecca by the hand and asked her to come with her, so they could give the doctor space to attend to Ambrose, Jarrod followed them as they walked into the waiting room in a bid to ease the tension.

Moments after they took their seats in the waiting room, Jarrod turned to Rebecca, and asked her if she's aware of these competing interests. Stacy muttered, saying everybody has a past, this is just a past lover laying claim to a man who no longer has affection for her.

Rebecca couldn't provide any response to Jarrod's question, rather she stood up and said she just need to make some phone calls. She then asked Stacy to come with her, but then told Jarrod they'll be with him in a minute.

"Please make those calls, and let's hope the day doesn't get weirder than it already is," replied Jarrod.

**Luciferian Annual Convention.**

In one of their global annual conventions in the United States where Luciferian leaders from across the globe meet, Brandon Moore who is the global Spiritual Head of the sect called Prophet Lucian Gaia aside for a heart-to-heart conversion. Arguably, Luciferians across Europe are now beginning to point fingers of accusations at Prophet Gregory Helsing, who has suddenly become the subject of most conversations among leaders of Luciferian communities.

Prophet Gregory Helsing served in Lucian Gaia's temple, while under Lucian, Gregory Helsing enjoyed fame because Lucian Gaia took Gregory Helsing with him to places and he became known to many other temple leaders. If Prophet Gregory Helsing's burst to fame became a concern, who better to discuss it with, if not Prophet Gregory's former spiritual father.

While these two prophets stepped aside for a heart-to-heart, in what looks like a two heads one heart, kind of thing, they soon got chatty.

"Your protégé, Gregory Helsing, when last did you have words with him?" Asked Brandon Moore.

Lucian Gaia interjected and said his conversations with Gregory of late isn't the usual heart to heart between friends, but then asked Prophet Moore if his questions about Gregory is a follow-up from their previous phone conversion.

"Of course, yes, we need to excommunicate him from the Luciferian community, because he's more of a Satanist than a Luciferian," Brandon Moore retorted.

Echoes of the happenings in the Bliss Camp reached the ears of Brandon Moore, and he's now proactively taking steps to address the matter. Prophet Lucian wasn't in a hurry to cascade his concerns about Gregory Helsing's posturing and his self-acclaimed altruistic worship to Lucifer. Lucian had to hold back on his prejudice even though his support for Gregory Helsing is no longer unalloyed.

Lucian Gaia projected him as someone worthy of being ordained a prophet in the order of Lucifer. Prophet Lucian Gaia is a top dog, who has a good number of Europe's politicians worshipping in his temple in Netherlands. He's the son of one of Europe's richest businessmen raised in the singularity of enjoying the pleasures of the world, and in essence, pampered, but his service to Lucifer made him quite single minded, without the stiff upper lip that characterises the top echelon of the European society.

Considering himself as some kind of inspiration, does not necessarily imply Prophet Gregory is grandstanding against his mentor, Lucian Gaia on the other hand, hasn't stopped biting his lips for erroneously allowing Prophet Gregory Helsing to toddle into the unknown. Lucian Gaia didn't at first consider his decision an error of judgement when he garnered support from Luciferian prophets far and near to attend the commissioning of the Bliss Luciferian Camp, but that decision is one he now regrets.

Regrettably, his support and the rallying presence of highly respected Luciferian prophets gave credibility to Gregory Helsing when he started the Bliss Luciferian Camp.

Arguably, fame cuts both ways, and just as it attracts praises, it also opens the door to criticism. Lucian Gaia on the other hand seem to have had enough of talking about this with Gregory Helsing, and said he's done talking. He then fixed his gaze at

Brandon Moore and suggested he should pay Gregory Helsing a visit and discuss his concerns with Gregory.

"Are you suggesting that I travel from the United States down to Europe just to have words with Gregory?" Asked Brandon Moore.

Brandon Moore's question seem to have an already-made answer, as Lucian Gaia advised Brandon Moore to pay Gregory a visit, and maybe, his presence might cause a change in Gregory.

Brandon Moore saw wisdom in Lucian Gaia's suggestion and decided to take it on board, and after spending some time chatting about other things, the men then joined the others.

# CHAPTER

## ELEVEN

*The loser's game*

Stacy and Rebecca strolled to the hospital's car park, to ponder upon how their little dark secret has suddenly unfolded. It's now embarrassingly obvious that the day of truth has come in quite a damning manner. The situation is changing, thick and fast, as Stacy subtly asked Rebecca what she thinks about this whole drama unravelling right before their eyes. She then reminded Rebecca that they both knew that this day will come, and there won't be any need playing hard and dirty with Winnie, because if they do, it will be at their own peril.

Stacy insisted that there's no need nosing about at this point, she'd rather they return to the camp straight away to avoid further ridicule. She was a bit damning when she reminded Rebecca, she might have thought that her relationship with Ambrose was for the long haul, but the love boat didn't sail far after all. Rebecca interjected as she tried to play down the magnitude of the situation, saying, of course they knew a day like this will come, but not for it to play out in this manner.

"Why don't we just get Jarrod and return to the camp?" asked Stacy.

Rebecca unwittingly became agitated following Stacy's suggestion, she then muttered saying she came here with her partner, and asked how she expects her to return to the camp alone. Stacy suddenly assumed the place of a counsellor, as she reminded Rebecca that she knows quite well that her love for Ambrose is real and losing him just on a whim is actually distressing, but at this point that relationship has just hit rock bottom.

Rebecca remained resolute, and insisting, love is a gift and not meant to be thrown away, particularly when that love came about from divine providence. They stared at each other for a while, as they looked each other in the eye, but the message from Rebecca's eyes was so reassuring in a manner of saying she'd this under control.

Stacy on the other hand has refused to play the part of a trained dog particularly now that the wall of her support for Rebecca's game has come crumbling down. Rebecca's plan to hold onto the stranger she found floating in the sea has soon become an albatross around their neck. Ordinarily the tail doesn't wag the dog and there wasn't a need to attempt the Samson act as this might mean pulling down the house on everyone.

Even at that, she remained unbowed, this is because Rebecca has just fallen into a chasm that has left a grim mark on her reputation. Arguably, Stacy isn't willing to play the devil's advocate this time because she sees what she considers a towering victory ahead for Winnie.

Stacy then burst into laughter and urged Rebecca to remember that this love came to her freely, and the same love is now leaving her without a cost, she then pleaded with her not to make this costly. Rebecca remained stubborn as she insisted that walking away empty handed is the only thing that will make this whole thing quite costly. She then fixed her gaze on Stacy for a second time and reminded her that what she had with Ambrose is something she holds so dear, and letting it go without a fight would be costly, because people fight for what matters to them.

Watching as staff of this hospital kept sniggering at them as they walked past, is nothing but an obvious message that Rebecca's arguments has gone beyond the point of rational thought, yet her last stand is an indication that she intends to rabbit on, until she runs out of steam.

Stacy looked at Rebecca with so much empathy but reminded her that Winnie doesn't seem ready to give up, she would rather fight dirty, and it's going to get ugly.

"Ugly you said, it's already ugly, maybe you and Jarrod should return to the camp; I need to see this through to the end," said Rebecca.

"You know I can't leave you alone all by yourself against them, I will have to stay with you," said Stacy.

Rebecca pleaded with Stacy to return to the camp with Jarrod, because she intends to fight until she wins this battle, she then muttered again saying, sometimes you just have to take what you can in this crazy world. Rebecca continued to weave a story out of the unfolding drama playing out before her, just to keep Ambrose strung to her apron.

Stacy was quite taken aback by Rebecca's doggedness, as she told Rebecca that the world is actually crazy but her insistence on holding onto Ambrose has just added to that madness.

Rebecca's dogged determination to keep Ambrose was predicated on the fact that she has been unable to consummate her relationship with Ambrose, something she kept from Stacy.

Stacy's furrowed brow was her way of expressing her shock when Rebecca unwittingly let slip that she and Ambrose haven't consummated their relationship.

"That's a lie, Rebecca, don't tell me that your posturing of a wild romance with Ambrose was all made up," replied Stacy.

Rebecca opened up and said Ambrose was reluctant in accepting her repeated romantic overtures and after realising he isn't reciprocating, she'd to limit their relationship to mere holding of hands, hugging and a bit of tickling. She then apologised to Stacy for making her believe otherwise, yet begged her not to ask her further questions about it. This terribly guileful posturing by Rebecca was a mind numbingly dumb thing to do, but Stacy did cut her some slack, because it's never fun when the tables turn. Her time with the Evangelist kind of put a lid on her ravenous appetite for sex as she was unable to get it from the Evangelist and didn't get it from Eric either.

As the ladies leave the car park and returned to the ward, Stacy pleaded with Rebecca that she wouldn't want Jarrod to be a part of this, at least to reduce the scandal since he has no clue of what they're up against.

Rebecca needed as much help that she could get and asked what if these people aren't really what they claim to be. Rebecca's comment came as a surprise to Stacy, who interjected and asked what she meant by that. Stacy on the other hand didn't really like the fact that Rebecca has chosen to remain illusory with the fact that they could get into a big trouble, as Rebecca continued to insist that those women ranting in there could be mere interested parties seeking to gain recognition.

Stacy stopped for a moment and reminded Rebecca not to join issues, as she told her that Winnie must be Ambrose's wife, because her face matches the one she saw online during Ambrose's purported funeral mass. She then insisted that if Rebecca consider Winnie's claim a stunt, then that stunt is insidious.

"I'm angry that this is all happening now, Jarrod should leave now, let the two of us handle this alone," said Rebecca.

Stacy wasn't particularly thrilled with the fact that Rebecca is now playing the victim's card, even when they both know she's the impostor in this whole kerfuffle. She then urged her to stop sounding as one peeved at herself and reminded her that other members of the Bliss Luciferian Camp could be on their way to see Ambrose, and what does she intend to do with them.

"I know you're suffering emotional dislocation, but this isn't how to go about it," said Stacy.

Rebecca had to confess to Stacy that she's quite aware that she's working on a tightrope with a possibility of a super pitfall, but she's emotionally attached to Ambrose and letting go seems quite difficult.

"This is a murky water, navigating it might not be easy," said Stacy.

"Maybe love has made me deluded and confused," said Rebecca, who suddenly became quiet, Stacy looked at her for a while and asked to know the reason behind the grave silence.

Rebecca began walking towards the ward again, and said she's just reminiscing her time with Ambrose, she then urged Stacy not to worry because she's like a cat with nine lives, insisting she will come out of this unscathed.

"Ooh, that makes you quite a fascinating character," said Stacy.

By the time they got to the waiting room where Jarrod was seated, Rebecca immediately suggested to Jarrod that it's best he returns to the camp.

Jarrod, though, has remained on the fence as he watched this whole drama unravel, yet didn't think running back to the camp when Ambrose isn't out of the woods is the humane thing to do. He immediately interjected and asked Rebecca why she would suggest a thing like that, insisting he's only here for Ambrose, and then asked what he should say to residents in the camp.

Rebecca immediately applied a more subtle tone, as she told Jarrod that Ambrose has a difficult past, and his past is coming up, and as such she would like to deal with this alone.

"Stacy and I can't just walk away, leaving you alone in times like this," said Jarrod.

Stacy interjected immediately, and said she will stay with Rebecca, so they both will sort the matter out with the nurses, woman to woman.

Jarrod was lost with the rhetoric behind this new line of conversation, as he insisted that he's sure the ladies will still need him to assist in one way or the other.

"Don't worry, Jarrod, I'll update you on the situation of things," said Rebecca.

"You're his partner, and the best person to handle this, maybe I should get going," said Jarrod.

Rebecca immediately gave Jarrod a hug and thanked him so he could be on his way and out of the picture as soon as possible.

Rebecca and Stacy continued scheming on how to limit the outcry from their dark and scandalous act, by asking Jarrod to return to the camp so they could deal with the matter on their own. Alisabel walked to Winnie, who's seated by Ambrose's bed side and informed her that the scan result is back. Winnie immediately stretched forth her hand so she could take a look at the scan result. Alisabel put up a brief smile as she handed the scan result to Winnie and said there isn't any major cause for concern.

"Says who?" asked Winnie.

"Says the scan result," replied Alisabel.

Even before taking a thorough look at the scan result, Winnie muttered, and said if there's no cause for concern, what about the excruciating stomach ache, and what's the cause.

Alisabel was more concerned about the good news from the result of the scan, yet said she has no idea of what could be the cause of the stomach ache. She then reminded Winnie she's a nurse and also able to interpret a scan result.

"Maybe nature just wants him to reunite with his family," replied Alisabel. Alisabel's comment was quite thought provoking for Winnie who tried not to be overly optimistic, yet she immediately asked Alisabel if she meant an episode of excruciating stomach ache, is the means through which her husband could find his family.

"Of course, I guess so, and if not so, why did the pain disappear?" asked Alisabel.

Winnie spent some time perusing the scan result, and found nothing either, she heaves a sigh of relief and then said she's glad he's stable, yet she finds it needling that this episode of stomach ache is responsible for his re-emergence. "That's a mystery we will have to deal with when he wakes up," Alisabel retorted.

Winnie reached for her phone for the second time, in her attempt to ring her boys to tell them about the good news but couldn't follow through with the call. She's keen on knowing more about her husband's story before getting her boys involved, particularly now that a strange woman is involved. She then fixed her gaze on Alisabel and said the fact that she came to work as a widow, but returning home with her husband who was presumed to be dead is quite a lot to take in and she's eternally grateful to God.

Alisabel observed as Winnie restrained herself from making phone calls for the second time, and sensed she's quite apprehensive, she then asked Winnie if she has informed Peter and Jordan about their dad. Winnie responded saying she'd wanted to, but wants her husband to be stable before breaking the news. Alisabel smiled and urged her not to manage the expression of her joy, because she can see happiness in her, and it's beyond expression. Alisabel continues to tease Winnie, saying she's happier than a lottery winner.

Winnie concurred as she burst into laughter saying her husband's return to her is beyond lottery. Alisabel then steered the conversation back to the contention for her husband and asked how she intend to deal with this other woman.

Winnie remained as calm as a cucumber, even though she's keen to see how this drama unravels further. She then asked Alisabel not to worry because she will put Rebecca in her place and promised that Rebecca wouldn't have a leg to stand on when she finishes with her. Winnie had to hold her nerves and said all that she wants is for her husband to be on his feet, and tell her his story himself.

"Sorry, there's something I didn't tell you about your husband and those in his company," said Alisabel.

"What about it? I need to know, please tell me, all of it," said Winnie.

Alisabel whispered to Winnie, saying she wouldn't like this, but she thinks it's best Winnie knows about it, that these people are satanists from the much dreaded and popular Bliss Luciferian Camp.

"Luciferians, as in vegetarians or what?" asked Winnie.

Alisabel muttered saying these aren't vegetarians; they're people proudly and openly in the service of Satan and walk around scantily dressed. This news got Winnie quite spooked, as she exclaimed, and told Alisabel that she has just dampened her joy with this new revelation.

She then stood up from her seat in confusion, asking herself, "How come her husband ended up in a community of half-naked Satan worshipers." She's now realising that the situation is much grimmer than she'd thought. Insisting her sons would probably hold their heads in their hand when they get to hear this. More so, preening this news still won't make it any better when her boys eventually hear of it. Rebecca might likely get an ear bashing from this. Sadly, by the time Winnie's relatives and her friends gets involved in this matter, Rebecca's situation will soon be likened to a person bleeding profusely in shark infested water.

Alisabel herself doesn't have the answer to the question Winnie seeks, but her only consolation for Winnie was for her not to let this sobering news steal her joy. This news got Winnie reeling from within, as she couldn't stop muttering, and describing Rebecca as an evil filth that has been indulging her husband and saying what a shame it is that she would have to deal with a smug like Rebecca. While Winnie and Alisabel were holding a conversation, Doctor Saul walked into the conversation, and asked Alisabel if the scan result in her hand belongs to Winnie's husband.

"Yes, of course, but there isn't need for any concern," Alisabel said, and then hands the scan result to Doctor Saul. Just as the doctor takes a look at the scan result, Winnie suddenly stood up and began walking away.

Doctor Saul immediately beckoned on her and asked where she's headed. Winnie on the other hand, seems to have a lot on her mind, but had no choice but to break the sweet and sour news to her boys, saying she needed to put her boys in the know, particularly about this new development.

Doctor Saul interjected and inquired about this new development she wants to tell her boys, as he urged her to have in mind that this news will unwittingly generate mixed feelings in her sons.

Winnie insists she has to bring her sons up to speed about their dad, stressing that no matter what the feelings are, their dad is back from the dead, and she supposes that this is good news enough for any son who have been unable to explain his dad's unexplained death.

"I see, you're ecstatic. your joy is unspeakable, and I'm happy for you, Winnie," said Doc. Saul.

Rebecca accosted Winnie as she walks past them. "Excuse me, excuse me, I need to speak to you," she said, as she rushed towards Winnie.

With a sustained frown on her face, Winnie stopped and wasn't in any mood for a conversation, particularly with this woman with whom she has bones to pick.

"What's it you want?" asked Winnie.

Rebecca didn't hesitate to remind Winnie she has come to ask her the same question, before inquiring why she's doing this. "Doing what? This is my husband, and I was just going to inform my sons that I have found their dad," said Winnie.

Rebecca continued with her claim on Ambrose as her partner, insisting that Winnie should stop contesting with her, and asking Winne what it is that's wrong with her.

"Did I hear you say partner, as in how, and how long you have partnered my husband?" asked Winnie. Rebecca became more belligerent than anxious as the conversation persisted. She immediately cautioned Winnie, urging her to stop making possessive sentences, insisting that she and Ambrose have been living as husband and wife for close to three years.

Rebecca's claim got Winnie reeling from within. "Really, husband and wife, this is a shame, and how did this come about?" asked Winnie.

"Because he's in love with me, and I suggest you move on because Ambrose now belong to your past, but not your present and won't be a part of your future either," insists Rebecca.

Winnie finds Rebecca's comment quite spectacularly cruel and without empathy. She immediately hushed Rebecca to stop engaging her in tiffs and witless argument, because she expects her to be contrite for stealing her husband. Rebecca wasn't quite perturbed even as Stacy told her earlier that she was walking on thin ice, yet she insisted on putting her feet down, and telling Winnie to say whatever she likes because she's no stranger to criticism.

Winnie seems to use every opportunity at her disposal to set the record straight, as she immediately interjected and reminded Rebecca that for the for the record the patient's name isn't Ambrose, his name is Fredrick Douglas and he's an Evangelist.

Rebecca smiled and urged Winnie to stand aside, "Fredrick is in the past, and Ambrose is in the present, get that into your head," said Rebecca.

In a bid to manage the reverberation from the scandal surrounding her husband whereabouts for the past three years and what he has been up to, Winnie told Rebecca, she might forgive her if she stops this madness right now. It's embarrassingly obvious that dredging this matter that was already consigned to the past wasn't an easy thing for Winnie to do. All she could hope for is for her husband to wake from his sleep that looks more like a slumber and tell her his story. Winnie then walked away but didn't go through with the phone call to her sons, she just cooled off a bit and returned.

The moment Rebecca saw Winnie coming back she followed her again, and not letting her off easily, Winnie on the other hand tried ignoring Rebecca as she said she's glad her husband is stable, and when he wakes up, he'll tell Rebecca about his wife and two sons.

"I'm not disputing your story, after all, people get married, they get divorced and they remarry," said Rebecca.

Winnie immediate steered the conversation into areas Rebeca might find uncomfortable, asking her what's it about her being a naturist, meaning she walks around naked.

"What about it? It's a lifestyle, good you know, Ambrose and I are naturists, which is one thing we have in common," replied Rebecca.

Winnie briskly inches away, and immediately asked Rebecca not to come any closer. She insisted that there's no cat in hells' chance for Rebecca to achieve her aim, saying Rebecca must be out of her tree to think she will leave this hospital and return to that God forsaken camp with the Evangelist. She became quite irritated by Rebecca, and the irritation actually made her skin crawl, as she muttered and told Rebecca it's a shame she spread her filth to her husband, but that filthiness ends today. Rebecca wasn't deterred by Winnie's characterization of her as some kind of filth, she informed Winnie that she doesn't think Ambrose would even recognise Winnie when he wakes up.

Winnie on the other hand had no knowledge that her husband lost his memory following the cruise ship accident, and that he unfortunately doesn't remember anything about himself before the accident.

"Why won't he recognize me, is anything wrong with him? Maybe it's time the police interrogate you," said Winnie.

"You sound funny, what if Ambrose tells the police he was married to you, but presently in love with me?" asked Rebecca.

Winnie was as calm as a cucumber earlier, but with Rebecca's recent utterances she's now at sea, and a bit agitated because she doesn't know what to expect when her husband eventually wakes up, as she insisted that whatever Rebecca may have done to her husband to win his heart loses its efficacy today. Rebecca isn't giving up either, as she insisted that Winnie may wish to take advantage of the fact that she works in this hospital to win sympathies to herself, but she will be hanging around to wait for Ambrose to wake up and be by his side.

Winnie began walking away from Rebecca, but walks back to her on a second thought. "Tell me something, why did you put on clothes on your way here, if decency is a good thing?" asked Winnie. Rebecca hesitated but immediately decided not to keep quiet.

"What do you care, living scantily dressed is a lifestyle, does it mean you can't walk about scantily dressed in a crowd of people?" asked Rebecca.

Winnie smiled in mockery at Rebecca's naivety, asking her if she still thinks she's moonlighting, and asked why she would do a thing like that, because it's nothing but an expression of insanity. Winnie then said' "I'm sick, and very sick indeed about my husband's association with Satanist filth like you."

Rebecca stopped closing the gap between her and Winnie, sensing that she's quite irritated by her lifestyle as a Satanist, and accusing Winnie that her divergent opinion about her belief as a Luciferian is nothing but an aggressive cynicism. Winnie thinks she has had enough of going back and forth with Rebecca and wouldn't want Doctor Saul to find her engaging Rebecca any further. She then turned around to leave but left a parting word for Rebecca as she said it's devious to keep a man under her sway, manipulating him to live the life of another.

Winnie then proceeded to be by her husband's side. At this point, Doctor Saul has finished with the Evangelist and moved on to other patients as he continues with his ward rounds. Alisabel on the other hand, allowed the Evangelist to continue in his slumber, and went about her work. Rebecca hated the fact that Winnie sees her as disposable, she then returned to Stacy who seems not too keen to speak on this subject until Ambrose comes around, as she fears, this might come to bite.

They then walked back to the waiting room as they continue assessing their options.

It didn't take long after the ladies got chatting that a phone call came in from Doctor Barran Steel, who called to inquire of Ambrose's condition. The conversation quickly got awkward the moment the doctor ended the brief exchange of pleasantries and began asking specific questions about Ambrose.

It's obvious at this point that Rebecca isn't overly fond of people nosing into what goes on in her relationship with Ambrose. She decided to put a sock in it and wasn't giving much out, but the doctor felt obligated because Ambrose was first his patient. Her attempt to walk this path alone meant she will continue to stone-wall in a manner that will leave members growing in anger.

The doctor held onto the phone still trying to make in-roads into Rebecca but suddenly became frustrated as she rudely interrupted him and became dismissive. There is no sense of humour left in Rebecca who is now bleeding of friendship at every turn. Stacy who stood by Rebecca's side nudged her with her elbow as a way of urging her to be calm and stop being overly dismissive with the doctor. She has no need to humour Rebecca but assured her that no harm could come to her reputation if she drops the attitude.

Moments later, Rebecca walked back into the ward and walked to Ambrose's bedside and met Winnie still sitting by her husband's bedside. Winnie immediately turned to her and asked what's it she's still doing loitering in the hospital premises, reminding her she has done enough damage already. Rebecca stood as if Winnie isn't there and didn't utter a word either, but after a moment of dead silence, she dismissed Winnie, and accused her.

"Your position in this matter is nothing but a childish sense of superiority, and paranoid grandiosity," Rebecca retorted.

Winnie obviously doesn't want Rebecca anywhere near her husband as she insisted that Rebecca's jaundiced view over this issue amuses her, and her conspiracy is more of an immoral and a subhuman conduct because her foolishness will soon land her in the police cell. Rebecca frowned at Winnie's possessiveness and asked why she's so engrossed in this needless, excessive fuss that's nothing but a clash of ideology of what they each believed to be the right way to live.

"I care not about your facial expression, your action is a flagrant disregard for my husband's belief, why must you strip him, leaving him scantily dressed and make him one of yours?" asked Winnie.

Rebecca is now beginning to reflect on Winnie's reaction towards her, as she pointed out to Winnie that she can see deep seated anger in her and that she isn't surprised, and after all, Christians are reputed for their disdain towards people who don't share their beliefs.

"Disdain you call it, stop sounding remorselessly shameless," Winnie replied as she attempts to walk away in anger.

Rebecca cautioned her not to walk out on her, as she reminded Winnie, she's woman just like her and they both cared about the Evangelist. Winnie continued to walk further away from Rebecca as she insists Rebecca should stop referring to herself as a woman, because she isn't, stressing that a woman who goes running about naked has impugned on her dignity as a woman.

"Why are you hurtling away? We're still in a conversation", said Rebecca who then screamed at Winnie as she walks away.

Winnie finds it profoundly insulting that Rebecca chose to engage her in a tug of war, as opposed to tucking her tail and cowering in shame for her criminal act. She hated Rebecca's guts and the thought about the latest revelation concerning Rebecca and her cohorts being Satanists will do nothing but kill brain cells for Winnie.

Worried about Rebecca's boldness in this matter, Winnie immediately reached for her phone and dialled her son, Peter, and asked if he's at home.

Peter replied her mum saying he's at home but still got an hour. His mum interjected.

"An hour for what?" asked Winnie.

"An hour to come pick you up from work," said Peter.

"Who is talking about your picking me up from work? Guess what, Pete," said Winnie who burst into uncontrolled laughter as she spoke to her son.

Peter immediately asked his mum to know the reason behind her hysteria, saying he really can't remember when last she displayed this degree of excitement. Peter soon joined his mum in the laughter even when he'd no idea of what's behind his mum's excitement, she then reminded her son that it's good he recognised she hasn't been this excited for a long while.

Peter on the other hand hadn't the foggiest idea of what his mum is up to, yet didn't waste time to remind her that the only time he remembered her displaying this kind of excitement was when dad was alive.

"Hmm, I'm displaying this excitement because your dad is alive," she said and burst out laughing again.

"What, dad is alive?" Peter asked and burst into laughter, thinking his mum is just being metaphorical. He then said he knows his dad is alive because as a Christian he died in Christ, but then asked his mum where the thought of his dad being alive came from, before subtly reminding her that this isn't a good joke.

Without further ado, Winnie immediately let the cat out of the bag as she told Peter that his dad is right here in the hospital, and that some people brought him in this morning.

Peter muttered, saying this must be a joke, but realising his mum never makes a joke of this magnitude, and neither is she an alarmist, he then became a bit more serious and asked if she's quite sure it is his dad she saw.

"You have to believe me, and it's my husband we are talking about, so I know my husband very well," said Winnie.

It soon dawned on Peter after he reminded himself that his dad's whereabouts has been a mystery, and after all, they only had a funeral without a body.

"Oh my God!" Peter exclaimed and burst into laughter, and inquired further from his mum as he's keen to know those who brought his dad in. Winnie didn't really respond to her son's question of who found his dad and how he ended up in the hospital, as she senses that the lesser her son know about those who brought his dad to the hospital, the better. She interjected and said they'll talk about how his dad got to the hospital later, but for now, she just wants him to know that his dad is right by her side, she has touched him, held him, and it's all real, she then burst into laughter again.

"Well, this good news makes today a good day, I'm on my way, mum," said Peter.

Peter couldn't contain his excitement as he hurtled around the house looking for Jordan to break the good news to him. He then rushed to Jordan's room in excitement, he was actually calling out to Jordan as he approaches the door to Jordan's room.

Jordan rushed to the door because the excitement and the mannerism in Peter's voice meant there's more to this call, and immediately he got to the door, he reminded Peter that there's something overwhelming in that voice. Instead of breaking the news of his dad's whereabouts, Peter asked his brother to get ready, that they're heading to the hospital right away.

"Why, is anything the matter?" asked Jordan.

"Dad is alive!" exclaimed Peter.

"What, dad is alive? Don't say things you know nothing about please, and you know it hurts," Jordan retorted.

"This isn't gibberish, it's real," replied Peter.

Jordan refused to be sucked in by his brother's excitement and reminded him that they've both been at home since morning, asking where this came from. Peter interjected and said their mum just called minutes ago, and that their dad is with her. Jordan then asked to be sure for a second time.

"You said, mum said this, then let me give mum a call?" said Jordan.

Peter couldn't hang around to dawdle any further, he immediately dismissed his brother's doubts and said he doesn't have the patience of spending one more minute here, insisting he's off to the hospital. It didn't take long for Jordan to realise his brother isn't messing about. "You mean, dad is truly alive?" Jordan asked, and then screamed, "I just can't believe this!"

Peter immediately urged his brother to get dressed, even as he told Jordan that their mum said some people brought their dad in this morning. Jordan interjected and asked who they are, and where they found him. Peter himself knew little or nothing about how his dad got to the hospital, all he could do was to advise his brother to be patient that all these questions will answer themselves when they get there.

"I still don't believe you, Peter, until I see dad myself and be sure he's real," said Jordan.

"Whatever, I'm waiting for you in the car, and I don't have all day," said Peter.

An hour later, the brothers arrived the hospital, and Jordan didn't even allow his brother to finish with the manoeuvring of parking the car properly, before he alighted from the car. He immediately rushed into the acute assessment unit, while Peter walked following his brother from behind. Funnily, Jordan spotted his mum immediately he walked into the ward. "Mum, mum, where is he?" asked Jordan.

"Ooh, Jordan, I knew you would come running; your dad is alive," Winnie replied to her son, laughing.

Jordan wasn't too keen on pleasantries with his mum, he just want to see his dad for himself, he immediately interjected and asked his mum where his dad is because he needs to see him now, and he can't wait.

"Mum, is he here in AAU" asked Peter.

"Yes, of course, come with me," said Winnie.

Jordan and Peter made their way to Ambrose's bed side.

"Hey dad," said Jordan who immediately turned to Peter, laughing, and said this is real, Peter, and that it's actually their dad. Funny enough, by the time they got to their dad's bedside, Rebecca has returned to the waiting room, as she feels quite uncomfortable that the hospital staffs are sniggering at her and her friend.

"Dad, dad," said Peter, who then turned to his mum and asked to know how they found his dad, and who did. Winnie immediately urged Peter not wake his dad up, telling them their dad has gone through a lot.

"A lot, you said, how did they find him?" asked Peter.

Winnie had to manage her sons' excitement and told them that how they found their dad and who did is a subject of an ongoing conversation. Peter couldn't wait to speak to his dad, he then proceeded to ask his mum how bad his dad's situation is and what's wrong with him.

Jordan became concerned and his excitement suddenly receded and changed into a frown as he asked what the problem with his dad could be and suggested their dad should come home with them.

Winnie didn't explicitly suggest to her sons' that there could be a problem with their dad, following Rebecca's utterances. She had to play safe by suggesting to them that when Ambrose wakes up and he's certified ok by the doctor, then maybe, they can begin the conversation about going home. Peter was lost as he tried to understand the hesitation in his mum's tone, he interjected and asked.

"Why the, maybe, is there anything you aren't telling us?"

"Not now," Peter, at least, it's a good thing your dad is back," replied Winnie. Jordan hesitated for a while but pointed out to his mum that she seems to be withholding something. He asked if their dad is dying or what, then insisted that it is their right know if something is wrong with their dad. The greatest chasm in this is that there is a hint of darkness, particularly with a strange woman in the middle of this reunion.

Now that her sons are becoming increasingly inquisitive about the unspoken story surrounding their dad's whereabouts for the last three years, Winnie realised she couldn't be economical with the truth any longer, and said if they must know, there's a woman in the waiting room who claims to be their dad's wife, and they have been living together for about three years.

"What, his wife! Why would dad do a thing like that?" asked Jordan.

Peter was also taken aback but subtly inquired to know how his dad met the woman in question, he then surprisingly prodded his mum with a question she finds strangely out of taste and asked if she's implying that their dad wasn't on that ship in the first place. Winnie herself was lost for words, but said she knew the man she married isn't such a man, and there was a first-hand account of people who saw her husband in the ship as well. All Winnie could say was that they're all burdened with questions but assured her sons that their dad will answer for himself when he wakes up.

"You said, she's in the waiting room, let me have a word with her," said Peter.

Winnie immediately urged Peter not to engage Rebecca in verbal exchanges. Peter promised his mum he isn't engaging in any conversation that's devoid of civility, then asked to know how he could identify Rebecca.

"She's wearing a blue silk shirt on a red skirt, and she called herself, Rebecca," said Winnie.

Peter then turned around and said he will soon be back, and he then left his mum and Jordan behind. Jordan sensed his brother might confront the woman in question, he then turned around as he attempted to follow his brother from behind yet urged his mum to come with them to manage any kerfuffle that could erupt. Winnie isn't keen to join issues any further, and said she isn't coming because she has had her fill of Rebecca's disgust, she just muttered and said she's only waiting for the Evangelist to wake up, so he could tell her what he has been doing with that woman.

Jordan immediately made his way to the waiting room, saying he needed to see this strange woman who has suddenly become an interest to this family.

Peter walked into the waiting room and sat on the empty seat next to Rebecca's.

"Hello, you're Rebecca, I guess?" asked Peter.

Rebecca interjected and asked Peter who he was and said she has never met him before.

"Not at all, but we have something in common," said Peter.

"In common, you and I, what is it?" asked Rebecca as she became quite inquisitive.

Peter muttered, and said, his dad is what they've in common, then said he's the son of Evangelist Fredrick Douglas.

"Ooh my goodness, you're Ambrose's son?" asked Rebecca.

Peter interjected immediately and reminded her he isn't the son of Ambrose, rather he's the son of Fredrick Douglas, he then asked.

"By the way, who is Ambrose?"

"The man in ward C, that a woman called Winnie is claiming to be his wife," said Rebecca.

Peter immediately said that's his dad, and that woman is his mum, and how come she's calling him Ambrose. Jordan angrily interjected with a harsh rebuke, as he told Rebecca to stop calling his dad Ambrose because his name isn't Ambrose.

Rebecca turned to Jordan who isn't having a laugh, "Ooh, you're another of his sons, and have you guys come to fight me!" exclaimed Rebecca. The clapback from Jordan was expected anyways, but this is more or less a realistic replay of Ambrose's dream coming alive. Retrospectively, the moment Peter and Jordan made themselves known to Rebecca, she immediately flashed back to Ambrose's dream of himself, a woman, and two young men, the dream is now playing out before her eyes.

Funny enough, what unwittingly got Jordan reeling from within and got him hopping mad, was the fact that if Rebecca is saying the truth about being is dad's wife, this strange woman could end up being his step mum.

Peter tapped Jordan on the shoulder, urging him to calm down, so they could hear her out because they aren't here to fight. He then turned to Rebecca and said he just want to thank her for helping them find their dad and for returning him to his wife and children. Stacy laughed, and asked Peter if he and his brother consider themselves capable of turning the hands of the clock backwards.

Peter wants to know how his dad ended up in Rebecca's embrace, and to avoid the possibility of a shouting match resulting from this conversation, he turned to Stacy and said no one is talking about turning the hand of the clock backward but then urged the ladies to tell him how and where they found his dad.

Rebecca became more benign than Peter had expected. She then said she thinks she owes them an explanation, but she doesn't mind being hated by Winnie and her sons who considers her to be nothing but a con artist taking their dad to the cleaners. Peter muttered and said he needed these answers to quench his curiosity, he then told Rebecca that his dad was in the ill-fated Octal Flamingo when the accident occurred. He narrated how the divers searched and searched and couldn't find him.

Rebecca didn't say much, as she reminded them that they've seen their dad, but then asked them why they need her to explain how she found him. Peter then turned to Rebecca and asked how come she's claiming to be his dad's wife. Rebecca held her cards close to her chest even as she asked Peter and his brother why they're in such a rush for answers. She then proceeded to say they should all be patient and allow Ambrose to wake up, and they'll find out if her claims are in line or not.

"Is this a joke? Stop messing with our family, these claims are ludicrous and laughable," said Jordan.

As opposed to stopping Peter from confronting Rebecca, Peter is now the one holding Jordan down and asking him to be calm, and then suggested it might be more appropriate if Rebecca explains her complicity to the police.

"Ooh, the police, don't bet on it," replied Rebecca.

Peter held Jordan, saying they should leave Rebecca to herself because she's a stubborn woman who deserves a deafening response. Jordan hesitated as he said he now knows why his mum wouldn't engage her any further. They then turned around and returned to their mum in the ward.

Immediately the boys returned to their dad's bedside, their mum asked if they saw Rebecca, and obviously, her itching ears meant she wants to hear what Rebecca said to them.

"It seems her mind is set," said Peter.

"Set on what?" asked Winnie. Peter told his mum that Rebecca's mind is set on their dad, and she is likely going to fight dirty. As opposed to kindness personified, they soon concluded that Rebecca is actually trouble personified, Peter then suggested to his mum that it's best to get the police involved.

Winnie insists she wouldn't do any such thing, and she isn't getting the police involve until she hears from her husband, she then turned to Peter and asked what if his dad is complicit in all of this.

Jordan immediately took exception to his mum's comment as he asked his mum why she's sounding like this, and does it mean she doesn't trust his dad. Winnie immediately urged her children not to join issues, she turned to Jordan and reminded him his dad's explanation will give them the best clue on how to go about this.

Peter wasn't quite impressed that his dad seems to be sleeping forever, and his desire for answers is something that kept him on the edge. He then asked his mum when she expects their dad to wake up. "Winnie is a nurse and works in the hospital, she immediately informed her boys that their dad isn't unconscious, and neither is his condition critical, he's stable, he's fine, and will wake anytime soon.

"Ok, let's be patient then, and it's a good day knowing that dad is with us, these grim realities mean nothing," said Peter. "You don't care?" asked Winnie.

Peter said he doesn't really care, and all that matters to him is that his dad is back from the dead, and that outweighs whatever stunt this woman is pulling.

While Stacy and Rebecca were seated in the waiting room, Stacy's utterances show that her support for Rebecca's cause is wavering, yet she trusts the outcome of this adventure with some sort of cautious optimism. She nudged Rebecca with her elbow and reminded her that the storm is gathering in momentum and then urged her to just let go of Ambrose. Rebecca interjected and reminded Stacy that she won't let go just because his wife and kids wish to bully her into submission.

Even when she chose to stay mum on the subject and remain head strong, Rebecca had no idea how the thoughts racing through her heart slipped out of her mouth.

"I'm the one being pilloried by that woman, Winnie, or whatever her name is, and she wouldn't stop until she makes a BBQ out of me, for my crime of passion," Rebecca muttered.

Stacy had to put the conversation back in perspective, and told Rebecca that she's quite aware that the only reason she's standing her ground on this matter is because she sensed Ambrose won't recognise his wife and kids when he wakes up.

"Yes, of course, that's going to be my selling point," said Rebecca.

Stacy understands quite well that Rebecca's stance in this matter is anything but benign and her stunt might rub off badly on the Romanian Luciferian Community. She then reminded Rebecca that she doesn't think members would love the path she's toeing in this entire circus, as a representative of the Luciferian Community.

Rebecca finds Stacy's remark hysterical and uncalled for, as her long side-glance did the job of subtly asking Stacy not to go there. She then cynically asked Stacy if she should just let Ambrose go because of what members would think. Stacy emphasised her earlier position on the subject as she reminded Rebecca that Prophet Gregory won't like this, and other directors won't like this either, more so, members of the Bliss will be hopping mad at her for the action she has just taken.

"What do you want me to do, and what do we tell members when they ask me about Ambrose?" asked Rebecca.

"Tell them Ambrose has reunited with his family," said Stacy.

Rebecca hesitated for a while and said Ambrose has no memory of his family, and she would certainly want to see him when he wakes up because if she walks away now, such revelation might be too much for him to take in.

"Ok then, I give you the benefit of doubt," said Stacy. It's now blatant to Stacy that Rebecca's appetite for contention is quite galling, and that unwittingly left Winnie hopping mad at Rebecca.

Stacy isn't oblivious of the fact that it's moments such as this that tests true friendship, she is now torn between making a run for it or standing by her friend. Rebecca pleaded with Stacy and urged her not to get bogged down with the feeling that her stay here would end in futility, she then proceeded to remind Stacy that Ambrose is the manager of the Bliss Luciferian Camp, and a lot more people would be interested in this matter than she thinks.

"Ok, but let's not be pig-headed about this," Stacy advised.

Hours later, same day, Winnie was still seated by Ambrose's bedside, when she observed Ambrose opened his eyes.

"Hey honey, you're awake," said Winnie.

"Ooh my head, my tummy hurts, where is she?" asked Ambrose.

"Hey honey, I'm here, and I'm glad you are awake," said Winnie, who immediately began checking Ambrose's vitals as he complains of tummy ache. Ambrose wasn't quite pleased with Winnie referring to him as her honey, he immediately asked who she was, and then inquired of Rebecca's whereabouts.

"Rebecca isn't here and why do you keep insisting on having her here? I'm your wife, I am Winnie," she retorted.

"Who, my wife? I don't know you!" exclaimed Ambrose.

"You mean you don't know me?" asked Winnie, with some emphasis.

"Who are you, and how am I expected to know you, have we met before?" Ambrose asked again. Winnie immediately muttered to herself, and asked what's happening, expressing her frustration as she became more exasperated by the minute. The Evangelist isn't some petulant teenager making a fuss out of nothing, this is a man whose memory bank was wiped out by the cruise ship accident.

Alisabel was some feet away as Winnie mutters in frustration, she then walked into the conversation, and asked Winnie what the problem was, and then inquired why she's muttering and grumbling. Winnie immediately said she has no idea of what could be wrong with him, and said her husband kept asking about the other woman and pretending not to know her.

"You mean he doesn't recognise you, and are you sure he isn't faking it?" asked Alisabel.

Winnie interjected and said of course, Ambrose doesn't recognise her, and his body language doesn't suggest he's faking it. Alisabel immediately suggested to Winnie to allow her do the talking maybe Ambrose might open up, she then turned to Ambrose.

"Hello Fredrick, how are you, I'm Alisabel, and do you remember me?" she asked.

Ambrose interjected immediately and asked who Fredrick is, and reminded Alisabel his name is Ambrose, he then asked her of Rebecca's whereabouts.

Alisabel sensed that the rubber has now hit the road, she then turned to Winnie and asked what she suggest they do about this, but then suggested they conduct another scan to be sure he's ok. Winnie saw Doctor Saul walked in, and then exhaled and said Doctor Saul is here.

"Of course, I'm here, what's it that need my attention, I'm glad he's awake, and how are you guys getting along?" asked Doc. Saul.

Winnie muttered, saying there's no getting along because her husband seems not to know her.

Doctor Saul exclaimed, and asked Winnie if she's sure about this. It's obvious that absence makes the heart grow fonder, but this isn't the case as Ambrose is suddenly looking like the bogeyman trapped by the roadside and scared of passers-by. It's quite embarrassing that her husband's inability to recognise her makes her day sort of flippant, and this really drives her up the wall.

Winnie now has no choice but to inform the doctor that she has tried, and Alisabel has equally tried, before suggesting they conduct another scan. Doctor Saul hesitated for a while, and then suggested to Winnie to get Rebecca, saying they need a better understanding of what transpired between when that cruise accident happened and now.

Winnie then turned to Doctor Saul and said while he speaks to Rebecca, she will need to get her sons to inform them their dad has woken up, and funnily this dim light of hope of having her husband back seem to be dimmer than she'd expected.

"Ok, while you speak with Rebecca, let me get my sons, maybe he would recognise them," said Winnie. Alisabel immediately suggested she prefers to be the one to call Rebecca in, to avoid making the already tensed situation a much more difficult one.

"Allow me to give my sons the privilege of meeting their father, before bringing this woman and her confusion in here," said Winnie.

Minutes later, Alisabel walked to the car park where Peter and Jordan were, and waiting for news about their dad and didn't find them there. She then walked into the waiting room and there they were.

"Peter, come with me," said Alisabel.

"What about me, is my dad awake?" asked Jordan. Alisabel turned to Jordan and said he can come as well, and as expected, Rebecca immediately stood up from her seat and asked if Ambrose has woken up from sleep. She then asked Alisabel why she isn't allowing her to see Ambrose. Alisabel turned to her and said she will come back for her, even as she urged Rebecca to calm down.

Stacy sensed Rebecca's anxiety, and gave her hand a slight squeeze, she then urged Rebecca to take Alisabel by her word for the benefit of the doubt and be calm. Peter and his brother then followed Alisabel, and moments later, they were by Ambrose's bed side.

"Hey dad, you're awake?" said Jordan.

Winnie immediately breaks the news to her children that their dad doesn't seem to recognise her, and this is another nightmare.

"What, why, and how?" asked Peter.

Ambrose looked at Peter and Jordan with this look of unease written all over his face, as he didn't really like the idea of strangers invading his space, because he really doesn't know who they are. Alisabel saw the surprise in the faces of these two young men who seem lost with what the problem with their dad could be. She then interjected and suggested to them not to push Ambrose so much, suggesting it could put him under intense stress because he's not fully recovered. Peter seems to think his mum hasn't done enough to make his dad remember.

Winnie immediately turned to Peter and urged him to try if he thinks he can, but didn't stop short of letting her son know that his dad has been asking for that strange woman.

Ambrose wasn't sick enough not to know he's the subject of the conversation between this woman and her children, he knows what they're about, but he didn't recollect having any dealing with them, not to talk of being their dad.

"You seem to be talking about me?" asked Ambrose. Jordan interjected immediately as he called Ambrose, dad, and said of course, it's him they're discussing.

"Dad, how are you feeling?" asked Jordan.

"How can I be your dad, have we met before? Because I don't know you," Ambrose retorted. "Dad, you mean you don't remember us?" asked Peter.

Ambrose immediately cautioned them from making spurious claims, saying he doesn't understand the game they are playing, and his facial expression shows he doesn't like the manner in which this woman and her sons invaded his space. He then urged them to please get his partner, Rebecca, for him if she's here.

"Oh my God, why is he pretending not to know us?" asked Jordan. Winnie stepped in and urged her sons to calm down, as she said this isn't pretence, and that their dad doesn't really remember. Ignorant they said is bliss, and Peters' earlier thinking that reuniting with his dad without Rebecca's support will be a walk in the park. Peter considered Rebecca to be overly ambitious, but he seems to have come to the sudden realisation that the situation at hand is more than a handful, as they now look like someone chasing the rainbow.

He then muttered asking his mum, "How can we make this tragedy go away?" Winnie immediately reminded her sons that this is what she's been dealing with. It's now obvious that Winnie has had her chance with Ambrose but failed, Doctor Saul then asked Alisabel to get Rebecca, so they could get more detail about Fredrick's condition from her.

Moments later, Rebecca walked into the ward with Stacy by her side.

"Ooh my goodness, honey, you're awake," said Rebecca.

"Yes, I am, just that my head still aches," said Ambrose.

Stacy breathes a sigh of relief and told Ambrose it's good to see him looking much better, because he gave them a hell of a scare this morning. Doctor Saul on the other hand, immediately excused Rebecca and said he wants to have a word her. Rebecca turned to the doctor and said she will be with him in a minute.

Ambrose interjected and reminded the doctor that Rebecca just came in, and then asked why he's taking her away. "Honey, I will be back, Stacy will stay with you," said Rebecca, as Winnie and her sons watched hopelessly in amazement. The drama playing out before Winnie's eyes suddenly left her suffering from a thumping headache, that left her in tears.

Funny enough, this family have been so busy doing absolutely everything they could but their inability to help their dad meant Rebecca still has him under her thumb, and attempts to glean more information out of Rebecca seemed not to have worked out as expected.

Moments later, Doctor Saul and Rebecca were in the doctor's office, he then asked Rebecca if she's aware of Fredrick's memory loss. Rebecca realised the odds are in her favour. She immediately began playing hide and seek with the doctor, as she reminded him, he's a doctor. She then asked why he's asking her about Ambrose medical condition and supposes he should know.

Doctor Saul refused to remain on the back foot in this conversation, and said every citizen of Romania, and most Europeans are aware of the fate of Octal Flamingo, and an eyewitness categorically said Fredrick was unconscious as at the time the ship sank.

Rebecca interjected and asked the doctor why he's telling her about this, and why she should concern herself about an ill-fated ship. She told them they'll have a long wait if they expect her to divulge how she met Ambrose and insists they would rather not think she would self-incriminate herself.

The doctor then accused Rebecca of taking advantage of an accident victim, and said this is a crime against humanity, and when the sordid details of her acts get out, the society will not only decry her action, but will be asking for her head on the plate. Arguably, her actions will equally make authorities to want to take a sneak peek into what goes on in that Satanic Bliss camp, and this treachery hatched and incubated in the Bliss Luciferian Camp will make ears tingle when words about this goes out. She then looked at the doctor and said instead of going on and on about the lack of benignity in her conduct, a simple thank you for her act of kindness towards Ambrose would suffice, because she helped Ambrose when he was down on his luck.

"What crime are you talking about? You can't bully me into talking to you," said Rebecca.

The doctor had to change tact and began talking tough as he told Rebecca that she'd better start talking, because they're thinking of taking the police to her camp, and he's certain her fellow members wouldn't want to be associated with this scandal. Interestingly, the doctor's tough talking didn't cause a change in Rebecca's stance, as she remained illusory and asking the doctor what scandal he's talking about, and if it's a crime to assist a dying man.

Doctor Saul immediately drew a distinction between helping a man and coveting him for her personal use, by taking advantage of his vulnerability. Doctor Saul paused for a second time, with his gaze fixed on Rebecca. He then said, unlike Fredrick Douglas, he's quite sure he isn't suffering amnesia and if his memory serves him right, Amnesia doesn't run in his family, and it's only those who believe in a future they've foreseen that makes a plan, but in this circumstance, she doesn't have a future with Fredrick Douglas. He smiled displaying the cheeky grin of a rambunctious teenager that got Rebecca quite uncomfortable and confused.

She feared that Winnie and her cohorts will be rubbing their hands with glee over her shame, particularly when Doctor Saul has made it clear to her that he doesn't have an atom of sympathy for her. He urged her not to let her imagination run away with her, after accusing her of displaying mood swings like a menopausal woman. Funnily, she took objection to the sexist description, and didn't take the qualification lying down.

"I'd wanted to beg you not to cut me into tiny little pieces with your sarcasm, but I rather not, because you might choke on it," said Rebecca.

Winnie on the other hand is keen for answers, and while the doctor and Rebecca were at it, she walks in and listened to them as they speak without interrupting their conversation.

Rebecca doesn't seem to like Winnie's presence, she then turned to leave, and said she hadn't the foggiest idea of what the doctor is driving at. The doctor looked at Winnie and could feel her frustrations in all of this, he then turned to Rebecca and said he finds it an arduous task convincing her to open up, now that there's a possibility of making this a sweet or bitter moment for herself.

Rebecca got to the door and stopped, and then said Ambrose was actually unconscious when she found him floating on water, and without any memory of his past. "You found him floating, and where precisely did you find him?" asked Doc. Saul.

Rebecca's stance is now beginning to thaw, as she opened up to the doctor that she found Ambrose at the seashore of the Bliss Luciferian Camp, the camp is sitting at the tip of the sea shore.

Doctor Saul immediately toned down the fiery rhetoric, and asked Rebecca why she didn't involve the police, so the police can help locate Ambrose's family and help restore his memory.

"What a sick woman you are, and how many other people have you coveted in your sick camp?" asked Winnie. Rebecca wasn't quite receptive with stunning rebuke like this one from Winnie, she immediately urged Winnie to stop saying what she knew nothing about. Rebecca then proceeded to say that there were indications that Ambrose had a skull injury, and the fear was that he was attacked, possibly a blunt force injury. More so, the fact that he lost his memory, exacerbated the fear of sending him back to his possible attackers.

Winnie dismissed Rebecca's excuses as lame and without substance, but now that she's armed with the truth about her husband, Winnie turned on Rebecca, accusing her of orchestrating a weirdly inexplicable dogma of balancing one tragedy with a more terrible tragedy.

Doctor Saul then interjected and asked Winnie to calm down, he then reminded Rebecca that it may come to her as a shocker, but she now knows that Fredrick has a family. He then suggested to her to help Ambrose reunite with his family. With Winnie becoming all fiery, Rebecca began playing her hide and seek again, as she asked the doctor what proof is there to show this is Ambrose's wife and the boys are his sons.

"We can get dirty, Rebecca, if you chose to play smart. I will make sure you go down for your crimes," said Doc. Saul.

Now that Rebecca have confessed how it came about that she coveted and took over another woman's husband, it's now obvious that the genie is now out of the bottle and can't be put back. She then muttered, and said she knows quite well that Winnie wants her head on a Plate for her failings. Winnie interjected and promised she would forgive Rebecca and let her go scot-free if she stops this game of hers right now, and then walks away immediately she finished stating her position.

Rebecca on the other hand was surprised to see Winnie hurtle away, and then asked where's she headed. Doctor Saul urged Rebecca not to worry herself with where Winnie is headed and reminded her, she's about to make national headlines for the wrong reasons, but the choice is now hers because members of the Bliss Camp would receive a national embarrassment.

"Ok, ok, let me speak with Ambrose," said Rebecca.

Now that Rebecca is willing to let go, Doctor Saul immediately urged her to hold on, and suggested they get pictures and videos of Ambrose with his family, to help jog his memory before Rebecca can speak with him.

"Ok, I will wait," said Rebecca.

Not long after the doctor and Rebecca concluded their conversation, they left the office, the doctor then walked up to Winnie, while Rebecca returned to the waiting room.

### Crime and Punishment

Alisabel got hopping mad when she learnt Winnie is letting Rebecca off the hook just like that without facing the consequences of her action. She called Winnie aside and said its time they have a little chat. Funnily, Alisabel just finished dealing with a pregnant and paranoid patient who won't stop taking the mickey out of her, there's this tired and old smile on her face, but then decided that her little chat with Winnie can't wait.

They made a beeline for the car park as they stepped aside for a heart-to-heart conversation. They stopped and stood in front of the hospital, under the Romanian national flag, with the flag fluttering above them as they had their conversation. She reminded Winnie that Rebecca isn't an invalid, and she didn't like the idea of her being treated as if she's wrapped in cotton wool, but then decided to apply some apt. She insisted that the decision to let Rebecca walk scot-free seems inept, because people don't just do a thing like this and get rewarded with a pat on the back and a pack of chocolate.

She then insisted that the decision to let Rebecca walk scot-free seems inept, because people don't just do a thing like this and get rewarded with a pat on the back and a pack of chocolate.

She looked Winnie in the eye and said Rebecca's action is nothing but a wicked indulgence, and consequences of actions like this sort should be harsh enough on Rebecca in a manner that will leave her body without the feminine vigour. Winnie asked Alisabel if her view of crime and punishment is all about finding solace, because she's aware that some people find closure only when perpetrators have been punished. She reminded Alisabel she's a Christian, she gave Rebecca her word that if she stops this nonsense right now, she wouldn't mind letting her go scot-free, and as a Christian, Christ's death on the cross is about forgiveness and second chance.

Winnie proceeded to say forgiveness only happen when either party has been wronged, she then smiled and said her husband was dead and now, he's back to life.

"You attended his funeral service, remember?" asked Winnie. Alisabel nodded in affirmation, saying she was at the funeral. Yet, she pressed on Winnie, insisting they aren't talking about some scruffy guy that fell off an open roof tourist bus, that she's actually referring to Evangelist Fredrick, a man on a mission for God, but Winnie interjected immediately and said God has the same level of love and care for that all-scruffy looking guy in the street as He does her husband. Alisabel isn't some kind of vengeful and vindictive person, she is just someone who expects that someone who has done this degree of incalculable damage is deserving of some retribution and insisted that the only reason why there's punishment is because sin such as this exists. She then urged Winnie to listen to reason, but what reason meant to Winnie is far from retributive justice.

Winnie wasn't dismissive, and even though she considers Alisabel's prejudice to be logical, she finds it more illuminating that her gratitude to God makes her forget whatever wrong that was done to her and her family. After having their little talk, they both walked back and returned to the ward.

The doctor then urged Winnie to get pictures and videos of her husband and his family, and suggest they use it to jog his memory.

"What about her, and what's her position in this?" asked Winnie.

"She's willing to cooperate," replied Doc. Saul.

Winnie immediately requested that a test for sexually transmitted infection should be conducted on her husband, but the doctor wants the contention sorted first, and asked Winnie if that is necessary. He however reminded Winnie that she doesn't have the all-clear yet to demand that a test be conducted on her husband because his consent is necessary.

Winnie insists her husband has been living with another woman in a morally debased environment, as husband and wife does. She insisted that her husband was perfect when he left her, but she doesn't know of Rebecca's health status.

"Good talk, but I would suggest we do that once we are done with the contentious matter at hand," said Doc. Saul.

Winnie then excused herself and left, but Stacy turned to Winnie as she walks into the ward and asked her of Rebecca's whereabouts.

Winnie muttered and said Rebecca is out there, but she better let Rebecca know that she wouldn't be able to stand her storm, when it comes raging. Peter immediately asked his mum about the outcome of Doctor Saul's meeting with Rebecca. Doctor Saul cuts into the conversation, and said Rebecca has agreed to help, and urged everyone to give Rebecca the benefit of the doubt.

"How does she intend to help?" asked Jordan. Doctor Saul insists he has told Rebecca to use her closeness with Fredrick, to help with his memory. Funnily, most of these conversations about Fredrick were held some distance away from him, but not audible enough for him to hear he is the subject of their conversation.

He's already agitated, having strangers who claimed they know him hanging around his bedside. However, the drama playing out before him, reminds him of his dreams where he kept finding himself in the company of a woman and two young men, and that became needling at a time, but he's now able to associate what's going on right now with his dreams. There's now a part of him that's telling him there is substance to Winnie's claim, just that he just couldn't bring himself to believe it.

It's now obvious that Fredrick has overstayed his welcome in the AAU, but still needs to remain under observation, Winnie then asked Doctor Saul when he's moving her husband to the ward, because it's obvious he can't stay in AAU forever.

"I am moving him to the ward, Doctor Oliver will take care of him," said Doc. Saul. Peter immediately reminded his mum that it's already her closing time, and then suggested to her that she and Jordan should go home, while he stays with his dad in the hospital.

"No way, I'm staying here with dad, and I want to be by his side," said Jordan.

"Whatever, your protest just reminded me I do not have monopoly of dad," Peter retorted.

Winnie agreed to go home, just to be able to get some pictures and videos of her husband as requested by Doctor Saul because that would help him restore his memory.

Since no one has explicitly mentioned what went on in the meeting between Rebecca and Doctor Saul, Stacy was keen to know what's going on. She then left Ambrose's bedside and returned and joined Rebecca in the waiting room, she then asked, "What's going on, Rebecca, and why aren't you coming in?" Rebecca owned up to Stacy, and said she has had enough trouble already, and she's leaving Ambrose with them. Stacy interjected and asked what caused her to suddenly change her stance, and said Ambrose is expecting her to come back to him.

Rebecca opened up to Stacy that they're threatening to bring the Bliss Camp into this, and that will put her in the crosshairs of Prophet Gregory. More so, the ensuing scandal wouldn't be good for the camp and she wants none of that.

"Then let's leave this hole, and return to the camp," said Stacy.

Rebecca muttered, saying she can't just tuck her tail and run off, and that she would need to help Ambrose reunite with his family. Now that it's embarrassingly obvious to Stacy that Rebecca's grandstanding is unwittingly a lost battle, Stacy needed more confirmation from Rebecca and asked how she intends to help Ambrose reunite with his family. Rebecca then told Stacy that the doctor has requested for past pictures and videos of Ambrose to help him remember his family.

"I hope they aren't sucking you into their game?" asked Stacy.

"What game are you suggesting?" asked Rebecca.

Stacy immediately suggested to Rebecca that the decision to stay back shouldn't be down to serendipity and said she hopes Rebecca isn't unwittingly giving Winnie the evidence with which to nail her. Suggesting, she wouldn't just want Winnie and her cohorts leading her into the rabbit hole.

Rebecca agreed with Stacy, and said she's equally pessimistic but there's some degree of sincerity in Winnie, and even the doctor, and suggested they do this.

"Do you see any credence in their assertions?" asked Stacy.

"Yes, and I wouldn't want to conclude this on a gruesome note," replied Rebecca.

Stacy had to revisit the obvious as she asked Rebecca what she suggest they tell members of the Bliss Luciferian Camp about Ambrose, when they eventually return to the camp. Rebecca isn't keen to obfuscate the truth any longer. She was quite self-effacing about it, as she said she will tell them Ambrose found his family and they have been happily reunited.

"I guess we should go home, and return tomorrow," said Stacy.

Winnie arrived home and realized she needed to inform Reverend Fitzgerald of the new revelations about her husband. She immediately reached for the phone and dialled Reverend Fitzgerald who picked the call almost immediately.

"Guess what, Reverend, my husband was brought in today," said Winnie.

"Aah, Winnie, you're getting married, and I knew nothing about it?" asked Rev. Fitzgerald.

"Married! Who's talking about getting married, I'm talking about Fredrick, your Evangelist?" said Winnie. Reverend Fitzgerald exclaimed and said he doesn't seem to hear her well and asked if she did say Evangelist Fredrick Douglas was in her hospital today. The reverend then proceeded to ask Winnie if they've recovered her husband's body.

Winnie burst into laughter again, even though she has been laughing all along as they had their conversation. She exclaimed for a second time and said Fredrick's body wasn't recovered, rather he was brought in alive, though sick, but he's fine and stable now.

"Oh my God, thank you lord, and great news!" exclaimed Rev. Fitzgerald.

"Yes of course, good news, indeed," replied Winnie.

Reverend Fitzgerald immediately asked how this happen, and who brought the Evangelist into the hospital, he proceeded to asked where Fredrick has been all this while. Winnie didn't hesitate to inform the Reverend that she herself is burdened with questions, and said she must confess, she doesn't have the answers to these questions.

"Why, and what's going on?" asked Rev. Fitzgerald.

Winnie had to tell the reverend all she knew about her husband so far, as she told him that a group of people brought him in but strangely, he seems to have lost his memory.

"Oh my God! He lost his memory, and how bad is it?" asked Rev. Fitzgerald. Winnie muttered and said the situation is pretty bad, bad enough that Fredrick didn't recognise her and her sons, saying she doesn't know how she's going to handle this. The reverend paused for a while, then said this is a pretty difficult one, but however difficult it is, this is good news, and it's worth's celebrating.

Winnie smiled and said she guessed he's right, as she affirmed that having her husband returned to her from the dead is quite a miracle despite effort to restore his memory.

"Did you involve the police?" asked Rev. Fitzgerald.

"Not yet, I don't want the hysteria overshadowing this joyful moment," said Winnie.

The reverend nodded in affirmation, and said he understands it's been quite a long and interesting day for Winnie and her sons, he then urged her to get some rest and he will join her the next day.

"Ok, I feel you should know, because this isn't just any news, it's good news," said Winnie.

It didn't take too long before the staff of this ward began to saunter in, one after another, in their bid to take a peek at this Evangelist once thought to be dead. Arguably, the surprise on the face of this Evangelist that has suddenly become the sensation of everyone around, was likened to that of a bird caught in a cage.

By Morning of the next day, Winnie resumes duty but had to check on her husband to see how he's doing, and immediately she entered the ward, she inquired from Peter about how his dad has been holding up. Peter stepped aside to speak to his mum, and said his dad is fine and improving greatly, just that he has refused to speak to him and kept asking for Rebecca.

"He hasn't recognised any of you yet?" asked Winnie.

Jordan interjected and said of course he hasn't, and said they brought Rebecca to be with their dad following his continued insistence. Winnie realised the situation is grimmer than earlier thought, after she asked her sons what they're doing cooped up in the waiting room, and Jordan told her they needed to allow Rebecca take charge while they watch from a distance. Winnie immediately walked to her husband bedside, and interestingly, Rebecca said hello to her immediately she walked in. Winnie didn't really respond to Rebecca's overtures, and asked Rebecca if she did talk about it with him.

"About what, specifically?" asked Rebecca.

"About us, about his true family, what are you waiting for?" asked Winnie.

Rebecca made light of Winnie's exasperation, saying she doesn't think it's a bad idea being Ambrose's partner for a few more hours, she then proceeded to ask Winnie if she did come with the pictures. Winnie muttered and said she did, but cautioned Rebecca to spare her of her illusion. She then handed the pictures to Rebecca, and said they should start off immediately. Winnie turned around and left Rebecca alone with Ambrose. Just as Winnie left, Ambrose curiously turned to Rebecca and asked her the very question he asked her earlier.

"Who are these people hovering around and confusing me, and saying I'm their husband and father, and why're they pestering me?" asked Ambrose. Rebecca immediately showed the photographs to him and asked him to take a look at these pictures, she then hands a catalogue of pictures to him.

"This is me and them, where did you get this from, and I don't remember taking these photographs with these people, what's going on?" he asked. Rebecca became more subtle in her approach, as she painstakingly narrated his past to him that the people in the photographs are his wife and children. She then proceeded to inform him he was involved in an accident, and he lost his memory in the process. Ambrose muttered, saying it's no longer news that he lost his memory but he really didn't remember any of this, and then questioned if the pictures are real. Unfortunately, he'd no idea Ambrose is a fraud, and his world in the person of Ambrose is about to unravel.

"These are your wedding picture," said Rebecca, as she showed him a particular page in the catalogue.

"You were married," said Rebecca.

Ambrose remained open-mouthed, as he confessed to Rebecca that he's taken aback with these new developments, and this is just too much to process. Rebecca then removed Prophet Gregory's ring from the Evangelist's finger, as she turns her back to her supposed partner of three years. "I need to hand this back to Prophet Gregory," said Rebecca.

Rebecca then played some videos and asked him to watch these videos, she played some videos of Ambrose before the accident. She then said that's him preaching in a congregation, that was his last church appearance before the accident and that's Winnie by his side in the church.

"Ooh my goodness, is that me? It seems to me I was a popular person," said Ambrose. Rebecca responded saying she suppose so, she also muttered and said she never knew he's this popular but she has long perceived there's something special about him.

"Then how did you come to indulge me? Because this whole complex situation is taking a toll on me," said Ambrose. Sanity is simple but madness is quite difficult to explain. Even at that, Rebecca didn't perceive her actions as anything close to letting the camel's nose under the tent.

Rebecca had to narrate how fate brought them in contact, and said it was one evening, she and Stacy were by the beach when they found him floating in the water and unconscious. The camp clinic revived him but realised he has lost his memory, that was how she stepped in to help him. Ambrose seems not impressed with Rebecca.

"When you realised, I had lost my memory, you then took advantage of me, or what?" asked Ambrose. Now that Rebecca herself, and by her own admission made it clear to Ambrose that she took advantage of his vulnerability, this relationship is now faced with a new twist. Rebecca tried to rationalise her action, and reminded Ambrose that someone needed to be there for him. She then told Ambrose that he was sick and remembered nothing, and the humane thing to do was for her to step up and fill the vacuum.

"This is too much to take in, give me some space, I need time to process this," said Ambrose.

Stacy was present all along but said nothing, she then interjected and urged Ambrose to calm down, and said they're here for him.

"Yes, of course I need to calm down, but I want to be left alone, please," said Ambrose.

Rebecca realised things has suddenly gone sour, and immediately asked Stacy to come with her so they could give Ambrose time to assimilate this news, and then suggests she doesn't expect him to be indifferent. They then left Ambrose's bedside, and just as Rebecca and Stacy walked into the waiting room, Peter inquired about his dad. Stacy was upfront in her response and said it's a lot for him to take in, and he requested they give him time to process the news alone.

"Where is your mum?" asked Rebecca.

"That's her coming, you know she's on duty and can't be seated here with us?" said Jordan.

Winnie came in, and immediately asked Rebecca how her conversation with Ambrose went. Rebecca was a bit cold in her response, yet told Winnie her husband is fine, but needs a little space to take the news in. Winnie seems not to like Rebecca's cold response, she immediately reminded her that if her plan wasn't thwarted, her husband would have remained under her spell.

Rebecca muttered, saying she thought they've moved past that, Winnie on the other hand said she's trying to put Rebecca's action behind her, but she has done so much damage, and that's something she finds difficult to reconcile. Winnie began to sob in a manner that got Rebecca a bit emotional. Rebecca began apologising, saying she's sorry about how she has made her feel, "I really do, but in two hours' time I will return to him, everything will be back to normal for you, but for me, it would leave me broken," said Rebecca.

Two hours later Rebecca turned to Peter.

"It's now about two hours I guess, I'm going in," she said. Jordan has this permafrown on his face since he knew about Rebecca's involvement with his dad, he immediately turned to her, "You seem to be enjoying this, aren't you?" he asked.

Rebecca wasn't pleased with Jordan's ingratitude, as she reminded him, she's working hard to reunite his dad with his family, then said this is also hard for her because she came here with her partner and she's now planning on returning home empty handed.

"Returning home empty handed is the price you pay for coveting another woman's husband," Jordan retorted.

Peter interjected and asked Jordan to stop the tackling, he then turned to Rebecca and asked if they can come with her. Rebecca thinks otherwise and suggested to Peter to allow her to go in first, that she will come for him, suggesting a smooth and willing reunion is advisable.

"Let's go in there, sort this out and return to the camp, I am exhausted already," Stacy muttered.

Rebecca and Stacy then left the waiting room and sat by Ambrose's bedside.

"Honey, how are you, oh sorry for calling you that, I just realised you have found your honey?" said Rebecca. It's now obvious to Rebecca that Ambrose is now critical of her and Stacy, she then decided to temper down on the humour.

Ambrose seemed calm enough to talk, he then asked Rebecca about the whereabouts of the young men claiming to be his family, and the woman in question. Rebecca was quite upfront in her response, as she said they are out there waiting for him to meet them and they're eager to do so.

"You mean they're eager to meet me? Please, bring them in," said Ambrose.

Rebecca immediately turned to Stacy, and then asked her to please ask Peter and Jordan to come in.

A moment later, Peter and Jordan walked in, and Peter immediately said, "Hello dad."

Ambrose looked at Peter and Jordan with so much love, and then apologised, saying he's so sorry, this whole dad thing is new to him, and he really can't remember being called dad. Jordan was taken over by his emotion, as tears ran down his cheeks.

"We missed you, we searched and searched for you after the accident, when we couldn't find you, we decided to hold a funeral," said Jordan.

Ambrose was shocked to realise a funeral service was held for him, he continues to apologise, saying he's so sorry, and that he remembers nothing of his past, and he still does, but they all should look for a way to move past this. Jordan interjected and informed his dad that he comes to this hospital to pick his mum every day, at the close of work, he then asked his dad if he didn't remember doing that as well. Ambrose looked lost and said he really didn't remember any of that.

Winnie walked into the conversation, "how is he?" She asked and she then turned to Ambrose. "Honey, do you remember us now?" asked Winnie.

Ambrose responded saying he still doesn't recollect anything, but after reviewing information about the Octal Flamingo incident on the internet, he realised the accident made a mess of his memory and said he's sorry, that he unwittingly began leading another life.

"None of this is your fault, and I'm glad you're beginning to come around, I'm busy right now, but I'll be back," said Winnie.

Ambrose pleaded with Winnie begging her not to go, that the evidence is overwhelming, he then held her hand.

"Let's see how everything I have lost can be restored," said Ambrose.

Winnie stood for a while, and fixed her gaze on her husband, she suddenly gave him a big hug and said she's glad to have him back. She then said she's on duty, and she will be back. "You and your sons can start some form of bonding," said Winnie.

Interestingly, just as Winnie leaves her husband's bedside, she spotted Reverend Fitzgerald walking in, and she then walks up to him.

"You are here, Reverend," said Winnie. Reverend Fitzgerald responded saying of course, he's here because he couldn't sleep, and he just can't wait another hour to see the Evangelist.

Winnie couldn't help the reverend manage his anxiety either, all she said was that the news is real, and her husband is right here. She then asked the reverend to come with her, he followed her and they walked side by side.

Immediately Reverend Fitzgerald got to Fredrick's bedside, he remained speechless as he gazed at the Evangelist for a while. He then muttered, "Thank you, Lord," before asking the Evangelist how he's doing. Ambrose was quite receptive and cheerful the moment the priest fixed his gaze on him, he sensed the priest is someone he's well aquatinted with. Ambrose welcomed the priest and said he doesn't seem to recollect the priest's face, but the photographs and videos suggests him and the reverend were quite close.

Reverend Fitzgerald said of course they were quite close, yet he couldn't stop muttering, that this is a miracle, and told Fredrick that he commissioned Fredrick's ill-fated missionary assignment.

"Are you a Priest? Your dress suggests so," said Fredrick.

"Of course, I'm a priest, and you're an Evangelist," said Rev. Fitzgerald, who then turned to Winnie, and asked how she found Fredrick.

Winnie burst into laughter, and said the whole thing is some kind of irony, as she told the reverend that Fredrick actually found her, she then pointed the reverend to Rebecca and Stacy, "courtesy of these ladies," said Winnie. Rev. Fitzgerald immediately turned to Rebecca, and thanked her, he then asked them where and how they found him.

Winnie interjected immediately and urged the Reverend to save himself the trouble because the answer to the questions he's asking will make his stomach churn. The reverend became quite surprised at Winnie's assertion, he then asked her to explain what she meant by the stomach-churning response he will get from these ladies.

Winnie had no choice but to satisfy the reverend's curiosity, and said they found Fredrick by the beach of a Luciferian camp, only to revive him and marry him, as against involving the police to look for his family.

"Who married him?" asked Rev. Fitzgerald.

Winnie immediately pointed to Rebecca and said she's the one who married her husband, then turned to the priest and asked, "who does a thing like that," converting an Evangelist into a Satanist. Funnily, Peter and his brother only knew their dad was living with another woman for the past three years, their mum intentionally spared them the lurid details surrounding the lifestyle their dad was leading all this while.

"What! You mean they're Satanists, mum, you didn't tell us about that?" asked Peter.

Winnie had to own up to her children that she knowingly kept that aspect of the story under wraps because it isn't a good thing to say to one's children, that their dad lived in a camp were everybody go about their business scantily clothed, in service to Lucifer.

Reverend Fitzgerald left Rebecca alone, and then turned to the Evangelist whom he thinks should know better, and asked Fredrick how come he ended up in a Satanist camp.

"Dad, why, do you have to live in a nudist camp?" cried Jordan.

Winnie interjected and said this has nothing to do with her husband, it isn't his fault, because he was found unconscious by the beach of the Bliss Luciferian camp, and when they realised, he has no memory of his past, they exploited his vulnerability. Obviously, the Bliss camp is notorious for a lot of terribly mysterious stuff happening to people in Europe, and learning that his dad, who is a known Evangelist has been living a normal life in the camp did rattle Peter's cage.

This latest revelation of Luciferianism and part-nudism got Peter reeling from within, he immediately began feeling sick and needed somewhere throw up. He isn't willing to let go of this matter so soon as he lashed out at Rebecca for a second time and said instead of helping a helpless man, all she did was destroy him.

Fredrick watched as the circus played out before his eyes, he then urged Peter and his brother to take it easy, and said he's here now, then suggested they should all look for ways to move past this.

The bashing became too much for Rebecca who suddenly became all teary, and said she knows they all blame her for everything, but they've also failed to see her effort in helping to keep Ambrose alive.

Jordan tried shutting Rebecca up by insisting her excuse is a lame one, as he asked "what effort did you put, other than pursuing your selfish goals?"

"I found him lifeless, he wasn't breathing and there wasn't any pulse either, everybody around confirmed him dead, I fought hard to ensure they take a further look at him," said Rebecca.

Stacy immediately put some words in for Rebecca as she told everyone in the cubicle that to be sincere, if not for Rebecca the man they see here wouldn't have been alive. Jordan took exception to the excuses put forward by Rebecca and Stacy, and said thankfully they pulled his dad out of the water, but no thanks to what they did afterwards.

"That does not justify her actions, and you know how dirty this would be if we bring the police into this," Peter chuckled.

Stacy urged everyone to lay down their swords and said what's done can't be undone.

Winnie concurred with Stacy and insists it's time for everyone to lay down their sword, but truth be told, this is a serious situation and Rebecca's handling of it befuddles the problem, confused it and even belittles it.

"Ok, let's think of moving past this, the past would bring us nothing other than pain," said Rev. Fitzgerald.

Now that she has succeeded in reuniting Ambrose with his family, Rebecca excused herself and said she thinks she should get going because she has done her bit.

Jordan immediately suggested to Rebecca not to be so quick in running off without first repairing all the damage she have created.

Rebecca insisted she has already kick-started the process of bonding, and there isn't any need for that nuance. The reverend turned to Jordan and insisted that his dad is beginning to come around, and that they should let Rebecca go. Winnie doesn't want this debate dragging on any further, she immediately told Rebecca she can, and that they will take if from here.

"Ok, but can I call you to find out how he's fairing?" asked Rebecca.

"There won't be a need for that, and you've done enough damage already," said Winnie.

Stacy immediately held Rebecca by the hand and reminded her that Ambrose's family has made their position clear and she doesn't have to bog people just to help them. She then urged Rebecca to come with her, so they can return to the camp.

Reverend Fitzgerald turned to Rebecca and thanked her, then asked her to please leave her phone number that they would contact her if there were a need for it.

Stacy urged the reverend to leave the police out of this, Winnie interjected and assured them that for now, this will stay this way, she then suggested that they would definitely inform the police they've found her husband, but they wouldn't drop Rebecca in it. Rebecca then thanked Winnie for her benignity and then left the hospital with Stacy. Immediately Rebecca and Stacy left, the reverend asked Winnie to get a Bible and hand it to the Evangelist, Jordan interjected and suggested it would've been more appropriate to give his dad a bible after his memory has been restored.

It was a bittersweet moment for this family, as they try to grapple with the reality before them, but the reverend insisted that the bible should be handed to Fredrick immediately, because reading the bible is what he's known for and the Bible will help him remember who he used to be, and God will perfect the rest. Winnie immediately reached for her bag and brought out a bible and handed it to her husband who took the bible yet knows not what to do with it. The Reverend immediately asked Ambrose to open the bible to the book of Isaiah, but the Evangelist struggled as he seems to have lost his idea of the bible.

The Reverend then took the Bible and opened the book of Isaiah 43:19 which reads "See, I am doing a new thing! Now it springs up; do you not perceive it? I am making a way in the wilderness and streams in the wasteland." The Reverend encouraged the Evangelist to read and reread and then meditate on this bible verse.

Jarrod rushed to Rebecca and Stacy the moment they arrived the camp, he then asked where Ambrose was. Rebecca was all smiley in a bid to put on a brave face, and said Ambrose is fine and has reunited with his family. "You must be kidding me, right?" asked Jarrod.

Stacy immediately reminded Jarrod he witnessed a woman protesting to be Ambrose's wife, Jarrod mumbled he did witness the woman making her claims but insisted Rebecca seems to be having none of that.

Stacy had to put Jarrod's mind at rest as she informed him that Ambrose's family came with proof, and they've got no choice than to let go of Ambrose.

Jarrod remained concerned about how the camp members will receive the obviously shocking news that Ambrose has reunited with his family. Rebecca, who on the other hand was busy counting her losses, said she doesn't think she owes anyone an explanation. Jarrod insists she does owe them an explanation, because she left the camp with Ambrose and returned empty handed and asked what that suggests. "It suggests nothing, and for your information we just realised Ambrose was a preacher, a Christian," said Stacy.

Jarrod smiled and said the new revelation about Ambrose being a preacher meant nothing. He insisted that Ambrose is a Luciferian and he loved everything about it, but then reminded

Rebecca that Prophet Gregory would love to hear about what happened to Ambrose.

Rebecca thought to herself that Jarrod was going on and on about Ambrose love for the Luciferian lifestyle because he'd no idea they just escaped prison by a whisker. She's still miffed by the drama she just walked away from, and even the fairy godmother won't see a thing like this coming.

Her disposition reflects this hopelessness that is likened to a smouldering candlewick, Rebecca has now come to realise that her relationship with Ambrose turned out to be a porcupine that will be difficult to digest. She then began walking away, saying she desires nothing else than a warm shower, a bubble bath rather.

"I was told Zeppelin called, requesting to know of Ambrose's condition," said Jarrod. Stacy was quite keen to kill this conversation, she immediately turned to Jarrod and said if Zeppelin wants Ambrose he should go to town and get him from his wife and kids.

"You don't have to be rude about it, and I would suggest that you manage your emotion," said Jarrod.

"I have to go, Jarrod, maybe we will talk about this later," said Rebecca, who then continued walking away from Jarrod with Stacy by her side.

Even as they walked away, Jarrod left them a word of advice, and suggested they should speak to Zeppelin about Ambrose. Losing Ambrose makes her more or less vagrant, and her looks like that of a wounded bunny, meant it's difficult to see beyond her deceptive innocence. Stacy on the other hand might soon realise that it doesn't look good on her as she plays the role of a nodding dog. Except for Stacy, no other person might be willing to fall on their sword to save Rebecca, even as she maintains a low profile and gave out less information about Ambrose.

Even as they parted ways, Jarrod expected Rebecca to be kicking and screaming, for someone who left the camp with her supposed partner but returned empty handed and without him.

A day after Rebecca left Fredrick behind and returned to the camp, Doctor Oliver walks up to Winnie and Evangelist Fredrick.

"How are you feeling, Fredrick, the photographs, the videos and even the stories you're being told, have they helped in any way to remind you of your past?" asked Doc. Oliver. No, just flashes, and difficult to piece together," replied Evangelist Fredrick.

"How do you feel about reuniting with your new family?" asked Doc. Oliver.

Evangelist Fredrick laughed even as he admitted it was kind of strange, but he's now beginning to like the experience of being with his real family.

"How far reaching has this helped you?" asked Doc. Oliver.

Evangelist Fredrick responded saying it has been wonderful to establish connections and bond, sort of, with his lovely wife and his sons. Even though he didn't object to undergoing a test, he'd to make sure of it, to let his wife know that there's no need testing for a Sexually Transmitted Infections because he didn't get sexually involved with Rebecca. Unfortunately, the result of the test is among the reasons of the doctors' visit. The doctor then turned to Winnie, and said her husband will be discharged later today, and that the nurse will handle the paper work later.

Winnie on the other hand thinks more should be done to help her husband remember, she immediately asked the doctor if her husband needs regular visits to the hospital for check-ups. Doctor Oliver affirmed and said of course more hospital visits will be arranged with a psychologist to help Fredrick with his memory and the nurse will tell her all about that.

The doctor handed Winnie the test result for sexually trans-mitted infection and said her husband is clean. It didn't take long before the doctor left Winnie and Fredrick, but the Evangelist seems keen to know more about himself. He then asked Winnie to tell him what kind of a man he was before the accident. Winnie smiled as she urged him not to worry about that because he's a good man, and a caring father.

Evangelist Fredrick was preoccupied about his past, and urged her to go on, pleading with her not to stop, but tell him more about himself, and about his marriage, him and his wife, them together.

"You're a loving, romantic and caring husband; you bring me to work daily and return to pick me from work at the close of the day, but you're a disciplined father," said Winnie.

"What about Peter, and Jordan, what was my relationship with them like?" asked Evang. Fredrick.

Winnie told him the relationship between him and his sons is a normal father to son relationship. She added that Peter always come to him for advice, and Jordan is fond of him as well, but always clinging to his mum. Evangelist Fredrick smiled, and said he looks forward to restoring his family the way it was before the unfortunate accident. Winnie gave him a big hug and held unto him and not letting go for a while, she then asked him about Rebecca, and what he intends to do about her.

The Evangelist didn't hesitate to let his wife know that Rebecca now belongs to his past, though, he felt betrayed, but still look forward to restoring all he has lost.

"How do you advise we help you get back to your old life?" asked Winnie.

Evangelist Fredrick suggested they take things one day at a time, and then asked about how to get his things in the Luciferian camp. Winnie squirmed and said, "that God forsaken place? No, no, you can't go back to that camp," she then reminded him he arrived the camp with nothing and it's better he leaves everything behind.

"If you say so," said Evangelist Fredrick.

Winnie then kissed him, and said she has to return to work, but she would be back.

Also, in the Bliss Camp, Zeppelin walked into the hospital and approached Doctor Van.

Zeppelin chatted with the doctor for a while, even as the doctor informed him, he just arrived in the camp that morning. Zeppelin then asked Doctor Van about Ambrose, and inquired about Ambrose's health, saying he couldn't reach him on phone, and he has been left in the dark.

"I guess you are right, Zeppelin, Ambrose isn't picking his phone, and Rebecca couldn't give me a concrete answer," said Doc. Van.

Zeppelin wasn't particularly impressed with Doctor Van's response concerning Rebecca, he then queried Rebecca's refusal to give a concrete response about Ambrose's condition.

Doctor Van immediately told Zeppelin that he learnt Rebecca is in the camp and he hope to pay her a visit in her camp room to speak to her further on the subject.

"Ok, I hope you find her, and I need to know what it is with Ambrose because I can't leave the camp without a manager," said Zeppelin.

Doctor Van got to Rebecca's door and knocked.

"Hey Rebecca, are you home?" asked Doc. Van.

"Of course, I am home, when did you return to the camp?" asked Rebecca.

Van immediately informed Rebecca that Zeppelin was in the camp clinic minutes earlier, and he wants to speak with her. Rebecca was a bit reluctant to speak with the doctor. She's more like a cat who will always land on her feet, particularly with the lucky escape she just had with Ambrose's family. At this point, she's like a woman reserving her energy for public display, while at the same time managing the struggles inside her.

Sensing that Rebecca was sounding a bit off, Doctor Van immediately dialled Zeppelin and hands the phone to Rebecca. "Hello Zeppelin, I learnt you have been trying to reach me, sorry, I've been indisposed," said Rebecca. Zeppelin wasn't pleased with Rebecca's choice of words and asked if she meant she has been indisposed to speak to him, and said he has been worried sick about Ambrose's condition just as she does. Rebecca thanked Zeppelin for his concerns for Ambrose, she then asked him how she could be of help.

"How is he, and when is he returning to the camp? I learnt you returned to the camp without him," said Zeppelin.

Rebecca had to break the sad news to Zeppelin and said Ambrose's family found him, and they have taken him off her. Zeppelin was taken aback with this new turn of event, he then asked Rebecca to give flesh to her story, because he wants to know how this happened.

Rebecca replied to Zeppelin, saying there's nothing to tell. Unfortunately, Ambrose's wife was among the nurses in the acute assessment unit attending to patients, that was how they found him.

"Is he coming back, or I should get a replacement for him? I can't leave the camp without someone in charge," said Zeppelin.

Rebecca suggested to Zeppelin she doesn't think Ambrose would, she then suggested they all should consider him gone, and for good, maybe. After his conversation with Rebecca, Zeppelin then asked her to give the phone to Doctor Van, so he could speak with him.

"Zeppelin, its Van on the phone," said Doc. Van.

Zeppelin immediately began a conversation with Doctor Van and said he knows Van is a busy doctor but he wants him to take charge of the management of the camp. He then proceeded to say, he will conclude this conversation with Prophet Gregory, before he comes to a conclusion on how this will work.

"Ok, Zeppelin, this is a difficult one, but I'll give it my best shot, and let me know the outcome of your conversion with Prophet Gregory," replied Doc. Van.

Zeppelin thanked Doctor Van for stepping in, he then said he will keep in touch with the doctor for further update.

Fredrick Douglas has now been discharged from the hospital, but the moment the Evangelist walked into the house and set his eyes on the golden lamp stand by his bed side, he had a recollection for the first time. He is overly fond of this lamp stand because this is what he uses to read his Bible and other Christian literatures daily, before the unfortunate cruise ship accident. So far, this lamp stand is the only thing the Evangelist remembered from his past.

Weeks later, after Evangelist Fredrick's discharge from the hospital, Winnie woke up from sleep one of the mornings and turned facing her husband.

"Honey, how are you?" she asked. The Evangelist who was still in bed, but was seated and reading a Christian literature then replied to his wife saying he's fine, and he's glad to be home. Now that he has spent some time with his family, it's obvious that the Evangelist has had a flavour of the family life he used to enjoy before the cruise ship accident, just that embracing that family life hasn't been a walk in the park for him. Winnie subtly pointed out to him, he has been unusually quiet in recent days, and his excitement is fading by the day.

"Why did you say that?" asked Evang. Fredrick.

"Having found us, you were happy to be home, but now your attitude towards the family is cold," said Winnie.

The Evangelist opened up to his wife and said her assertion isn't far from the truth, saying his struggles grew by the day. She looked at him for a while and said he's sounding a bit morbid but she's all ears, and then urged him to get his concerns off his chest. It's obvious to his family that since he returned home, he has been nothing but a wallflower. Winnie exclaimed asking her husband, how and why the struggles. She immediately urged him to share his worries with her, so they should talk about it.

"Since I got home, evidence of my previous lifestyle before the accident makes the life I lived in the Luciferian camp an abomination," said Evang. Fredrick.

Winnie tried to comfort her husband, telling him the accident, and what happened to him in the wake of it, at that God forsaken camp isn't his fault. Evangelist Fredrick Douglas turned to his wife who seem keen to hear him out, he muttered to his wife that he himself has written a number of Christian writings condemning wild and abominable lifestyle like the one he led in the camp. He paused for a while, then said this is the third Christian literature written by other people he has studied since his return, and all he could deduce from these books is that he's no longer worthy.

"Honey, no, you don't have to think that way, the God you served and preached all over the world won't hold this against you because people took advantage of your vulnerability," said Winnie. Evangelist Fredrick muttered again, asking himself if he could ever return to the man he used to be before this unfortunate accident. He then insisted that returning to his former self might be a bit easy, but living it won't be. Winnie held her husband by the hand and said for what it's worth, he can't win a race looking backward even as she pleaded with him to look to the future and be expectant.

"I'm trying, but it's just not working," insists Evang. Fredrick. Winnie struggled to keep up with the conversation, she then steered the focus of the conversation to something more general as she asked him about his sons.

"How much time do you spend with them, that's one way of moving on," said Winnie.

"Yeah, we've been spending some time together, maybe not as much, just that our first outing was a bit awkward," said Evangelist Fredrick.

Winnie wasn't briefed by her sons that their outing with their dad was kind of awkward, she immediately asked her husband how come he concluded that his outing with his sons was awkward.

The Evangelist smiled as he narrated to his wife that they were seated in this restaurant, looking at each other and waiting for who speaks first.

"Who spoke first?" asked Winnie.

"Hmm, Peter did, but I took over and we discussed a range of issues, we talked about what we like, they told me about my likes and dislikes, and some of their funny or rather awkward moments with me," said Evangelist Fredrick. Winnie immediately exclaimed and said that was fun, and she'd loved to be a part of that outing, just that her work is an impediment but promised to be a part of their next planned outing.

Evangelist Fredrick suddenly suggested to his wife that a cup of tea will make this conversation more interesting. Winnie immediately got up from bed and said she will rather make two cups of tea because she needed to make herself a cup of tea as well, and just as her feet touched down, she turned to her husband and jocularly urged him to stay put and not go anywhere. She then said she will be back and burst into laughter to lighten the ambience in the bedroom.

"Ok, I'm waiting," said Evangelist Fredrick.

Days later, Reverend Fitzgerald visits Evangelist Fredrick, immediately he alighted from his car and walked to the door, he knocked and asked if there's anyone at home. Peter opened the door.

"Hello reverend, please come in," said Peter.

"Ooh thank you, Peter, how are you, and how is your dad settling down?" asked Rev. Fitzgerald. Peter smiled and said his dad is settling in better as the days go by. Reverend Fitzgerald walked into the house and sat down. After ushering the reverend into the house, Peter went to inform his dad that the reverend is here to see him. Interestingly, since Evangelist Fredrick's return, Reverend Fitzgerald had only been following him up on the phone, and this is the reverend's first home visit.

"Hello Evangelist, how are you getting on?" asked Rev. Fitzgerald.

Evangelist Fredrick smiled and reminded the reverend that he has been referring to him as an "Evangelist" and videos of him and the reverend shows the reverend addresses him as such.

"Yes, because that's what you are, as you learn more about yourself, you would soon come to terms with your past," said Rev. Fitzgerald.

Evangelist Fredrick thanked the reverend for his support during these difficult times and said he's eternally grateful.

The Reverend on the other hand, said he hasn't done anything special to deserve a thank you, and insisted they're in this together. The reverend was quite emotional because he isn't a custodian without a conscience, as he frankly told the Evangelist he shares in the blame of whatever happened to him, but he must say that his return was a miracle indeed.

Evangelist Fredrick was enthusiastic about having the reverend whom he shared a great deal in common with, yet he didn't really find his survival from the accident to be something fascinating. He expressed his exception in a clearer term as he pointed out to the reverend that referring to his survival as a miracle doesn't sit right with him. This is because he felt that his being alive can't be a miracle since he's still grappling with the gap between his lifestyle as an Evangelist and the abominable life he lived in that God forsaken camp, when placed side-by-side.

"You were meant to be dead, Evangelist, we've held a funeral for you, and now you're alive and breathing," said Rev. Fitzgerald.

The Evangelist was quite upfront with the reverend, as he reminded the reverend that his reference to his experience as a miracle is nothing but platitudes, and that this isn't a good thing for him. He then proceeded to say that he still remained to be convinced but he's needled by his inability to get his head around why he descended this low, spiritually and morally. The reverend immediately realised Fredrick is dealing with a lot inside him, he reminded him that without coincidences life wouldn't make any sense, before urging him to focus on the future.

"Maybe we should talk about your sufferings, and your pain," said Rev. Fitzgerald.

"I'm actually struggling within, since you want me to talk about it," said Evangelist Fredrick.

The reverend had no choice but to let the Evangelist know that Winnie told him about his struggles, the reverend then suggested that maybe it's time to engage the Evangelist with some evangelical activities. Evangelist Fredrick interjected and said maybe that should wait a little while, and suggested he get use to his home, his wife, and sons, first before venturing into something else. Reverend Fitzgerald elaborated further saying, doing evangelical work will help the Evangelist take back control and assume his old lifestyle of evangelism, and help him forget about what he lost living in that camp. The Reverend suggested they do it together, and at least the Evangelist will have a friend to keep him company to help him get his mind busy.

The reverend did agree that his suggestion of knowing his family better before any evangelical work isn't misplaced but taking him around sometimes shouldn't be out of place either.

"What do you suggest?" asked Evangelist Fredrick.

"I suggest you get dressed, let's go around town together," said Rev. Fitzgerald.

"Ok then, maybe that will help me to reconnect with you," said Evangelist Fredrick. He then went inside, got dressed and left the house with the reverend. A lot of effort was put in, to help the Evangelist put his past behind him. Regrettably, those effort didn't go far enough to help him forgive himself for the life he led while in that camp, and he hasn't forgiven Rebecca either.

Months after the visit of Lucian Gaia, Prophet Gregory's spiritual father, the activities of the Bliss Luciferian Camp continue to be something of a concern begging for action. Even though Brandon Moore thought it wise to observe Gregory Helsing from a safe distance, he now has no choice but to dip his feather in the flutter.

It was just sun set, on Sunday evening when Prophet Gregory was on his regular botanical walk, that he got a message that Brandon Moore will be visiting the Bliss Luciferian Camp, just a week from that day.

Gregory Helsing knew what this visit meant, and you don't just get the global head of Luciferian prophets paying you a courtesy visit just like that. This visit is more like Moloch himself paying him a visit. Arguably, visits of this nature are rare, this visit is more about whipping him into line, than giving him a pat on the back. They all live a voodoo-like life, shrouded in mystery, so Gregory himself perceived this visit to be the biggest challenge of his service in the Luciferian Order.

Gregory Helsing already got a hint from Lucian Gaia that Brandon Moore finds him to be sort of menacing to the body of the Luciferian Order.

Unfortunately, the visit is happening and nothing can stop Brandon Moore visiting, all Gregory Helsing has to do, is to wait for the big man to come.

Just exactly a week after the notice that Brandon Moore is visiting, Brandon Moore arrived at the Bliss Luciferian Camp, in the company of a number of Luciferian prophets. Immediately Brandon Moore alighted from the car, Gregory Helsing and Noel Zeppelin were on hand to receive him. They bowed in reverence, and kissed Brandon Moore's ring. They then showed him to the dining table that was already set for a lavish lunch. Even the residents of this camp can sense it that a big beast, a dinosaur rather, has visited.

After their meal, Brandon Moore and Gregory Helsing then walked into the temple for a one-to-one. "I suppose, you know why I'm here," said Brandon Moore.

"Your lordship, I suppose so," replied Gregory Helsing.

'I sent Lucian Gaia to you, but you haven't changed your approach," Brandon Moore retorted. Gregory Helsing had to inform the lordship that came visiting that he had an encounter with Lucifer who ordained him himself, on a separate ordination and instructed him to make sure the churches are empty, because the judgement at the great White Throne is at hand.

"Yes, I get you, but the mannerism of your call to Lucifer is too pronounced, it's more like Satanism," said Brandon Moore. Gregory Helsing couldn't help but reminded his lordship that they are Satanists, and the term Luciferianism is just a posh way of presenting themselves. "No, don't say a thing like that, we aren't Satanist, we venerate Lucifer, he is the bringer of light, the Guardian and the Librator," Brandon Moore retorted.

"But as Luciferians, we hex people, we do spiritism, we do vodoo, we strike people with mysterious illnesses, and cause mishap for peoples, aren't these Satanism?" replied Prophet Gregory.

"Of course, we do all you just mentioned to people, but we still don't regard ourselves as Satanists," Brandon Moore insists. Gregory Helsing immediately began pointing his guest to a mosaic of news info on the board in his office.

"You see this, we are behind this accident that killed thirty school children on a school trip in Italy, the school is managed by the church, and a lot of people blamed the church for negligence. Many Europeans renounce their Christian faith as a result of this singular act.

There is currently a movement across Europe, encouraging Christians to resign the church, that's my hand work.," said Gregory Helsing, who also reminded his lordship "I suppose you are aware of a number of priests who say they are pastors in Christian churches but don't believe in Christ, that's also my hand work."

"Sometimes we send people to seduce vulnerable priests, we film them and create a scandal from it. What followed in the wake of each of these scandals is some kind of prejudice in the hearts of people, that caused people to drop the Christian faith, and leave the church in droves," said Prophet Gregory.

He informed his guest that he won't stop until Europe turns its back on Christians, because Christianity is Lucifer's nemesis, which he's determined to confront.

"I don't mind causing an accident and make people blame it on the church or use boys and girls to seduce priests and create a scandal from it, or possibly get compromising video, documents or information concerning government officials and use it to blackmail them into doing our biddings," said Prophet Gregory.

"Then what's your bidding?" Asked Brandon Moore.

"Use government officials to make laws that limit Christianity," replied prophet Gregory.

Brandon Moore was silent as he listened keenly to Gregory Helsing self-profiling himself. He appreciated Gregory Helsing's effort to discredit the Christian faith, but told his host that his approach is petty, and more like pick pocket. Brandon Moore considers Prophet Gregory's approach to be sort of a hodge-podge that leaves everyone confused. He doesn't like the idea of Luciferians operating in penny packets, before suggesting what considers to be a better alternative.

Brandon Moore then pointed out to Gregory Helsing that the bliss camp will make more impact working with government figures, who will use their influence to make policies that will kick Christianity out of people's lives across Europe, starting from Romania. Brandon Moore then boasts to Gregory Helsing that he's behind most of the polices that limits the practice of the Christian faith in America, and currently expanding policies that separate children from their parents, wives from marriages, and make marriage to be something mundane.

Gregory Helsing remained as bold as brass, and decided not to keep quite as he made light of Brandon Moore's achievements. He was a bit cheeky in the manner he went about it, he reminded his host that changes in government, and push back from Republican politicians in the United States, coupled with constant push back from conservative American Christians has impeded the lordship ability to record the kind of success he has just mentioned.

But he, Gregory Helsing, has had the most impact on Christians, and that not even twenty Luciferian prophets put together has reduced Christianity in the manner he has impacted on the Christians faith. Brandon Moore soon realised that this meeting isn't going to be a breeze because the comparison kind of irked him, and the sudden perma-frown on his face shows his discontent.

He emphatically made it clear to Gregory Helsing that what he's doing is a monstrous throwback to the byegone age, describing him as a kind of vile ogre to the Luciferian Order, and distancing themselves from him is now the only way out. The tension between them didn't abate, it continued like a simmering saucepan, but their conversation suddenly became heated when Brandon Moore informed Gregory Helsing of his plans to excommunicate him, but has decided to put that decision on hold for now. He then suggested that Gregory Helsing should be reporting to him, until he's satisfied with his approach to gathering audience for Lucifer.

Gregory Helsing muttered in response to this decision and said that this is an attempt to cage him, and deny his ability to serve Lucifer in the manner he sees fit, but his guest insists his decision on the matter is final. This decision didn't sit well with Gregory Helsing, who wouldn't want others shovelling their thoughts about Lucifer into him, he then stormed out of the meeting, and left his lordship standing. Brandon Moore felt slighted by Prophet Gregory's decision to walk out on him. He waited for a while, he waited to see if the prophet will return but he didn't, he then returned to his entourage, and they drove out of the Bliss camp without the courtesy of a goodbye from his host.

Every dog has its day, but this visit to the Bliss camp isn't one of such days for Bandon Moore, who prefers the loyalty of others more than anything else. On the other hand, Gregory Helsing's perception of Brandon Moore as some kind of big harmless doll that could be poked without due regard was his Achilles heel, and a big error of judgement.

Prophet Grogory's rabid devotion to Lucifer has been called into question, and yet Brandon's Moore's botched attempt to curb his excesses, has largely failed. Just a few minutes after Brandon Moore left the camp unceremoniously, Zeppelin walked up to Prophet Gregory and pointed out that it seems his meeting with his lordship didn't go as planned.

"His lordship, you said, I'm sorry to disappoint you, Zeppelin, because I am now unable to tell if the lord is in the ship or the ship is in the lord," Prophet Gregory replied humorously.

The Prophet then hinted Zeppelin that Brandon Moore's effort to shut him up proved underwhelming, then said the meeting was more of a damp squib anyway.

# CHAPTER

## TWELVE

### *Rebecca's sin*

Days later, after Winnie have left the house to work, Evangelist Fredrick left a note addressed to his wife in the living room, went into his car and drove off. Not long after his dad drove out of the house, Jordan walked into the living room and saw the note his dad addressed to their mum. Jordan immediately rushed to Peter's room holding the note his dad left behind in his hand, he anxiously handed the note to Peter and asked him to read this because it's about their dad and it seems urgent.

"What is it, Jordan?" asked Peter.

"It's dad, but you'll need to read this for yourself," said Jordan. Peter immediately took the note from Jordan, and read through.

"Oh my God, I hope dad isn't attempting to do something stupid?" said Peter.

Jordan immediately suggested to his brother that they should get their mum involved right away.

"Wait a minute, I suggest we handle this calmly, and maybe I should have a word with dad before getting mum involved," said Peter.

Arguably, these young men didn't know their dad to be a man with a one-track mindset, but it's obviously looking like that this time. This move isn't about bluster or some sort of bravado, he's just a man feeling kind off messed up by others.

Jordan insists that won't be possible and said he doesn't think there is time for them to handle this with tact.

Peter on the other hand had no knowledge that his dad has left the house, he pressed his brother to let him speak with their dad, and after all, he's right there in his bedroom. Jordan had to inform Peter that their dad isn't in his bedroom, he then explained to his brother that he saw their dad drove off just before he walked into the living room and found the note.

"When did he leave? I didn't hear the sound of his car," asked Peter.

Jordan reminded Peter that he didn't hear the sound of the car because the car was parked across the road, so he wouldn't hear. Peter then decided he would have to call his mum to let her know what's on ground. "Please do," said Jordan. Peter immediately reached for the phone, and he then dialled his mum, and asked if she's busy.

Winnie's response was quite expected, as she reminded her son, she's at work and should be busy but she is free at the moment. Peter didn't hesitate to let his mum know the phone call is about his dad who seem to be losing it, and said it's important she know.

"What is it about your dad, I just finished speaking with him," said Winnie.

"Ooh, he called you, what did he say to you?" asked Peter.

"He just called saying he wants to hear my voice, is anything the matter?" asked Winnie.

Peter replied his mum saying he's afraid there's a problem, and that Jordan found a note he left in the living room.

"Note, what about the note?" asked Winnie.

Peter immediately suggested to his mum that he would rather read the content of the note out-loud to his mum. Winnie urged

Peter to be fast about it, because he's already scaring the hell out of her. Peter then reads the content of the note to his mum.

"Winnie, I'm so sorry, I feel I can't go on being a servant of God, after running around scantily clothed in the service of Lucifer and living a morally debased life of another for years. Those responsible for this must provide the reasons for their actions because they've succeeded in pulling me away from my God," the note reads.

Winnie had to think on her feet, as she informed her sons that she's aware of the fact that their dad hasn't been able to come to terms with his activities in that camp.

Peter Interjected and asked his mum what she thinks they should do now because their dad could do something stupid. Winnie immediately told Peter that their dad could be heading to that camp, possibly in search for answers. She reiterated that these people aren't overly fond of Christians, and this could get ugly.

"Mum, maybe dad doesn't' have any intention to pick a fight," said Peter.

Winnie remained worried sick that her husband is returning to the very people that worked tirelessly to kill the light of God in him. She immediately suggested to Peter to take Jordan with him and trace their dad to the camp right away because he obviously won't get the answer he seeks. Peter interjected and asked his mum if they should drive through the hospital and pick her up, so they could go after their dad together, if she desires to come with them.

Arguably, this family's entire nightmare has just been rolled into one, and this whole drama suddenly left Winnie befuddled, but without a galling feeling towards her husband. She couldn't tolerate any dawdling at this point, as she insists there isn't time, that she would rather go with Alisabel's car. Interestingly, her place of work is about thirty minutes closer to the camp, and she will possibly get there before her husband does.

"Ok, mum," said Peter, they then rushed to the car and left the house.

Stefan was returning from walking the woods bordering the Bliss camp, he was assigned by Prophet Gregory to cull badgers in what was meant to be a pest control measure. Stefan was returning from one of his badger culling rounds and had a gun in his hand when he saw Ambrose alight from the car. News that Ambrose was a Christian preacher suddenly made Ambrose enemy number one as far as this Satanist camp is concerned. Ambrose is now everything this camp is against, Stefan immediately pointed his gun at the Evangelist, threatening to shoot if he doesn't leave the camp right away. Ambrose hesitated and seem bent on getting the answers he came for.

This was a guy that has spent all day shooting badgers, shooting this Christian preacher is just one more bullet, and underestimating Stefan might be at the Evangelist's peril. Stefan seems convinced that the Evangelist is off his trolley for setting his foot in the camp, and decided to teach him a little lesson. He obviously was serious about shooting the Evangelist, maybe not to kill him, but to at least leave a scar, and it will be foolhardy for Ambrose to return to the camp to seek answers that aren't there, and he's now in a situation where there is no good outcome. The shouting match attracted a number of residents which includes Rebecca, and while the drama between the pair unfolds, Ambrose drew close and took advantage of proximity to wrestle the gun away from Stefan.

By the time Winnie arrived the Bliss Luciferian Camp, her husband was already there and now pointing the gun he retrieved from Stefan, pointing a gun at Rebecca and a group of other Luciferians in the camp. She had to run as fast as her legs could carry her, but the distance between where she parked the car and where her husband was, meant that by the time she could catch up with him the damage would have been done already.

"Ambrose, what are you doing?" asked Rebecca. Evangelist Fredrick hushed Rebecca, asking her not to refer to him as Ambrose because that isn't his name, but then continued asking

Rebecca repeatedly why she coveted him, even after she saw a bible on him as at when they pulled him out of the water.

Ambrose couldn't let go of the gun, he held onto the gun as a means of defending himself, in case they attempted to lynch him. Serendipitously, this whole drama is happening on a day Prophet Gregory is out of town. He's on a courtesy visit to Prophet Lucian Gaia in Netherlands. Berger felt bad that this is happening on a day like this because if the prophet had been in the camp, maybe he would have eaten the Evangelist for breakfast.

"Glad your prophet is out of town, and at least, Rebecca will tell me about her little conspiracy with the prophet to make me one of you," replied the Evangelist.

Unfortunately, residents aren't obliging of Ambrose anymore. He used to be one of them, but they now see him as someone making a stir fry, without actually stirring the fry, and this doesn't bold well with the friendship they had either. Seeing the man she shared her life with for three years pointing a gun at her and her friends scared the hell out of Rebecca, as she kept screaming and asking the Evangelist what sin is it, he's talking about.

Jarrod on the other hand was out and about in the camp when he saw people gathered from a distance and some showing signs of panic but had no idea of what was keeping them on the edge, and then decided to walk into the scene, "Ooh my goodness, Ambrose, what are you doing with a gun?" asked Jarrod. The Evangelist muttered, saying he's only seeking answers but Stefan wanted to shoot him because he's a Christian, and that he shouldn't have set his foot inside his camp, but he wants answers for every wrong done to him.

"Ambrose or whatever you call yourself, what's wrong with you?" asked Orla.

Jarrod interjected and immediately urged Orla to stop provoking Ambrose so as not to exacerbate the already inflamed situation, because that isn't the best way to address a man with a gun. "Hey Orla, I'm not here for you, I just want to know how I ended up becoming a Luciferian," said Evangelist Fredrick.

Jarrod urged everyone to stop describing Ambrose as some kind of character, he then turned around as someone in shock, as he implored them to stop giving Ambrose the treatment of a mouse on the butcher's window because he has got a gun in his hand. Rebecca realised she's now in the Evangelist's cross hairs, particularly now that Stefan attacked him first. She now had no choice but to plead with the Evangelist to please calm down, suggesting they can talk about this, and reminding him they used to be good friends.

"You all took advantage of my memory loss to make me one of yours," said Evangelist Fredrick.

Orla turned to Rebecca, and accused her of being behind this unfortunate drama, and then suggested it's best she dance the music alone. "You caused this, and I suggest you take Ambrose to the side and face the music alone," she muttered. Rebecca is now pressed on all sides even as she had a gun pointed at her, and Stefan. Yet she's able to give Orla her long side-glance, and said she's aware Orla has some reservations about her, but reminded Orla, that this isn't the best time for her rhetoric.

Berger turned to Rebecca and Orla, and reminded them they all have a gun pointed at them, and unfortunately, they both find it appropriate to be at each other's throat at a time as this.

"I wish Eric was here to see how your escapades take a new turn," said Orla.

"Never mind, this is part of the twist and turns of life, my life is a story that has just taken an ugly turn," said Rebecca.

"Good you know this might turn ugly if you don't provide the answers to my questions," said Evangelist Fredrick. By ugly he's implying getting the police involved, but residents seem to mean the Evangelist is talking about guns blazing.

This Evangelist isn't into some kind of vulture culture, but he'd to hold onto the gun for as long as possible as he plans his escape. Holding onto this gun for longer, has suddenly cast this Evangelist as the aggressor, unbeknownst to these residents, he's thinking of dropping the gun and making a run for it because he doesn't have the heart to shoot his friends.

For what it's worth, Evangelist Fredrick looked like someone moonlighting, as he pointed his gun at these people longer than necessary and knowing full well that he isn't going to shoot. He stood and watched as his old friends argue among themselves, and some of them are beginning to realise he obviously can't pull the trigger. The Evangelist was scared stiff even with the gun in his hand, he stood statue still and looking more like a totem pole.

Jarrod pleaded with Ambrose and urged him to remember they were good friends, asking him not to do something he would regret. Berger seemed to want to take on the Evangelist, saying they have had enough of the Evangelist, and they don't want anything turning ugly. He then began stepping forward towards the Evangelist asking him to just return the gun to Stefan, and leave because they don't want any trouble.

"Step back, Berger, I advise you all to stay put," said Evang. Fredrick.

Winnie drew closer to where her husband was, and saw him pointing a gun at a bunch of Luciferians, she became quite exasperated, and asking herself where he got the gun from. She immediately began running towards her husband.

"Honey, stop, stop, don't do that, please put down the gun," said Winnie.

Rebecca immediately pointed to Winnie, as she made her way towards them. She then told the Evangelist his wife is coming and she is asking him to put down the gun. "Please, listen to her," said Rebecca.

"I heard her voice, and she can't stop me from protecting myself from you lot, and I need the gun to protect my wife," Evangelist Fredrick retorted. Winnie was just meters away from her husband even as he had his gun pointed at his old friends, Winnie then began to plead with him saying.

"Honey, stop, put down the gun".

Immediately Evangelist Fredrick shifted his attention to glance at his wife, Rebecca and the others attempted scampering to safety, and Stefan stepped forward and about to tackle the Evangelist.

The Evangelist panicked and accidentally fired a shot a Rebecca, and immediately became fearful that he has fired a shot at Rebecca in error, the shot hit her in the arm. Rebecca stopped running, fearing that the Evangelist is crazy and will shoot to kill if she attempts running again. Winnie then rushed and stood between Rebecca and her husband, the Evangelist then decided to put the gun away, saying the shot wasn't intentional, but then accidentally fired a second shot that hit his wife in the arm coincidentally.

"Ouch, ouch my hand, honey, you have to stop this right now. This is madness, and you must stop this," Winnie retorted.

Immediately his wife became his next victim, he unwittingly dropped the gun and suddenly became worried and rushed to attend to his wife. "Ouch, my hand, my hand," Winnie screamed at her husband, saying she knows how grave the actions of the camp members against her husband is but this isn't the way to go about it. She then turned to Rebecca.

"Are you ok?" she asked.

Rebecca muttered in response and said how can she be ok when she's bleeding.

"He shot me in the arm," said Rebecca.

Winnie immediately went for the gun, took it off him, then put the gun away, even as she continues to calm her husband, saying, "It's ok, honey, you don't have to do this."

The crowd observed that Winnie has successfully disarmed her husband, they rushed out of their hiding to assist Rebecca and Winnie to stop their bleeding from gunshot wounds.

"Why did you take a bullet for me, I thought you hated me?" asked Rebecca.

"I don't hate you; I only hate what you did and your lifestyle as well," replied Winnie.

Jarrod collected the gun from Winnie, then asked Berger to please hold the gun while he sorts this whole thing out. Rebecca unwittingly became overwhelmed by Winnie's benignity, and suddenly turned to her and thanked her for staking her life for hers.

"You deserve to live; we all do, despite your faults," said Winnie.

The atmosphere between these former friends is now adversarial, and anything is expected. Stacy immediately stepped in and said she's calling the Police because this attack on their camp shouldn't go unpunished, insisting they'll be pressing charges against the Evangelist. Stacy then reached for her phone, in her bid to call Prophet Gregory and inform him of what just transpired, and obviously, the prophet would have run as fast as a speeding bullet to give Ambrose a taste of his own medicine. Rebecca interjected and said she'd rather not, because there isn't any need for that.

"What about his wife that took a bullet for me?" Asked Rebecca.

Stacy seems to be having none of it and asked who the hell Ambrose think he is, and insisted that Ambrose can't just walk away freely after causing her harm and disturbing the peace of this camp. Rebecca immediately toned down the fiery remark coming from Stacy by reminding her she's the injured party here, and what Ambrose just did, made her realise Ambrose is going through so much pain inside him and as such she won't be pressing any charges.

Berger immediately suggested they rush Rebecca and Winnie to the camp clinic for treatment right away. Jarrod turned to Winnie, and reminded her it was her he saw at the hospital on the day they brought Ambrose to the hospital.

"Of course, it's me, and his name is Fredrick, don't call him Ambrose," said Winnie.

"Can I help you with that, you're bleeding," asked Jarrod.

"Ok, thank you," said Winnie. Jarrod helped tie the gunshot wound to stop the bleeding, while Berger suggested for a second time that Winnie and Rebecca should be taken to the camp clinic for treatment. Fredrick interjected, and said his wife will not go in there, and that he'd rather take his wife to the hospital outside this camp.

Berger then went to Rebecca, and offered to take her to the clinic, saying she's bleeding, and something needed to be done about her arm.

"Ok, thank you," said Rebecca.

Evangelist Fredrick then turned to his wife and suggested to her that she shouldn't have put herself in the line of fire. "I know you have been struggling with coming to terms with all that have happened to you, but firing a shot at her isn't the best way out of this," said Winnie.

The Evangelist helped his wife up, and apologised, saying he's so sorry and that he never intended to fire a single shot at anyone. He then offered to take her to the hospital. Winnie muttered and told her husband that when he reunited with his family, she thought their troubles are over, she'd no idea a drama like this one was waiting to happen, she then asked him to take her to the hospital.

Just as Winnie and her husband are about to make their way to hospital, Berger informed the Evangelist that the gun will be with him for now, and the Evangelist isn't going away with it.

Stefan interjected and immediately prevailed on Berger to hand his gun over to him, promising to keep it far away from crazy Ambrose. Berger then handed the gun to Stefan yet said if Ambrose returns to the camp in an attempt to pull similar stunt, then they will have no choice but to shoot him, or get the Police involved.

As Winnie and her husband approached the car park, Peter and Jordan drove into the camp, Jordan saw his parents approaching and immediately rushed out of the car just as Peter attempts to park the car properly. Jordan then rushed to his mum, asking her if everything ok, pointing to her hand, and said she's bleeding.

Though in pain, Winnie didn't make a fuss about her bleeding arm, as she told Jordan she's ok, but things would've been worst if she hadn't gotten to the camp on time.

Moments later, Peter got out of the car, and asked his mum if the residents of the camp caused the injury in her arm. Winnie shook her head and said the residents of the camp obviously didn't cause the injury but their dad did, and she's glad their dad didn't erroneously kill Rebecca.

"Seriously, mum, you mean dad shot at you, and why would he do a thing like that?" asked Jordan. Evangelist Fredrick interjected as he quickly absolved himself of any deliberate attempt to shoot his wife, and asked Jordan of why he would want to kill his mum. He then told his sons that he inadvertently fired the shot at Rebecca but their mum put herself in the line of fire, in her attempt to save Rebecca. He then apologised, saying he's sorry for putting his family through this.

"Your dad is right, I put myself in the line of fire to save her," said Winnie.

"How bad is it?" asked Peter.

"Bad enough as you can see, but I'm glad the bone isn't fractured," said Winnie.

Peter became worried sick that his dad may have hurt a lot more people, he then asked his mum if any other person was hurt by his dad's action. Winnie had to open up to Peter that Rebecca was also injured. Peter became quite exasperated about the level of damage his dad may have caused, he immediately inquired about Rebecca's condition from his mum.

Winnie had to put his mind to rest, as she told Peter that Rebecca was shot in the arm as well but she can't tell if it fractured her bone but she has been taken to the camp clinic.

"Where is she? Let's take her to the hospital, and I don't want this turning into a police case," said Peter.

"No, stop, don't go any further, they're all scantily dressed in there, and it's not a sight to behold, I wonder how your dad would've lived in a place like this," Winnie retorted.

Evangelist Fredrick immediately suggested they get going, and that there isn't any need dawdling around any further because their mum needs to start going to the hospital, to get treated.

Peter turned around and suggested to his mum to go with his dad to the hospital, while he will drive Alisabel's to the hospital and then turned to Jordan before urging him to carefully drive the car they came with home. With this, they wouldn't have any reason to pay a second visit to the camp, and minutes later, they all left the camp.

By the evening of the same day, Orla dialled Eric's phone as she's keen to let Eric in on a little gossip, after all, he now has the last laugh.

"Hey Orla, how are you?" asked Eric.

Orla couldn't wait to dispense of all pleasantries, before accusing Eric of shying away from the camp because Ambrose and Rebecca were at the helm of affairs in the camp.

Funny enough, Eric didn't contest Orla's assertion about why he has stayed away from the camp all this while. He then said since she knew about his decision to stay away from the camp, why then Is she revisiting the matter because it makes him uncomfortable.

Orla laughed, even as she prodded Eric with more questions, and asking if it meant he signed out of his Luciferian belief over a minor tiff with Rebecca.

Eric suddenly got chatty with Orla, as he asked her, what's it she expects since Ambrose now runs the camp and Rebecca is his partner. He then opened up to her that he really doesn't enjoy people sniggering and making mockery of him as some kind of a loser, whenever he comes around.

"What about your other friends in the camp, did you turn your back on us as well?" asked Orla.

Eric burst into laughter, and reminded Orla he wouldn't do a thing like that, insisting he has a lot of friends in the camp even before Rebecca joined the Luciferian society.

Orla didn't hesitate any further before letting the cat out of the bag, and immediately suggested to Eric that he can return to the camp now that the fairy tale of Ambrose and Rebecca's relationship has taken a fatal turn.

"What do you mean, a fatal turn, did anybody die? Please fill me in," said Eric.

Orla agreed with Eric and said it's actually been a year since he visited the camp, but he doesn't need to have his ears on the ground to know the happenings in the camp.

"To start with, Eric, Ambrose no longer manages the camp," said Orla.

"What, how, and why was he removed?" asked Eric.

Orla found thrill in narrating Ambrose's story, saying he was sick and was taken to the hospital, only for the nurse attending to him to discover it was her husband who was presumed dead that was just brought in for treatment.

"What, this must be the biggest joke of the century, is Ambrose still living in the camp?" asked Eric.

"Not at all, his family took him in, and helped him with his memory," said Orla.

Eric was taken aback by these new twists, and asked when this happened, Orla narrated further that the Ambrose thing happened about three months ago.

"But a story like that should have been in the news, and why didn't I know of it?" asked Eric.

Orla continued to give flesh to her story and said the camp authorities pleaded with Ambrose's family to keep it quiet. More so, Ambrose's family don't want the news of him running around in a Luciferian camp were hordes of people move around in the camp, scantily dressed, coming out in the open.

"Ambrose is a nice guy, Rebecca just took advantage of his vulnerability, and how is she?" asked Eric. Orla didn't hesitate to let Eric know that Rebecca is in the camp clinic nursing her bullet wound.

"Bullet wound! How come, and who shot her?" asked Eric.

Orla didn't stop until she put the icing on the cake as she tells her story, in a bid to let Eric know how Rebecca's actions stinks to high heaven. She then proceeded to tell Eric that Ambrose returned to the camp seeking answers, but disarmed Stefan and then pointed the gun at members and he shot Rebecca in the process as she escaped with a bullet wound to her arm.

"As much as I hate Rebecca's actions, I feel for her," said Eric. Orla wasn't quite pleased that Eric still felt for Rebecca in the manner he just did, she immediately reminded him Rebecca brought this on herself, and asked why he has to feel for her.

It's embarrassingly obvious that Eric isn't as cruel as Orla wants him to be, he interjected and said it's a shame that this much has happened within a space of three months and he knew nothing about it.

"If you'd kept in touch, you would have known," replied Orla.

"No worries, I will visit the camp one of these days to see you and know how Rebecca is fairing," said Eric. Orla exclaimed and didn't hesitate to accuse Eric of planning on returning fast to the camp, because the competition is off. Eric smiled and said he's returning fast because he cares about Rebecca and just want to be sure she's ok.

"Ok, see you when you come around," said Orla.

"Ok, thank you for the gist, though it's heart wrenching," said Eric.

Lucky enough the bullet from the gunshot spared Winnie's bones and there wasn't any fracture because the bullet pierced through her flesh and came out from the other side. Her treatment went well, and she immediately decided to do something about her husband to see if there's a way out of his dilemma.

A day later, Winnie dialled Reverend Fitzgerald's phone.

"Hello reverend, how are you doing?" she asked.

"I'm good, Winnie, how is my Evangelist doing?" asked Rev. Fitzgerald. Winnie replied to the reverend that her husband is doing great, but then suggested to the reverend to have a word with her husband. Reverend Fitzgerald interjected and asked Winnie if anything is the matter and then inquired to know if the Evangelist is ok. Winnie reminded the reverend that her husband is facing too many struggles inside him, and told the reverend that her husband returned to the camp yesterday seeking answers, and by the time she got there he had a gun in his hand.

"A gun, what for?" asked Rev. Fitzgerald.

Winnie paused for a while, then said the gun was retrieved from a resident of the camp who first pointed the gun at him, he in turn tried using the gun to protect himself, while requesting answers from Rebecca. This sudden revelation struck a raw nerve in the reverend and left him quite exasperated as he interjected saying he hopes the Evangelist didn't go ahead with it. Winnie had feared that there's a certain inevitability that her husband might slip further into depression if nothing is done to help him. Sadly, Winnie had to open up to the reverend that her husband did hurt someone with the gun, and if not for her intervention it would have been worst.

"What! You meant he hurt someone?" asked the reverend.

"Yes, he did, he shot Rebecca in the arm, and if not for the fact that I took the second bullet he would have killed her," said Winnie.

"Bullet? Don't tell me your husband shot you," said Rev. Fitzgerald.

Winnie smiled and said she's only smiling because God intervened that's why the drama of the previous day didn't turn out to be ghastly, and then concurred she took a bullet in the arm but she's fine since her arm isn't fractured. Reverend Fitzgerald got all panicky, and even as he held the phone by his ear, his hands were a shudder as he paused to listen to all Winnie had to say. But after a while he proceeded to ask Winnie if she's calling him from the hospital or what.

Winnie on the other hand could sense the reverend's anxiety from his voice, and decided to put his mind at rest. She immediately told him she's fine and already at home after being treated in the hospital yesterday, and after all, it's a mere flesh wound because she's lucky the bullet didn't break any bone and didn't get the best of her.

Reverend Fitzgerald muttered and said what just happened implies they'll need to do a lot of praying, and he will have a word with the Evangelist, he then urged Winnie to continue trusting God for her husband, promising her that everything will be fine.

"Thank you, reverend," said Winnie.

Immediately the phone call with Winnie ended, the reverend decided to give Evangelist Fredrick a call but stopped suddenly, he stood up from his seat and walked around his living room, with too many questions running through his mind. The Evangelist's difficulties left the reverend worried sick and shaking the heaviness of guilt is also a big ask. Interestingly, instead of calling the Evangelist immediately and talking to him about what he just heard, Reverend Fitzgerald went into intense prayer and fasting as he tried to understand from God, how to deal with the debacle his beloved Evangelist found himself.

By the cool of evening, few days later, Winnie returned from work and walked to the back garden where her husband was seated, with a Christian Literature in his hand. He was still cheesed up in the wake of his disappointing act in the Bliss camp, just days before.

He welcomed her from work and asked how her day went.

"Your hand, how is it?" he asked, sombrely, and reminded her she should've waited to be healed of her injuries before resuming work. Winnie played down his concerns, and said she's fine, and it's just a mere flesh wound.

Acting in haste and repenting later is now the Evangelist present circumstance, but Winnie seems not to be holding his feet to the fire for his failures. She kind of empathised with him, and didn't give him the dressing down, to avoid exacerbating the troubles inside a struggling man. But his wife's silence speaks volumes, and he knows it, he then gave his wife this look that speaks volume, like saying "he might be out but not down", and she doesn't need to burst a blood vessel to get him to understand how grim things are.

Going back to what he's used to, is like a person returning to a comfortable pair of shoes, and that to him, is a perfect rational thought that makes a lot of sense, but embracing his new life still seem difficult and remains a struggle.

The Evangelist visited the camp the week before, thinking the answers he will get will detoxify the negative emotions within, but that trip was nothing but a damp squib. This whirlwind of hurt didn't go away, and arguably, the Evangelist went into a camp that's hostile to Christians, and expecting a soft landing. Winnie kind of understand the fact that her husband is still a bit rough around the edges, as per what's expected of a Christian, but he isn't anything like a loose cannon.

Instead of allowing him to blunder through, she reminded him he needed help and she has had words with the reverend, and he didn't' make a fuss about his wife decision to reach out to Reverend Fitzgerald. He's glad to have his wife be the voice of caution that will always have his ears, particularly now that he's trying to adjust to something that's perfect semblance of a normal family life.

It's now two months since the visit of Brandon Moore to the Bliss Luciferian Camp that ended rather on a bizarre note. Unfortunately, Brandon Moore was unforgiving and had decided to do something about Gregory Helsing. It's sunset, with the night fast approaching, Brandon Moore is preparing a hexing ceremony for midnight.

A ceremony meant to teach Prophet Gregory Helsing a lesson of his life, for walking out on him, and most importantly, for not giving him his due reverence of kissing his ring as a way of saying goodbye to him. This isn't Brandon Moore reaching for his sword and not intending to pull it out of its scabbard, he actually intends to use his sword this time, as he visits his wrath on Prophet Gregory.

Once this night is over, and dawn sets in, the very energetic Prophet Gregory Helsing will find out if his vigour is still intact, and if he's lucky, he might escape with some scratches.

Prophet Gregory Helsing woke up the next morning, feeling quite poorly, and so sick that he couldn't get down from his bed, he'd wanted to get an ambulance but felt it wouldn't look good if members of his camp perceived their all-knowing prophet is sick and unable to heal himself. He immediately asked his driver to help him out of bed and take him to the hospital immediately. It didn't take long before they arrived Genesis Medical Centre which is closest to the Bliss Camp.

The doctors began attending to Prophet Gregory immediately he was wheeled in. Hours later, a full body scan result was ready, followed by a brain scan, and it isn't good.

The doctor's disposition tells it all, as the scan result revealed Gregory Helsing has two sudden aggressive brain tumours that are inoperable.

"Doctor, what's the problem, it's like the scan result isn't good," asked Prophet Gregory.

The doctors have no choice but to disclose the result of the scan to the prophet and said the scan reveals he has two aggressive brain tumours that are now inoperable. The doctors then informed the prophet that what makes these tumours rather bizarre was that they looked like horns. The mention of the tumours looking like horns brought about the sudden realisation that he has been hexed by Brandon Moore. Unfortunately, Gregory Helsing had no knowledge that Brandon Moore did actually perform a hexing ceremony on him the night before, and the sudden tumour was the result of that ceremony. Yet, he has to explore the options available to him.

"Doctor, if you say the tumour is inoperable, what other treatment options do I have?" Asked Prophet Gregory.

"I am sorry, there's nothing we can do," replied the doctor.

It now dawned on Prophet Gregory that his time is out. He then asked the doctors how much time he has left. The ambience was quite eerie when the doctor replied him, saying he has just two weeks at most. Arguably, this is where his walking out on Brandon Moore got him, death, slow and painful death. Walking out on Brandon Moore isn't anything short of walking out on Moloch himself.

# CHAPTER

## THIRTEEN

### *The Master Planner*

A week after Winnie informed Reverend Fitzgerald about the gun-pointing incident, the reverend received a phone call from Evangelist Fredrick.

"Hello Evangelist, it's good to hear from you," said Rev. Fitzgerald. He then told the Evangelist he's aware of the incident at the Luciferian camp and he has been praying for him since then.

Evangelist Fredrick seemed to have gotten a grip since the incident that took place a week before, he assured the reverend that his action was a foolish act that won't repeat itself, and that's in the past now. Reverend Fitzgerald knew for sure that God is already working on the Evangelist, but then acknowledged he's aware of Fredrick's struggles and then urged him not let it get into his head.

Evangelist Fredrick then steered the conversation away to the reason he called the reverend in the first place, and said he had a revelation the night before.

"A revelation! Please, tell me all about it," said the reverend.

The Evangelist immediately began narrating to the reverend that God told him He deliberately led him to that camp just to show him the extent to which Bliss camp has infiltrated Europe, and the terrible things they do to Christians, and that God instructed him to sort out the decay close to him instead of going on a far missionary assignment.

"And this decay is the Luciferian camp, I guess?" asked Rev. Fitzgerald.

"Yes, of course," said Evang. Fredrick.

Reverend Fitzgerald immediately realised his fasting and prayers to God concerning the Evangelist has been answered, but asked the Evangelist for a second time if he meant God said he deliberately sent him to that camp. Evangelist Fredrick continued and said he has learnt many things in his troubled life, and knows when God speaks.

He then said he asked God why He should take him so low to the point of living in a squalor that looks like a nudist camp. The Evangelist made it clear to the reverend that he actually expressed his mind to God, saying He should've told him what he wants him to do instead of making him to live in the camp as Satanist and away from his family while presumed to be dead.

The reverend listened keenly and nodded as the Evangelist narrated his encounter with God, and funnily, after this encounter with God, the Evangelist woke up the next morning and suddenly realised that majority of his memory has been restored, he could now remember a lot about his past.

The Evangelist then proceeded to say God said He used Rebecca to make him live in their mist and earn their trust.

Arguably, God knew that if the Evangelist's memory is intact, he would have struggled to live among these Satanists.

"To what purpose?" asked Rev. Fitzgerald.

Evangelist Fredrick replied, saying God wants him to stop every Satanist practice that goes on in that camp, as well as stop every lifestyle of nudism in that camp and build a church in the camp for him. Reverend Fitzgerald soon realised that his decision to reroute the Evangelist's missionary work wasn't his, but God's. He has been beating himself up for setting this rollercoaster of cacophony of setbacks in motion, but this light-bulb moment meant he has now come to terms with himself.

The Evangelist told the reverend that God specifically told him that the Bliss camp is the biggest threat to the Christian faith in the entirety of Europe. He reiterated that this camp has suddenly become a gangrene that God needed to cut out. "Reverend, do you know the Bliss camp is behind most scandals against the church? It's behind most freak accidents for which the church was accused of negligence. The Bliss camp is behind the mass exodus from the Christian faith in Europe, in the last decade," said the Evangelist.

He also tried to disabuse the Priest of any erroneous perception of him as a conflicted man, he immediately informed the priest that the gun incident wasn't intentional, it was rather serendipity, because he disarmed someone, only to use gun to protect himself but panicked at a point and the gun went off.

The Reverend interjected and asked the Evangelist how he intends to go about this, because the church doesn't associate with violence, and shooting his way like he did days ago isn't the way out. He then assured the priest that violence isn't his thing.

"God said he has positioned a woman to help me achieve this," said the Evangelist.

"Are you suggesting, Rebecca?" Asked Rev Fitzgerald.

"I think so, because I don't know of any other woman," replied Evangelist Fredrick.

Evangelist Fredrick immediately urged the reverend not to worry about the fall-out from this, and assured the reverend that everything will be done peacefully. Suggesting he intends to talk with them as an insider, as one of them, and that's the reason God made him live in their midst.

The sheer drudgery associated with this task makes the Evangelist the best candidate for this assignment, and God didn't make a mistake to have chosen a man whose will is already sold out to the service of Jesus Christ.

"I have been praying for you, and I'm glad to hear it's all the Lord's doing, and we'll have to talk about the best way to approach this," said Rev. Fitzgerald.

"Ok, reverend, thank you," said Evangelist Fredrick.

Just as he's about to drop the phone, the reverend asked Evangelist Fredrick if he has discussed this revelation with Winnie, but the Evangelist replied to him, saying no, he hasn't but he will.

"Ok, please do," said Rev. Fitzgerald.

By the evening of the same day, the family was at the dining table, and having their dinner. Immediately after taking his last bite of the steak in his plate and drinking some water. He then cleared his throat and said he was on the phone earlier today discussing his revelation with Reverend Fitzgerald.

"Revelation, what it's it about? Please, share it with us," said Winnie.

Jordan interjected and asked his dad what the revelation was about. Evangelist Fredrick calmly told them God is just making a meaning of why he found himself in that Satanist camp. Jordan interjected again, with a little sarcasm this time, as he asked his dad if there can be a positive reason for living in the mist of scantily dressed people. Winnie immediately urged Jordan to calm down, and allow his dad to share his revelation, she then turned to her husband, and urged him to please tell them all about it. The Evangelist then proceeded to say God wanted him to see the terrible practices going on in that camp, and the far-reaching impact of their actions on Christians near him while he's travelling to other nations to tell people about God.

Peter immediately echoed his brother's earlier exception, and asked his dad that if God wants him to see this despicable life style, God should have communicated it through other means instead of sending him to that God forsaken camp, unconscious, and making him live as one of them.

Evangelist Fredrick smiled and said they can't question God because He's all-knowing, but then said he asked God a similar question, but God said he showed it to him, and he asked God when He did that. God then reminded him of the day Luciferians advocating nudism came to the national television station during the news broadcast, and God also reminded him of the day he read about the Satanic activities of the Bliss Luciferian camp in the papers.

As they speak of these past events, it suddenly dawned on Evangelist's family that he could remember. Something that left his family speechless because they find it to be alarmingly miraculous. Even as they celebrate the return of the Evangelist's memory, the conversation at hand remains on the table.

Winnie confirmed that God is right about nudists coming to sell their lifestyle on the national broadcasting television channel. She reminded her husband of when a couple of nudists who openly claimed they are Luciferians were invited to the television channel to talk about their lifestyle. Yet she pointed out to her husband that they didn't support it and that they actually find it to be despicable as well. Glad that the Evangelist memory is back and he remembers what Winnie was alluding to because it was aired as part of the news hour, when most citizens will have to watch it.

Evangelist Fredrick affirmed they did watch that news and proceeded to say that God said they only hated what they saw and just as many other Christians, but did nothing about it.

"We did pray and asked God to intervene, to bring an end to this wickedness and filth in our nation," said Winnie.

Her husband replied her saying, he did remind God that he and his family spent considerable time praying concerning the activities of nudists in their nation, after watching their effrontery to bravely take up the news hour, but God chastised him saying, yes, they did pray concerning the airing of the Satanists lifestyle on the television just like many other Christians did, and He answered their prayers, but it all ended there.

And that didn't go far enough because praying alone about the situation isn't enough. On hearing that God answered their prayers, Winnie heaved a sigh of relief, but the Evangelist proceeded to say that God said He answered their prayers, but they needed to have taken a stand to bring the answer into manifestation. He then insisted that God said he expected them to take a stand, and He God Almighty will then go ahead of them to cause the change they prayed about to happen. Like Shadrach Meshach and Abednego who took a stand and God could not ignore but send his son to preserve them from the heat of the fire.

God had to send His son even before his appointed time of unveiling because these three Hebrew Children decided to take a stand for what they believe in.

Jordan immediately reminded his dad that his missionary work must count for something.

"Does it mean God didn't recognise your Evangelism in this nation and missionary work abroad as taking a stand for Him?"

The Evangelist immediately put Jordan's mind to rest and said God did recognise he has done a lot, yet said He singled him out for this assignment.

"Because He knows I'll do anything He asks of me," said Evangelist Fredrick.

Winnie was impressed to learn that it was God dealing with her family all along, and was glad that her husband's sojourn, though not palatable, ended in praise because God has put the sun over the cloud of darkness on this family.

Interestingly, this family accepted this revelation whole-heartedly, because God didn't only reveal his intentions to the Evangelist, he completely restored his memory, as a way of making it known to this family that he's restoring this Evangelist to his former glory.

"Hmm, you've been busy talking with God," said Winnie. Her husband nodded in affirmation and with a smile, and said of course God finds it worthy to put this assignment in his hands, and, "He has obviously made clear what He expects of me," he said.

But what riles his wife and sons the most is the fact that he has suddenly regained his memory after this encounter with God, which made his wife to belief him the more. Their celebration of this miracle isn't out of place because his encounter with God isn't in doubt. Winnie interjected and asked further as she's keen to know the granular details of the assignment her husband is referring to, but she suddenly paused to allow him finish his sentence.

He then continued, and said God wanted him to live with them, make friends with them and earn their trust.

"To what end is this revelation," asked Winnie. The Evangelist then said God wants him to win residents of the camp to Him and also build a church in that camp. Winnie interjected again and asked her husband how he intends to achieve this assignment without scuffles. There's this unspoken concern about how he might carry out this assignment without butting heads with residents of the Bliss Luciferian Camp, not to forget that Stefan had wanted to shoot him for returning to the camp.

Just like Van gogh, Pablo Picasso, Leonardo Da Vinci or any other artist, the most important feature of an artist is that they have a picture in their mind, even before the first stroke of the brush is applied on the canvas, so is this Evangelist who seems convinced that God has already handed the camp to him. He sees victory, that's why he accepted this challenge, and all he has to do is just to make the move while God will take it from there.

The Evangelist then said there is work to do, and that he'll rather get on with God's instructions than cower away in fear. After all, his wife has pulled herself up by the bootstraps and she is willing to go the whole hog with him. The Evangelist muttered and said he will need to win back his friends. Jordan interjected, for a second time and reminded his dad, if it's Rebecca he's talking about, he shouldn't forget in a hurry that he just shot at her days ago.

Evangelist Fredrick told his family that he will have to rely on the grace of God, to get back the friends he has in the camp. Funnily, his family seems supportive as Peter suggested to his dad, he would have to return to being Ambrose to get back his friends, but not necessarily scantily clothed like them. Winnie on the other hand, suggested they'll need tact and charm to achieve this, and assured her husband she's with him in this.

Jordan was a bit cautious, as he reminded his dad that the hatred he had for himself will be nothing compared with what the members of the camp now have for him. He then urged his dad to be cautiously optimistic. Evangelist Fredrick appreciated their contribution and then thanked his wife and his sons for their support.

Moments after their table talk, the Evangelist then headed for the bedroom, Winnie followed him as they continued their conversation.

"Now, I know why," he muttered.

"Why? What are you insinuating?" She questioned.

"Why I didn't get romantic with Rebecca, God held me back from consummating my relationship with her, he'd it in mind to return me to my family," replied the Evangelist.

"I'm glad God had our back all along," replied Winnie.

Days later, at the Bliss Camp, Stacy walked into the gym centre and saw Rebecca keeping fit, and going about her day as though nothing happened. Stacy cheekily asked her if she's fit enough to be here. Rebecca burst into laughter and asked Stacy if there's any law banning a person with a gunshot wound from the gym centre. Not long after they dispensed of all pleasantries, Stacy asked her how she's feeling and said the drama of the other day is still a nightmare.

"Yeah, tell me about it, my life has always been a tale with too many dead ends," said Rebecca.

Stacy smiled and asked Rebecca if she considers her relationship with Ambrose one of those dead ends. Rebecca interjected, and said of course, the death of her husband in the prime of his life was one dead end, and the abrupt end of her budding relationship with Ambrose happens to be another.

Stacy on the other hand considers Rebecca lifestyle to be nothing but a tedious waste of good judgements. She immediately reminded Rebecca that it would've been better if they both agree that her dead ends, isn't life serving her its cruellest but because she made too many bad choices.

"Bad choices, hmm. My husband isn't, but Ambrose, maybe yes," replied Rebecca.

Stacy gave Rebecca a trip down memory lane and reminded her of the day she told her this would blow up on their faces one day. Her prodigious posture of holding onto Ambrose can be a kiss of death because this stranger's story is still unfolding. Rebecca smiled and accepted Stacy did warn her, but said unlike Turkeys, she thought she could prevent Christmas, but things went embarrassingly ugly and almost fatal. Stacy wasn't quite pleased with Rebecca's decision not to press charges against Ambrose, as she continues to insist, she still doesn't understand why Ambrose should be let off the hook after causing a scene in this camp. Rebecca thinks there's no need for such degree of censure, insisting it's up to her to press charges and she isn't going to do that now because the circumstance presents itself. She then asked Stacy what if Ambrose's family had pressed charges against her, and after all she was first in the wrong.

"It implies, your action can best be described as shooting yourself on the feet," Stacy retorted. It's arguably obvious that Rebecca didn't find Ambrose's company tedious, as she still has fond memories of him and despite all that has happened, she's still convinced that no love was lost between them. She proceeded to inform Stacy of her intention to pay Ambrose a visit.

Stacy always finds Rebecca highly disagreeable and didn't hesitate to remind her friend that she's about to add to her catalogue of bad decisions, pointing out to Rebecca that Ambrose specifically said he doesn't want her referring to him as Ambrose.

"Yes, I understand, but I've gotten so attached to that name, and letting go of that name will take some time," said Rebecca.

"You mentioned paying Ambrose a visit, to what end, if I may ask?" asked Stacy.

Rebecca opened up, and said she intend to visit him because she wants to tender her unreserved apology to him and to his family, and maybe that will help him find closure. Stacy burst into laughter at Rebecca's naivety and said three years together with Ambrose is a short period of acquaintance, but to Rebecca it's something that looks more like a lifetime.

She then urged her not to make the mistake of thinking she knows Ambrose that well, and what if he attacks her again because people never find closure to things like this, particularly for a man who went full tonto in the camp the other day. Rebecca reminded Stacy that Ambrose isn't a violent person, and that the gun entered his hand by chance, but then insists it's a chance she's ready to take. She made it clear, she needed to appeal to his conscience so they can put this behind them.

"You want to keep this quiet to prevent the management of the camp taking this matter to the board?" asked Stacy. Rebecca interjected and said of course, and she's quite glad her name didn't make headlines when the family of Ambrose discovered him. She didn't stop short of suggesting to Stacy that the board and even the prophet must have been furnished with the granular details of Ambrose's action, but why they stayed quiet on the subject is what riles her.

Stacy wasn't as benign this time as she did before, this time she prodded Rebecca with her questions. She proceeded to ask if she didn't find it paradoxical to think Ambrose will love being in the service of Lucifer after they found a bible on him, on the day they found him floating in the sea, and good to hear she's looking for a quiet way out of this.

Days later, Rebecca and Stacy dressed up and looking their best as they paid Evangelist Fredrick a visit, they stood by the door to Evangelist Fredrick's house, and knocked on the door, and asked if there's anyone home.

It didn't take long before Peter opened the door.

"Hmm, it's you, and what are you doing here?" he asked.

Rebecca immediately apologised to Peter, saying she's sorry if he feels bothered by her presence, but then asked him if Ambrose is at home. Peter wasn't quite a welcoming host, as he interjected and questioned who Rebecca is referring to as Ambrose. He then cautioned her not to refer to his dad as Ambrose, and that his dad's name is Fredrick Douglas.

"Oh, Fredrick, I get it, sorry about that, and is he home, please?" asked Rebecca.

Peter replied to her, saying his dad is at home but he doesn't think her coming to see his dad is a good idea considering her last encounter with him. Rebecca agreed that the odds aren't in her favour, and said she understands her visit might be perceived as offensive, but she doesn't intend to cause any trouble, just that she wants to apologise to him for everything that happened.

Stacy interjected subtly and told Peter not to give way to such a gloomy thought, and said Rebecca is only here to make things right, she then urged him to please give her the opportunity to do so. Rebecca isn't some kind of debt collector that has come to collect, she's just a woman showing contrition.

"Ok, you can come in," said Peter. Rebecca and Stacy then walked into the house and made themselves comfortable. While Rebecca attempts to sit on the couch, she turned to Peter and asked if his mum is at home.

"Of course, she is, let me get my dad," said Peter, who then walked to the door of his dad's bedroom, and told him Rebecca is here to see him.

Winnie got up from bed and inquired to know which Rebecca Peter is referring, before asking if he's referring to the Rebecca from the Luciferian Camp.

"Yes, of course," said Peter.

"I hope she's fully clothed?" asked Winnie. Peter understands the nuance in her mum's question to mean nothing but banter and said Rebecca obviously won't come to town without having her clothes on.

"What's she doing here? This woman has guts," Winnie muttered.

Peter seemed to have come to terms with Rebecca's visit and said she has come to apologise to his dad, he then urged his mum to give her the opportunity to do so. As opposed to his wife, Evangelist Fredrick immediately got up from bed, and said he would by no means send them away, saying he's glad she's here, and it's a good thing this meeting is taking place. Winnie was out of spirit, and insists there can't be anything good about Rebecca's visit.

It wasn't tongue in cheek this time as she asked her husband what's good about this meeting, and that the sound of gunshot was what she heard in their last meeting.

"I'll need her help in fulfilling God's plan for that camp," said Evangelist Fredrick.

Winnie nodded and said if her husband thinks Rebecca is of value then so be it, she then walks to the living room. Rebecca is no longer considered an encumbrance, but a guest.

"Hey Rebecca, you're welcome," said Winnie. Rebecca turned around and said she admired Winnie's forbearance, and for not treating her so contemptibly, she then thanked Winnie for accepting her into her home.

"You're already in, my son allowed you in not me, but you're welcome, and how did you locate our place?" asked Winnie.

Rebecca told Winnie she looked it up from the open register. Winnie became jocular as she asked Rebecca, she hoped she'd her clothes on when she left the Bliss camp. Stacy obviously doesn't like Winnie's benign sarcasm, as she reminded her, they obviously don't go about town nude or scantily dressed.

Winnie steered the conversation away from the platitudes of banter, and asked Rebecca about the injury on her arm, inquiring about how the gunshot wound is healing. She drew closer to her to take a look at her injury. Rebecca made light of her injury, saying as Winnie can see, she's better, and lucky enough the bullet didn't get the best of her, and thanked Winnie for her intervention. Winnie interjected and said maybe they're both lucky, she then asked her guests to make themselves comfortable, before asking what she should offer them.

Rebecca wasn't expecting any form of hospitality from her host, and immediately told Winnie that this isn't a social call, and offering them something won't be necessary either, because she's just here to see Fredrick briefly.

Stacy subtly interjected, saying she's aware that this family has long desired their absence, but their visit isn't one of comfort, but more like damage control, insisting they're only here to see if they can fix that which can't be fixed. Winnie first suggested a cup of tea, but realising that the weather is a bit hot, she decided to offer them an alternative.

"A glass of non-alcoholic red wine won't do you harm," said Winnie.

While Winnie attended to her guests, Evangelist Fredrick walked into the conversation. He turned to Rebecca and said hello to her, and then asked if he should welcome her, or say sorry about the other day but whichever way, she's welcome. Rebecca immediately appealed to Ambrose that she won't take much of his time, then exclaimed suddenly.

"Oh sorry, Fredrick, my bad, I don't know why I keep referring to you as Ambrose," said Rebecca. Fredrick didn't hesitate to say he'd no idea why Rebecca keeps calling him that, saying the name Ambrose reminds him of something unpleasant.

Rebecca agreed that the name Ambrose reminds the Evangelist of the bitterest moments of his life, yet urged him not to worry. She promised she soon will get used to calling him Fredrick, but she's just here to apologise for the past. Evangelist Fredrick dismissed each of Rebecca's concerns, saying the past is past, but Rebecca remained convinced that people don't just put the past behind them in a whim and her last encounter with him makes her understand he's still struggling with the past, and she has come to make things right.

The Evangelist muttered saying heaven forbids that he will condescend to the barbarity of the previous week, that is nothing short of a bullyboy in the playground and insisted he has actually put all of it behind him and he's looking forward to the future.

"Please, I know I can't re-write the past but in future I will do better, and please pardon all my excesses," said Rebecca. Evangelist

Fredrick thanked Rebecca for coming, and also apologised for his actions against her. He then proceeded to say, that it is just days ago that he realised that their coming together was divine.

"Divine, how do you mean?" asked Stacy. This line of conversation isn't something Stacy expected, life isn't about coincidences but this serendipity needed to be explored further.

Evangelist Fredrick didn't see it fit to bore his guest with the details of his divine adventure and assured Rebecca, he'll tell her more about that in their next meeting, he then urged her not to be in a rush.

"Next meeting, what for?" asked Rebecca.

The Evangelist nodded and said things are a bit sketchy for now, but yes, there will be a next meeting. He then suggested that Stacy can come with her if she likes, but he just wants her to know he has got no grudge against her, and the past is already in the past. Winnie comes with a bottle of non-alcoholic wine and four glasses.

"Here you go," said Winnie, she then served herself, her husband, Rebecca and then Stacy.

Rebecca thanked Winnie for her kind gesture, and she then turned to the Evangelist and urged him to give her an idea of what this meeting is all about.

Stacy also thanked Winnie for her hospitality, Rebecca suddenly came to the realisation of how she admired the quintessence of Ambrose's family. After spending about an hour, Rebecca and Stacy left and returned to their camp.

Days later, Evangelist Fredrick had a second meeting with Rebecca and Stacy, this time they're seated in a restaurant. "Thank you for coming," said Evangelist Fredrick. Stacy didn't hesitate to ask what's it he want to talk about. In Rebecca's bid to avoid more awkward moments, she interjected and asked the Evangelist if his wife is aware of this meeting, saying she doesn't want any more of her trouble.

The Evangelist assured Rebecca that his wife is aware of the meeting, and after all, his wife was there when he told her about the need for a second meeting. He urged her not to worry, and that his wife understands that residual emotion between ex-lovers is easily rekindled, but this isn't one of such cases. Stacy muttered for a second time, but this time to sing Winnie's praises, as she said that Winnie is a woman with a large heart, and that if it were some other women, she wouldn't want her husband to ever meet with Rebecca again.

Rebecca is now bygone and a relic of the past. The Evangelist on the other hand seemed convinced that there's no way he would allow himself to be lustfully compromised by Rebecca as he returned to be in the company of his old friends. He's now a man on a mission but common sense demands that discretion is necessary. He then used his hand as gesture to request the attention of the waiter, and it didn't take long the waiter was by their side to take their orders. He then asked Rebecca what she wants the waiter to get them.

"Get me a bottle of water, he said and then turned to Rebecca and Stacy, and then asked them to tell the waiter what they cared to have.

Rebecca requested for a bottle of water just as the Evangelist, but Evangelist Fredrick immediately turned to them and urged them to eat something, saying this restaurant serves good meals, and they shouldn't bother with the fact that he's having just a bottle of water.

After much persuasion from the Evangelist, Stacy then turned to the waiter, and requested for beef lasagne. "What about drink?" asked the Waiter.

"Just a glass of coke," said Stacy.

Rebecca immediately changed her mind following Stacy's order, she then requested for some spring rolls, and a piece of chicken, and it didn't take long before the waiter brought their orders.

As they enjoyed their meals, the Evangelist then decided to talk about the reason behind their meeting. He then informed them of his intention to build a church in the Bliss Luciferian Camp.

"What, a church! Is that why you brought us here?" Stacy retorted.

Rebecca interjected and asked the Evangelist what he's getting at with this move. She blatantly asked if he thinks Zeppelin or even Prophet Gregory will let him anywhere near the camp, insisting there's not a cat in hell's chance that they would allow any attempt to build a church in the Bliss Camp. Evangelist Fredrick subtly reminded Stacy and Rebecca that he intends to go about this the right way, because he's going to speak to Zeppelin about this, and he knows for sure that this is a daunting task but he wants to begin with the two of them just as he's doing now.

Rebecca doesn't want to be taken for a ride, she needed all the cards on the table, and would rather not dive into the deep end of this plan with her eyes closed. She then asked the Evangelist what the end game is, insisting she sees the Evangelist going beyond just building a church. For what it was worth, the Evangelist isn't being dishonest about his intention, and said if given the opportunity he intends to do more than merely building a church. Stacy doesn't seem to like the direction of this conversation, she then stood up angrily and attempted to leave because she feared that Prophet Gregory will eat her and Rebecca for breakfast for being a part of this.

She immediately accused the Evangelist of planning to make Zeppelin chase them out of the camp, and hinting that he's climbing the wrong ladder. She then reminded him that Prophet Gregory Helsing sense of charity does not extend to people displaying acts of brigandage inside his camp.

Evangelist Fredrick knew that Stacy is establishing value, and had to tread softly, as he urged Stacy to calm down, saying there will be a plan in place for every resident of the camp, and that he also intends to speak to Prophet Gregory, after his meeting with Zeppelin. He then pleaded with Stacy, urging her to please stay, so they can talk about this. Funnily, Stacy continued standing and itching to leave, but Rebecca interjected and urged Stacy to come back, so they could hear him out.

Stacy is convinced that lives will be lost if Prophet Gregory learns of this, more so, Zeppelin will never give his blessing to this plan that's nothing but a dark rabbit hole, and urged Evangelist Fredrick not to expect them to follow him down this ugly path. She didn't take kindly the fact that he's torturing their ears with such an unthinkable wickedness, and if at all, this is one thing she will never acquiesce.

Rebecca constrained her friend urging her to sit down, saying there's no need to be too agitated, after all, nothing unsavoury is being shoved down their throat. Stacy has unwittingly become a sensitive goldfish that wouldn't want anything upsetting the status quo, she hesitated for a while, then returned to her seat. She then continued in the conversation, Evangelist Fredrick then began by telling them he was a missionary before the shipwreck that brought him to the camp, saying he's used to travelling around the world, to help people get back on the feet, and primarily to bring them closer to God.

Rebecca confirmed she has seen videos and pictures of him which suggests he's man of impressive personality and a man of wit. The Evangelist assured them he will help them find a place, and also help them find a better life, as opposed to the life they live at the moment.

"Didn't you see the peace in my wife, Winnie?" asked Evang. Fredrick. Stacy interjected insisting there's nothing wrong with living in a camp where people are scantily clothed, and in service of Lucifer, but he hesitated for a while before asking Stacy to look around the restaurant. Then muttered and said people are meant to live and go about their business clothed, and not remain cooped in a secret camp.

"That's a choice, and the choice is mine," replied Stacy.

Evangelist Fredrick then subtly asked her why she clothed herself while leaving the camp to meet with him in this restaurant. Stacy still didn't see any need for the hue and cry from the Evangelist, as she insisted that the only reason she left the camp clothed is just to stop the stereotyping.

The Evangelist turned to Stacy, and said she clothed herself before coming to town, not just because of the stereotyping but because she felt it isn't decent going about wearing close to nothing. Rebecca interjected and suggested to Stacy that they should give Ambrose the opportunity, maybe it's time for a change, insisting that this has nothing to do with abiding in Ambrose's indignation.

Stacy immediately got all riled up, as she became quite upset with Rebecca, accusing her of taking sides with him because he's her ex. It's obvious that Rebecca still has a soft spot for the Evangelist.

"I thought you and I were in locked steps," said Stacy.

"Hmm, Ambrose, I suggest you speak to Zeppelin, leave Stacy to me," said Rebecca. Evangelist Fredrick didn't belabour the subject further, to avoid the whole thing going out with a whimper. He then changed the subject to something else, and it didn't take time, the warm ambience returned. After spending some time with Rebecca and her friend in the restaurant, they said their goodbyes, and left.

Prophet Gregory Helsing was quite shaken by the latest diagnosis on his health, his health was deteriorating fast, and time is now of the essence. He immediately sent for Zeppelin, who visited the prophet almost immediately. The frail looking Prophet Gregory opened up to Zeppelin that Brandon Moore hexed him two days ago over the little disagreements they had during his visit.

"I'm dying, Zeppelin, Brandon Moore killed me, and I am reporting my own murder to you," Prophet Gregory reported. Zeppelin was quite emotional, seeing how poorly his prophet suddenly become, he then asked what the diagnosis was.

"I have less than two weeks, Zeppelin, two aggressive brain tumours, inoperable," said the prophet.

It's obvious that people don't rely on the kindness of their enemy, something prophet Gregory realised when it's already too late. With his face looking more like a man robbed at knife point, sympathy from Zeppelin is now the least of his concern. This prophet has to say goodbye to his Satanist camp that have awfully served as a bed of passion for most Luciferians in Europe. Members of the Bliss camp cosseted Prophet Gregory with their love, praise and loyalty, but those niceties are now a thing of the past.

Zeppelin was lost for words, as he imagined life without Prophet Gregory, who said he's now putting his house in order, and that there won't be any need going into any hospice for end-of-life care. Unfortunately, reporting his murder to Zeppelin is meaningless because Zeppelin don't have what it takes to confront Brandon Moore, the man currently holding the position of Moloch. Brandon Moore is a proud man, whose pride is obviously more than that of a peacock. His ego has been hurt and has obviously decided to teach Gregory Helsing a little lesson. More so, Lucian Gaia, Gregory Helsing's spiritual father, wouldn't be happy about how the meeting turned out, his deferred hope about this meeting obviously left him befuddled.

# CHAPTER

## FOURTEEN

*Charting a new course*

A week after his brief meeting with Rebecca and Stacy, Evangelist Fredrick decided it's time to start from the top of the food chain, and that would mean engaging Prophet Gregory. Instead of starting with the prophet, he decided that Zeppelin might provide the soft landing he needed, to kick star this process. Zeppelin is the big boss of the Bliss Luciferian Camp. Arguably, the Evangelist had no knowledge that God has already used Brandon Moore to take out Prophet Gregory, whom he feared could be his nemesis.

Immediately Evangelist Fredrick got to the entrance to Zeppelin's office, he turned to Zeppelin's secretary, and said hello to her.

"Hello, how can I be of help?" She asked. The Evangelist replied her saying he's here to see Zeppelin. The secretary welcomed him but asked if he has an appointment.

For what it's worth, this is his very first visit to Zeppelin's office outside the camp, most of the camp managers' dealings with Zeppelin are usually limited to the Bliss Luciferian Camp. And for personal reasons, Zeppelin ensured that his Luciferian dealings and proclivities are limited within the camp.

The secretary immediately dialled Zeppelin to let him know about the Evangelist's presence.

"Yes, Piper, I am listening, speak up," said Zeppelin.

"There's a gentleman here who wants to see you," said Piper.

Zeppelin asked if the gentleman in question has an appointment, but the secretary said he doesn't. Zeppelin interjected and asked who this gentleman is since there is no appointment, Piper turned to the Evangelist and asked.

"Your name, please?" asked Piper.

"Fredrick Douglas, I guess," replied the Evangelist. Piper finds Fredrick's response to be quite hysterical, and then asked the Evangelist if he's having a laugh, before asking if he's guessing his name or Fredrick Douglas is actually his name.

Evangelist Fredrick replied saying, he isn't guessing, just that Zeppelin might not know him by that name but by a different name, like, Ambrose.

Piper muttered and said this is quite strange, but then returned to the phone and continued her conversation with Zeppelin.

"He's Fredrick Douglas," said Piper. Funnily, the name Ambrose didn't strike a chord in Piper, she knew the name Ambrose as the name of the man managing the Bliss Luciferian Camp. Even though they haven't met face to face, she still didn't connect the dots enough to know that it is the same Ambrose that's standing before her.

But while the Evangelist had his conversation with Piper, he saw a bible on her desk and sensed the bible is hers, but even as they talked, he didn't make reference to the bible on Piper's desk.

"Fredrick Douglas, you said?" replied Zeppelin.

"Yes, of course, but he said you might know him with a different name, maybe, Ambrose, I guess," said Piper.

"Ooh goodness, Ambrose? Please, let him in," said Zeppelin.

The Evangelist walked into the office, and said hello to Zeppelin, then said it's been quite a while.

"What a visit, thoughts of you keep flooding my head, and how are you?" asked Zeppelin.

"I'm fine, Zeppelin, your office looks lovely," said Ambrose.

Zeppelin was quite ecstatic to see the guy he put in charge of the Bliss Luciferian Camp once again, saying he's glad to see the Evangelist after his un-ceremonial exit from the camp. He began by thanking the Evangelist and his family for keeping the Bliss Luciferian Camp away from the media storm when he reunited with his family but then asked what his visit is about.

The warm ambience suddenly turned sour as things took a rather bizarre twist when Evangelist Fredrick held his Bible up visibly and said he has come to sell God to him.

Zeppelin asked the Evangelist if he really meant he has come to sell God to him, he then chuckled saying, that sounds a bit cheeky. Evangelist Fredrick smiled and said he agrees with Zeppelin that what he just said might sound cheeky but he's serious about it, and Zeppelin is aware he's never been this serious. Zeppelin's smile dissipated immediately and morphed into a frown, as he frankly asked the Evangelist what sort of joke, he think this is, and then questioned if he told the Evangelist he's lacking a God that he would boldly walk into his office to talk about selling God to him.

He proceeded to ask the Evangelist if he's here to perform some visual illusion, then said he'd rather spend his time attending to a man showing him new tricks on cognitive illusion as opposed to the ruse that's coming from him. "You must be off your rocker, I suppose!" Exclaimed Zeppelin. Evangelist Fredrick maintained his cheerful disposition even as Zeppelin became quite incensed with the purpose of his visit, the Evangelist then urged Zeppelin not go all squawky with his next comment. Zeppelin then stopped for a moment and listened keenly to hear what the Evangelist's next comment is. The Evangelist then said God wants Zeppelin to work for him and "He said I should tell you this," said Evangelist Fredrick.

Zeppelin muttered and said he was bereft when he lost Ambrose's company, yet cautioned the Evangelist that allowing him to walk into his office doesn't give him the effrontery to start speaking gibberish to him. The Evangelist paused for a while, then told Zeppelin if he has asked about his whereabouts since he left the camp and the circumstances surrounding why he didn't return to the camp.

"Ooh, that's a good angle you're coming from, and why don't you tell me all about it?" asked Zeppelin.

Evangelist Fredrick then began by reminding Zeppelin that he's aware of the fact that the Bliss Luciferian Camp took advantage of his vulnerability to make him one of theirs.

Zeppelin didn't hesitate to let the Evangelist know, that making him one of them should be a thing of honour. Zeppelin got cheeky and took a dig at him as he reminded the Evangelist that his proposal isn't less ridiculous as attempting to sell a truck load of snow to Eskimos in the month of January. "You have said nothing, but doubling down on your stupidity," said Zeppelin. He proceeded to ask the Evangelist if he knew he did try their patience when attempted to murder members' resident in the camp with his gun pointing act.

The Evangelist immediately apologised over his action, and said he actually regretted going to that camp for answers and pointing the gun he retrieved from Stefan at residents in self-defence, but he expected that incident at the camp to be the first topic he should've confronted him with. He then proceeded to ask if such silence about the incident in the camp is because he's concerned about the political schism that will follow in the wake of such incident. He however urged Zeppelin to constrain himself from thinking a repeat of that might occur.

Zeppelin insisted he didn't make the gun incident to be the first matter he would like to talk about because he isn't a man known for brooding, and said the attempted murder of camp residents by the Evangelist cancels the injustice done to the Evangelist at the camp, and that's why he didn't bring up the matter. Evangelist Fredrick accepted Zeppelin's rationale, and said he considered the degree of attention Zeppelin placed on reputation as a reason for keeping the scandal under wraps.

Zeppelin interjected and said he's grateful for the Evangelist's thoughtfulness but it's time for the Evangelist to take his leave. Evangelist Frederick insisted that his Christian faith is the fig leaf that defined his personality, but then fixed his gaze on Zeppelin and said it's surprising that he's a Luciferian Chief Executive who employed a Christian Secretary. He then asked Zeppelin what he's playing at, and if he's living in denial, or just shying away from the truth. Zeppelin didn't take likely the fact that the Evangelist is questioning his choices, and his lifestyle. It's obvious to the Evangelist that Zeppelin is getting hot under the collar as he questions Ambrose's audacity to bring this anathema to his office.

"You've got a lot of nerve walking into my office to lecture me on my beliefs," said Zeppelin. He immediately picked up his phone and dialled his secretary, and said this man here has overstayed his welcome, and urged her to come and show him the way out.

"Is it because Prophet Gregory is indisposed, and you waited for a time like this to come up with this fib, because you consider me a low hanging fruit?" asked Zeppelin. The Evangelist immediately asked Zeppelin what he meant by Prophet Gregory being indisposed, and didn't get any response from Zeppelin.

Piper walked into the conversation and didn't hesitate to inform Fredrick, that she thinks it's time he takes his leave, and the door is open. Evangelist Fredrick subtly reminded Piper she's a Christian, and asked how come she's in Zeppelin's employment. His question did touch a raw nerve that set Piper on edge. He kind of suggested that Piper may have been lured by Zeppelin, who went about presenting his liberal values in colourful wrappers, in a virtue signalling manner, that without doubt makes a mockery of human dignity.

Piper immediately accused the Evangelist of making uniformed speculation, and didn't unequivocally deny the claim but asked where this assertion comes from. She then questioned how he came to the conclusion that she's a Christian. Evangelist Fredrick made it clear that this isn't innuendo but the truth because he saw

Christian symbols on her and a bible verse in full display by her corner, insisting she's either feigning it or confusing it.

"Where do you stand, and who are you?" asked the Evangelist.

"That's for me to worry about," replied Piper.

This Evangelist couldn't fathom how this office secretary who boldly displayed the Bible verse of John 14:6 by her corner, happened to be working for a man who openly declared he's in the service of Lucifer. He just couldn't get his head around the interplay between these quite contrasting personalities.

Just as the Evangelist attempted to leave Zeppelin office, he stopped at the door and urged Zeppelin that it's time they do things differently, insisting that God would want him to build a church in that camp.

Unbeknownst to Piper, the man she was meant to show the way out was fighting in the same corner as her, and funnily, the Evangelist had no idea that Piper isn't just a secretary but Zeppelin's wife. The meeting didn't end badly for the Evangelist, because he didn't leave with his foot in his mouth.

Moments after Evangelist Fredrick left, Piper returned to her desk, picked up her bag and closed for the day, without her boss's say so.

When Piper got home from work that evening, she went straight into her room, shut the door and went on her knees. She prayed for hours inquiring from the Lord about Frederick Douglas' visit.

"Lord, you said I should hold on, and not leave this marriage, is Fredrick Douglas the man you're sending to help me shut the Bliss camp?" asked Piper. After three hours of intense prayer, God confirmed to her that Fredrick Douglas is the man He promised. Now that she got her confirmation, that the auspicious moment has come, she got up, praising God.

By the close of work, Zeppelin returned home to his wife, who obviously is in a moment of deep reflection. Interestingly, his encounter with the Evangelist hours earlier, remained fresh in his memory, and the time that has past seemed not to have calmed his nerves enough, not to revisit the matter.

Zeppelin isn't the vilest of men, yet he remained sullen that this matter was even discussed in the first place. It's general knowledge that children avoid stepping on a bed of roses, for fear of thorns. The options presented to Zeppelin is everything benign and smells only of roses as far as this Evangelist is concerned, but Zeppelin sees nothing but the thorns in the roses, which makes the Evangelist's proposal a handful for him. Zeppelin was quite down in the dumps, looking like a captive and even more pathetic in his sullen disposition.

He continued fuming and saying this Evangelist must be out of his tree, for him to have come to him to talk trash, he then turned to Piper, "Can you imagine this?" asked Zeppelin. Piper subtly asked Zeppelin what he expects, insisting that this man was directed specifically to him and the Evangelist is not being flippant, and then accused her husband of stalling in stubbornness. Zeppelin became jocular as he begged her not to cut him into tiny little pieces with her sarcasm, because there was never a time she walked around and looking like a wet weekend and then harshly asked Piper, if she's suggesting he fall for this trash from Ambrose.

"You call this trash? He's establishing value, and trying to lead you to God, and away from hell, and from utter darkness," said Piper.

The porosity of the camp after the sudden absence of Prophet Gregory Helsing left Zeppelin feeling quite vulnerable, particularly now that his wife and the Evangelist seem to be running rings around him. "Why then did you continue to marry me after realising I'm a Luciferian, and yet you won't let me be?" asked Zeppelin. Piper wasn't insisting of being axiomatic as she stated that for the record, she never knew he's in the service of Lucifer as at the time she married him, and accused Zeppelin of hiding that aspect of his lifestyle away from her.

"And you went ahead with the marriage, after you knew I'm in the service of Lucifer," said Zeppelin. Piper had to open up to her husband that he's a good man with a good heart, and that she liked him, even before marrying him. Yet said God constrained her from withdrawing from the marriage after she learnt about his lifestyle just to save him from damnation. She proceeded to suggest that maybe God blindsided her from knowing about his Satanist belief.

"The actual plan of God for man, is for human beings to live and go about their business naked, this changed when they sinned against him," said Zeppelin.

"Stop being deluded, God himself used skin to make clothes for humans, when the need becomes necessary because he doesn't want them running around naked," replied Piper.

Zeppelin continued justifying his ownership of the Luciferian camp as he has always done. He pointed out that his camp has helped distressed people who enjoy naturism, and give them a place to display their lifestyle, and liberate them from the shackles of the Christian religion.

Now that the Evangelist opened the door of this conversation, Piper decided to make the best of it, and didn't stop prodding her husband with questions, asking him, if he thinks Satanism and nudism are good why didn't he allow their children to be a part of it. Zeppelin stood up from his seat and asked her how she expects him to allow their children to be a part of the lifestyle, since all she does is spread fear and hatred about Luciferians. He however expressed his frustration over his wife's refusal to share in the experience.

Piper stepped back from her husband, who seemed to inch closer as he attempts to talk some sense into her. She then muttered, suggesting it might be more appropriate if they go their separate ways, because she doesn't seem to see a future. Zeppelin became mortified by his wife's sudden squawky decision to bin their marriage.

"Why the sudden U-turn, Ambrose appeared from the blue, and you suddenly realised our marriage is good for nothing?" asked Zeppelin.

It's obvious to Zeppelin that his wife is out to roughen him up, by tightening the screws on him a bit.

She looked sort of crumpled in the corner and her nose scowling with this remarkable awkwardness that suggests trouble.

Piper seemed to want to distance herself from her husband's sullied reputation of being a Satanist even if he'd no idea he has no reputation to preserve, insisting that continuing in the marriage will be nothing but folly. She hesitated for a while, and then subtly told her husband that Ambrose's visit might just be a watershed moment and the rude wakening she needed to make the bold move she appeared to have shelved all this while. Zeppelin suddenly became irate and flounced back and forth in his bedroom, saying he's having none of it, and the kids won't allow this to happen either.

With a pitiful gaze, Piper reminded Zeppelin that the decision to remain in the marriage isn't for him to make, and after all, he knows for sure that his kids aren't a fan of his lifestyle.

Zeppelin asked his wife if he hasn't been a good father to warrant being put is such a difficult situation, and then asked his wife what else she wants. Piper became emotional, and all teary as she reminded her husband that her daughter is in a wheel chair, and needs a miracle, but he's standing in the way of that miracle.

"What a joke! You Christians, what's it with you, and why're you optimistic she would be healed if the camp is shut down?" asked Zeppelin. Piper insists she's a mother who is joining her faith with her daughters' faith to see the impossible happen in her daughter's life. Zeppelin stopped speaking for a moment, as if he's trying to reason out what's going on. He then asked his wife if after telling her about the health condition of Prophet Gregory the other day, she saw it as an opportunity because the Achilles heel is out of the way, and then connived with Ambrose to force him into shutting down the Bliss camp.

Zeppelin may have taken his wife for a ride all these years, and now that her time to put her foot down has come, it will be foolhardy for Zeppelin to be careless about what the wounded dog in corner might do.

She then turned to leave, but Zeppelin beckoned on her and asked where is it she's going while they still had their conversation. Piper continued walking away, and her response was that she's retuning to the living room and she's glad the scales have just fallen from her eyes. Zeppelin muttered over and over and accusing her of using divorce to force his hands into doing the wishes of Ambrose. Piper left the door ajar but stopped again in her attempt to enlighten her husband, and said Ambrose was here to liberate him from the sham he called a liberated lifestyle, and then urged her husband to open up, to allow Ambrose help him with some illumination. Piper seemed to have touched the last remaining nerve in Zeppelin, he unwittingly caved in, and eventually urged Piper to ask Ambrose to see him tomorrow.

He reminded his wife that this isn't some kind of Scooby doo moment where things are zapped into place in a matter of minutes. He then pointed out the fact that despite Prophet Gregory's incapacitation, other directors still have a say on how things will eventually play out, and they might not feel good about this move, and might veto it.

Piper pressed her husband to go ahead with the move and reminded him he's the major financier, and Prophet Gregory who obviously would've made this move impossible, is now serendipitously out of the way. More so, the property is his, to decide whatever he intends to do with it. Zeppelin walked back to his seat but told his wife that she has just placed a heavy moral burden on him, and perhaps a grave one too heavy to bear. It's obvious that Zeppelin conceded to his wife request with a sense foreboding in his voice. Piper on the other hand reminded him that his lifestyle is nothing but a scandal, and this scandal is a blot on them, his wife and children.

The next day, Evangelist Fredrick walked in to see Zeppelin, and said hello to Piper, and immediately confessed to her that he was surprised when she called to inform him Zeppelin requested that he should see him today.

Piper was quite welcoming as opposed to her disposition the previous day, saying she's glad the Evangelist honoured the invitation.

Fredrick was quite amazed and told Piper he suspects she said something to Zeppelin that made him change his mind, "Did you?" he asked. Piper opened up to the Evangelist and said his comments triggered a whole debate between her and Zeppelin. Evangelist Fredrick smiled and said he arguably understand the debate that could result from a clash of ideology, but he still couldn't get his head around why a Christian woman would choose to be the secretary to a CEO of an Oil firm who practices Satanism and supports a lifestyle that's close to nudism. While the Evangelist began exploring the morality surrounding the interplay between Zeppelin and his secretary, she immediately asked if he's the one He is sending to help her out.

"Sorry madam, I don't get you, who is sending who, and to help you out with what?" replied the Evangelist. She opened up to the Evangelist and said his conversation with her boss yesterday begs for an answer because God promised her, He's sending someone to help her shut that filthy camp down, but she just wants to know if the Evangelist is the one. Piper obviously has gotten a confirmation from God, but she obviously wants to know how much revelation the Evangelist received from God concerning this whole thing.

Piper had to give the Evangelist a trip down memory lane, and said she was working with Zeppelin because she's his wife, and she knows this would come to him as a surprise.

This news did come to the Evangelist as surprise, as he exclaimed, he'd no knowledge she's Zeppelin's wife, and asked how come he never met her. Piper confessed they never crossed each other's path because she deliberately stayed away from Zeppelin's circle of friends. More so, she works as her husband's secretary in his oil firm and doesn't in anyway deal with anything that relates to his Luciferian activities, and even the camp.

"Are you regretting marrying him, even when you knew he's in the service of Lucifer?" asked Evang. Fredrick. "I realised he's a Luciferian, or a Satanists rather, after our marriage and as a Christian, I don't believe in divorce and more so, God constrained me to remain," said Piper.

This Secretary can tolerate Zeppelin and his Satanists friends limiting their naturist proclivities to the Bliss camp, but one thing she will never acquiesce is for Zeppelin to bring his Satanist liberated proclivities to her office, in the heart of Bucharest. If he dares, she wouldn't mind screaming blue murder to all who cares to listen, and if that doesn't work then she might go a step further to do something about it.

Evangelist Fredrick smiled and said he knew she was being skittish the previous day but he's glad she added her voice for a good cause. Piper tried to reason out what's going on in the head of the Evangelist, and asked what he meant by his pursuit of a good cause.

It's obvious that secrets eat a person from inside, and it's now obvious to Piper that she needed some sort of confirmation as she assured this Evangelist who seems to pride himself on the niceties of God's grace, that he now has both her permission and her gratitude at the same time.

She then proceeded to ask him if he's the help God promised to send her way, and funnily, this question did rile the Evangelist up, but he'd to buckle down without any atom of ingenuity. The Evangelist obviously doesn't look like a man blowing smoke, he sure looks like the steady hand on the tiller, as he assured her that his message to Zeppelin was actually from God. In quite an unflattering tone, he told her he likes her enthusiasm, because it's enduring and contagious, but God didn't really mention her in his message, then said he has just come to realise that God kept people in his path to help him achieve this assignment and that seem to include her.

The Evangelist then said he's wondering how she came about working for her husband as his secretary, that most women would rather work in another capacity, and not as their secretary. "I was his secretary when we fell in love and got married, and we just decided things should stay that way. Evangelist Fredrick muttered again, saying that's rare because most ladies would want something more, particularly when their husband is the CEO of an oil firm.

Piper smiled and said she and her husband aren't competing, and at least it helps her to keep a closer eye on him. The Evangelist then smiled and said there's wisdom in that, suggesting it's not a bad idea.

Piper then interjected and said Zeppelin is free, and he can go in if he wants, he then left her and opened the door to Zeppelin's main office and entered. Zeppelin thanked Ambrose for coming, but Evangelist Fredrick interrupted immediately to correct him, as he urged Zeppelin to please refer to him as Fredrick and reminded him that the name Ambrose was given to him when there wasn't a name to call him.

"Ok, now that you're here, bring your argument forward," said Zeppelin. With things falling in line for Piper, Zeppelin gave the floor to the Evangelist to bring forward his argument. Evangelist Fredrick fixed his gaze at Zeppelin and said before going ahead, he wants to assure him he doesn't mean any offense to the point of stirring up disagreement between him and his wife. Zeppelin seems not to be a fan of platitudes, and immediately admonished the Evangelist, asking why people always say they don't intend to be rude only when they are about to be rude.

"This is an exception, now back to why I'm here," said Evang. Fredrick.

Zeppelin was a bit harsh in his questioning of the Evangelist as he asked, "Why do you think I should build a church in the camp? I consider this conversation absurd," said Zeppelin.

The Evangelist interjected and said he isn't befuddled to hear that Zeppelin finds this conversation to be absurd, but it isn't, and that it only opens up channels for new ideas. The Evangelist then began speaking as an insider when he said he realised that most people in the camp, just like Rebecca, were taken in by the Bliss Camp when they were vulnerable. The Evangelist's comment seems to suggest that the Bliss Luciferian Camp does more than just helping people explore their closeness to nature but also sell them the ruse of a better alternative to Christianity.

The thought of slapping him down with a feather is something Zeppelin had rather not think about because of the harm it would cause to his marriage. Zeppelin worries about what will follow in the wake of this decision to give Ambrose's suggestion a go, he considers it a blank cheque and doesn't really like the idea. Zeppelin thought to himself that if Prophet Gregory Hesling, who obviously is spiritually stronger than him, could be whacked on the head by Brandon Moore during a hexing ceremony, then he has no chance to escape the wrath of Brandon Moore, if he allows the Evangelist to go ahead with this. He knows too well that those sure-footed members of the Bliss Luciferian Camp wouldn't for any reason acquiesce that this kaleidoscope be shaken.

In his bid to dismiss the Evangelist's claims as utter nonsense, Zeppelin immediately questioned him. "When does assisting vulnerable people become an issue?"

The Evangelist refused to be on the back foot in this conversation, he paused for a while, then mentioned a few residents who came to the camp with a monkey on their back, and then asked. "What about you, what do you think, and is it just about others, or do you have reservation about being a nudist?" asked Evangelist Fredrick.

Zeppelin responded, saying he doesn't know what to think any longer, and said his wife has made him doubt his beliefs as someone who loves to be in the service of Lucifer.

Evangelist Fredrick sensed he hasn't only succeeded in getting under Zeppelin's skin, but he also has succeeded in exposing his vulnerability after Zeppelin opened up about his doubts. The Evangelist made it clear that he isn't here to rub his hands in glee over the pickle Zeppelin found himself, but then assured Zeppelin that he understands his concerns, and wouldn't want to shove his Christian beliefs down the throats of others.

"Isn't that exactly what you are doing? Shoving your beliefs into me," asked Zeppelin.

"What if you allow me to put my arguments before camp residents?" asked Evangelist Fredrick.

Zeppelin didn't hesitate to tell the Evangelist he wouldn't do a thing like that, because that would be one sided, but he would rather it's a balanced debate. This doesn't need telling residents tales about how the leaves came tumbling down from the tree, and instead of pursuing consensus, he'd rather go for a democratic process where the winner takes the day. "Meaning?" asked Evangelist Fredrick.

Zeppelin then stood up from his seat, to let the Evangelist know how this will eventually play out, and said the Evangelist should argue against the existence of the camp, while the Bliss Camp will get somebody to argue for the continued existence of the camp, and the winner takes the day.

"Not a bad idea, though tasking, but I accept the challenge," said Evangelist Fredrick.

Zeppelin now has his cards laid out, and said at least, he's being democratic, and reasonable about this. The Evangelist thanked Zeppelin for the opportunity to argue his case before camp residents.

"It's now up to me to convince them, you have done your bit," said Evangelist Fredrick.

He then leaves Zeppelin's office. Interestingly, Piper who awaits nothing but a positive outcome accosted the Evangelist immediately he left Zeppelin's office, and asked how the meeting went. Evangelist Fredrick smiled and said it was fruitful, and God has already begun what He promised. He then told Piper that her husband gave him a task of putting his argument forward in a debate and it now behoves him to win camp residents to God's side.

"This is daunting, are you sure you can win this debate? I'm counting on you, and I can't wait to see these nudists and Satanists, leave our property," Piper retorted.

The Evangelist assured Piper that God has a hand in this, and the success so far wouldn't have been possible without God, and He will perfect what he has just started. He urged her to continue praying, then told her that God just gave him a favour similar to the kind of favour God gave Nehemiah in the hands of the king of Persia (Nehemiah 2:5), and he's sure the rest will work out to the glory of God.

Later that day, Evangelist Fredrick received a phone call from an unlikely source, he picked the call, and while trying to pin the voice on the phone to a face, the caller introduced herself as Piper, Zeppelin's wife. The Evangelist immediately continues the conversation where they left it, and Piper didn't hesitate to inform the Evangelist that she did a brief internet search about the Evangelist and the church he attends, and realised he's man who has done so much in the service of God. She hinted the Evangelist that God might have picked him for this task because he's the sharpest knife in the draw. She opened up and confessed she really didn't know much about the Evangelist, and said, that for sure is her loss. Evangelist Fredrick smiled and said people don't go about with badge of their achievements on their shoulder, particularly when that service is to God. She muttered to herself saying she didn't know much about the Evangelists' time in the camp either because she has never set her foot in the camp and knows nothing about who does what in the camp. Piper had to open up to the Evangelist that she's calling to see how they could form an alliance.

"To what end is this alliance?" he asked. Piper interjected and told the Evangelist they have common interest, as they both want the camp shut down for good, and a church erected in its wake. After spending time brainstorming on the way forward, they agreed a meeting, as Piper promised to pay the Evangelist a visit in his home.

Later, same day, while at the dining table having dinner with his family, Winnie exclaimed in excitement and said she's glad Zeppelin requested for a second meeting with her husband after turning him down a day earlier. She then asked him how his second visit to Zeppelin's office went.

He didn't respond immediately until he finished chewing the soup he had in his mouth, and said it went well, and that the whole thing is playing to his favour, and he can actually see the hand of God in all of this. Winnie had no knowledge of the dynamics between Zeppelin and his Secretary, all she knew was the information her husband passed on to her a day earlier which continues to befuddle her. She immediately muttered saying why on earth should a Christian woman who is proud enough show off her faith, work for a man like that, as his secretary. The Evangelist didn't hesitate to bring his wife up to speed on the new twist between Zeppelin and his secretary, he interjected and told his wife that the woman in question, the secretary, is Zeppelin's wife.

"What! How come she calls herself a Christian, after marrying a man in the service of Lucifer, and runs a camp that encouraged people to go about scantily dressed?" asked Winnie.

"She married him not knowing he's a Satanist, he actually hid that aspect of himself away from her," said Evangelist Fredrick.

"He actually did that?" asked Winnie.

"Yeah, he did," said Evangelist Fredrick.

Peter interjected and said that's cruel, then asked why then did Zeppelin's wife continue with the marriage after realising that her supposed husband is in the service of Lucifer. Peter finds it gut wrenching that the interplay in this relationship is rather in contrast with being considered fascinating.

Evangelist Fredrick decided to expatiate on the supposed interplay between the couple, and said Piper remained in the marriage hoping she can change Zeppelin for good. Peter sighed and said, "what a futile effort it is for a Christian to falsely hope she will change her unbelieving husband." He then said a lot of Christians make that mistake but end up disappointed as he suggested the marriage is sort of a smoke screen. Evangelist Fredrick on the other hand looked at the complicated relationship between Piper and her husband from the lenses of God's eyes, and said Piper's effort isn't futile, it's beginning to pay off because it was her who encouraged her husband to give heed to his proposal.

He however cautioned that on no account should a Christian get involved in and remain in a false marriage like Piper did, but emphasised that Piper's case is exceptional because it was divinely orchestrated.

"But how come she works as his secretary, and why should a woman accept such enslavement?" asked Jordan. Winnie turned to Jordan and advised that everything shouldn't be about one person enslaving the other, as he has always asserted, and life isn't always black and white.

Evangelist Fredrick proceeded to inform his family that Piper has a special needs child whom she has been believing God for her healing, but believes her husband's abominable acts is preventing the miracle they so desire. "Her husband is busy playing the clown at a time the family is trusting God for a miracle," said Jordan.

Evangelist Fredrick paused for a while, and said, "life is not fair, people would always say," he then said Piper now saw him as a window of opportunity to shut the camp down, once and for all.

"Meaning she has been fighting her husband to shut the camp?" asked Peter.

"Yes, of course, I don't know how she succeeded in forcing him to yield to this," said Evang. Fredrick.

Winnie turned to her husband and appreciated his effort so far, but then said, the elephant in the room has been left out in their conversation so far, and this elephant is one that can't be ignored, and that's Prophet Gregory. The Evangelist affirmed to his family that Prophet Gregory is obviously the biggest stumbling block in his path, because he's highly revered and feared, and his say so, is final. Even at that, the Evangelist is optimistic that God has the final say, if he has promised to do it, then it will come to pass, but he'd to begin with Zeppelin to see where it leads.

Winnie then inquired from her husband about when Zeppelin will commence the shutting down of the camp. Evangelist Fredrick chuckled as he interjected and said Zeppelin is allowing this to go down, but not without a fight. Winnie on the other hand asked her husband what sort of fight he's referring and asked if Zeppelin is stalling. The Evangelist told her that Zeppelin wants a debate, as he's keen to make the process democratic, and the winner takes the day.

Peter needed more clarity as he asked his dad who he's debating against, that's if Zeppelin has his way with Prophet Gregory.

Funnily, his dad replied him saying, so far, he hadn't the faintest inkling of who he will be going up against, but Zeppelin will appoint someone to debate for the continued existence of the camp, while he on the other hand will debate against that. Jordan interjected suggesting they will need to put heads together to help his dad build a good case, because building a good argument will make some sense in this regard.

All hands to the pump should have been more ideal, but the Evangelist thinks otherwise in the current circumstance, as he turned to Jordan and said he doesn't think brainstorming to build a case would be necessary.

He then suggested that maybe the reason God took him to that camp was for him to know a lot about them and give him reasons to build an argument. Winnie was also keen on how this whole thing will play out, and then asked her husband when he intends to hold this debate, yet asked if she and her sons will be allowed to be a part of the debate. Evangelist Fredrick replied her saying hopefully, in a matter of weeks, and he will arrange that with Zeppelin, but suggested he doesn't think it will be ideal for his family to be involved in this.

He isn't in anyway attempting to play the heroes' card by making himself the star player making all the moves. He's just a bit concerned about getting his family mired so soon in this murky water.

"Why, dad, would Zeppelin object to this?" asked Peter.

Evangelist Fredrick turned to peter and shook his head, and said this isn't about Zeppelin, insisting it's him that's objecting, and this is because shutting down a camp with close to ten thousand members, of which over fifty of them are residents, would mean contending with lots of bad blood in that camp. Peter then muttered as he confirmed that they obviously can't sit on two chairs at once, yet asked his dad if he's suspecting the possibility, that this could turn ugly. His dad added his voice and said moreover, it's a camp where people go about their business almost nude, and it isn't the kind of place he would want his family to visit.

Winnie interjected immediately as she tried to dispel every concern, she then said she sees sense in her husband's view on the matter, before suggesting they should approach this with utmost caution. She then turned to Jordan and asked him to clear the table.

This move by God is likened to a dinner bell that alerts believers to the fact that God is now in the process of reclaiming the Wastelands of Europe. In pursuant to reclaiming this wasteland, God had to bust every anecdotal myth of portraying Lucifer as some kind of hero deserving of reverence. That is where this Evangelist comes in, and with Zeppelin's as a reliable enabler, Evangelist Fredrick Douglas intends to inundate residents with the word of God, until the myth is busted.

A day later, someone was at the door and Jordan went to get the door and it was a lady with her daughter, bound in the wheelchair.

"Hello, what can I do for you?" he asked.

"This is Evangelist Fredrick Douglas's home, I suppose," said Piper. Jordan smiled and said of course, this is the Evangelist's home and proceeded to say it's his dad she's talking about. Even as he listened keenly to what she had to say, he didn't have the slightest suspicion that this visitor could be Zeppelin's Secretary they talked about, and neither did he suspect her to be one of his dad's mistresses from his time in the camp. She interjected and said she wants to see his dad. Jordan on the other hand excused her and went inside to get his dad, and it didn't take long the door opened again and it was the Evangelist at the door.

"Hello Fredrick," said Piper.

"Hello, please come in," said the Evangelist. He received her into his home and helped push the wheelchair into the house, even as he said hello to the little girl in wheelchair. Not long after they made themselves comfortable, Winnie walked into the living room, and the Evangelist formally introduced her to Piper. Winnie was quite welcoming, as she turned and engaged Piper's daughter for a while and didn't hesitate to tell Piper her husband has said a lot of nice things about her and her effort to shut the Bliss Luciferian Camp. Piper opened up and told Winnie a little about herself and the steps she took in her attempt to end her relationship with Zeppelin the moment she became aware of his proclivities, but God constrained her not to end the relationship.

She proceeded to tell of how she was quite mad at God for insisting she remain in this relationship, and it's arguably incalculable to ascertain the degree of damage her husband's Satanist support for the liberated lifestyle of nudism has done to her and her children. Evangelist Fredrick interjected and said God wants to use her to shut the camp and save more souls, because if she'd left her husband the conversation about shutting down the Bliss Luciferian camp wouldn't be on the table.

Winnie was opened mouthed because she knew God can do anything, but she hadn't the slightest inkling that God could go as far as sending her husband to that camp, and even made this woman to remain with a Satanist husband just for a time such as this. Winnie asked her guests what she could offer them, Piper requested for a cup of coffee.

Moments later, Winnie got the cup of coffee and some cookies on the side, and then brought a glass of orange juice for her daughter. Moments after Winnie brought her the cup of coffee, Piper told them she visited so they could discuss how they will go about achieving a successful outcome in the upcoming debate.

Winnie immediately inquired from Piper if Zeppelin has spoken about this whole thing with Prophet Gregory, because getting past the prophet, or underestimating him might be a fatal mistake, and that she sees the prophet as the main stumbling block in all of these. Piper paused and said unfortunately, Prophet Gregory has just been diagnosed with inoperable brain tumour, and he has just less than two weeks to live. The Evangelist was quite shocked to learn of the untimely death that awaits the prophet. He felt some sympathy for the prophet, after all, they once worked together, and it was good while it lasted.

He then cast his mind backwards to Zeppelin's comment, referring to the prophet as indisposed. Piper took her time to inform this couple that Prophet Gregory's demise and the Evangelist's visit to her husband's office requesting he shut the camp, happened at about the same time, and that is what proved to her that God is in the process of shutting the camp. He knew that there's no way this will get past Prophet Gregory without taking a fatal turn. So, he used Brandon Moore to take him out, and that while Brandon Moore was serving his own ego, he had no idea that he has just inadvertently been used by God. Yet, members of the camp had no knowledge that Brandon Moore was behind Prophet Gregory's health debacle, after a brief falling out.

"You mean Luciferians destroying each other, and having no knowledge that they're making way for the closure of the Bliss Camp?" asked the Evangelist.

"All things work together for good, this is just like the days of Jehoshaphat, in the Bible book of 2 chronicle 20:23 when the Ammonites and Moabites rose up against the men from Mount Seir and destroyed them," said Winnie.

It's now obvious that they no longer have to worry about Prophet Gregory, it's only Zeppelin, they have to contend with. Piper was quite upfront in saying, she could feel it that God brought the Evangelist her way to help bring her request to pass. Evangelist Fredrick then told her that his family is already praying and fasting towards it and they're pleading with God to go ahead of them to speak to the hearts of residents in the camp before the debate happen.

He then suggested to Piper that they needed to make the whole thing water-tight, then urged her to join his family in the fasting until the debate happened. She interjected and said she's up for it and was quite glad to see God working towards shutting the camp for good. Piper's total commitment to see this camp shut down for good was welcomed by the Evangelist and his family, she is now an active player in this alliance.

They prayed together, and the Evangelist then spent some time praying for Piper's daughter that was wheelchair bound. He then suggested to Piper to make another visit, so he could introduce her to Reverend Fitzgerald who's also a mentor to the Evangelist, as this whole thing unfolds. After spending time with the Evangelist and his family, Piper returned home.

Days after her visit to Evangelist Fredrick's home, Piper drove straight to the Reverend's resident where the Evangelist was already waiting for her at the car park.

"Evangelist, how are you?" asked Piper. They exchanged pleasantries briefly and the Evangelist then helped to get Piper's daughter, Sarah, wheelchair out of the car and then helped Sarah sit in her wheelchair, before they proceeded to see the reverend. It didn't take long before they were all introduced and seated, then began holding a conversation.

"The Evangelist told me about the active role you played to make your husband agree to this," said Reverend Fitzgerald. Piper interjected and said she's honoured to be a part of what God is doing right now and said her encounter with the Evangelist was divinely orchestrated.

She narrated how God constrained her from leaving Zeppelin, as she told them of how she packed her bags and loaded them up in the car and then headed to her parents' place. "I couldn't bear the shame, no one in their right senses can," she muttered.

"For one week, I couldn't sleep, God came to me daily asking me to go back to Zeppelin, and said through me, he will shut the camp and lots of people will come to Christ, and lots more people will be spared the temptations of abandoning their Christian faith, and becoming a Luciferian in the future," she said.

"God pointed me to Jonah whom he sent to Nineveh, to a place he didn't want to go and a place he didn't want to be, He also pointed me to Hosea (Hosea 3:1) whom he made to take back his prostitute wife," she said.

The reverend then muttered and shook his head as he listened to Piper, narrating the pickle she was in, to this reverend who cared enough to listen. The reverend then muttered a second time and said God must have really constrained her in a manner that's quite convincing.

She constrained herself from describing her husband as idiosyncratic but having given her new found friends a hint about how she came to catch a glimpse of the darkness within Zeppelin, not long after their marriage, and how things went down like a lead balloon. It now makes sense not to rush into passing judgement on why she remained in the marriage.

The Evangelist confessed to Piper that the first time he set his eyes on her, all he saw in her eyes was a soul dwelling in fathomless sense of reason, but that emptiness seems to have suddenly disappeared because her waiting time is over, and that the light at the end of the tunnel is now, and within a touching distance. She interjected and said God kept assuring her during this period that in due course He will send someone to help her shut the camp and her husband will eventually give his life to Christ.

"To be frank with you, I refused to go back Zeppelin, then God got angry with me, I'd to pack my bags immediately and return," she said. It now dawned on the Evangelist that Piper is the woman God told him about, unfortunately he'd erroneously fitted Rebecca in that mould.

This meeting also brought about an opportunity to have a panoramic view of how they might want things to play out once God hands the camp over to them, particularly now that Prophet Gregory is out of the picture. The reverend then intimated to Piper that they've planned to help residents who wouldn't want to have anything to do with the church find a job.

Piper loved the idea and was upfront as she suggested she and her husband might help some residents get jobs in the oil firm her husband manages. Piper obviously isn't a woman of a limited talent as she bought her expertise to bear. She informed the reverend that this move will unwittingly provoke backlash from the labyrinths in this nation who hadn't the foggiest idea of what God is about, but she will be ready with press statement that will keep them quiet. The reverend assured Piper that God is already in the driver's seat and there might not be a need for a press statement because the people will willingly surrender the camp to God.

# CHAPTER

## FIFTEEN

### *The Debate*

Two weeks later, Zeppelin visited the Bliss Luciferian Camp and was addressing residents, as he stood in their mist. He started by saying he wish to thank every member of this Luciferian camp who have endured criticism from those who are against what they stood for. "I suppose, you're all aware of the unfortunate death of our beloved Prophet, Gregory Helsing, he died yesterday, and his death is a big loss to this camp," said Zeppelin.

He then proceeded to say that he also wishes to state that recent events have resulted in his consideration to build a church in this camp, and being a democratically minded person, he would rather ignite a debate in which the man with the highest votes carries the day. Berger interjected in quite a harsh tone, and asked Zeppelin who is it that's proposing the building of a church inside a premises where services are offered to Lucifer, and where the crazy thought came from. They obviously don't need a shrink to tell them, after all, the Evangelist was standing right beside Zeppelin.

"Fredrick or Ambrose, whatever you call him, are you guys aware he's a Christian Evangelist?" asked Zeppelin. It didn't take long before Zeppelin realised, he's stepping on a land mine, as residents accused him of being a sell-out, in such a harsh rebuke. Residents gathered around him, and began chanting shame, shame, shame, saying he couldn't wait for Prophet Gregory to die before selling them out.

Stacy interjected in an audacious tone, saying of course, they're already aware Ambrose is a Christian, but they've just lost their spiritual father, and without an opportunity to mourn his death. She unblinkingly accused Zeppelin of making a mockery and having a laugh about the prophet's death.

They aren't only murmuring their disquiet, they're rather contending with a chorus, and at this point Zeppelin had to tell these protesting residents of his abiding memory of Prophet Gregory Helsing. Zeppelin tried as much as he could to correct any perception of him as not showing any sympathy for the dead. He narrated to them that since the diagnosis, he has visited the hospital daily, and wept for his friend and prophet, Gregory Helsing, until he took his last breath in his arms. Zeppelin was deeply saddened by Prophet Gregory's demise and in a touching tribute to the beloved Prophet Gregory, Zeppelin said the prophet will be greatly missed.

"Let the angels of Lucifer continue to sing his praises into Lucifer's ears," he concluded.

Jarrod hushed Stacy as he insisted that some of them didn't have the slightest clue that Ambrose is a Christian and accused Stacy of cover-up for keeping such news to herself. Zeppelin immediately stepped in to calm things down, and said at least they now know, he then turned to Jarrod and informed him that Ambrose will argue for the building of a church in this camp, while Hubert will argue for the preservation of the camp the way it has been, and against the building of a church.

"Why are you doing this, Zeppelin? This isn't right, we are Satanists, and don't co-exist with Christians, why then are you talking about building a church?" Jarrod protested.

Arguably, the church and Luciferianism can't co-exist. After all, the bible book of 1 Samuel 5:2 told us that Dagon, the god of the philistine got decimated after attempting to share space with ark of Covenant, and the philistines were punished until they stayed clear of the ark of Covenant.

This isn't some kind of righteous indignation, it's a fear for the obvious, and there isn't any desire to allow this to flower out. Zeppelin sensed the ambience have suddenly gone sour, and tried to assuage Jarrod of his concern, saying he shouldn't be afraid of a debate with Ambrose, as he made jokes that fear only makes the wolf bigger. He suddenly stopped laughing, and said his hands are tied, then asked Jarrod if he's married.

"For now, I'm not married, but I have a son," Jarrod retorted.

"Where's he?" asked Zeppelin.

"He's with his mum, my ex," replied Jarrod.

There and then, Zeppelin began exploring Jarrod's relationship, and asked why he didn't continue the marriage or relationship with his son's mum. Jarrod wasn't too comfortable announcing the odds of his relationship to everyone, but had to tell Zeppelin that his ex-wife doesn't approve of her son's dad being a Satanist. Zeppelin knew of Jarrod's story long before now but he explored Jarrod's circumstance to prove they have something in common, he then told Jarrod he's in a similar situation.

"My wife also doesn't approve of my Luciferian beliefs," said Zeppelin.

It's obvious to these residents that this speech by Zeppelin is nothing but letting the dog see the rabbit, but the Evangelist has to keep his eyes peeled for the likes of Stefan who isn't overly fond of Christians. Even as Zeppelin urged residents not to conflate the matter at hand with the supposition that some are dogs and others rabbit, residents remained furious with him for paving the way for Ambrose to walk all over them.

Stefan's instinctive revulsion to Christians is a feeling shared by many in this camp, even at that the Evangelist seem to have left an impression of himself that created a ripple of anxiety amongst residents. No virtue signalling, nothing pugnacious, and pursing a knock-out might come across as arrogant. The stage is now set and it doesn't matter whose ox is gored.

Amy is the fiery type who would rather not sit idly and allow someone pull the wool across her eyes, particularly when she thinks Zeppelin is being doubly dishonest to them.

"If prophet Gregory had been alive, you dare not do this, if you had tried, you would've been jumping at shadows and hiding under your bed, because he would come after you like a ton of bricks and chase you into the rabbit hole where you belong," Amy retorted. Cavalier is her thing, particularly when navigating life issues in a world she considers quite hostile. Amy recently cancelled her planned wedding to her fiancée whom she once described as not the scintillating type of man, because he'd rather they have dinner in the bedroom than explore the outdoors with her, and even telling her fiancée to his face that gossip has it, that he's as lazy as a cat.

Berger accepted that they're still in mourning for their beloved Prophet Gregory, yet in such a theatrical move, said he's confident about the future, and asked Zeppelin, what if they win, and Ambrose loses. Zeppelin held his cards to his chest, and said if Hubert wins, then that's it, and Ambrose will return home a loser. Amy finds this stunt by Zeppelin not just to be needling but quite telling, she'd this eerie feeling that Zeppelin's sudden suggestion for a debate means they're on their way out of the camp. She then turned to Zeppelin as she voiced out again saying she doesn't like this idea.

Funnily, Zeppelin didn't respond so as not to provoke her further, because he's already aware that this move will be likened to stirring the hornet nest. She then turned to Ambrose, who stood on the side-lines and has remained silent all along, and asked why he has come to disturb their peace.

Zeppelin continues to assess the mood of the people, with his smile smouldered in hubris, a smile that's visibly present whenever he's down to be cheeky.

Scarcely is Zeppelin's sarcasm deemed offensive, yet he does always have this cloud of emotions laced in hubris with no tenterhooks. It's obvious to Zeppelin that residents aren't obliging of Ambrose, yet he allowed Ambrose to try his luck and tire himself out.

"Amy, please call me Fredrick, I haven't come to disturb your peace, and I suppose you hear me out, then make your choice," said Evangelist Fredrick.

Amy was a bit snappy and irritable, she immediately cautioned Ambrose, that his abiding indignation for Luciferianism won't go unpunished, because the squawky reaction that will follow in the wake of this move will be much more than he'd expected. This debate is a blank cheque handed to the Evangelist, and even as he hopes to make the best out of it, Amy is here assuring him that the rambling response from members will show the world his intention is warped. Amy didn't stop as she poured out her heart and said this could turn out to be a cautionary tale of a Christian spy who came to live in the Luciferian camp out of hate for their liberal lifestyle.

Berger muttered in frustration and said he's tired of the chicken and egg game. He then suggested they go ahead with it, so they can put this behind them. Zeppelin concluded by saying the next one month will allow each person to campaign for what they believe, before the day of the voting proper. He then reminded them that he has given Ambrose the permission to return to this camp and he mustn't be harassed. The odds are quite stacked against Ambrose, particularly when he'd to preach to someone like Amy who is quite resentful of privileges that aren't earned. Amy is a cold fish at best, and doesn't like people running rings around her.

Pinching away their primordial belief on the altar of Christianity, is something Amy finds too hard to swallow because this isn't some kind of zero-sum game. Rebecca stood on the side and watched as Amy ran amok, displaying her revulsion towards Zeppelin's move, and hurling hurtful slurs at Zeppelin. She couldn't bear but got involved, as she reminded Amy that there's no need bemoaning Zeppelin action as infantile, for his unwillingness to put his head above the parapet for their sake.

Amy seemed convinced that this move by Zeppelin did nothing but give wind to Ambrose's sails, and instead of allowing the Evangelist help Zeppelin achieve his egocentric trip, she made it her personal business to scuttle whatever plan the pair hopes to achieve.

In her bid to take the wind off their sails, she turned to Zeppelin and inquired whether members who aren't resident in this camp can vote. "Yes, of course, whatever decision we take here affects them, so they're welcome to be a part of the process, and I'll ask Doctor Van to put the news up in the camp's website," said Zeppelin.

Amy is still not letting Zeppelin get away with this, as she insisted that her hunch tells her he favours Ambrose's position and that's quite scary, because it makes her uncomfortable. Zeppelin on the other hand doesn't have an appetite to engage the already incensed Amy further. Yet his silence didn't deter Amy, who prodded Zeppelin further by asking if he considers them an embarrassing encumbrance, before suggesting to Zeppelin that, what if they engage in fund-raising to pay him off and keep the camp for themselves.

Funnily, she'd no knowledge of the interplay between Zeppelin and Evangelist Fredrick who knows he's outnumbered, but with the stage set, he's certain that the wallpaper is now up, and it's time to fight to take the camp over. It's arguably obvious to the Evangelist that the ambience has turned quite sour and he needed to calm things down, Zeppelin then told Amy there's nothing to be scared about, as he assured her in quite an ingenious fashion that Ambrose is only proposing they build a church in this camp. While Zeppelin continued to assure residents that no love is lost, just for cool heads to prevail, Amy interjected again saying she can now see that this is much more than building a church, because Satanism and Christianity don't co-exist in any shape or form, she then concluded that the church story is just a ploy to kick-start the process of sending them packing out of the camp.

The idea of building a church and having Christians co-exist alongside them kind of gives her the creeps because the power of Christ might come to bare on the camp in a manner that would obviously breaks the magic and the spell behind Luciferianism.

"Amy is making some sense, allow us to raise funds, pay you off and retain the camp," said Jarrod. Zeppelin then opened up as he apologised to Jarrod, saying he's sorry, because paying him off isn't among the options on the table, and that this is as good as it can get.

Berger seemed confident that the debate is the way out of this quagmire, and was quite eager to hit the ground running, as he asked what day in particular is the debate taking place. Zeppelin immediately declared the process open, and said people who wish to commence campaigning, can start mobilizing support, he then thanked them for their time.

Amy took offence in the hilarity of Zeppelin's approach as she insisted that his action is everything but benign. She then turned to Zeppelin and said every other person here is scantily dressed except Ambrose, "Why isn't he undressed, this is a nude camp, if I must ask?" asked Amy.

"You've all seen Ambrose scantily dressed in the past, he went about his business amongst you scantily dressed for three years, but he's no longer one of us, and he's in his right to be clothed," replied Zeppelin. Fredrick Douglas walked through life's tragic circumstance into a glorious outcome, in a manner that seems quite emblematic of the finger of God. He isn't here to make an exhibition of himself but to preach God to the people he still considered his friends. This time, he's more like Goldilocks becoming the bad guy, and they aren't treating him with the kindness of a big puppy dog.

Amy continued referring to the Evangelist as Ambrose even when he has told them not to refer to him as Ambrose. She didn't stop but continued plaguing Zeppelin with her opposition to Ambrose's presence, as she insists that the fact that Ambrose is dressed and not looking like the rest of them shows he's an outlier, and he shouldn't be here. Zeppelin seemed to have had an earful of what he considers Amy's farcical claims, he then began walking away, but even as Zeppelin walked away, Jarrod followed him, accusing him that his decision of showing preference for Christianity is a decision taken at the expense of humanity. It was crazily amazing in the manner in which Zeppelin kept walking without looking back. It's more like a dog barking as the caravan moves on.

The moment Zeppelin left, the Evangelist followed to allow members come to terms with the news they just heard.

Within hours after he left the Bliss Luciferian Camp, Fredrick Douglas visited Reverend Fitzgerald to brief him on the outcome of his visit to the camp. Immediately after they finished exchanging pleasantries, the Reverend asked how his visit to the camp went, then said he suppose it was fruitful. As they had their conversation, they both walked to the conservatory where the Reverend loves to relax. The Evangelist was upbeat and in good spirit as he made himself comfortable. He then confirmed to the Reverend who's quite happy to have his Evangelist back, that the debate is on, and he hopes to make a convincing case. The Reverend immediately asked if he needed any form of support, and if he wants him to come along.

"No, no reverend, it's not a place for you, they are all scantily dressed in there, and the sight isn't a good one," replied the Evangelist.

"Hmm, how then will you be able to cope in such an environment?" asked Rev. Fitzgerald. Evangelist Fredrick assured the Reverend that God has given him the grace to cope, and that he unfortunately was one of them and the sight of scantily dressed Satanists going about their business isn't new to him.

"Ok, I get it, we'll support you from a distance, and when it becomes necessary for us to come in, you should let us know," said the Reverend.

Evangelist Fredrick then steered the conversation on the way forward, and then asked the Reverend of what alternative they should offer these Luciferians and camp residents to make them abandon their old ways.

"You know I've been out of circulation for some time now, and haven't returned to work, and have nothing to offer in that regard," said Evangelist Fredrick.

Reverend Fitzgerald immediately responded and said it's good they start talking about an alternative for residents living in the camp. He then assured the Evangelist that it's now glaringly obvious that God will deliver the camp to them, and those Satanists who used to be Christians and love to return to their faith will be retained and employed to work for the church. He then muttered, saying he prefers referring to them as Satanist, because the term Luciferians are just some made up name, meant to make a bad word sound nice to the ears.

"What about the non-Christians?" asked Evangelist Fredrick. Reverend Fitzgerald responded saying he will help these groups of residents find work with companies and resettle them outside the camp. "Ooh, that's great, and all sorted then," said Evangelist Fredrick.

Reverend Fitzgerald then steered the conversation to the obvious, as he asked the Evangelist about Rebecca and Stacy, and asked if they gave him the expected support. Evangelist Fredrick nodded as he assured the priest that they of course supported him, but he hasn't been able to talk them out of being Luciferians. After spending some time talking about how to go about shutting down the Bliss Luciferian Camp peacefully, the reverend once again steered the conversation to the Evangelists' wellbeing, asking how he's coping with his family. The Evangelist on the other hand has no qualms with his health, saying he's now as strong as a bull, and his memory is great, and after all, they now talk about things they share in common before the cruise ship incident.

Days later, Evangelist Fredrick Douglas visited the camp as he began his campaign to win friends over.

"Friends, I've come to you as an ex-Luciferian, who has lived and shared the same values with you for three years."

Amy interjected and asked the Evangelist why he's taking the stage, and said she expects him and Hubert to take the stage side by side. The Evangelist was quite subtle this time as he insists, he didn't stop Hubert from making a case for his argument, and Hubert can do that whenever he chooses.

Amy became verbally abusive out of frustration, as she suddenly began bantering the Evangelist, saying she's quite aware that Ambrose is socially insecure and looking for a way to burn out his doldrums and questioned why he's doing this. Evangelist Fredrick smiled and said he likes her sarcasm and won't take any offence at her explosive remarks. Hubert got wind of Ambrose's presence and rushed to the scene, he immediately turned to the Evangelist and muttered saying, Orla just informed him he's already spreading his religious poison.

The Evangelist smiled and told Hubert he's welcomed to join in the debate, but he's only here to present to them the splendour of heaven.

"Can you imagine this bigotry? He isn't even dead, and without a single clue about heaven, yet he's offering us the splendour of heaven," said Hubert. Evangelist Fredrick continued smiling to maintain a warm ambience, and said he was found lifeless at the beach here in this camp, he then turned to Hubert.

"Don't you think I caught a glimpse of heaven, during that short period of lifelessness?" asked Evang. Fredrick.

Hubert accused the Evangelist of being hubristic and jocularly asked if Ambrose is here to tell them he saw God during his brief moment of unconsciousness. Evangelist Fredrick burst into laughter, and then turned to Hubert and said he's meant to put his case forward, but this seems to look like an interview session.

"Hmm, what do you expect? I'm walking on sunshine," Hubert replied jocularly, and then burst into laughter. Orla immediately frowned at Hubert's ineptitude, reminding him that this isn't some kind of circus show, as she urged him to be serious because Ambrose is here to send them packing out of this camp, and insisted he stops making a joke out of this.

The Evangelist immediately focused on Orla and urged her not to allow herself to be so worked up unnecessarily, he then fixed his gaze at her.

"I offer you God in exchange for Satan, I offer you morality in exchange for decadence, and I offer you a life of openness for the life of secrecy you all live in this camp," said Evang. Fredrick.

"Can you hear this heretic speak about offering us what he himself doesn't have?" asked Hubert. Orla also saw this as an opportunity to even her score with Rebecca, she immediately began pointing at Rebecca, as she directed the attention of all residents at Rebecca before suggesting to them to blame her for this drama coming from Ambrose.

"Blame me for what, and what drama are you talking about?" asked Rebecca.

Orla isn't letting Rebecca off the hook that easily, as she reminded everyone present that Ambrose was dead, but Rebecca selfishly revived him and shamefully betrayed Eric. Rebecca immediately tried to exonerate herself from Ola's accusation and asked what Ambrose's action has got to do with her, and asked Orla when she'll stop speaking for Eric. Stacy who has passively observed the debate between the Evangelist and Hubert, didn't hesitate to speak up in defence of her friend. She then asked Orla to allow Rebecca some breathing space, and accused her of orchestrating a sustained verbal attack on Rebecca even when she remained mute.

"I know the two of you are cut from the same cloth, tell her to take her sick and twisted mind somewhere else," replied Orla.

Feeling quite exasperated by the possible consequence of this debate, Orla turned to Ambrose and inquired why he's bent on pushing this deranged conspiracy through Zeppelin.

"There isn't anything deranged about this, it's just an attempt to save your soul and show you other options to life and a better one for that matter," said Evangelist Fredrick.

Hubert suddenly became serious with the debate following Orla's outcry, he then turned to the Evangelist and said his vicious intent to demonise their beliefs and way of life shows he's nothing but a man who has lost touch with reality. Unfortunately, he lived amongst them, not as a conformist but as someone brought to the shores of the Bliss camp by the hand of fate. He remained unwaveringly resolute preaching the need to embrace monotheism in a supposedly Satanic plural society.

Stefan stood up from the log he was sitting on, and didn't hesitate to decry the Evangelist's sense of reason, describing the Evangelist as an alarmist, and pointed out that he's doing this at an apocalyptic proportion.

"I'm only telling you as it is, Stefan, if you die today, what next?" asked the Evangelist.

"I don't know, obviously, when I die then I will see what follows," replied Stefan.

"I am sorry to announce to you, that life after death leaves you with only two options, eternity in Heaven or eternity in Hell. The Bible book of Hebrews 9:27 says "And as it is appointed unto men once to die, but after this the judgement." The evangelist retorted.

Things are becoming heated, and the anger within is now coming to the surface.

"Ambrose, I advise you to let us be, just take your poisonous ideology out of this camp," said Jarrod. Hubert paused for a while as if he's empathising with the Evangelist but then said the world is not in books they say, and suggested they live it out one day at a time just as they've been doing but Ambrose here wants them to live their life based on a book called the bible.

"My friends, that's all for today, we'll continue this campaign in the next few days," said Evangelist Fredrick.

Hubert was taken aback by the Evangelists decision to call it a day and accused him of chickening out at a time the debate was becoming quite interesting. He then turned to the Evangelist and pleaded with him not to come back.

"Ambrose, go and live your life, and let us be," he retorted.

Strangely, while the conversation was ongoing Eric whose name was mentioned earlier, walked into the gathering. Rebecca sensed someone suddenly stood by her side, she immediately turned to see who it was and realised it was Eric, she then nudged him with her elbow.

"Hey Rebecca, what's up," asked Eric. Rebecca smiled and told him it's been close to a year since he visited this camp, then asked what he's doing here.

"How are you doing? I learnt about Ambrose's attempt to kill you," he said.

Rebecca didn't need to see a shrink to know how Eric got wind of the incident between her and Ambrose, she immediately pointed out to Eric that it was Orla that gossiped about the incident to him, and that she is well aware of Orla's ravishing appetite for gossip. She then suggested that Eric seemed to have come too late because she's better now. Eric hesitated because he isn't keen to hang Orla out to dry and insisted it doesn't matter how he knew about the incident, but he did feel bad when he learnt about Ambrose's attempted to kill her. Rebecca on the other hand made light of Eric's concerns, saying that's in the past now, but asked if Orla also informed him that Ambrose has reunited with his family. Eric accepted he was told Ambrose has reunited with his family, and he wanted to come over to see her but he wasn't chanced.

"To see me?" asked Rebecca.

"Of course, I still have that soft spot for you despite the ill treatment you gave me," said Eric.

Rebecca pretended not to hear what he just said, but then steered the conversation and asked him if he has come for the debate. Eric muttered and said he'd no idea a debate is going on, that he just came to see how she is doing, and the debate is just a coincidence. Rebecca immediately turned to Eric and said she will be back in a minute, that she needed to speak with Ambrose before he leaves. Immediately she took some steps towards Ambrose, she turned to Stacy, and asked her to come with her.

This could become a slam dunk but with his family by his side, he's going to make the best out of this opportunity presented to him on a Plate. Moreover, his promise to provide an alternative accommodation, and his insistence that he isn't just here to scare the horses didn't go far enough to stop stiff opposition coming his way.

Rebecca and Stacy followed Evangelist Fredrick as he attempts to leave, he saw them coming towards him and stopped. Funnily, immediately Rebecca got to where the Evangelist was, she didn't hesitate to speak out, saying she doesn't think she can go along with him on this plan to kick innocent residents out of their homes. Evangelist Fredrick immediately urged her to please refer to him as Fredrick. He then turned to her, "But why? I thought we have been through this before," said Evangelist Fredrick.

Rebecca had to voice her concern asking him where these people would go if things go as he'd planned. The Evangelist returned his car keys back to his pocket and began assuring Rebecca that there are better places to go, better things to do and a better life ahead.

"Tell me all about it," said Rebecca. Evangelist Fredrick told her he saw Eric, and asked if they're getting back together. Rebecca smiled and asked the Evangelist if he thinks it will ever be possible for her and Eric to be together again, considering the manner she left Eric to be with him.

The Evangelist confidently assured her that nothing is impossible with God, he then said he's praying for her and Stacy. Stacy insists on not being selfish, and asked the Evangelist if his concern is just for her and Rebecca. She then questioned what his intention is concerning other members resident in the camp.

"It's natural to be agitated when change is on the horizon, even when the change will be for good," said Evangelist Fredrick. Rebecca muttered repeatedly saying, even though she's falling for his ideas, he's yet to fully convince her that there's light in what he's proposing. The Evangelist assured her repeatedly that they both know that living life scantily dressed in the service of Lucifer is debasing and reminded her they spent time the other day at the restaurant, and asked if she remembered how beautiful life is out there.

"Yeah, but it doesn't mean they don't have troubles, and I was out there before, you know," said Rebecca. Evangelist Fredrick reminded Rebecca that staying in the camp doesn't mean her troubles have gone away, and reminded her they were a couple for about three years. Stacy interjected and urged the Evangelist to speak in a clearer term, asking him to lay out the possible options available to the people. Realising that Rebecca and Stacy are instrumental in his getting this right, he'd to open up to them that some of them under the employment of the Camp, like Stacy, will be placed under the employment of the church.

"I guess you would love to work for God," said Evangelist Fredrick. Rebecca turned around and saw Eric approaching, she then said they'll continue this conversation in the future because Eric is waiting and she needed to join him. Eric caught up with them eventually and didn't hesitate to ask Rebecca if she's still friends with Ambrose after his attempt on her life.

Rebecca immediately repeated her earlier comment saying she has put that behind her and "I guess you've put my actions against you behind you?" asked Rebecca. Eric on the other hand realised, his attempt to stir up bad blood between the pair didn't work as he himself also confirmed to Rebecca that he's trying to put the past behind, but she did treat him shabbily.

Eric became a bit cheeky with the Evangelist, as he asked him if he thinks Europe is still interested in the Christian faith he preaches, suggesting a lot of Christians in Europe have ditched the faith. The Evangelist on the other hand, hinted Eric that he worked with the late Prophet Gregory Helsing, and he knows the activities of the Bliss Luciferians Camp.

He pointed out to Eric that most Christians ditching their Christian faith over petty issues such as the errors of other Christians, and even church errors, are oblivious of the effort put in by these Satanic agents to make them lose their faith. They'd no idea that their Christian faith is the most precious gift they have, and each time a person lost his faith, it is a win for the devil, at least one more candidate accompanying the devil to hell.

After the Evangelist left, Eric became cheerful and said even though he was pained by Rebecca's actions, he had to move on and not remain in the place of a loser. Rebecca was circumspect not to make a fool out of herself, she then began prodding Eric with questions that will illuminate her on Eric's love life.

"You didn't come with her?" asked Rebecca.

"Come with whom?" asked Eric.

"Your partner, I guess you moved on and got involved with someone else," said Rebecca.

Stacy doesn't seem to like veiled comments and decided to be more direct as she interjected and asked Eric if he's still free, and suggesting Rebecca wants to know if she still has a place in his heart.

Rebecca muttered and asked Stacy to stop being forward, as she asked her how she knew what's in her mind. Stacy became jocular after bursting Rebecca's bubble, urging Eric not to mind Rebecca, she then opened up to him that Rebecca wants to get back with him but doesn't know how to go about it.

"For your information, Rebecca, I'm still single, but your actions towards me made me stay away from women," Eric retorted. Rebecca became emotional with her face looking down, as she confessed in quite a subtle tone, that she knew she acted badly, and she's sorry about how shamefully she treated him. Eric replied that her action did deal a great blow to him, but her malicious ridicule wouldn't turn him into a vengeful character, he however didn't mention his failed adventure with Loana.

Shawn Tristan got wind of what Zeppelin has been up to lately, he then called Zeppelin immediately to register a protest.

"Hello Zeppelin, it has been a while," said Shawn.

Zeppelin smiled the moment Shawn said hello to him, "What a surprise, Shawn? I actually expected this call, and you did call," said Zeppelin. Shawn wasn't smiling back at Zeppelin, and funnily, the conversation wasn't a friendly one from the moment Zeppelin picked the phone, Shawn felt slighted by Zeppelin as he asked if he doesn't deserve being consulted.

"You mean I should've consulted you? Maybe you're right and I'm sorry about that," said Zeppelin. Efforts to pacify Shawn with sweet talk failed because Shawn was keen for answers, as he kept asking Zeppelin where the thought of building a church in the camp came from. Shawn is one of the three directors of the camp but has been visibly absent in the running of the camp.

Zeppelin became defensive and began asking Shawn when he last visited the camp and wanting to know where his sudden interest in the preservation of the camp comes from. Shawn dismissed Zeppelin's submissions, and insisted he has a stake in that camp because he's a member of the Bliss Luciferian Camp, and more so, he's a member of the Board of Directors of the Bliss Luciferian camp.

Shawn hesitated for a while, and accepted he seldom call to discuss matters relating to the camp, but that shouldn't be a reason for the brash decision. He muttered and said Zeppelin made this whole thing look like it's quite above his pay grade to have a say in this matter, in a manner that he might probably have to sell one of his kidneys to assume that role.

Without expressly asking Shawn to continue bluffing away, Zeppelin knew for sure that his idea of collapsing this elephant in one sweep seems too much for Shawn, and even Shawn himself knew Zeppelin is calling his bluff but seems to be going about it benignly.

Zeppelin's approach to collapsing this camp is producing a squawky reaction, more like the sound of a hammer shattering glass. This approach is rather hyperbolic than linear, instead of starting with the directors where one thing will lead to the other, he's rather collapsing the whole thing in one go.

Shawn inquisitively asked to know what side Zeppelin's bread was buttered on, and the apparent simplification that this move isn't motivated by a fist full of cash from the church isn't something many find logical. He muttered, yet reminded Zeppelin that a cash bonanza from the church to sway and incentivise people to return to their old Christian faith is felonious, and more like placing a loaded gun on the table during a negotiation. As far as Zeppelin is concerned, this isn't situational and neither is it anything close to placing a loaded gun on the table. After all, he is convinced that he isn't charging into the camp and chasing residents out like a bull in a China shop.

Shawn then intimated to Zeppelin that his actions can be interpreted that he'd secretly wished that Prophet Gregory is out of the way, so he can do as he please with the camp. Zeppelin on the other hand asked Shawn where he was when the Prophet took his last breath, and reminded Shawn, the Prophet took his last breath in his arms, showing how much he cared for the prophet.

Zeppelin remained upbeat and said he's glad Shawn acknowledged the fact that he distanced himself from the activities of the camp, and the few occasions they spoke was only when he called Shawn to discuss matters relating to the camp. Zeppelin seems to have a lot on his chest, but decided to put a sock in it, yet muttered to Shawn that the tail won't be wagging the dog this time, before urging Shawn to let this matter be. Shawn couldn't take the insult lying down, he continued his protest and said as a director he deserved to be in the know of whatever goes on in the camp.

It's embarrassingly obvious that Shawn finds it quite puzzling that Zeppelin dared to make an audacious decision of building a church in the camp designated for the service of Lucifer without consulting him. He was left needled by the perplexing feeling that Zeppelin subtly gave him the middle finger, and this left him reeling from within. Zeppelin assured Shawn that there's no love lost between them, as he reminded Shawn of when he last contributed towards the financing of the camp.

"Are you implying, this decision is an attempt to humiliate me?" asked Shawn.

"No, not at all, this decision is about a change for good, let's do things differently," replied Zeppelin.

Shawn's disposition began to thaw after Zeppelin repeatedly pointed out to him that there's no need rocking the boat at this point. Quite perplexing as it might seem for Shawn who then proceeded to speak in a tone, saying he isn't disputing Zeppelin's commitment towards the running of the camp, but insisted, the directors deserved to be carried along when a major decision of this nature is on the table. He then asked Zeppelin if he has discussed this move with Mitchell, the other member of the board. Funnily, Zeppelin affirmed he did discuss the matter with Mitchell, and as expected, Mitchell is ok with the idea of building a church in the camp. Shawn immediately muttered in frustration that Zeppelin has railroaded Mitchell into coming onboard and said he can see that Zeppelin didn't bother to accord him the same regard he accorded Mitchell. Shawn however returned to his earlier position on the matter as he questioned why he wasn't also consulted.

While this conversation rambles on, Zeppelin decided it's best to go softly on Shawn, he then apologised to Shawn that he's sorry about his failure to consult him, and said he meant no offence, then urged him it's best they move on from this. Shawn then toned down the outburst and asked Zeppelin what he intends to do with camp residents who don't intend to be a part of the church thing.

"They will be resettled, and those that want to be a part of the Christian fold, will be employed by the church," said Zeppelin.

"How, Zeppelin, I need to know?" asked Shawn. Zeppelin paused as he attempts to choose his words carefully so as not to inflame the situation further. He opened his mouth and assured Shawn that he'll work with the church to work out modalities of employment for those that choose to return to their Christian faith.

The great chasm between what Zeppelin turned into in relation to what was expected of him is indicative of a man on a mission. His willingness to put his head above the parapet was quite audacious and tellingly naïve, but that didn't in anyway make his old friends perceive him as a charlatan. Not minding the humour and candour associated with fairytales, it remains common knowledge that happily ever after doesn't even work in fairytales.

Shawn immediately smelt a rat and didn't hesitate to accuse Zeppelin of tricking the people back to their old Christian faith, and he then put it directly to Zeppelin and asked if he's returning residents to their old faith against their will.

"Not at all, they're all adults and can make a choice for themselves, and I'm not coercing anybody," said Zeppelin.

Shawn gave a long pause, and after a while, he then asked Zeppelin if this is his way of saying goodbye to Luciferianism and the Liberal lifestyle. Zeppelin interjected in his attempt to play down any assumption that he has won, as he suggested to Shawn that they shouldn't be too quick to jump into conclusions, and the future will now depend on the outcome of the debate. He however persuaded Shawn that there's no need for concern, saying this move will not in any way result in a tide of people leaving the camp, and after all, there are only fifty residents in the camp.

"Obviously, you seem to have said goodbye to your service to Lucifer, long ago," said Zeppelin.

"Why did you say that?" asked Shawn.

"You don't participate, you don't come around, and you distanced yourself in most cases," said Zeppelin.

Shawn then decided it's best to wait and see the outcome of this debate before they can conclude on the way forward.

### The Debate

Days later, Evangelist Fredrick was at it again inside the Bliss Luciferian Camp as he continues with his pursuit of winning the people to his side. He had a Bible in his hand as he spoke out loud and said, "So bounteous is the joy of serving God, rather than running around this camp half naked."

Hubert wasn't far away, as he hushed the Evangelist, urging him to stop menacing their ears with the fallacy of making it look like Christianity is all they needed to live a happy life. Hubert then walked a few steps forward, and said he was a Christian, they all were, but nothing to show for it.

Evangelist Fredrick smiled; he then raised his bible as he entreated the people to join him as he introduced them to the splendour of heaven. Hubert didn't stop short of referring to the Evangelist as a plague and demanded that he must be removed from amongst them immediately, saying he's bewildered at his pretended piety. Unfortunately, some of the residents are overly fond of the Evangelist who used to be the manager of the camp and hurling him through the fence, and out of the camp, is something to which they'll never acquiesce. The Evangelist then proceeded to say he has put himself in a position where they will love to hate him and hate to loath him, but he's here to show them tolerance as opposed to hiding away in this camp.

Hubert insisted that the Evangelist is shrouded in duplicity, and tragically pursuing a morally twisted course while pretending to love them. The Evangelist on the other hand didn't hesitate to say he isn't duplicitous, but God wants to show Himself to the people of this camp and he's ready to go the whole hog until God takes his place in the affairs of nations, and in the life of members in this camp. He admonished them further saying, any freedom without God is a corrupted freedom. "Your kind of freedom give you a sense of something that is satisfying, and yet leaves you worrying that something about life isn't right. This leaves you in a state of continuous pursuit and self-seeking," said the Evangelist.

The Evangelist wasn't messing about, he was succinct, and didn't hold back his views as he pontificates on the stark difference between Christianity and Luciferianism, as more like day and night. He now feels more comfortable than anxious, as he placed Christ on a high moral pedestal before he began admonishing residents saying, Jesus Christ is the truth, and Lucifer is nothing but a liar destined for hell, reminding them that Lucifer has been judged and condemned, but the unfortunate thing is that Lucifer wants them to accompany him to hell.

"We aren't talking about a God whose mercies, grace, and resources are finite, the God of the bible is infinite in his resources. He loves to see you smile, He loves to see you prosper in good health, and even in earthly resources, and wants you to live a life that is right," the Evangelist announced.

"You keep telling us, Christ is the truth, by whose authority is that?" Asked Mortiboys.

"God's authority," replied the Evangelist.

"Is that the truth because God said it is the truth, or God said it is the truth because it is the truth?" Asked Mortiboys.

"It is the truth because God said it is the truth," replied the Evangelist.

Tobias Little wasn't ingenuous and without tongue-in-cheek in his critical thought, interjected. "Are you suggesting that God caused the shipwreck and killed all the passengers of the Octal Flamingo just because God wants you to preach to us?"

The Evangelist response had to be illuminating, as he said of course not, God didn't kill the passengers of the Octa Flamingo just to drag him by the collar so he could preach to residents of the Bliss Camp. The truth is that God has it in mind to bring him to the Bliss camp at some point, and the devil needed to stop that from happening. He then alluded to the fact that the devil caused the shipwreck to stop him but God turned things around by fast forwarding his sojourn to the Bliss camp.

"There is no need pounding the sand because God will always have his way and definitely, He will drain this swamp," the Evangelist cautioned.

It was a moment of stillness in fear when darkness and utter darkness pervades Europe that God picked this Evangelist to go up against what the reverend described as a brood of vipers. At a time when Christians find it difficult to put their chest forward in righteousness and push back on the anti-God doctrines in their cities. He emphasised that Jesus brought heaven down but the nations of Europe has vehemently rejected this free gift of heaven.

Mortiboys once came to the camp with a northern lass, who had a nasty case of expectations meeting reality after she arrived the Bliss Camp. Her experience didn't leave any room for nuance as she accused Mortiboys of being blind to his own blindness. Mortiboys didn't go after her, hoping she will come back to him, as he insisted that decisions made in anger are repented in leisure and surely, all things come to those who waits.

There was this undercurrent of anger, that looks like everyone was about to let loose, and arguably, the Evangelist got everyone telling him off, and he got so much telling off, that he was almost choking on it. This push back came particularly from Mortiboys, as he stood beside the Evangelist, who considered this camp to be nothing but a moral junkyard that must be shut down.

Mortiboys is an English man who regularly travels from England to the Bliss camp because he treats his Luciferian lifestyle as some sort of escapism. The permafrown on Mortiboys' face was palpable but not enough to leave the Evangelist spreadeagle because looks don't kill.

The Evangelist was standing beside Mortiboys while addressing the crowd, and the Evangelist whom Mortiboys refers to as the preacher-man sensed Mortiboys was bearing down on him in quite a threatening manner. He then took some steps away from Mortiboys to avoid being on this angry residents' face, as he made sure of it, to leave a safe distance between him and Mortiboys.

The whole thing is now looking more like Goldilocks and the Big Bad Wolf, with residents assuming the place of the victims even as they point fingers of accusations at the Evangelist who has suddenly taken the place of the Big Bad Wolf.

Mortiboys is a sort of self-acclaimed elitists Luciferian, and the feeling of helplessness isn't something he associates with himself, which explains his actions. Even at that, Mortiboys wouldn't allow his emotion to corner him into punching the preacher-man on the face, but the temptation to roughen the preacher-man a bit becomes one he couldn't bear. This meant the safe distance didn't do much, after all. Mortiboys didn't disappoint on-lookers as he walked up to the Evangelist and grabbed him by the collar of his well-ironed office shirt.

"You keep going on and on about the splendour of heaven, show me the splendour of heaven," Mortiboys retorted.

"The splendour of heaven, is **Jesus**, I bring you **Jesus**," said the Evangelist.

"Jesus? What nonsense!" Exclaimed Mortiboys. He then let go of the Evangelist's collar.

"I bring you **Jesus**, the man of peace and the only way to God, **Jesus** won't judge you and his arms are open to receive you because he wants a friendship with you.

"How? is your Jesus interested in becoming a Luciferian?" asked Orla.

"There are better alternatives to a life of nudism in service to the devil, but a relationship with Jesus opens your eyes to the beauty of Christian living," he replied.

The Evangelist then proceeded to admonish them as he encouraged them to accept Christ, and that it doesn't matter how bad and how unworthy they see themselves, Jesus has a way of restoring them back to the light, and a life of peace.

The Evangelist didn't stop but proceeded to remind residents that everyone one, the rich or the poor, the pretty or the ugly, the handsome or the not so good-looking guy, the tall, the average in hight or even the short. It doesn't matter what we desire or what height we aspire to attain, everyone wants something to make them feel fulfilled. And even when our innermost desire has been achieved, we seem to still want something because there's always a drive for something that we think will make us complete and funny enough, even when you have achieved that which you hoped will make you complete, you will come to realise that the feeling of desiring something that will make you complete is still there, and never goes away.

"Are you saying you have come to make the feeling go away?" Asked Mortiboys.

"Using this camp as some sort of escapism hasn't made that feeling of seeking fulfilment go away. Yes! There's a part of every man that is connected to God and when that connection is broken, man will continue to be in need and will never stop pursuing," replied Evangelist Fredrick.

Realising that members don't seem willing to throw the Evangelist out, following his instructions, except for Mortiboys who roughened the Evangelist a bit. Hubert didn't want to wallow in the embarrassment, he then became a bit confrontational as he shouts out to the people that a man with such a strident tone, and spouting extreme religious view is not one to be followed. Evangelist Fredrick continued to maintain his meek posture even as he asked Hubert why he's scoffing at his proposals, and belittling his ideas without offering an alternative to a better life, he then muttered. "This makes you a character indeed," replied the Evangelist.

Hubert on the other hand, made it known that they're already in the service of Lucifer, and there's no better life than what they already have.

Even your Lucifer is subject to God. In the bible book of Job 1:6, when the sons of God came to present themselves to God, Lucifer also came to present himself to God. "Doesn't that tell you who is in charge? God is supreme, when your Lucifer stands in the queue to be judged, you also will be judged and every man on his own. Unfortunately, Lucifer has been judged already, he's just taking you guys with him. Why then will you guys leave the God that's in charge to worship a fraudulent Lucifer?" asked the Evangelist.

"God was unjustified for kicking Lucifer out of heaven and we aren't happy about that," said Mortiboys.

"Unfortunately, there's nothing you can do about that. God remains God irrespective of what anyone thinks, and how anyone feels. But one thing is sure, God is good, and always right," replied the Evangelist.

The more the Evangelist unravels, Hubbert could see nothing but mystery wrapped in imagination that has been unleashed on them. He just couldn't get his head around how this once fragile Ambrose suddenly became the man butting heads with their Lucifer.

There wasn't a dull moment as residents engaged the Evangelist in this delicate subject. Yet the Evangelist was upfront as he reminded residents, God loves them even before their decision to become Luciferians, and He still loves them even now that they are in the service of Lucifer.

"Albeit your association with Lucifer might want to make you hesitate, God still loves you anyway, and if after this democratic process you intend to remain a Luciferian, God's hand of love is still stretched out to you because God wants a fellowship with you. That door closes when you die, and no one knows when death will come knocking," the evangelist retorted.

Kosi was the only person of South American descent resident in the Bliss camp, and he didn't take likely the fact that Ambrose who was once one of them is here to tell them they are no good.

"Can you imagine this annoyingly arrogant White privileged American, returning to this camp to tell us what to do? Please take your good news somewhere else," Kosi retorted.

"Kosi, I have lived amongst you, I was one of you, and you and I were friends, but I am only here to tell you of a better alternative to the life I once lived," replied the Evangelist.

He stopped and said the hollow stare on their faces isn't something new, because that was something they once had in common, and he wasn't speaking in the finger wagging sense. He was rather empathetic as he pointed them to the collective pain they once shared. Ambrose needed an opportunity to prove to them he isn't here just to get their goat, he then stopped with his hands clasped, before he decided to try a little humour, in the face of this stiff opposition. "We all need a smile sometimes, don't we? Because it makes the world a better place," asked the Evangelist.

"It doesn't matter, just go away and leave us alone," Kosi retorted again.

"Kosi, I understand your prejudice, and I implore you to consider an alternative to this camp, I leave with you the words of Apostle Paul in the bible book of Philippians 4:8.

'Finally, brothers, whatever is true, whatever is noble, whatever is right, whatever is pure, whatever is lovely, whatever is admirable--if anything is excellent or praiseworthy--think about such things," said the Evangelist.

The Evangelist continued to explore the subject further. "You may feel frustrated with life, your marriage may have crashed, you may have lost a loved one and struggling to come to terms with your loss, or your life is just hard and things aren't just working out, and perhaps life may have been unfair to you, and believe me, sometimes it looks like that to everyone. We all feel overwhelmed some times, and even men of God do feel overwhelmed.

Maybe you're in mess and all effort to get yourself out of it hasn't panned out, and it seems to you like you are in a room without doors and windows, and the walls are closing in on you. There is only one way out, and that way is Jesus. He understands what you're going through, He will give you hope even in your darkest moment and he will give you peace. He might not make your troubles go away because in this world you will have troubles, but Jesus will walk with you and help you find peace as you deal with the troubles of this world.

I don't know how and why many of you ended up in this camp, but running to the Bliss Luciferian Camp for succour won't help and Lucifer can't help you either.

Jesus Christ is the only Way and the only Truth."

"I love to go to heaven, but asking us to live our lives in a certain way is ridiculously out of order, and God has no right to do that," Natalie retorted.

As far as this camp is concerned, Natalie is someone in the fringes and speaks from the fringes, she isn't an audible voice, not the likes of Orla who will always put her two pennies in, even when not needed.

"I understand your question, Natalie, what about your own choice to decide what you want, and you feel God has taken that choice away from you?" asked the Evangelist.

"Of course, yes, I suppose so," replied Natalie.

"In every facet of the human society, there are always requirements, and you must meet certain criteria to access certain privileges. There are rules everywhere, there are laws and there are conditions that needs to be met. Be it a space in the market place, you must meet certain criteria put in place by the council, or if you desire a place in the university, you must sit and pass your GCSE exams to go to the university, and for the lawyers, you must take the Bar exams to be called to the Bar, or for the Doctors, you must take your medical exams to practice as a doctor. If the human society operates by rules and laws like this, how come humans deem it ridiculous that there are certain requirements to make heaven," said the Evangelist.

Amy got hopping mad at Natalie for suggesting she loved the idea of heaven, and decided to remind her what they are. "What has gotten into you, Natalie? We are Luciferians and shouldn't have anything to do with God's heaven," said Amy.

Natalie was unbowed by Amy's fierce rebuke, as she muttered in her response stressing that there's no need being speculative about the intentions of others, and she then hinted that she has no intention of rushing off to hell in hand cuffs.

"Please let's not allow our imagination run away with us, and please I beg you to desist from telling God off, because God is God, in His own class and beyond human imagination and comprehension. We humans unfortunately, are nothing but mere dust. The fact that God loves human so much does not in any way translate into God and man being at par," said the Evangelist.

He did frantically try to correct the erroneous impression they have of God as a patient father that can be addressed without regard. He stopped and watched them bleating out as they speak noisily and wildly, he then alluded to the fact that God is obviously a Lamb, but He is also a Lion when He chooses to act.

This Evangelist isn't some kind of self-seeking glory hunter, he's a man carrying out God's instruction. "We don't have to live our lives by the dictates of the bible. God should allow humans to discover themselves by themselves," said Hubert.

"Man know thy self, I suppose. Socrates, isn't?" Asked the Evangelist.

"Of course, Socrates," replied Hubert.

"Socrates himself didn't discover himself, he was still seeking when he died," replied the Evangelist.

"That's heresy, Ambrose, Socrates is a respected philosopher," replied Hubert.

The Evangelist then proceeded to say that Socrates was no doubt a sage, and aside his mention of sacrificing a rooster to Asclepius, in his last moments. He was talking about praying so that his life after death will be a fortunate one, and when you're praying for a certain outcome, it means that outcome is outside your control.

"If you read his last words, you will discover that Socrates was hoping that his transition will turn out well. That shows he wasn't hundred percent certain of how things will turn out.

Unlike Socrates, if you die in Christ, you're sure of transitioning to heaven. You don't need to pray for your transition to be a fortunate one.

The worst thing that will happen to any of you, is for your friends and even the government to pat your back into Hell. They might be telling you that your values are fine and wonderful, and that it's great to be different rather than helping you to better yourself to avoid Hell. Frankly speaking, Hell is the worst thing that should happen to any man.

Even if we die today, we can't escape judgement because death isn't the end, judgement transcends death. So, don't think you can do as you please here on earth and when you die, you have escaped God. After death, there lies judgement," said the Evangelist.

While Hubert and the Evangelist were at it, and the crowd listening keenly, as this pair make their case, there was a sudden pandemonium, and this time, it was Wopi chasing a mouse. Obviously, the mouse flustered the crowd in a manner that got people jumping off the ground, and thumping. This cat is a known mice hunter, bred from one of the species of wild cats, and even as the mouse makes an escape by mingling and weaving through the crowd and between their feet, that didn't deter Wopi who seems quite determined not to miss out on this possible meal.

Wopi didn't stop but followed the mouse, and that sort of created the pandemonium that left people who have phobia for mouse squirming and scampering. Jarrod quickly dashed towards his cat and swooped Wopi off the ground into his embrace, but the determined cat leap-frogged from Jarrod's embrace as she continued her pursuit, and it didn't take long before the mouse was between Wopi's canines.

Wopi is Jarrod beloved cat, Wopi is famous for keeping tabs on all the mice in this camp and even those in the adjoining bushes. This cat could smell a mouse from a mile away, and all the mice in this vicinity know it. Wopi hardly eats conventional cat food, she has a special appetite for mice, and it's no surprise to Jarrod that mice are Wopi's special delicacy.

After the hullaballoo with Wopi, that had a highly profound impact on the calm atmosphere, the debate eventually resumed, and Hubert still didn't take the disturbance of minutes ago likely. He then proceeded to ask Ambrose if his intention was to invade, subdue and forcibly convert this camp into a church. Amy stood by the side and fuming at the refusal of camp members to throw the Evangelist out of the camp. She interjected and accused the Evangelist of taking advantage of the unique and thrilling privilege of working in this camp, to worm his way into their hearts.

The Evangelist immediately decided to set the record straight and said he didn't worm his way here; he was actually on a missionary assignment but God brought him here.

Amy drew closer and finger pointing at the Evangelist, as she reminded him that God has better things to do than bring him to a naturist camp. "And to do what, if I may ask?" asked Amy. He then focused his attention on Amy and said it's no longer news that he was a victim of the Octal Flamingo, then said he's a Christian missionary who found himself unconscious by the beach of a Luciferian camp.

Amy took this whole thing personal, because she finds it frustrating to be at the mercy of the church. The Evangelist could sense the build-up of anger in Amy, as she prodded him further with questions about what his botched missionary assignment got to do with building a church in this camp. Evangelist Fredrick is known for his charismatic nature, and maintained a warm ambience all along, as he assured Amy that God specifically told him he brought him here to see the moral decadence close to him while he was busy travelling around the world on missionary assignments.

The debate suddenly became rowdy as Orla added her voice to Amy's, asking the Evangelist why God would bring him to a nudist camp housing Christians who has ditched the faith.

"Your cruel and vile assertion leaves me baffled," said Evangelist Fredrick.

Hubert interjected and urged the Evangelist not to be baffled and said he has been attentive all these while and many of them have been, but they haven't heard God speak before, asking if hearing God is exclusive to the Evangelist. Residents present then burst into laughter, but Rebecca seemed not to like the sniggering, and decided to break her silence as she admonished the people to stop acting tone-deaf and dumb by not listening. She then urged them to listen to what Ambrose will have to offer if he has his way.

"Ok, Rebecca has brought up an important point," said Berger, he then turned to Ambrose and asked, if they allow him to build a church in this camp, then what happens to them.

"Those of you working in this camp that love to return to your Christian faith will be employed by the church," said Evang. Fredrick.

Hubert didn't hesitate to hush the Evangelist up and asked him to keep his alternatives to himself, insisting many of the people here don't want anything to do with his Christianity.

Evangelist Fredrick continued and wasn't deterred by what he called Hubert's damn-low banter, and assured them that the church will help those who chose not to have anything to do with the church to get a job out there, and that's for those who aren't already working. Allowing residents who aren't returning to their Christian faith to remain in the camp was a compromised path, that isn't an option for Reverend Fitzgerald and even the Evangelist.

"You have our lives planned out, what gives you right to think you can think for us?" asked Amy.

"Zeppelin will be a part of whatever the church does, and I promise you, none of you will be left out," said Evangelist Fredrick.

Hubert turned around with his hands spread out to attract the attention of the people to himself, and asked the Evangelist what makes him think anyone in their right senses will like these plans. The Evangelist wasn't giving in either as he assured onlookers that whatever he has got to offer is better than running around in this camp nude.

Amy suddenly began to weep, and accusing the Evangelist of being cruel to them. She then pointed at Ambrose and said he's pushing his argument over the ethical cliff, and he's doing this with a healthy dose of fear. Evangelist Fredrick wasn't apathetic to Amy's feelings, he tried explaining to her that he was one of them, and they weren't happier than those in the regular society. Yet, they lived in secrecy because they're always scantily dressed. Amy turned around to leave, but promised the Evangelist she will do everything within her power to ensure he doesn't have his way, as this will be decided by a vote.

The obvious division among residents is beginning to surface the moment Berger reminded Amy that it's not up to her, as he insisted, he's ready to go with Ambrose and many others might as well be thinking of doing the same. Amy then stopped and asked Berger what happened to him, asking him what Ambrose did to him that made him fall so cheap.

Residents had their heads spinning, the moment Berger breaks rank. "Ambrose didn't give a dime to me, I use to be a Christian, but now, I'm trapped in this Luciferian lifestyle, and I'm glad to find a way out," said Berger.

Hubert overheard Berger's comment and wasn't particularly pleased that Berger bought into the ruse Ambrose was selling to them. He then asked Berger why he still remained in this camp against his better judgement when he realised his Christian beliefs is contending with his service to Lucifer. Berger didn't hesitate to let his fellow residents know that the amount of pressure that brought him to this camp, is still the same amount of pressure required to force him out of this camp.

He then told them that the ferocity of Ambrose's push is what he needed to make the sudden change he needed. Rebecca immediately became an enabler, by adding her voice to Berger's to make the echoes of support louder, as she announced to residents that Ambrose seems to be the pressure, she herself needed to redirect her life and possibly what many of them actually need as a way out of this rot. Hubert was quite disappointed and got hopping mad at what he described as dissenting voices from Berger and Rebecca, asking if they're acquiescing to religious proclivities to assuage their misplaced trepidations.

Convinced that the truth never wilts, he wasn't frazzled by the veracity of whatever falsehood perpetuated in this camp for years, he remained resolute despite push backs from residents until their resolve began to melt. The Evangelist observed that the stiff resistance is beginning to thaw, and the table is about to turn. He immediately invited those that are willing to give their life to Christ to join him make a difference in this camp, saying this is a clarion call to spiritual awakening, as he reminded them that his survival is a clear and unassailable testimony.

Berger took some steps forward as he is determined to give his life to Christ, in what his fellow Luciferians considered a jaw dropping moment, but he suddenly stopped and walked back. Orla's spine-chilling rebuke was nothing but a chilling warning to Berger, who suddenly realised his move will put him at Hubert's cross-hairs. Berger has inadvertently become a recluse, following his sudden interest in the Evangelist's message.

He realised he will definitely be mobbed by residents if he attends to the alter call, he then decided to walk back. The Evangelist read Berger's mind and realised he feared for his safety and decided not to push any further until the ballot happens. He then deferred the alter call until Saturday, to avoid putting anyone in danger.

"We don't want to live in bondage of Christianity any longer, and please allow us to express the freedom that being Luciferians offers," said Hubert.

The atmosphere was quite electrifying, more like something out of a disaster movie and this isn't some kind of a game between the dog and the Vet. The Evangelist is now itching to wrap the day's debate, as he retorted and said the word freedom is a hydra-headed monster, a cankerworm that has no destructive limit, and reminded them that freedom isn't actually free.

Sensing that the debate of the day is coming to an end, Hubert assured the Evangelist that his irrevocable commitment means he'll work assiduously to retain the true happiness they enjoy in this camp. The Evangelist immediately stepped down from the stand and said by Saturday Zeppelin will be here for the voting.

"I beg you all who abandoned your Christian faith for this camp to return, God wants you back to Himself, and He said, I should tell you this," the Evangelist retorted.

"This man's rhetoric is nothing but a retrogressive propensity that stocks the embers of hatred in our world today, and I urge you not to fall for him," said Hubert. Berger interjected and thanked everyone, and said they'll meet at the polls by Saturday, yet reminded them that one-on-one campaign is still allowed, and it didn't take long before members began dispersing.

The Evangelist avoided exacerbating the situation but understands the possible ramification of postponing Berger's opportunity to give his life to Christ because tomorrow might be too late. As Rebecca walked him to the car, he immediately called Rebecca aside and pleaded with Rebecca who was a bit hesitant to please bring Berger to meet with him at the park, later that day.

Hours later, it was sunset at the busy park, and not long after Rebecca and Berger met Evangelist Fredrick who was already waiting for them, they got talking. The Evangelist hinted him of the need not to postpone an opportunity to receive Christ into his life because tomorrow might be too late.

He proceeded to remind Berger that they're both witnesses to how Prophet Gregory sends priests all over Europe to encourage people to seek liberal Christianity, and the deconstruction of the Christian faith. Albeit ignorantly, many in the West are taking the bait, thinking that deconstruction is their personal decision to drop the Christian faith, unbeknownst to them, they have inadvertently just enrolled into Lucifer's camp, because there's no middle ground, and you are either here or there.

He then pointed to one of the benches in the park and they stepped aside and took their seat.

After making themselves comfortable, the Evangelist continued with admonishing Berger, as he acknowledged that the rabid desire of camp residents to kill this conversation meant any resident coming forward to accept Christ will incur the ire of these angry residents.

"Look around you, what did you see?" asked the Evangelist.

Berger who obviously had no idea of what the Evangelist was getting at looked around and said he didn't see anything, except lots of people going about their business, some catching fun and others just moving on.

Great! But do you know that a hundred years from now almost all these people will not be here, they will all be dead, and if Christ tarries, this place will be replaced by other people and might still be as busy as it is today.

"Yes, Fredrick, you are making sense, but what are you getting at?" asked Berger.

He also touched on the perennial topic of human being having the final say when it comes to God, the Evangelist suddenly smiled and said, fighting with God is liking to a person taking a water gun to a gun fight.

"This earth belongs to God, and life after death also belongs to God, and all the people you see here today will account for their time here on earth," replied the Evangelist.

He then proceeded to itemise the three common questions people ask when they are dying.

What happens after I die?

I have always heard people talk about heaven and hell, are they real?

I have never believed in God, will He accept me?

"I understand the folly of the human heart, I understand the pride of life, the intelligence of the human mind, the beauty and wonder associated with human beings, but remember that this wonderful creature called human is nothing but a quintessence of dust. From dust we all came and to dust we all will return, but the real you, I mean our soul, will answer to God in judgement.

He then quoted the Bible verse of Psalm 24:1-2. "The earth is the LORD's, and everything in it, the world, and all who live in it; for he founded it on the seas and established it on the waters".

Realising the wheels are obviously coming off the Bliss Camp, and in quite a conciliatory tone, the Evangelist posited to them that God has no place for Universalism. He then admonished Berger, as he elucidated that God is in the process of reclaiming the wasteland of Europe and this camp that epitomises a moral junkyard, is nothing but a wasteland.

His message resonated quite well with Berger as he admonished them further with the word of God. The message was dished out raw, nothing choreographed, and nothing farcical. Rebecca suddenly finds herself holding the Evangelist's hand and asking him to pray for her.

He then led them to Christ before they returned to the camp as they await the democratic process that's just a day away.

# CHAPTER

## SIXTEEN

### *The Open Ballot*

It's Saturday, it's time to vote, and Zeppelin was on hand to
supervise the much-anticipated democratic process. He stood
in the mist of members of the Bliss Luciferian Camp and began
addressing members. Zeppelin began by reminding members
that the voting is slated for today, Saturday, to allow members
who aren't resident in this camp to be a part of the democratic
process because today's decision affects them. Amy became seemingly exasperated by the fear that Ambrose will have the day, she
immediately rushed to Zeppelin, and suggested they wait an hour
longer to enable members on their way to be a part of the process.
Zeppelin on the other hand affirmed that it's obvious that they
already have more crowds than expected, but Amy seemed overly
cautious and suggested that twenty more minutes will be good.

"We can't wait any longer, we've given a thirty-minute period
of grace, let's get on with it," replied Zeppelin.

Hubert was upbeat because he's convinced the odds are to his
favour, and after all, who will want to vote for this bigot spouting
nonsense about God. He then asked Zeppelin to enlighten them

on how the process will happen. The Evangelist isn't taking a stab in the dark, he sees a towering victory ahead, and Hubert seems not to take the Evangelist seriously, saying his proposal leaves much to be desired.

Zeppelin immediately focused his attention on Hubert, and said it's just a simple open ballot, those with Ambrose on the right and those with Hubert should go left.

Eric has suddenly become a regular in the camp after mending his friendship with Rebecca, he stood beside Rebecca asking where she intends to vote.

"What do you think? With Ambrose of course, maybe if the camp is converted to a church, I will go with you and live in the heart of Bucharest," said Rebecca. Eric smiled and said it's good to hear Rebecca proposing to come with him, he then said he'll vote for Ambrose, since he's Rebecca's choice.

Rebecca who has suddenly assumed the role of a flunky, continued her manoeuvring as she left Eric and walked up to Stacy, and asked who she intends to vote for. "All the time spent in this camp hasn't made me a happier person as envisioned, I will go with Ambrose," said Stacy.

These ladies have done some manoeuvring of pulling some strings to win friends and sympathisers to Ambrose before now, but now that the hour of reckoning has come, they still needed to confirm that their loyalty to Ambrose is unshakable.

Orla moved to the left in support of Hubert, she then turned to Jarrod who seemed to be dawdling around, and beckoned on Jarrod, asking where he's headed, and reminded him he belongs to Hubert's camp.

Jarrod dawdled for a while, and said he don't know what to think anymore, saying if the church will resettle him, maybe he will opt for a change because he will love to return to the city. Amy was shocked to see those on her side creeping away and queuing behind Ambrose, and even as she stood behind Hubert she screamed, "Shame on you," at Ambrose, and accused him of using Rebecca and Stacy to win members to himself. The

Evangelist was quite amazed to see Jarrod and many other residents queuing behind him, he then shook hands with those that find his offer attractive. It suddenly dawned on Hubert that things aren't as easy as they seem, the Evangelist has suddenly become a man whose bluff they can't call.

Moments later, members were distinctively separated into two groups, with a clear line of demarcation. Those in support of building a church queued behind the Evangelist, while those who want the status quo to remain queued behind Hubert. Zeppelin then conducted a head count, and funnily, it was a tie.

"We have a tie, each side has one hundred ninety-four votes each, what do we do?" asked Zeppelin. Hubert immediately suggested to Zeppelin, that Zeppelin would have to vote to break the tie because he's now the decider. Amy dialled her voice in support of Hubert's proposal and suggested to Zeppelin that his vote will make all the difference, and it's time they sort this out and put Ambrose where he belongs.

Zeppelin hesitated for a while, insisting he'd wanted to remain neutral in all of this, but since they all wanted him to vote, he then decided to go with Ambrose.

"Huh, no Zeppelin, that's a bad decision that will impact on many who trusted you," said Hubert. Arguably, it takes a steady hand to hold a full cup, and it just dawned on these Luciferians that Zeppelin should have been courted rather than wrestled, because his contrived oddity of using this stranger who strayed into their camp has serendipitously turned this camp into a bear pit.

Rebecca didn't hesitate to give Ambrose a big hug, she was awfully excited, as she screamed on top of her voice that a decision has been made and it's time for a change. Zeppelin interjected in his bid to manage the ambience that has suddenly gone sour, and immediately urged Rebecca to be nicer to those who lost.

Amy hushed Zeppelin, screaming shame on him, and said he messed everything up. Stacy was quick to put Amy in her place, reminding her she doesn't have to be rude, and after all, Zeppelin has promised he will work something out for them. The flare and flavour of this debate was such that left Amy without joy.

Even as they perceived the Evangelist's message to be crooked in boundless bigotry, his words seem to have permeated through the darkness in their hearts. Yet his victory is now a success that wasn't celebrated as the whole thing is now knotted in controversy. Zeppelin is by no means rubbing his hands in glee over this move that might see some of the residents adjusting to a new life different from the one they'd preferred. He then turned to Hubert and his group and assured them he has got plans for everyone.

Zeppelin waited for a while, for things to calm down a bit, and for Hubert and his group to come to terms with their loss. He then addressed the people, saying a decision has been made but everyone is a winner under the circumstance. He then proceeded to declare that hence forth this camp ceases to be a Luciferian camp, and this is now a church premises and any service to Lucifer is now prohibited. Zeppelin urged those that want to return to their Christian faith to remain in the camp while the rest of them will be settled with jobs and accommodation. He then preceded to say that henceforth, anyone found walking out and about in the camp nude or scantily dressed, will be asked to leave the premises immediately or forcibly removed. Minutes after a decision was made in favour of the Evangelist, social media posts began popping up online.

Unbeknownst to Zeppelin, Shawn Tristan was keeping tabs on the happenings in the Bliss Luciferian Camp, but he'd no idea that the keen eyes of Brandon Moore are also watching from afar and following the events in the Bliss Camp.

Brandon Moore got wind of the recent happenings in the Bliss Camp, and that got him kicking off, he couldn't stop kicking himself for taking Prophet Gregory out, after realising he just paved the way for a church to take over the Bliss camp.

He'd wanted Prophet Lucian Gaia who already has a Luciferian temple in the Netherlands to manage the Bliss Luciferian Camp in Romania, for the time being, until he finds a suitable prophet to oversee the affairs of the Bliss Luciferian Camp.

The death of Prophet Gregory Helsing left Brandon Moore quite happy as a clam. They say, "it's better to be a warrior in a garden than a gardener in a war," but unfortunately, Brandon Moore just learnt the wisdom in the former, and he's incapable of being both.

Brandon Moore's hissy fit seems to have cost the Luciferian Order the Bliss camp. He regretted the haste to dish out punishment which was quite a childlike, petulant and tantrums throwing act, that lacks the benignity of a leader. Brandon Moore was convinced that Prophet Gregory was a problem, and that if he removes Prophet Gregory, he removes the problem. He'd no idea that he's obviously paving the way for the church as the problem serendipitously seems to have become bigger, and he now needed someone to fight his corner. Hours after the democratic process ended in the camp, with winners and losers emerging from the process, Brandon Moore immediately reached for the phone and dialled Shawn Tristan. He then ordered him to do something to stop Zeppelin's move from going ahead.

Removing the lynchpin from the Bliss Camp was an error of judgement that has inadvertently left Brandon Moore scraping the bottom of the barrel. Shawn wasn't forth coming but the ferocity of Brandon Moore request meant he can't argue but play the part of an obedient dog, he then takes up the task of stopping Zeppelin. Getting this done is like gold dust, but Shawn very naively went ahead with this instruction in which Brandon Moore has already made a nonsense of.

Brandon Moore stood confused and insanely befuddled, looking like he has been shot out of a cannon, he felt quite incapacitated in his bid to stop the church from taking over the Bliss camp. He held back from hurting Zeppelin, more so, the scatter gun approach of hurting anything and everything meant he might kill everyone, with no one left to run the camp.

He has learnt his lesson from the haste to punish Prophet Gregory, which is the reason behind using Shawn Tristan to fight Zeppelin, their conversation was a bit cranky, but the message was well communicated. Curtseying to Brandon Moore, isn't limited to gushingly reverencing his presence, it also includes doing as told.

Zeppelin just threw himself into a minefield of political correctness, and he'd no idea he has inadvertently enrolled himself for the punches. Unbeknown to him, God needed a man to take the plunge and he just did. Just as Zeppelin returned home, after a brief business meeting with some chief executives at the golf club, he received a phone call that didn't come to him as a surprise.

"Hello Zeppelin," said Shawn.

"Hi Shawn, I suppose you're aware that members have voted to build a church in the camp," said Zeppelin.

Shawn immediately told Zeppelin who'd no idea that something is in the offing, that his victory will be short lived, and this isn't a friendly call, assuring Zeppelin that he'll be hollowed out by the time he finishes with him. Zeppelin had no idea he has just upset the labyrinths behind the global push to embrace liberal values. This has nothing to do with revenge, served ice cold, but a man carrying out the instructions of another.

Zeppelin is now the sore thumb these Luciferians had to deal, with Shawn Tristian now the bellwether, Zeppelin has suddenly become a cornered animal.

"Cui bono, you asked?" Zeppelin retorted.

"Of course, yes, whose benefit, is it?" Replied Shawn.

"I don't know, ask Ambrose, but God's benefit, for sure," replied Zeppelin.

"Zeppelin, don't think you've won, and I promise you, you'll wet your pants by the time I hit you with what's coming," said Shawn.

Zeppelin interjected and inquired from Shawn about what it was that he's droning on and on about. Shawn told Zeppelin he's flying in from Moscow with Luciferians from around Europe to protest against his action. Shawn has suddenly turned himself into a hero, and he's now idolised by residents who has suddenly made themselves his fans, and now adore him for fighting their corner.

"Why're you doing this, Shawn? I supposed I've appealed to your good conscience," said Zeppelin.

With Shawn's new threat, Zeppelin soon realised he's about to find himself living his life in a fish bowl. He immediately stood up from his seat and walked through the door, to where Piper was seated. Muttering to himself that he can see Brandon Moore's finger in Shawn's action, and that this is an indirect attack on him. He knew Brandon Moore would've reached out to him to halt what he just did with the camp, but his killing of Prophet Gregory meant he has burnt that bridge because Prophet Gregory must have told him of who is behind his strange illness. He then turned to his wife, who obviously is keen to know what troubles him.

"I told you this might come back to bite, and I hope I didn't make a fool out of myself?" asked Zeppelin.

"Is anything the matter, and what's it that's coming to bite you?" replied Piper.

Zeppelin was only repeating the voice echoing in his head, and that voice was that of Shawn Tristian, promising to butt heads with him. Zeppelin reminded his wife of the fact that he told her of the possible objection and squawky reactions from other directors of the Luciferian camp, but she made him plough through, and now, Shawn Tristan is organising something big, the largest gathering of Luciferians to protest against him. Piper immediately calmed him down and assured her husband that there's no cause for concern, because God was behind what happened with that camp. She told her husband that she may not have told him all the details, but Evangelist Fredrick's mission was sanctioned by God, and God Himself confirmed it to her.

"Then what do you suggest we do? You need to speak to your God, ask him to make this national insult go away," Zeppelin retorted. Piper immediately reached for the phone, and dialled the Evangelist's phone.

After saying hello to Piper, the Evangelist proceeded to inform her of his intention to arrange a meeting between himself, Reverend Fitzgerald, herself, and her husband, to discuss how to proceed after their victory in the Bliss camp.

"Erm, Evangelist, we have a little problem," Piper muttered.

"Problem, you said, please go on," replied the Evangelist.

Piper then told the Evangelist that there is a planned protest to reverse todays' victory, and that one of the directors who felt aggrieved is organising the largest protest of Luciferians in Bucharest.

"Which of the directors are you talking about?" asked the Evangelist.

"Shawn Tristian, and he's threatening to get his friends in government to reverse our victory," she retorted.

The Evangelist immediately assured Piper that this is God's victory, and there's nothing to be worried about, but it's going to be an opportunity for a counter protest, and after all, the press hardly covers Christian events these days. He then suggested that while the press is covering the Luciferian protests, they will equally be covering the Christians preaching Christ to the Romanian nation.

"Piper, tell Zeppelin not to worry, we will remain in our place of prayer, and whatever Shawn is planning will fail," said the Evangelist.

Shawn reached out to his Luciferian friends across Europe, and in a matter of days he was already in Bucharest with his friends making headlines. This success seems to be short-lived as those who voted for the camp to remain a Luciferian camp finds this result to be wholly intolerable. They're pained, aggrieved, and then decided to take to the streets to protest what they described as the greatest and unacceptable ambush against their service to Lucifer. Some members of the Bliss Camp who didn't take likely the fact that their primordial belief has inexplicably been made an object of mockery, now find themselves side-by -side with other Luciferians and Satanists from around Europe, making their voice heard.

Now that Luciferians from across Europe has flocked to Romania, to make their presence known in the city of Bucharest as they held protest rallies. Interestingly, the contingent of Luciferians that came from England seem to have the most impact. In their submissions, they insisted that this move by Zeppelin will blatantly inhibit the freedom to express their service to Lucifer. Shawn Tristian has suddenly become a rallying point in this protest, he finds Zeppelin's action to be quite discriminatory, as he continues to protest the fact that he didn't have a vote in the decision to convert the Bliss Luciferian Camp into a church.

The rapacity of wokeism, has meant that liberals far and near in Europe had to unswervingly converge in Bucharest to fight this orthodoxy. Reverend Fitzgerald, who unsurprisingly, is a reliable and avid enabler of Christians holding onto their orthodox Christian views, isn't backing down either. Funny enough, Bro Paul and Bro Marius took permission from the reverend to preach Christ to the protesting Crowd, they then went before the crowd and held up a sign and began preaching Jesus Christ.

The mind-boggling idea of building a church in this Luciferian camp is something some residents find beyond belief and consider anathema, and they will go the whole hog to scuttle whatever plan Zeppelin has up his sleeve. Arguably, the audacity of Bro

Paul holding up a banner for Christ is something these Luciferian protesters find particularly insulting. The debate on who does what, as society strive to brush over the barrier of stereotyping task into a blue or pink task, isn't the subject of this national discuss.

The hue and cry were loud enough to precipitate an immediate debate among Romanians, particularly those in the state capital, Bucharest. This time the conservatives in Bucharest and those sympathetic to liberal lifestyle are at each other's' throats. This city is now faced with a moral war, steeped in ignominy as many now describes this as a battle between good and evil.

This whole protest unwittingly became repulsively charged and was suffused with antagonism. The national pulse is now one that is rife with antagonism between liberals and conservatives, and doesn't allow standing on the fence as Romanians take their sides on this debate.

This isn't a star-studded crowd, and neither is this some kind of rag tag army attempting to enforce street justice, in a manner that got on-lookers feeling panicky. These are Europe's liberals protecting their proclivities and their primordial belief.

Zeppelin has always been a role model to most of these residents, but now the boot is on the other foot. Attempts to ban him from social media in a bid to shut him out of the information highway, largely failed. Interestingly, some Luciferians who knows someone with access to the corridors of power, decided to call in some favours, and with few strings pulled, the Minister of Culture turned his attention to the demands of the protesters.

The government's sudden intervention in the just concluded democratic process that happened in the Bliss Luciferian Camp, meant that this conversation has morphed into a national conversation. Luciferians, Satanists, and liberals from across Europe, who are keen to limit the reach of Christianity, flocked to Romania, and made their presence known in the city of Bucharest as they held protest rallies. The minister of culture who prides himself on fairness and isn't swayed by the flattery of men, seemed to have been cornered this time, the press did a good job of getting him to foray into this dispute.

Alexandru Nicolae, the country's minister of culture immediately issued a statement informing Romanians of the government's interest to address the requests of the protesters, by looking at what happened at the Bliss Luciferian Camp, and the breach of the governance code by the Board of the Bliss Camp.

This minister, who seemed to have climbed the political tree faster than his contemporaries proceeded to assure protesters. "The Romanian government is looking into an allegation of a possible breach of corporate governance code," said Alexandru Nicolae.

In a follow-up, the press immediately posed a question to the minister of culture, about the proposal by some residents who suggested to pursue a fund raising in a bid to pay off Zeppelin and keep the Bliss Luciferian Camp to themselves.

"I'm aware of that proposal, and the government is looking at the possibility of handing the camp over to Shawn Tristian, the main aggrieved party, once this fund raising succeeds," replied the minister.

This protest has suddenly turned into a fly wheel that has inadvertently precipitated reinforcement of political correctness by liberals. The Minister of Culture taking sides with Liberals caused Conservative Christians to take to the streets in support of the Evangelist, as they chose not to stay mute in the face of this storm.

Anatolie Bogdan quipped when he saw the wave of protests, he's among the few cabinet ministers who said they'd rather not partake in this posture of antagonism against the church.

It was such a dramatic nail-biting moment in Bucharest, that could be perceived as someone making some kind of move on the big chessboard. Sensing this could be the hand work of Reverend Fitzgerald, a known orthodox priest, he immediately made a phone call to the priest.

This isn't a priest that needed an off ramp to get out of this and asking the minister to give him one. The conversation between Anatolie Bogdan and the priest was quite conciliatory, with the minster pledging his support for the priest.

While Shawn was busy leading the crusade against Zeppelin, he didn't realise he'd made so much headlines in Romania in a manner that attracted his wife, Natalya, who is Russian and based in Moscow where Shawn's family lives. The news that her husband was a Luciferian, engaged in some Satanic proclivities came to Natalya as a big surprise, because she had no knowledge that her husband has something of this sort going on the side.

She immediately picked up her phone and dialled her husband, and then ordered him to make his way to Moscow immediately, if at all he still wants to have a family by the end of that week. It's obvious to Shawn that his wife isn't blowing smoke, he has just been busted, and his chances of congregating with his friends to discuss their planned meeting with the minister of culture has now been ruined by Natalya's involvement.

Obviously at every fork in the road, where there is an opportunity for compromise, Shawn did turn the other cheek in what was erroneously perceived as weakness. This time, he's out to roughen Zeppelin up, in a show of strength, but with Natalya's involvement, he'll obviously attempt getting off this escalator.

As far as Shawn is concerned, this reaction from Natalya wasn't unexpected, he knows her to be a no-nonsense family-oriented woman, with orthodox inclinations. Unfortunately for Shawn, she finds his excuses for leading the protest for liberal values to be a mere ruse, or porkies of some sort. Shawn obviously won't get a Pulitzer Prize for this stunt, particularly now that his wife took the wind out of his sails.

The move to fight for the sustenance of his liberated lifestyle has suddenly become Shawn's Achilles heel, because the reverberation from this move wasn't limited to Natalya, but also from her parents who took so much liking in Shawn. The relationship between these in-laws hit rock bottom immediately, as Natalya's parents barred Shawn from coming anywhere near their dwellings but left Natalya to decide for herself how she intends to deal with her husband.

Shawn's in-laws are orthodox Russians, with orthodox Christian values, they have profoundly played an important role in Shawn's life, in helping to mould him into a highly regarded man in the society. This recent revelation about his Satanists proclivities came to them as a surprise, and seems to cast him as a man with a sullied evil reputation, and a disgusting character.

Shawn is a Romanian, but his Russian in-laws have had a profound impact in Shawn's life. They mentored him in the manner of behaviour and career pursuit, from the moment Shawn married their daughter, encouraging him through financial support and advice. Funnily, they'd no idea he has such an appetite for nudism and Satanism. Shawn's parents died in auto crash, not long after his secondary education. He became a bit adrift with life, until he came into contact with Natalya, who at first was just a friend with a shoulder to lean on. Their friendship morphed into a relationship, and that was when Natalya's parents took over parenting responsibilities in Shawn's life. They then sent Shawn to the university and groomed him into a man with good footing in the society.

Arguably, Webster was Shawn's friend and mate in the university, and he seemed to have pulled Shawn into his Satanists proclivities, and strung Shawn along all this while, even though Shawn isn't much of a Satanist.

After his phone conversation with his wife, it didn't take a shrink for Shawn to know that he's in for trouble and his indiscretion might cost him dearly. More so, the sudden realisation that he can't fight Zeppelin and Natalya at the same time, meant he needed to address the opposition at home first. He then turned to Hubert and Webster, and said he needed to hurry back to Moscow to address an urgent need, and then asked them to continue working with the minister of culture until he returns. It didn't take long before Shawn Tristian boarded the next available flight to Moscow, in his attempt to deal with the perceived crises brewing in his household.

The brazen decision by the minister of culture to hand the Bliss Luciferian Camp to Shawn without listening to Zeppelin to hear his own side of the story got him spooked.

Zeppelin didn't keep his concerns to himself, particularly when the minister of culture threw his weight behind Shawn after a friend of Shawn called in some favour from the high and mighty in Romania. Now that Shawn and his cohorts have called in some favours from some shenanigans of government, Zeppelin was now tempted call in his own favours, and after all, he's a big gun in the oil and gas sector with some great degree of clout in the society. Yet, he'd to exercise some restraint, and even at that his concern was quite palpable.

It is undoubtedly true that we live a crazy world where the strong take whatever they want and the weak are left with nothing. Some who may have been classed as being weak but with access to the corridors of power would pass as strong, which informed why Zeppelin suddenly felt strong-armed by the sudden involvement of the minister of culture.

The protesting crowd aren't only baying for the return of their camp, they are also baying for Zeppelin's head. Besides, the devil is an old foe, who is now using this protest to call Zeppelin's bluff, Zeppelin thinks he was an eye flicker away from success until things took a different turn.

Zeppelin was quite concerned about the fact that his assumed spotless reputation is now being placed under the microscope and scrutinised by the media. He told his wife that Shawn was masterful in the manner he went about his campaign against him, running around and telling a cacophony of lies about him. He then muttered in such a suggestive manner, before saying that the too much stuff in Shawn's head seemed to have clouded his judgment.

Piper immediately arranged a meeting with Evangelist Fredrick Douglas despite his earlier assurances that God is in control, but Zeppelin's concerns meant that there's a need to review how they would address the minister of culture's involvement in the matter.

This meeting isn't about fleshing out the statement the church will put out to silence the army of opposition out there, it's about assurances, and Zeppelin got the assurance he needed, to whether this storm.

"Piper, you need to calm down, I told you already that God is in control, and you know it," said Evangelist Fredrick.

"I know, but my husband couldn't get hold of himself, and that leaves me worried," replied Piper. Reverend Fitzgerald interjected as he added his voice to assure Piper that they've been praying, and still praying, that God will steer the hearts of all those who have a say in this matter and put a wedge among them as he did with the Tower of Babel, quoting Bible book of Genesis 11: 7.

The Reverend was quite confident and also quoted the Bible book of proverbs 21:1, "The heart of the king is in the hand of God." They then prayed together, and after some words of assurances, Piper left them and returned home, and carried the message of assurances from the priest and gave them to Zeppelin, who suddenly became hopeful that things will eventually work in their favour.

The priest did a good job of assuring Zeppelin that the ministers' involvement is nothing but a slight hiccup, and that God have sorted things out in advance. His advice was a subtle reminder that there's no need butting heads with Shawn Tristian just to make a point as that will count as nothing but doubling down on stupid.

Through their association with Piper, Reverend Fitzgerald got to know about Brandon Moore and the clout he possessed, the reverend made it his point of duty in a place of prayer to take Brandon Moore down, and interestingly, he's determined not to stop praying until God brings Brandon Moore and his cohort down.

It was quite a surreal moment for Shawn the moment he walked through the door to answer his wife's call, as his children avoided him like a plague. His kids were all in a tizzy the moment he stepped into the house, and that left him speechless. They were running away from him, and didn't want him to touch them, and even his wife blatantly asked him to stay away, and not come anywhere close to her. It was as if he's a goblin and about to gobble his kids up.

"Natalya, what's going on, and why're you guys avoiding me?" asked Shawn.

"No, no, step back, Shawn, I say step back, and don't come any closer," replied Natalya.

"Why're you doing this, and why're you keeping my children away from me?" Shawn retorted.

"Oh my God! You're a Satanist?" she asked desperately.

Natalya immediately asked the kids to stay behind her as she shields them away from their dad whom they now treat as a plague, they wouldn't want to touch him with a ten-foot barge pole. Shawn immediately realised his wife's red lines have been crossed.

While the back-and-forth continued, Natalya and her kids walked away from Shawn and into the children's bedroom, and left Shawn by himself in the living room. Yet, left Shawn a subtle word of caution, as she asked him not to step his sullied self into their bedroom, and also informed him her parents has also barred him from their house.

Shawn isn't in anyway keen to be Brandon Moore's lackey. He wouldn't be happy to be used as a battering ram either, but he'd no choice but to play the role of an obedient dog this time.

Natalya on the other hand isn't overly benevolent to self-acclaimed liberals and her reaction doesn't pass as uncommon cruelty either. She just doesn't suffer fools gladly, even Shawn suddenly became circumspect of his association with this protest.

After his wife held his feet to the fire for his indiscretions, Shawn was left confused and needed someone to talk to. He decided to give his friend a phone call and narrated his current ordeal to his friend, Vladimir.

Funnily, Vladimir's perception of the situation seems not to have made the situation any easier for Shawn, because Vladimir's wife took offence with her husband for his association with someone as filthy as Shawn. Nothing got them reeling from within like Shawn's' support for nudism. Vladimir narrated what transpired between him and his wife and reminded Shawn that the situation is quite bad, and urged him to give Natalya and the kids some space to allow things cool down. After his phone conversation with Vladimir, Shawn decided to sleep on the couch, as he passed the night in the living room, at least to avoid exacerbating the situation further.

By morning of the next day, Shawn decided to visit his in-laws whom he'd a very good relationship with, to see if they could talk some sense into their daughter. Unfortunately, this visit wasn't well received as his enraged in-laws gave him the boot. He was shocked in the manner in which his father in-law asked him to take his filthy feet off his balcony and leave their property immediately.

The treatment Shawn received from his father in-law left him in shudder, and the whole thing hollowed him out immediately. He lurched to his car as he managed to stay away from the wrath of his father in-law. Arguably, the scary thought of driving back home in that condition became a concern. He immediately thought of calling Vladimir to come and drive him, but then changed his mind on a second thought. He then managed to brave it and drove himself home. He bemoaned the treatment he received from his wife, and now his father in-law, yet was unable to do a thing about it. His wife and her parents seem to have thrown a collective spanner in the works of this protest, and his experience in the hands of his in-law was a watershed moment that gave him a cause for a rethink.

On his return from his in-laws, Shawn was quite distraught to realise his loved ones have suddenly turned their back on him, and on getting home, he just couldn't go inside the house to face his wife. He then turned to the only person whose ears he has at this point in time.

"Vladimir, my father in-law called me, 'a sullied person,' after asking me to not set my evil foot on his property, because he doesn't want me desecrating it," said Shawn.

"You mean your father in-law said that, the same man that calls you his best friend?" replied Vladimir.

"Yes, of course, and I don't know what to do, because my family is slipping away from my hands," Shawn retorted.

Vladimir then interjected and suggested to Shawn that making restitution is the only way out of this. Shawn was lost with the bizarrely vague and ambiguous suggestion of a restitution. He immediately reminded his friend that contrition doesn't have to result in restitution and asked Vladimir how he expects he go about making restitution, and to whom. Vladimir is the calm and collected type of guy, he proceeded to advise Shawn that instead of running to his wife or father in-law to blab about how he erroneously got himself in this pickle, he should make his way to Bucharest and renounce Luciferianism and naturism before the world. He made it known to Shawn Tristan in no uncertain terms, that the juice didn't worth the squeeze, particularly now that his wife is on a war path.

Shawn didn't really find Vladimir's suggestion to be sort of helpful, and he'd no idea Vladimir just saved his bacon. He finds the suggestion to be sort of hysterical, but after realising that the only healing his family and loved ones needed at a time like this, is for him to renounce Luciferianism, and tell the world he hates Lucifer, and that he's only helping to keep the camp buoyed up as a favour to friends. He urged Shawn to get on with it and assured him that he will muddle through somehow. Vladimir did leave quite an impression on Shawn, after encouraging him to tell his naturist friends that the Bliss camp deserved to be permanently shut, and that was the reason he distanced himself from the camp all these years.

This isn't just some kind of facade, this is a mission sanctioned by God, and any man standing in God's way will incur his wrath. Shawn returned to Bucharest and joined his Luciferian friends who are on the streets protesting and requesting the reversal of Zeppelin's decision. Immediately Hebert sighted Shawn approaching, he rushed to him.

"Shawn, the minister of culture wants to have a word with you, so he can put the Bliss Camp under your care," said Hubert.

"Under my care, you said?" asked Shawn.

"Of course, we pulled some strings and we've won, Shawn," replied Hubert.

Shawn was thrilled that the protest he orchestrated have produced the result he desired so much, but he's now in a limbo over what to do with this success. The cheeky grin on his face was Shawn's way of showing he loved what he just heard, but that didn't sit well with Hubert who seemed rather surprised that the good news he just gave Shawn didn't provoke the much-expected rapturous response from Shawn.

Shawn muttered and said he needed to make a speech. He immediately urged Hubert, and Webster who came from England in support of the protest to get the protesters together, that he has a speech to make. Hubert, Iain, and his friend, Webster, called out to the protesters and urged them to congregate because Shawn has a victory speech to make. Shawn immediately beckoned on the members of the press present, and urged them to make sure they cover his speech. It didn't take long before Shawn got the cameras facing him, and all others listening attentively to what he'd to say.

**Shawn:** I want to say this to my family, my friends, the Luciferian community, the Romanian people and the Minister of Culture, that I supported Zeppelin's move to shut the Bliss Naturist Camp.

There was a sudden silence that pervades the air, as it dawned on them that the much-expected victory speech, wasn't what they'd expected because the speech has suddenly been replaced by a loser's speech. The crowd suddenly began to jeer at Shawn, followed by successive boo at Shawn as many of them screamed betrayal.

Hubert was quite disappointed at Shawn whom he'd so much faith in, and among others, Iain and Webster were hit the hardest by Shawn's audacious move. This is because they travelled from England to support Shawn's cause. Arguably, Shawn just succeeded in lifting a huge stone, only to shamefully drop it on his feet. Hubert was worried sick at Shawn's sudden U-turn, and he's now convinced that this move was also the result of a fist full of cash, that may have changed hands.

The journalists present, immediately inundated Shawn with questions about the sudden U-turn. He kind of muddled through as he told the world that he has come to realise that his decision to challenge Zeppelin was the consequence of a temporary lapse of judgement. The jeers and the boos that pervaded the air meant that Shawn got the opportunity he seeks, as he hurriedly left and rushed into his car. Even as he rushed to his car, Hubert followed him, and prodded him with questions about why he cruelly betrayed them in such a mean-spirited manner.

Shawn was spectacular and rather self-indulgent in the manner he waffled through, and no one obviously was able to make sense of what he was getting at because of the too many piffle in his words. Hubbert had to prod him further as he accused him of double standard at the finest.

"Hubert, I'm returning to Moscow, and I am hoping that I still have a family by the time I get home," Shawn retorted.

"Your family, I don't seem to get you, and does it mean your family had no idea of your association with Lucifer?" replied Hubert.

"No, not at all, this protest has cast me in bad light, and I must confess that it did open a rotten can of worms that I have to deal with," Shawn confessed.

In a moment of truth, Shawn then told Hubert that he really isn't much of a Luciferian, and that he has stopped associating with the Bliss Camp for a long time. He reiterated that his desire to challenge Zeppelin was just a fight for his right as a board member and less about his love for Lucifer. He then apologised to Hubert for deceitfully stringing them along, and it was quite telling as those behind Shawn soon realised that he wasn't a steady hand on the tiller after all.

Hubert did acknowledge that Shawn had stayed away from the Luciferian lifestyle for a long time and wasn't regarded as a true Luciferian because he hardly associate himself with them, and his sudden desire to play the hero in his bid to challenge Zeppelin did astound him. Yet they're glad to have someone of Shawn status fighting their corner. Shawn had to excuse himself to avoid further awkward moments with some of the protesters who felt disappointed in them.

Immediately after Shawn's car drove off, the protest began to peel away, as the sulking crowd began dissipating, and it didn't take long before there wasn't any protester left, and even the journalists soon realised there was nothing else to cover and had to pack up their gear and left.

Iain and Webster turned to Hubert as they made their way to their cars and questioned how things bizarrely went south, because they seem not to understand how the wind was taken out of Shawn's sails. They remained miffed and flummoxed, particularly because the favours they called worked out well, yet things suddenly went down the pan.

The direct involvement of Brandon Moore was meant to scare the hell out of Zeppelin and leave him enfeeble, rather he inadvertently made way for Zeppelin to break this Luciferin myth rule that has kept residents in check.

Shawn eventually returned home to his wife and opened up to her about how he got himself mixed up with Luciferians through Webster, but he has long ago dropped those proclivities. He assured her that what he did wasn't out of support for Lucifer but just to get back at Zeppelin for not consulting him in the decision making.

After having had a frank conversion, and the fact that his stunt came at a great cost to his relationship gave Shawn quite a scare. Natalya eventually forgave Shawn's indiscretions, particularly after his brave decision to tell the world on camera that he supported Zeppelin's move to shut the Bliss Luciferian Camp, and that building a church in its place is what our world needs.

Following Shawn Tristian's withdrawal of his objection to Zeppelin's move, the Romanian minister of culture had no choice but to stay out of the matter and allow Zeppelin's decision to run its course.

Now that Shawn was unable to achieve the success Brandon Moore so much desired, Brandon Moore decided to do something fast about Zeppelin. Because of his association with Reverend Fitzgerald, Zeppelin now enjoys the blessings of God's preservation, and consequently, Brandon Moore's attempt to curse and hex him failed. Considering the Bible book of Numbers 23: 8. "No one can Curse what God has Blessed."

He performed exactly the same type of hexing ceremony to punish Zeppelin, but soon realised the hex didn't have any effect on Zeppelin who obviously is enjoying cover from his praying wife, the Evangelist, and the Reverend. It didn't take long before Brandon Moore realised that the battle to keep the Bliss camp is lost, the horse has bolted and the camp is now gone forever.

Months after God restored his memory, Evangelist Fredrick returned to his job as an architect, and more interesting is the expectation from his colleagues that he will be behind with regards his performance on the job after a long time away from work. They were all amazed to learn that the Evangelist's performance on the job improved greatly, as compared to his performance before the accident. He outperformed his colleagues who have been steady on the job, and they then began teasing him, saying it's like he went on a job-related course during his time of absence, for him to have recorded this level of remarkable improvement on the job.

After allowing time to pass, in one of the evenings, Natalya and Shawn paid a visit to Shawn's in-laws after his wife mended the bridges between her parents and her husband. Shawn took advantage of this visit to apologise unreservedly to his father in-law and promised to do better. With the dust now settled, Zeppelin then had a meeting with the reverend to conclude arrangements on handing the camp over to the church, as well as resettling residents of the Bliss camp.

Some of the aggrieved residents who want to retain their primordial Luciferian belief decided to leave, and that includes Hubert, Orla and Amy, while some other residents willing to return to their Christian faith were employed by the church. Zeppelin and his wife helped to get a number of residents gain-fully employed.

In an eerie twist of fate, a low-level investigation into misuse of charity funds by Larissa Nicolae, the wife of the minister of culture, Alexandru Nicolae suddenly became notorious. The case seemed to have been dormant for a while, but serendipitously gained traction and inadvertently became a national conversation.

The case morphed from the abuse of office by Larissa Nicolae to one in which the minister himself is now an accomplice as documents revealed he and his family went on holidays at the expense of a Charity on cash crunch. It suddenly dawned on Alexandru Nicolae that his position as the minister of culture is now inexorably untenable, for which he resigned disgracefully.

The Church then embarked on a one-month daily prayer walk, and held vigils in that camp, in its bid to dethrone Lucifer and enthrone Christ in that territory, before they commenced the work of building a church in the camp. The name "Bliss Luciferian Camp" which is now a thing of the bygone age, was eventually changed to "Church Arena," and now houses the largest church in Romania. Rebecca and Eric later got married, and interestingly, Reverend Fitzgerald was the officiating minister, while Evangelist Fredrick Douglas gave some words of advice to the newly wed.

Two years after the Luciferian community lost the Bliss Camp to the church, there was a federal investigation into child sexual assault that happened in the temple Brandon Moore officiates as a priest in the United States. Investigators discovered that Brandon Moore has no hand in the act, but he covered it when the assault came to his knowledge. Some sixteen, and seventeen years old, accused Brandon Moore's brother in-law of sexually assaulting them. Brandon Moore tried to settle the matter privately and then covered it up when he got to know about the assault. He tried to keep it quiet, to protect his flawless public reputation as a liberalist.

The judge found Brandon Moore culpable for covering the assault when it came to his knowledge, the judge also ordered that the temple where the assault occurred be closed down. Brandon Moore called in some favours from friends in the corridors of power, but the conservative judge that presided on the case wasn't having anyone stopping him from handing Brandon Moore a custodial sentence.

Brandon Moore was eventually sentenced to five years imprisonment, and the largest Luciferian temple permanently closed. Reverend Fitzgerald just finished his Saturday morning gardening and decided to relax in his conservatory. He then picked up one of the newspapers he read cursorily within the week and began reading in a more detailed fashion. He suddenly stumbled into the news of Brandon Moore's sentencing by a court in the United States. The reverend was taken by surprise at the news but was also excited to realise his prayers had been answered by God. He immediately went on his knees, and thanking God for still being in control of what goes on in the affairs of men. He then got up, reached for the phone and called Fredrick Douglas, to inform him of the supposedly good news, but instead of telling the Evangelist the reason for his phone call, he just kept quoting the Bible book of Matthew 16:17-19, "I will build my church, and the gates of hell shall not prevail against it."

From that moment, Brandon Moore lost his clout, and his name was never heard again, even among what was left of the Luciferian community.

The Evangelist listened in for a while as the reverend excitingly repeated his quote and then told him that Brandon Moore has been sentenced to five years imprisonment and his temple closed permanently. They celebrated the news as they acknowledged God's determination to preserve his church, and said the world had no knowledge that it was God that took Brandon Moore down. More so, God always have the last laugh.

Reverend Fitzgerald concluded their brief conversation by saying, instead of God allowing the Bliss Camp to continue being an infection that continues to spread and corrupt Christian families in Europe, God decided to treat it like a disease He had to contain.

Zeppelin created his own sense of morality, and being on the same side with the reverend didn't improve his religiosity either. He jocularly asked the reverend to knock himself out, after he handed the Bliss camp to the church. Zeppelin did put an end to his Luciferian lifestyle, but didn't immediately give his life to Christ despite giving up his property to the church. He did give his life to Christ three years later, on his daughter's thirteenth birthday, the day she miraculously walked out of the hospital on her own two feet. Her daughter's miracle tarried, but with prayers, the miracle did happen, and that was the watershed moment that got Zeppelin surrendering to the Lordship of Jesus Christ.

It was such a remarkable moment for Zeppelin's family after Sarah underwent a surgery that got her back on her feet. Before now, Sarah had three previous surgical operations after which the doctors put their feet on the brakes. Doctors in Europe, and as far as the United States, had ruled out the possibility of any further surgery for Sarah. Zeppelin has the money and was willing to pay whatever amount for surgery, but that option for surgery was ruled out because it will worsen Sarah's condition. His closeness with Reverend Fitzgerald meant he was encouraged by the reverend after time of prayers to put forward his request for surgery one more time. Interestingly, one of the hospitals that turned down his request earlier, accepted to perform the surgery, this time it was a success and Sarah was back on her feet.